THE DESERT ROAD OF NIGHT

V. E. MARÉS

Original Publication
This work was originally published as sections titled *Orpheus, Underworld,* and *The Labyrinth* in the novel *The Beautiful World of the Alive* by V. E. Marés.
First Edition: May 2023

Marfa Lights Press
Registered Office:
5203 Juan Tabo Blvd. NE, STE 2B
Albuquerque, NM 87111

Library of Congress Control Number: 2025901797
ISBN 978-1-967018-00-0 (ebook)
ISBN 978-1-967018-01-7 (paperback)
ISBN 978-1-967018-02-4 (audiobook)
Cover Photography: V. E. Marés
Edited by: Z. Scot (developmental editing)

There are years that ask questions and years that answer.

— ZORA NEALE HURSTON

PROLOGUE

We are the Watchers. We see all. We are the Beloved, now watching from outside of time.

Here, *We* wait for the day when he is led to a spot where the land is flat and the desert landscape glows gold.

That will be the day when the sky is at twilight.

His eyes will burn from staring at the sun setting on the horizon.

He will smile.

It will be December 21, 2014, *Our* wedding day.

Until then...

❧ I ❧
ORPHEUS

What are the roots that clutch, what branches grow
Out of this stony rubbish? Son of man,
You cannot say, or guess, for you know only
A heap of broken images. ...

— T. S. ELIOT

❧ I ❧

THE PROVIDER

THAT IS WHAT HIS THOUGHTS HAVE FELT LIKE SINCE RELAPSING: "a heap of broken images"—memories of a life that no longer exists—scattered, coming one after another, and another.

How did he get here, in the dark woods near Big Stone Gap, standing in front of the Matriarch's grave, surrounded by tombstones? How he arrived at the grave was as unreal as the vast night sky, but not as unreal as the sky in New Mexico. There, in the pockets of darkness, in dazzling clusters scattered across the night, the stars shone brighter. God came through in the shine.

There was no shine in Virginia. No shooting stars.

A long time ago, Emma, his shooting star, had said:

"There was something so beautiful about his devotion to Eurydice. It would get to me that a man could love a woman so much that he'd try to bring her back to life.... When I was a little girl, I wanted a love like that to be real. I prayed for love like that—a love that was so powerful, so strong, that it would drive my soulmate to go to the End of the World, into the Underworld, to come back for me, even if I were a lost cause. That's real love."

His undying love was real.

His undying devotion compelled him to walk away from the Matriarch's grave, get into his car parked nearby, sit in the driver's seat, and begin the journey toward the End of the World.

JULY 15, 2001

Emma ended their call. He turned off his phone, took a deep breath, and swallowed. He leaned against a terminal window at John F. Kennedy International Airport and gazed out at the distant glow of Manhattan's skyline to the west. Beside him at the window was a young woman with freckles and braided hair. She was on her phone, pleading, "Don't go, please, don't leave me. I can't be by myself." She made eye contact with him and then walked out of earshot.

He stepped away from the window and sat down. Moments later, the young woman returned and sat a few seats away, her head resting on an armrest.

She glanced at her phone, then sat up and dialed, holding it to her ear to make another call. "It's me again; I don't mean to keep bothering you. It's just that... I thought... I mean, you said I was your soulmate. I was your One... I understand—you'll never hear from me ever again."

The young woman dropped her phone to her side, threw her body back against the seat, and curled up. After a few moments, she straightened up, grabbed her phone, and dialed again. "I'll be boarding soon. If I get on this plane and it crashes, I want you to know that I was thinking about you until the very end. Goodbye."

He stared at his phone, wondering if he should turn it back on.

JANUARY 9, 2001

He ended the call with Emma. He turned his phone off, took a deep breath, and swallowed. He leaned against a terminal window at Denver International Airport and gazed out at the last rays of golden light, cutting to black. The sky was no longer at twilight. Flight attendants invited passengers to board. He stepped away from the window to join the line forming at the gate.

Moments later, he was in his seat toward the back, waiting for take-off. Once in the air, turbulence made the plane rock violently for an hour. The plane began its descent into Albuquerque. It hit an air pocket that made the flight attendant sitting next to him grab his hand on the armrest and call out to God.

The plane was in a nosedive, heading toward the Sandia Mountains. The flight attendant pleaded with God not to let her die. He closed his eyes. He anticipated the moment of impact against the mountain and everything cutting to black. The pilot pulled the plane out of its dive. The flight attendant stopped screaming. She held his hand until they landed.

At the gate, she looked over at him and laughed nervously. "I'm sorry... It's never that bad."

"No need to apologize; we're only human," he said, smiling.

She gave an awkward shrug, then stood up to help the passengers off the plane. He followed them into the empty terminal and walked to the rental car counter at the end.

He handed his driver's license to the agent, who then asked, while reviewing his reservation paperwork, "Is this your first time in our lovely state?"

"Yup," he replied.

The agent chuckled to himself. "Well, let me be the first to welcome you to the Land of Enchantment—or, as we like to call it, the Land of Entrapment."

"Why's that?"

The agent looked up and held out the keys. "You'll see, and when you do, you'll understand why, no matter where you go from now on, you'll end up back here."

He snatched the keys from the agent's hand and walked outside. Once in his rental car, he began driving north along the desert highway toward Santa Fe. He became mesmerized by how the moonlight lit up the landscape, making the Sandia Mountains stand out against the vast night sky. He remembered a few lines from *The Waste Land,* a poem he first read after randomly grabbing a book out of a box while rushing through an air terminal in Saudi Arabia in the lead-up to the Persian Gulf War:

> *Ganga was sunken, and the limp leaves*
> *Waited for rain, while the black clouds*
> *Gathered far distant, over Himavant.*
> *The jungle crouched, humped in silence.*
> *Then spoke the thunder.*

He imagined the Sandia Mountains as Himavant. He began repeating to himself the endings of both *The Waste Land* and *The Upanishads,* the sacred scripture that inspired What the Thunder said:

Shantih shantih shantih

He never imagined that having a six-figure career would not bring him peace.

He never imagined that being a provider would be the cause of Emma's unhappiness; she was angry that he was leaving her behind when she needed him the most. Earlier that night, as he was packing his suitcase and preparing to leave for LaGuardia Airport, Emma asked, "How are we gonna deal with this? This isn't like Chicago. I don't know when I'll see you again."

He sighed. "I know."

"Is that all you've got to say? 'I know?' You're not sad?"

"Of course I'm sad."

"But you don't act like it."

"What do you want me to do?"

"I don't know... Tell me that it's gonna be alright, that you'll find a way."

He looked at her, her face pleading for an answer. Instead of giving her one, he shut his suitcase and walked out of their bedroom.

Emma raced around him to block him from leaving their apartment. After a long stare, she threw her hands up and moved away from the door. "Fine, whatever. Do what you need to do, but you need to be back home before I pop."

THE WAY THE LONG ROAD RAN INTO THE NIGHT DREW HIM BACK into the moment. It was as if the earth had joined herself at the horizon to a vast sky filled with dazzling clusters of bright stars.

He never imagined meeting a woman who would join herself to him and show him the meaning of the word shantih: the peace that surpasses understanding.

A shooting star streaked overhead. He pulled over to the side of the road, got out of the car, and stood on the shoulder. He looked at the vast sky until more shooting stars flashed above. He smiled as he took out his phone, turned it on, and dialed, staring into the night while waiting for Emma to answer.

"Hello, can you hear me?" he asked.

"I can hear you," she replied. "What took you so long? I called—I left you a message—I was worried. You better have a good excuse."

"I don't... I'm still trying to deal with how we left things."

She sighed. "Me too."

"I'm sorry for putting us in this mess."

"Don't be. It's not your fault... I've been thinking: What were you supposed to do? You love everything about me. What you did to Paul shouldn't have surprised me. If this is the price I've gotta pay for having one of the good ones, then so be it."

"What if it doesn't have to be? Nothing's stopping you from moving here."

"No, I guess not," she said.

"Would moving to New Mexico get in the way of writing your dissertation?"

"No, I can do that from anywhere. Why not there? And if I need to meet with my advisor, I can always email her, call, or even fly back to New York, right?"

"Yup, but that'll become a lot harder the closer you get to your due—"

"Yeah, yeah, yeah—I know, and it's okay. I can always call or email if I can't get back for whatever reason."

"That's what I thought," he said.

"Wait a minute—where are you? You better not be driving."

"I'm not—I'm standing alongside a desert road."

"Get your goofy-ass back in the car! We didn't go through all that temperature-taking bullshit for you to get run over."

He laughed. "I know, but I had to pull over—I saw a sign."

"You did?"

"A shooting star."

"That's a big sign!"

"It's the biggest, and that's why I'm standing out here. I had to pull over to tell you how we're gonna deal with this."

"I'm joining you!"

"Yes! And since the firm is paying for everything, it'll make moving that much easier. We can set something up with the landlord so that we can continue paying our rent there on time."

"Leave that to me; I'll handle it," she said.

"I should've told you I was gonna find a way—that we don't have to be apart—but I still can't get over how we have it like that now. We can have two homes. We've got money."

Emma laughed. "Yeah... After everything we had to go through—"

"The doctors—"

"The needles... I forgot that we do... It feels like yesterday we were trying to figure out how to make forty dollars last between us, and here we are."

"Here we are—how soon can you get here?" he asked.

"As soon as I see my OB-GYN and get her permission to travel and live at that altitude, and after you and I have a long talk with Lydia, I'll be on the first flight out."

DECEMBER 21, 1994

It was a Friday night. He was making what felt like the longest walk from the Montrose Avenue subway station in Bushwick to his new apartment building, rushing inside for warmth. He raced up the steps to the top floor.

Elisa opened the door before he could finish unlocking it, greeting him with a bright smile that faded as he passed her and entered the family room. "What happened?" she asked, closing the door behind her.

He turned to face Elisa. "I was late again. I got fired."

"That's it?"

"Yeah, that's it."

"You came through that door like it was the end of the world."

"It feels like it."

Elisa waved dismissively. "It's really not a big deal. Come on, I made dinner."

He followed her from the family room into the kitchen. "You're not mad?"

Elisa paused in front of the stove, turning to face him with playful eyes. "Should I be? I mean, it was a bullshit job."

"It was still a job."

"Were you going to make a career of it? Was the commute worth it?"

"No."

"Okay then, don't worry. They did you a favor."

"Are you sure?"

"Yes, I'm sure. I did fine before you moved in, and I have a great job. I've got us covered."

"But it doesn't feel right," he said.

"Good—that's all I need to know about you. That it doesn't feel right. I know you'll do the right thing. Besides, I didn't ask you to move in because I needed help with the rent or with Myra. Fuck that. I asked you to move in because you're fun to be with and because I love you."

He smiled with relief. "I love you too."

"You'll get your break, and when you do, you'll make your money. I believe in you. Now, go shower and get comfortable. I made you your favorite: cheese fries."

❧ 2 ☙

MEET HER AT THE LOVE PARADE

JULY 18, 2001

IT HAD BEEN THE SAME ROUTINE SINCE ARRIVING IN BERLIN ON Monday: he worked at the client's site near the Berliner Dom until late. Due to the sensitivity and confidentiality of his work, no personal phones or laptops were allowed. He had to wait until he returned to his hotel room to check for messages from Emma. When he did, he found none.

He called his mother, Petra, in New York to see if she knew what was going on, but she didn't answer. The silence was becoming too much. He began to pace around the room. Did Emma relapse? Why was his mother sending his calls to voicemail? He hated himself for becoming a man who, by suspending disbelief and surrendering to the mysteries of the universe, had—through the power of love—become a believer in magic:

Soulmates are real.
He wanted to die now more than ever.

The pain was like a souvenir of all the broken dreams of what was to be.

The Gift Shop was now closed.

No joy seemed possible ever again in life.

There was no way to keep busy at this time of night.

No more TV to watch, no more music to listen to, no more books to read, no more thoughts to examine—over and over, playing in his mind on a loop.

There was nothing more.

He went into the bathroom and pulled out a razor blade from his shaving kit. He stripped until he was naked and got into the tub. He sat motionless as the hot water poured from the faucet, steam covering the mirrors. His hands were shaking as he held the razor above his wrist. He took a deep breath. He was about to cut himself open when he looked up and saw a moisture spot forming on the ceiling—it was in the shape of a small turtle.

He dropped the razor on the floor beside the bathtub, took a deep breath, and swallowed. He turned off the faucet and sat in the tub, head resting on his hand and elbow, staring down at the razor. The water became cold. He got out and moved as far away from the razor as possible. He sat naked at a desk by the window, fighting the urge to go back and cut his wrist open. Instead of giving in, he turned on his laptop, logged onto America Online, and searched for chatrooms devoted to coping with grief and loss.

They were all empty.

He found a chatroom for people living in Berlin and entered, introducing himself as "31/M/from NYC."

He received a direct message from Sif81, who asked:

SIF81

Are you here for the Love Parade?

SOLDIERBOY

No, I'm in the city for work, but I'd like to know more.

The Love Parade is a celebration of life. People come from around the world every year to visit the Großer Tiergarten and lose themselves to music. Are you interested?

Hell yeah! I came here looking for a way to deal with some stuff going on back home, and dancing has always brought me joy.

Then you should come.

Where's the Großer Tiergarten?

Do you know where the Brandenburg Gate is?

I know it's near my hotel.

It'll be in that area. By the way, my name is Ina. I can come down and show you myself. We can meet in the lobby of your hotel.

Maybe. What are some other places I should check out?

He sat at his desk, staring at the screen, waiting for Ina to answer. When she didn't, he logged out and tried to fall asleep.

JULY 19, 2001

The next day, he woke up to the same routine: he worked until it was late, then returned to his hotel room. He checked his messages to see if Emma had responded but found none. He called Elisa and asked to speak with their four-year-old daughter, Daphne. After talking with her, he asked Elisa if she had heard anything about Emma or his almost eleven-year-old son, Andy.

"Last I heard, he was with Lydia," Elisa said.

"Can you call my mom and see what's up with him? With Emma?"

"Call her yourself."

"She's not answering my calls. No one is."

"I don't want to talk to that woman."

"Please, it's important."

She laughed. "Not my circus, not my clowns," she said before hanging up.

Given Elisa's history with Emma, he understood her reaction was one any normal person would have and chose not to focus on it. Instead, he dialed Emma's number again. The call went to voicemail again. The urge to go back into the bathroom and grab the razor from where he had left it began to grow again. Instead of giving in, he went to his laptop and logged onto America Online.

The moment he appeared active, Ina sent him a message:

> Hi! I was hoping you would log back on. You
> disappeared! And I wanted to chat!

He wrote:

> I waited, but you never came back.

> My baby woke up, and I had to put her back
> to sleep. I'm sorry for that. It's only me. Her
> father is a sergeant in the army. We met when
> I lived in Landstuhl, and he was based there.
> When he was sent back to the United States,
> he left us without an address where I would
> be able to find him.

> That's fucked up!

> I know. Anyway, I was going to say that you
> should check out Friedrichshain. It's
> interesting. I live there with my mother and
> father; they help me. We had just moved to
> Berlin. It's a lot better than Landstuhl.

> I think I will.

> Can I ask you a question?

Sure.

You still haven't told me your name or asked
me what I look like. Why?

Because that's not what I'm here for.

Then why are you here?

I'm trying to keep busy—trying to deal with
some stuff without losing my mind. I need to
be home, but I'm in Berlin because I also need
to work. I can't afford to lose my job. It has me
all fucked up and sad.

I'm feeling all fucked up and sad, too. My
baby's father promised to take us back with
him. We were going to be a family. But he got
what he wanted and left us behind. He threw
me away.

I'm sorry you're going through this.

It is what it is—I think he has a wife already. I
need to change the subject, or else I'm going
to cry. Can you tell me what you look like?

I can do that—I'm stocky, with a crew cut. I'm
Puerto Rican.

Like my baby's father. He's Puerto Rican.

I was a sergeant too.

You could be my next big mistake!

He was at a loss for words and didn't respond.

> I know you're not here for this, but I'm going
> to tell you anyway: I'm skinny and blonde with
> short hair. I'm cute. How tall are you?

> How skinny are you?

> Don't worry. I'm thin, but I have enough meat
> on my ass to please any man.

> K

He logged out right away. He stood and began pacing around his hotel room, pulling out his phone to call Emma again. When the call went to voicemail, he tossed his phone on the desk and went to bed.

JULY 20, 2001

He couldn't sleep. He stayed awake until morning light began coming through the windows of his room, and it was time to leave for work. He worked at the client's site until late, and after a short walk, he was back in his hotel room. Instead of obsessing over Emma for another night, he convinced himself to change his clothes and go out for a late dinner. He went to his laptop to check his email one last time.

A direct message from Ina popped up on the screen.

> Where did you go last night? I was going to
> ask, instead of meeting in the lobby of your
> hotel, you can… maybe… meet me at the
> Love Parade? It's tomorrow, and I'm going to
> be there, alone. Come and dance with me.
> Let's be sad together.

He sat back in his chair, staring at the screen, wondering what it was about him that Ina wanted. Her interest, her desire for him, was strange. He was just a username on a computer screen. She didn't even know his real name.

He knew what he wanted:

She closed her eyes, moved her arms from his waist to his shoulders, and began singing along to the song playing. "Breathe love into me... Breathe love into me."

He asked himself, *How can I go on living in the aftermath of what we've lost without letting the pain eat me up, make me wanna kill myself? I need to carve out joy from the pain—from the grief—that's how. Maybe that's what Emma's doing now. She's got no choice, especially after she begged me not to get on the plane—not to go to Berlin—but I ignored her. I left her behind because of a job I can't lose, that pays me six figures, and that's why she's not responding to any of my messages. She has all the power to deal with our loss by carving out her own joy... Maybe she's too busy doing it.*

His freight train of thoughts was interrupted by Ina sending a message typed in all caps:

ARE YOU THERE?

After a moment, he typed:

I'm still here.

What happened last night? We were about to have some fun.

Nothing. I was tired and went to bed.

Okay? Do you still want to meet me at the Love Parade?

Sure. Tell me when and where.

Tomorrow—18:00—Brandenburg Gate. I'm sending you a picture, so check your email. When you meet me, I'll be wearing the same white bikini top that's in the picture.

Got it.

So, what do you think?

You're cute.

I told you! Now send me a picture so that I'll
know who I'm looking for.

He sent Ina a photo of himself standing alongside Emma on the crest of the Sandia Mountains. Their faces glowed gold from the setting sun. Emma wore a yellow maternity sundress that draped over her large belly, with a crown of sunflowers wrapped around the top of her curly auburn hair.

He logged out before Ina could respond. Leaving the room, he went to a nearby restaurant for a late-night meal. After finishing, he returned to his room, checked his email, and found an empty inbox. Then, he went to bed and fell asleep.

JULY 21, 2001

He woke up late on Saturday morning. He called Emma before brushing his teeth. When the call went to voicemail, he hung up and went to the bathroom. The razor was still on the floor where he had left it. Instead of picking it up and finishing the job—escaping the pain and grief he knew Emma was dealing with on her own—he went to his laptop. He sent Emma another email and waited all afternoon for her reply. He watched TV until it was time to leave. Before heading out the door, he made one last call and checked his email one last time. Again, nothing.

He left the hotel and walked the backstreets toward the Brandenburg Gate, arriving on time. Ina was nowhere to be found. Just as he was about to leave, a sudden rush of people—all with high expressions of love and ecstasy on their faces—swarmed him, pushing him away from the meeting spot.

He closed his eyes and focused on the way people swarming around him moved to the beats blaring from the massive speakers set up throughout the area. The sheer number of bodies pressing against him overwhelmed his senses. When he opened his eyes, he realized he had drifted toward the Victory Column. He was far from the meeting spot, but it didn't matter; he began dancing as if he were twenty-three years old again.

Suddenly, a small redhead with freckles approached. She wrapped her arms around his shoulders, buried her face against his chest, and began to dance with him. Her hair smelled like it had been wrapped in a crown of sunflowers. When she started singing along with the song playing, *"Breathe love into me... Breathe love into me,"* he stopped and looked longingly at her. She looked at him with soft eyes and asked, *"Geht es dir gut? Warum hast du aufgehört?"*

"Sprechen Sie Englisch?" he replied.

"Are you okay? Why did you stop?"

"Déjà vu."

She smiled as if that brought her tremendous joy. "I remind you of someone? Who?"

He pushed her away gently. "I need to leave."

She grabbed him by the arm to keep him in place. "You need to stay."

"But I've gotta go."

"No, you don't."

"I'm in a relationship."

She pulled him back, wrapping her arms around his shoulders. "And I'm engaged. We're not doing anything wrong. All we're doing is danc-ing, that's all."

"That's all," he said, reminding himself.

"It's all I want for now, so relax and go with it. Just go with it and breathe love into me."

For hours, they danced into the night, swaying their bodies to the beat of one song after another. The way the laser lights synced with the blaring music, flashing across her face, hypnotized him.

She smiled with her eyes closed, as though she were plugged into a universe of sound flowing through her. When she opened her eyes, she slowed their dance to a sway, as if moving would distract her from studying his face.

"I've been trying to figure out what you are," she said.

"What I am?" he said.

"Yes... Where are you from?"

"Guess."

"Tangier?"

"Not even close."

"Then where?"

"New York. I'm Puerto Rican."

She flashed a big smile. "That's even better."

"Better?"

"Yes, better."

"How so?" he asked, confused.

"I've never met someone like you. You're *exotic*."

"Exotic?" he said, laughing.

"Not many of *you people* are where I'm from."

"And where's that?"

"Johannesburg... Now, I really must know your name."

"But I don't wanna know yours."

"Too bad—I'm Alene."

"And I'm here."

"Seriously, what's your name?"

"Seriously, I'm here."

"Okay, Mister 'I'm Here,' can I ask you a question? And forgive me, please, but I'm curious."

"Go ahead."

"Do Puerto Rican men like white women, or do your people prefer to keep to your own?"

He laughed. "What?"

"I'm being honest."

A tap on the shoulder made him turn from Alene to the tall blonde smiling behind him.

"It's me, Ina!" she yelled over the music. Before he could respond, Ina shoved Alene into the crowd and pressed herself against him. "Sorry I'm late. I couldn't find a babysitter, and I was looking for you—"

Alene returned, yanking Ina to the ground by her hair. She hammered Ina's face over and over with her fist. Everyone dancing around them ignored Ina's screams for Alene to stop. Alene relented, stepping back from Ina.

Ina pushed herself up from the pavement. She stood tall over the two of them, blood pouring from her nose, covering her chest, and staining her white bikini top. Her left eye was bruised shut as she looked at him. "How could you let her do this to me?"

"I don't know you, and I'm not going to touch either one of you," he replied.

"You're not a real man!"

"You're late, she's here, and I'm trying not to lose my fucking mind and kill myself! I've got my own problems! I don't need yours!"

With hesitation, Ina looked at him, then at Alene with fear, before turning and running away into the crowd dancing around them.

Alene faced him with a smirk. "Where did you meet her? In a chatroom?" When he looked away, saying nothing, her smirk became a wicked smile. "How did I know? Does your *girlfriend* know you went on a date?"

He looked back at Alene. "You didn't need to beat her up."

"Oh, spare me. That wasn't about you; it was about respect. Miss AOL pushed me like I was nothing, and I had to correct her. So keep your opinions to yourself. No man is worth fighting for."

"No woman is worth the trouble."

Alene laughed. "*Wat ook al, Meneer Bullshit*—want to grab a drink? My fiancé won't mind."

"I wanna keep dancing."

"Me too, but you're the reason Miss AOL came here, so we have to hide now. Trust me, she'll be back with the *Polizei,* and they'll be looking for you as well. So why don't we get a drink while we hide? Yes? You can't say no—come on." Alene grabbed his hand and led him away from the crowds on the street, down a dark, tree-lined path in the Großer Tiergarten.

❧ 3 ❧

A-OKAY

HE WANDERED AROUND THE WINE LOUNGE, WISHING HE WERE HOME with his family. He decided to stop by the bar and order a drink. Just as the bartender served him, his supervisor—a tall woman with a sleek black bob and a dress that emphasized her curvy figure—sneaked up from behind. She snatched the wallet he had taken out to pay for his drink and quickly tucked it into his front pocket, her fingers lingering against his groin through the thin fabric.

"Keep it in your pants for now," she said.

He forced a grin, acknowledging he had no choice.

"Fancy seeing you here with the rest of us drunks. I'm surprised your girlfriend let you come out and play."

"She understands this is part of the job—part of the game," he said.

He held his frozen expression until she withdrew her hand and laughed. "You should've brought her down."

"She's got better things to do."

"That's too bad. I'm a fan of her work. I would've loved to have met her." The supervisor glanced at his drink. "Is that all you're going to have? No whiskey to my Pinot Noir?"

"I'm good with the soda, but thanks."

"I don't trust a man who doesn't drink." She placed her hand on his shoulder. "Maybe you shouldn't be involved with client demand planning. Is Paul here? Maybe I should have a word with him; you're not to be trusted."

"I don't like to drink... I can't handle booze."

"Oh, really?" She smiled and took his hand. "Let's grab a bottle and see where that takes us."

She tried pulling him away from the bar but stopped as a group of men entered the lounge. They were tall, with slicked-back hair, dressed in suits tailored from vicuña to fit their athletic frames. Immediately, they were surrounded by a throng of women who wanted to talk to them and men who wanted to be recognized by them. It was as if she was compelled by desire; the supervisor dropped his hand to thrust herself into their orbit as well.

He laughed at being forgotten so quickly and began to walk around the lounge, making small talk with his coworkers. Whenever they asked about the rumor that the client was slashing their workforce demands, he would cut them off rather than risk his facial expression confirming the truth.

Once the projects related to the Y2K bug were completed, the client would no longer need all the consultants the firm had placed on site. The days of laughing, drinking, and getting together at lounges and strip clubs, followed by discreet one-night stands—with everything being billed back to the client—were coming to an end. Most of his drunken colleagues in the lounge would soon be losing their jobs.

That was why he canceled his plans with Emma, Elisa, and the kids to be there instead. He needed to be seen. He couldn't risk having his name end up on another list—one he wasn't aware of and didn't manage—all because Paul and senior management might not see him as a team player for wanting to spend what little free time he had with Emma and the rest of his family. He had heard that by not drinking and doing drugs—not "playing"—he created the perception among his coworkers that he was trying to act as though he were better than them. In the corporate world, perception is reality.

To build upon that reality, he stepped away from them, out of the lounge, and through a set of patio doors onto a deck alongside the Hudson River in Battery Park City. He leaned against the railing and gazed at the Twin Towers looming high against the vast night sky.

A coworker, wearing the uniform of a corporate grunt—a white shirt with a loose tie hanging at the collar—approached and stood next to him, leaning back against the railing to gaze at the towers with him. After a long moment of silence, the coworker sighed and said, "Can you imagine being trapped up there while the towers are on fire? What would you do—jump or burn?"

"What do you want?" he said without looking at him.

The coworker sighed again. "I'm sorry... I know that was a weird thing to say, but I've been having these strange dreams where I'm trapped in a burning building, trying to find a way out, and—"

"Why are you telling me this?"

"I don't know. Maybe because I don't have anyone to talk to? Maybe because that's the way I feel? Trapped? I mean, I bought a house—"

"You bought a house... And?"

"Fuck it, I'm just gonna say it—whatever the list, please, I can't be on it."

"I don't know what you're talking about."

"Bullshit," the coworker said. "Paul loves you."

"Paul loves money."

"Stop it, man... He loves you. I've crunched the numbers. I know how much money you've put back in his pockets... You're his golden boy."

"No, I'm not—"

"Yes, you are, and it's funny."

"Why?"

"Because we took bets on how long you'd last, coming at everyone the way you have. I even overheard one of the senior managers complain to Paul about you."

"What did he say?"

"'Who does he think he is? He's nothing but an analyst.' But Paul told him to shut the fuck up and give you what you needed, saying that you were acting on his orders."

"Okay? And? Where are you going with this?"

"Paul doesn't talk to people like me. He doesn't even talk to your supervisor, and she's an associate partner and the motherfucking Director of Human Resources, but he talks to you, and that's because you know what's up. So don't play with me. I know change is coming."

He shifted his attention away from the Twin Towers and back to his coworker. "I've gotta get out of here—my kids are waiting."

The coworker grabbed his shoulder to keep him from walking away. "Look, man... I know you're a professional and wanna do a good job, but... Dude, I just bought a house. I have a wife and a little girl. You have a little girl, right?"

"She's two and a half."

"We're fathers... All we care about is providing a good life for our families, right? So, if you see my name on a list, all I'm asking is, can you look out for another father and warn me? You know? I could at least look for another job? 'Cause I don't wanna be here, but I have to, or else people will talk shit, and I'll stand out, and I don't wanna stand out. You and me, we're not like these idiots. We wanna do our jobs and go home—not drink and party."

After a long pause, he sighed and then placed his hand on his coworker's shoulder. "I need you to listen closely to what I'm about to say."

"Okay..."

"You're right... We're not like them. We have families. We should be with them... So, go home, Marco. Trust that everything's gonna be alright: I'm going home to be with mine."

Marco paused, appearing unsure, until he seemed to understand what was being said to him and smiled. "Dude, thank you!"

He smiled as he left Marco—the coworker—on the deck and exited the lounge. He walked back to Wall Street and caught a ride into Brooklyn with the firm's car service. The driver dropped him off in front of a pizzeria near Elisa's apartment building. He brought a pizza pie back to their home and sat down for a late dinner with Myra, his eleven-year-old stepdaughter; Daphne, who was two and a half years old; and Elisa, his ex-girlfriend.

For the rest of the night, he sat on the floor of the family room, watching TV with his daughters. He braided Daphne's hair while she held the baby doll Emma had given her as a family heirloom until she fell asleep, drool spilling from her mouth. He carried Daphne to bed, kissed Myra on the crown of her head, and gave Elisa a long hug before leaving her apartment. Then he walked to the Montrose Avenue station and boarded the L train to Manhattan, where he would join the rest of his family at their home on the Lower East Side.

MARCH 19, 2003

It was night, and he lay half-asleep in bed in his room with walls painted blue. The TV on the nightstand opposite him played music videos in the background. On the floor, scattered pictures of his old life in New Mexico lay next to half-opened books of poetry written by Emma, his shooting star. In the family room down the hall from his Blue Room, Elisa sat on the floor drawing with Daphne while Myra and Andy watched a cartoon sitcom on TV.

Elisa looked over at Daphne's drawing. "You're doing a great job. You're so talented."

Daphne looked up from her paper. "Can I show Daddy?"

"We don't want to wake him."

"But he needs to see this."

"Sweetie, no."

"I show him." Daphne jumped to her feet and dashed from the family room to her father's bedroom. She leapt onto his bed. "Wake up! Look!" Daphne waited for him to open one eye, holding her drawing in one hand and her baby doll in the other. When he did, she pressed the paper against his face. "I drew you. See? Do you like it?"

He opened his other eye. "I love it."

"You do?"

"Of course; the colors are so pretty. My love, you did a fantastic job. You bring me so much joy."

Elisa rushed into the room, grabbed Daphne—causing her to drop her baby doll next to him—and carried her away as best as a mother could carry a six-year-old in her thin arms.

He could hear them going down the hall and into the family room, with Elisa saying, "What did I tell you?"

"But Mom, Daddy isn't sad anymore, and that means everything's gonna be alright—Daddy's gonna be A-okay, right?"

Elisa didn't acknowledge Daphne's question or her need for reassurance. Instead, she asked Daphne to begin working on math exercises from a workbook he had bought during one of his rare, lucid moments.

Hearing Daphne think everything was going to be A-okay and seeing Emma's baby doll—now Daphne's—lying in a disjointed position next to him, pain welled up in his chest. He sat up, grabbed the remote from where it had been wedged beneath his pillow, and began flipping through the channels on the always-on TV. He paused at a commercial playing a song he had only heard in his sleep and dreams.

In the commercial, a car raced down a long desert road before slowing to enter a neighborhood that seemed to have materialized, like a mirage, from out of nowhere. Children played on slides set up on the front lawns of each house the car passed. It continued rolling slowly through the neighborhood, passing two little girls sitting on the curb. Behind them, a woman with auburn hair and a yellow sundress sat at the bottom of a slide, holding a small boy with a bowl haircut. They all waved and smiled.

He waved back at the TV but stopped when he realized it was just another manifestation of what his doctor had called his delusion. He changed the channel before it could suck him in further and landed on a news channel. What kept him from switching channels again was the pundits' muted excitement over the destruction—the loud, bright explosions and large plumes of smoke—broadcasted live from Baghdad.

Seeing how the pundits reported the horror with a tone similar to sportscasters giving play-by-play commentary on a football game—describing the destruction on screen—and how one pundit, in a detached voice only possible from the comfort of a news studio, said, "It's A-Day in Iraq; shock and awe is finally underway," he screamed at the TV.

He threw the remote as hard as he could at the screen, cracking it.

Elisa, Myra, and Andy rushed into the room and pushed him onto the bed.

Myra grabbed his arm.

Andy took hold of his ankles.

Elisa snatched his medication from the nightstand before jumping onto his chest.

He thrashed beneath her weight, swinging Myra hard against the wall and kicking Andy to the floor, knocking the wind out of both of his children.

Elisa popped open the bottle and poured out a pill to jam into his mouth.

He shot the tranquilizer out like a bullet and yelled, "I need to be awake!"

"No, you don't!" Elisa motioned for Myra to grab the pills from the floor and return them to her.

"But it's got his spit," Myra said.

"Get them now!"

Myra did as she was told. She handed her mother the wet pills.

Elisa stuffed the tranquilizer back into his mouth, clamping his jaw shut as if he were a pit bull. "Go back to sleep. Go back—the fuck—to sleep."

Elisa sat on his chest until he stopped thrashing and fell silent. She climbed off and backed away with Myra.

Andy stood up to look at his father before glancing back at Elisa. "I hate you! I want my mom!" He shoved Elisa out of his way and ran out of his father's bedroom, heading upstairs to his own.

Elisa sighed before following Myra out, joining Daphne, who had never left the family room. She was oblivious to the chaos, absorbed in what she enjoyed most: playing with numbers in her math workbook.

For Myra, everything was back to being A-okay. Elisa had returned the Minotaur to his deep sleep.

A fragile calm had returned to their lives.

AUGUST 27, 2014

He held onto the wheel, steering his car down a long road that disappeared into the night. Up ahead, a blue sign welcomed travelers to Tennessee.

His phone, resting against the dashboard, pulsed with bright light from an incoming text message. He grabbed it to look at the screen.

It was from Daphne. The message read:

ESTEFANIA

Dad, wherever you are, I hope you're A-okay. I love you.

A heap of broken images, all taken from memories of a life that no longer exists, continued to flash through his mind in a series of scattered visions:

JUNE 26, 2001

She opened her eyes and looked into the eyes of her father before closing them. ...

AUGUST 22, 2014

She looked into his eyes and smiled. ...

AUGUST 27, 2014

The memories of his loved ones' final moments caused him to lose control of his car, skidding off the road and coming to a halt.

He rushed out, dropped to his knees, and vomited along the shoulder.

He coughed and gasped for air until he stopped.

On hands and knees, he looked up at the vast night sky for any sign that she was out there, watching.

But there were no shooting stars in Tennessee tonight.

There would be no more signs of life, love, and joy.

There was only karma and the memory of how he met his shooting star—his Emma.

❦ 4 ❦

EURYDICE

IT WAS A FRIDAY NIGHT. HE WAS SEATED AT A TABLE IN A DIMLY LIT room somewhere on the Lower East Side of Manhattan, watching the emcee of the poetry slam scan the crowd from the stage.

The emcee announced, "Once again, for those who are new, my name is Reginald Superstar. Thank you for making The Loft a part of your night. No disrespect to our featured readers—they're all brilliant—but I think they'd all agree that we've saved the best for last."

"No, we don't!" someone yelled from the back.

Reginald laughed. "It's all a matter of opinion. I'll leave it up to you good people to decide. Put your hands together and give it up for Sylvia."

The audience clapped as she walked onto the stage, dressed in a black tank top and blue jeans.

Part of the reason he was at The Loft was because of her. He had seen Sylvia's picture in a magazine, in an article about spoken word poetry, while in the waiting room of a veterans' hospital. The more he looked at the photo of her yelling into a microphone like a punk rock star, the more he felt compelled to solve what had become a riddle for him:

Why did he feel like he knew her?

Why did he feel the need to return to her?

Why did she feel like déjà vu?

It was something he hoped to find out.

Sylvia grabbed the microphone from Reginald and pushed him out of her spotlight. She turned to face the audience and began laughing, seemingly amused by their enthusiasm.

"Settle down, people, settle down. It's not that serious," she said.

Her face became expressionless as she waited for everyone to do as she asked. All became quiet.

She brushed curls of auburn hair away from her face, held the microphone close to her full lips, and with closed eyes, whispered, "An ode to my hairy pussy."

When someone from the back laughed and said in a low voice, "What the fuck?" she opened her eyes and said, "Yeah, I wrote a poem about my hairy pussy. Got a problem with that? If you do, I don't care.

"Lovers have asked, 'Why did I let myself go?'

"Am I trying to put out, through my scent, amplified, that I'm the baddest bitch around?

"That's true,

"Especially in this room.

"But that's not why I've let myself go.

"Fuck you for even thinking that!"

She began to pace the stage.

"Maybe I don't want her to get sick.

"Maybe her health is more important to me

"Than your need

"To reduce me to a prepubescent,

"Which is creepy as fuck.

"No!

"I don't give a shit if my pussy is beautiful or not."

She returned to the spotlight and scanned the audience until she made eye contact with him and smiled.

"Think of a lock of my pubic hair

"As a souvenir

"From the Gift Shop

"That is my body."

She looked away to point at a man standing in the back.

"You can show it off to your friends.

"You can say, 'See? I fucked her.'

"And you'd be wrong."

She began to laugh.

"I'm the one who would've fucked you.

"I like to fuck.

"It's no business of yours who.

"You don't pay my bills,

"Not that I'd let you, no!

"You've not been there through my wars!

"You've not been there through my pain!

"You have zero impact on my life!

"You're about as disposable as they come!

"I won't remember your name after I'm done—"

Sylvia paused her performance to take a step back and cover her mouth, trying not to show how amused she was with herself. When the audience began to laugh at how much she struggled to keep a serious face, she couldn't hold back anymore and burst out laughing.

"I can't bullshit you people," she said.

"I was going to go on and on as if I were making some grand political statement. The truth is, I haven't had a boyfriend in a long-ass time; I'm super lazy, and it's a lot of fun making shampoo horns out of my pubes while I'm in the shower."

She looked at him again and smiled.

"My name is Sylvia Hadid James

"And now you know.

"Peace."

The audience erupted in applause as Reginald walked on stage and reached for the microphone. Instead of giving it to him, Sylvia dropped it and walked away. Reginald laughed, grabbed it from the floor, stood up, and announced the start of the open mic portion of the night.

Sylvia made her way to the bar in the far corner of the room, where a bartender handed her a glass of water. Other performers approached her, trying to get her attention, but she didn't seem interested. She shifted her focus away from them and toward him, staring for a long moment before offering a welcoming smile, then turning away.

Throughout the night, they exchanged glances until she seemed to grow impatient. She stepped away from her admirers and approached him. He rose from his seat and met her in the middle of the dark room. He towered above her. Sylvia raised her head to meet his gaze. Her face—with copper undertones and heavy-lidded eyes—flashed a bright smile.

"I feel like we've met before," she said.

"I was just thinking the same thing," he replied.

"You were? 'Cause I was just saying that."

"You mean you lied to me? How could you?"

"But I had to," she pleaded mockingly. "I didn't know what else to say, and something told me you're kind of dumb, and that I needed to make the first move, which is something I'd never, ever do—especially since you're not my type."

He pretended to be offended. "What do you mean, not your type?"

"I don't like guys who look and dress the way you do, with your silver earrings and pretty-boy clothes, and hair all slicked back—you're a player."

"I'm not a player."

"Yeah, you are. Shouldn't you be at a club instead?"

"I should," he said. "There'd be a lot prettier girls there."

She smiled, pretending to be offended. "If you feel that way, then tell me, why are you here? I know your goofy-ass can't read or write."

Just as he was about to respond to her playful teasing, Reginald called his name from the stage.

"Is that you?" Sylvia asked.

"Yeah," he replied.

"Then you better go."

"I'll be back—don't go anywhere. Gotta bomb on stage real quick."

"You do that!" she yelled as he walked away,

He stepped onto the stage to a scattering of claps and took the microphone from Reginald. He stammered as he introduced himself to an uncaring audience.

Sylvia came over and sat at a table in front of the stage, looking at him with bright, curious eyes.

He smiled at her. "I was gonna share a poem dedicated to my asshole father, but since I look like someone who doesn't know how to read, I'm gonna freestyle something off the top of my head instead."

Someone yelled from the back, "Nobody cares!"

Sylvia swung around in her seat. "I care!"

All became quiet.

He brushed strands of his dark hair back into place, pushing his undercut into a perfectly coiffed position. He held the microphone close to his lips and said, "It seems like I ring.

"The same doorbell and pick-up

"The same girl, and we go to

"The same café with

"The same guitarist playing

"The same sad songs as we sit at

"The same table, next to another couple doing

"The same thing, and I ask my date

"The same question about her interests, and she gives me

"The same answer: 'I have none,' and after dinner, we leave the café and walk down

"The same path through

"The same park, and I try to hold my date's hand, but she repeats

"The same gesture of withdrawal, and I feel

"The same doubt about whether this date is going well or whether it's not, and I hear

"The same voices echoing in my mind over and over, wondering why I am doing

"The same thing, all the time, as we finally reach my car, and I open the door for her, and I wait for her to settle in before closing, and she does

"The same shuffles in her seat and forgets to unlock my side of the door, leaving me feeling

"The same sense of apprehension about the game,

"This fucking game, as I drive up

"The same highways, and I try to find out if we like

"The same things, but everything I say is met with

"The same look of indifference as I exit the highway and drive up

"The same avenues and pull-up before

"The same building, and I park, and we get out of the car, and I walk her to

"The same door, with her giving me

"The same invitation to go upstairs, but that's not what I want. It's no longer what I need. Since I was thirteen, it's been

"The same thing, and I'm twenty-three now, and after everything I've been through and everything I've survived, I'm tired of it always being about sex...

"I'm looking for love."

He focused on Sylvia.

"How big of a number does it have to be before the soul longs for something more?

"I don't know about you, but I've tried doing the math, and I've lost count. And I don't know what effect that'll have on me and my ability to connect with women when now, what I need the most is to love and be loved."

He paused, letting the words hang in the space between him and Sylvia before looking at the rest of the audience, now paying attention.

"If love is what I need, then I'd have no choice but to walk away from

"The same invitation to go upstairs.

"To walk away from anyone who thinks I have only one thing on my mind.

"Because I'm playing a different game.

"I want to meet a woman who also has love on her mind.

"I wouldn't give a shit if she'd lost count at some point in her life.

"It's priceless to win the love of a woman like that because, to win her, a man would have to understand it's about more than the giving of her body;

"A man has to show he's worth the giving of her soul,

"The building and the giving of her trust

"And that's what I want.

"I want her surrender,

"And I would want to surrender to her because,

"After facing death,

"I want a woman who also wants more,

"Who needs more than boring small talk.

"Who's not afraid to live hard

"And love hard

"All within boundaries.

"Who, in the space between our bodies,

"In a sacred tantric posture,

"She'd find her life's meaning

"And show me mine."

He focused on Sylvia, who looked at him with wide eyes and her chin resting on her hands, making him feel like they were the only ones in the room.

"I want a woman who will join me

"In carving out joy

"From this ordinary world

"In such a passionate and exciting way

"That we will both realize

"We've been living

"All this time

"In a beautiful world of the alive.

"Players don't think like that,

"But lovers do.

"And that's who I am...

"Thank you for listening."

Sylvia's lone clapping boomed over the hushed sounds of drunks talking over each other. She got up from her seat to meet him as he came off the stage.

"What do you think?" he asked.

"I think a hit dog hollers the loudest," she replied.

"What does that even mean?"

"It means I'm still not convinced."

"Still?"

"Yeah, but I can be."

"What else do I need to do?"

"Oh, I don't know... Maybe you can dance with me? Do you like to dance?"

"I love to dance."

"Great! I know a spot around the corner. We can go there. But first, I've gotta go backstage and get my stuff." She stopped talking and stared at him for a long moment.

"Is everything okay?"

She looked into his eyes and smiled. "Yeah... Something tells me you shouldn't talk anymore, so stop. Can you meet me outside?"

"I can do that."

"Great! I'll be with you in a few."

He left Sylvia behind and pushed his way through the smoke and the crowd until he was outside, standing in front of The Loft. She appeared moments later, dressed in a faux leather jacket.

"Is it safe to talk?" he asked.

"Oh my God, yes," she replied. "I'm so sorry. I know that was weird, but it was a gut reaction to this voice in my head."

"Voice?"

She nudged him. "Shut up; you know what I mean."

"I know. I'm just fucking with you."

"That's okay. I can fuck with you right back." Sylvia grabbed his hand and began leading him away.

"Where are you taking me?" he asked.

"Robots," she replied.

"I know that spot."

"You do? I've never seen you there."

"That's because I could never get in. I don't have any juice."

"Well, it's a good thing you know a hotshot now 'cause I'm up to my eyeballs in juice. You'll see."

After walking down the street and around the corner, they arrived at an old, gated storefront on Avenue B. Sylvia approached a large bouncer who opened the door for them.

They went downstairs and found themselves in a dark basement. The floor was both slick and sticky. People danced in every corner of

the large room, with a giant strobe mirror ball hanging from the ceiling, making everyone's eyes twinkle like stars. The way Sylvia's eyes—
one blue and the other dark hazel—twinkled the brightest filled him
with so much joy, with so much want, with so much hunger and need
that he pulled her close to look directly into them and see where the
land of his dreams could begin.

"Hey," she said, laughing in his arms.

"Hey, what?" he replied.

She relaxed her body and smiled. "I don't know you like that, to be
pulling me."

"You do now. What's my name?"

"You're gonna try to get me to do that?"

"I'm not disposable—you're gonna remember my name."

"Oh, is that right?"

"Yeah, that's right. So say it."

After a pause where she acted as if deep in thought, she looked at
him with eyes like shooting stars. "Does it start with the letter A?"

"It sure does."

"Does it end with an S?"

"Yup."

"I know! It's Andrés! Your name is Andrés!"

"That's right."

"What's my name?"

"Sylvia."

"Say it again, this time, with a little more *oomph*."

"Sylvia!"

"And don't you forget it."

"I won't. You're gonna show me what you got going on down
there."

"I am?"

"Yes, you are. I need to see that hairy mess for myself."

She laughed, turning her face away to hide her surprise at how
direct and raw he was with her. She looked back at him with fake exasperation. "You just can't come at me like that. What happened to
romance?"

"This is the romance."

She laughed. "Whatever—just shut the fuck up and dance. Just dance with me. I need to feel if you're gonna be worth it. And when I do, I'll take you to the Gift Shop."

Sylvia held Andrés tight as they began to sway to the sensual drumbeats playing over the sound system, with a disembodied voice chanting, *"Breathe love into me... Breathe love into me."* Sylvia and Andrés continued to sway in the dark room, their bodies feeling as one while slowly circling beneath the strobe mirror ball. It was as if they were stars, making their eternal turn around the bright core of the Milky Way Galaxy.

❧ *5* ❧

THE SHAME GAME

AUGUST 27, 2014

HIS PHONE VIBRATED LOUDLY ON THE DASHBOARD AND COULD BE heard outside while he was on his knees, remembering the night he met Emma, wondering where it had all gone wrong.

JULY 22, 2001

Andrés followed Alene as she cackled maniacally, running and jumping over branches and rocks until they emerged from the darkness of the heavily wooded park onto the lamp-lit streets. He kept up with her as she led the way past other revelers still crowding the streets to a lounge near the Gendarmenmarkt. She told him this was where they could hide from the police. Once inside, the hostess guided them past other couples at tables—some laughing, others in quiet conversation— to a booth in the back with soft cushions and dim lighting.

He looked around before sitting down. "This is nice."

Alene looked behind her before turning her focus back to him and sitting down as well. "I know... it's too nice to be here with a stranger. I still don't know your name."

He laughed, remembering how he had introduced himself to her earlier in the evening. "It's Andrés."

"It's nice to meet you, Mr. Andrés. Are you here for the Love Parade?"

"I'm here for work. I'm a tech consultant."

"What a small world—so is my fiancé."

"Is he?" Andrés reached into his wallet for his business card and handed it to her.

She glanced at it, then looked back at him, confused. "What am I supposed to do with this?"

"I'm always networking. I'm sure your fiancé would want you to do the same."

"I don't think so."

"With the way things are going, guys like us are scrambling for work. Client demand is dropping everywhere. Ask him."

She placed Andrés's business card in her designer handbag. "I don't think so, especially when you're going to be my big secret."

Before Andrés could respond, a waitress approached to take their drink order. Alene asked for Pinot Noir, while Andrés asked for whiskey. The waitress took his credit card and left.

Alene appeared amused. "Whiskey? Do you also own a pickup truck?"

He sighed. "I've never needed a shot more than I do now. I don't drink, but this month has been the worst. This week has been just as bad."

"If I may ask, why?"

He hesitated before answering. "What's the worst thing that could happen to you?"

Alene was silent, as if lost in thought. Then a surprised expression appeared on her face. "Did someone die? Is that why you want to kill yourself?"

Andrés had forgotten that he had revealed this not only to Ina when she accused him of not being a "real man," but also to Alene. He realized this wasn't how he wanted their conversation to go, especially since he had gone to the Love Parade not to dwell on death but to carve out joy and keep himself alive.

"Forget I said anything," he said.

"You're the one who brought it up," she said.

"Then I'm changing it up: Are you here for the Love Parade?"

She said in a flat voice, "I live in Berlin."

"I thought you were from Johannesburg."

"I moved here last year."

"That's nice." Andrés yawned.

Alene arched an eyebrow. "Am I boring you? Because you're boring me too, and I didn't come here for that. So, here's what I'm thinking: I saved you, and now you owe me."

"Owe you?"

"Yes, owe me. I have a sister who met a guy like you in one of those chat rooms. She bombarded him with all this love and attention, convincing him that she was his 'One.' Now he supports her and my niece, and because my sister had stopped taking the pill, they have a baby. Miss AOL had the same plan for you."

He chuckled. "I don't think so."

"Where did you say you met her again?"

"In a chat room."

"Yeah, I saved you. All men are the same: weak."

"The men you deal with are weak. I can control myself."

She reached across the table to grab his hand. "So, if I were to say, 'Lothar is in Paris, let's go back to my place,' would you say no?"

"In a heartbeat."

"You say that, but we both know you can't turn me down."

"Oh, yes, I can."

"But I'm beautiful."

Andrés pulled his hand back. "No one is more beautiful than my Emma."

She chuckled. "You say that because you're in love, but you can't fool me. I felt you get hard while we were dancing. You know you want to fuck me."

"No."

"There'd be no strings attached; I promise. Your precious Emma will never know."

"But I would."

"Come on... I've never been with someone *exotic*."

"No."

"Real men never turn down pussy unless they're gay. It's okay if you are... are you?"

"Excuse me, but I need to use the toilet."

She leaned back, frustrated. "Go on... I'll be here."

Andrés stood up and rushed past the waitress approaching their booth with drinks. He dashed down a long hallway into the bathroom, leaned against a sink, and stared into the mirror.

"What are you doing?" he said to his reflection. "You know none of this makes any sense. There's nothing special about *you*. You're just a thirty-one-year-old man with a bit of a gut and a boring-ass haircut. Something's up. You better go! Get out!"

Andrés gave his reflection one last look before washing his hands and leaving. When he returned to the booth, his glass of whiskey sat on the table in front of Alene, next to her Pinot Noir.

"You're back."

"I am, but I've gotta go," he said.

Alene grabbed his arm. "Wait! I know I got weird, but I was trying to make this fun. I'm coming off a dreadful week, too. You don't know how close I came to hurting myself. I need an escape." She tugged at his arm. "Can you sit? Please?"

How could he say no? Alene was at the Love Parade for the same reasons: to carve out joy and avoid hurting herself. Andrés did as she asked, ignoring the warning he had given his reflection, and sat next to her.

Alene looked relieved. "Thank you. I know you have to go, but I've been struggling. I've had no one to talk to, no one who could help me figure out, before Lothar comes home, whether I should stay or go. The people I do have are those I've met because of him, and they would either judge me or push me to consider what's best for him. I feel trapped... Dancing with you hasn't helped."

"What did I do?"

Alene fiddled with her hair. "You've helped me understand why I feel the way I do... I know it's going to sound silly, and I know I should be happy. Lothar is a nice guy who makes great money and would make an excellent dad, but when I'm with him, I don't feel that spark—that passion. Lothar is not my soulmate... He doesn't like to dance."

"Did you tell him how you feel?"

"I've told him that sometimes I feel alone. He sends me flowers as if that's a solution. I don't think it matters anymore. So as long as he gives me a comfortable life, that's what counts, right? Especially if I want children, right? And I can still look when I'm married—still have my fun, right? I mean, real fun." She smirked. "I could start a fight, make him feel like he's to blame, and tell him we need a break, then leave for a few months. When I'm ready to come back, I could get him to apologize for making me feel alone—for putting his work before me—and we can move on."

"If you feel this way, then why are you getting married?"

She shrugged. "I don't know, but there are things I want from life that, if I don't act now, I'll never get. I'm getting older. My soulmate says he loves me, but he refuses to give me what I want the most. I've had to move on, and here I am, now in Berlin... Maybe it's for the best... My soulmate is a bum who only remembers me when he wants to dance and have sex, which we still do whenever I go back to Johannesburg."

"That's fucked up."

She sighed. "I know, but my ex is like that one beautiful drug. He has me hooked, but I can't deal with any more of his bullshit. To get what I want, I need stability. I want comfort. Yes—Lothar is the man who can give that to me."

"You're using him."

"No, I'm not."

"It sounds like you are."

"You're a man—you don't get it."

"Yes, I do."

"Is Emma your soulmate, or did you also have to settle?"

Andrés smiled, remembering happier times. "From the moment we met, we both knew there was something supernatural about our connection. No matter where we were in our lives or in the world, we could sense what the other was going through. But it took us years to feel safe enough to call each other soulmates. But now, I'm scared... I can't feel her anymore... I'm afraid she may have hurt herself."

"Have you called her?"

"I have, but she's not answering. She hasn't responded to any of my emails. Something is wrong."

Alene rolled her eyes.

"You don't understand," Andrés said.

"Yes, I do—death—but did she pick a fight with you?"

"It's not just any death... Something's wrong."

"If it's that bad, and you knew there was a chance she could hurt herself, then why did you come to Berlin? Shouldn't you be at home with her instead?"

"With all the medical bills we're facing, I need this job now more than ever."

Alene waved him off, annoyed. "Excuses... I'm so tired of hearing it. Lothar said the same thing before leaving. He needs the job, and I told him I didn't move here to spend so much time alone. He left anyway. And here I am, at an after-hours lounge with a stranger, feeling dead inside too... If my soulmate had lived in Berlin, he would've made time for me. He would've gone to the Love Parade with me. I came with friends instead."

Andrés scoffed. "It's easy to make time when you're a bum, but when you have to pay for something like that *Hermès* handbag you keep letting touch the floor, men like your fiancé know what's up. They have to keep that cash flow going."

Alene laughed. "You know your brands? Are you sure you're not gay?"

He laughed. "I bought a purple one like that for Emma. She didn't want it and got so mad at me for spending so much money on something that, in her words, was trivial—especially when we were paying out of pocket for so many of her medical procedures. But once she held it and felt the quality, she started strutting around like a super-model, like she was invincible. After working hard for most of her life and everything she'd been through, I wanted her to have nice things. She deserves nice things."

"Lothar said the same thing to me!" Alene's face became sad as she paused to think. "I love him so much... I hate myself for comparing him to my soulmate, but what am I to do? If I can't have everything I want, I need to be happy with what I can get, right? And for what I want in life, Lothar needs to travel. But still, I miss dancing."

"Why can't you make things work with your soulmate? Even if he's a bum, who cares?"

"He has nothing to offer except dancing and dick."

"So what? Neither did I. But Emma stood by me, and before our lives fell apart, we had built a beautiful life together. She believed in me; I believed in her. Why can't you do the same for what's-his-name?"

"Liam."

"Give Liam a chance."

Alene stopped talking, her eyes drifting from side to side as if daydreaming about family life with her soulmate. After a moment, she shook her head, rejecting the vision her daydream had given her. "You know what? I don't have time for that. I want to be a mom. I want to build a home with a man who'll provide for our children—who isn't prettier than me—who won't have mistresses or illegitimate children. Lothar is an immensely decent and trustworthy man. I can build my life with him, and I'm so lucky he loves me with all my flaws."

Alene began to smile. "You've helped me think it through. There's more to life than passion. I think it's good that he doesn't love music the way I do. He balances me out. Lothar brings me peace... I'm not sad anymore."

"I'm glad to be of help," Andrés said.

"Immensely helpful. I can finally message him back. Lothar has been bombarding me with emails all week, asking if everything is fine with us, and I've had to ignore him."

"At least acknowledge him."

"For what? So he could ask me why I went silent, pressure me to tell him? I don't think so." Alene paused, then burst out with a wicked laugh.

"What's so funny?" Andrés asked.

She took a sip of wine before saying, "I think I know why your girl-friend isn't responding. Have you considered that maybe your Emma is in a lounge with another guy, trying to figure things out too? Maybe she met him while dancing and is trying to get him to fuck her, like I tried with you. Maybe Emma said, 'I don't care anymore' because she's sad and in pain from her soulmate abandoning her to face death alone. I don't know who died, but when my little brother passed away, I watched my mom deal with it alone while my dad went back to work like nothing had happened. I think that's why she's ignoring your calls. You're an asshole who cares more about your job than her."

It was as if Alene could read him—his mind, his situation—how everything she said mirrored what he and Emma had been through. There was no way Andrés could respond to Alene other than by grabbing his shot glass filled with whiskey and gulping it down, as if drinking would help him forget the overwhelming shame of aban-doning the woman who had devoted herself to him—who had given him his first feeling of oneness while slowly circling beneath the strobe mirror ball the first time he danced with her, making what felt like their eternal turn around the bright core of the Milky Way Galaxy—who, from their first moment together in her Purple Room, had surrendered and given him the most valuable thing she had—her vulnerability—all so he could get on a plane bound for Berlin and abandon her just to avoid dealing with his emotions in front of her.

The room began spinning around him like a carnival ride. He stood and stumbled away.

From the booth, Alene yelled, "Go on! Do what you do best! Leave!"

Andrés approached the bar to settle the tab and retrieve his credit card. He struggled to keep his balance, stumbling out of the lounge.

Outside, he tried to figure out where he was and how to get back to the hotel. Music from the nearby Love Parade blared in the distance, and stragglers from the event roamed the streets.

Alene appeared from behind and grabbed his shoulder. "I can't believe you actually walked away. Where are you going?"

"Back to my room."

"But the night's not done. We're not done."

"Yes, we are," Andrés said, waving at passing taxis, but they all seemed occupied.

"You're going to leave me behind, looking like this?"

"Yup."

Alene blocked his path. "But I'm alone."

"Okay, and?"

"I left my friends to dance with you!"

"So?"

"How am I supposed to get home?"

"The same way you got here."

Alene stomped her foot. "I can't! Look at me! Look at me!"

For the first time, Andrés saw Alene as she truly was—not as the spirit conjured by the magic spell of their dance, but as a person at her most vulnerable. She wore a sheer yellow top and knee-high yellow boots. Her short skirt hung below the waistline of her almost emaciated body.

Alene began to plead. "Can't you see? It's too late for me to ride the U-Bahn alone, and even if I get a taxi, I wouldn't feel safe. I know you don't know me, but I left my friends so I could dance with you. I wasn't planning on leaving the Love Parade, but we did—and that's because of you. Now you owe me. You can pay me back by taking me to your room. I promise—I'll sleep on the floor, the couch, whatever. I don't care. I just don't want anything to happen to me on my way home. Please, don't be that guy who says no. Be a real man!"

He sighed. "You can have the couch."

She hugged him. "Thank you, thank you, thank you! I knew you were a real man. Where are we staying?"

"I'm at the Four Seasons."

She giggled. "We don't need a taxi. Your hotel is down the street. I'll take you there."

Alene wrapped her arm around his waist and tried to lead him away. But after a moment of drunken walking, Andrés stumbled and fell onto the pavement.

"I don't know what's going on," he said, struggling to push himself up.

"You said you're not a drinker. What did you expect?"

"I don't know, but not this," he said, slurring his words.

She helped him stand and kept him propped up as they staggered through the streets. Eventually, they arrived at the hotel. He leaned against her as they entered the lobby. She steered him into the elevator. Each time he tried to press a button, he missed.

"I got it. Which floor?" she asked.

"Top, top, top," he replied.

The motion of the elevator made Andrés slump into a corner. When they reached the top floor, he crawled out. Alene followed him down the hall to his room. She reached into his pocket for the key and opened the door. Inside, he crawled to the bed.

She turned on the TV. Music from the last channel he'd watched began to play.

He closed his eyes.

A paralysis began to spread through his body—the kind he used to feel as a little boy when he couldn't tell if he was awake or dreaming, if he was in the Land of the Alive or the Land of the Not-Alive.

If he was still asleep.

In the background, the TV played music, its melodies anchoring his senses to the present and making the dreams he felt himself slipping into seem less like *a heap of broken images*. He tried to make sense of it all, of a woman's voice whispering, "Relax, I'm good at this."

The voice wasn't Emma's, and because of that, and because he hadn't given Alene his permission, it made what she was doing to him wrong—so wrong—that it made Andrés scream, "No! Stop!"

It made him keep shouting, "No! Stop!" as if he were being hacked to pieces by a maenad in a frenzy.

But no sound came out.

He yelled at himself to wake up, and when he did, he found Alene on her knees and elbows, stroking him off into her mouth. The room appeared to spin—a physical force that kept him pinned to the bed.

Alene locked her eyes on him. She sprang from her knees, grabbed his wrists, and mounted him.

He had no power to push her off, to move her—to make her stop pulling hard on his hair, to get her hands off his mouth.

She bit her bottom lip harder with each forceful grind of her hips against his paralyzed body. Her mouth turned red. Blood dripped onto his face. Her inner pulse induced him to ejaculate. She let out a high-pitched screech, her entire body flushing red. She fell against him, unmoving, breathing hard against his chest.

After several deep breaths, she sat up and wiped the blood from her mouth with the back of her hand. Color began to fade from the rest of her body, as if something within Alene was returning from a frenzy, and she was back behind her mask.

Her freckled face was gaunt and pale again. She pushed herself off him and lay beside him, placing a pillow under the arch of her back.

He stared at her, wide-eyed and unable to move.

Alene turned to him and chuckled. "You look so funny lying there... I can see what you're thinking, and no, I'm not desperate. It's just that I've never had sex with someone so *exotic* before. I know, I know—there are plenty of foreign men in Berlin, but I've never met one who's Puerto Rican, and I've heard stories. The moment I first saw you, I knew I had to have you.

"After you turned me down, I got wet thinking about taking you like this instead. It's a lot more exciting. Like big-game hunting. Taking down a big, pretty boy like you... It makes me want to stay and play some more, but I don't think that's a good idea. Once the drugs I used to spike your drink wear off, there's no telling what you'll do. So I'm going to go."

Alene got up from bed and went into the bathroom to clean herself up. When she came back, she tossed the razor blade that had been on the bathroom floor onto the bed next to Andrés on the bed.

"I found this," she said, getting dressed.

Once finished, she looked at him again. "I can't help but think that if you'd done the right thing and stayed with your *girlfriend,* we wouldn't have met. But we did. I'm glad you're a piece of shit—I got what I wanted. You can kill yourself now."

She walked to the door and picked up the yellow handbag she had dropped earlier.

Before leaving, she gave him one last look.

"For the record, you were my *Junggesellinnenabschied*. I didn't come here with friends, and my car's parked in a garage. Ciao!"

SEPTEMBER 10, 2001

After spending the summer in Berlin and arriving directly from the airport, Andrés spent the rest of the evening with his daughter and stepdaughter at Elisa's apartment. As he was about to leave, she stopped him. "You need to call in; tomorrow is a big day for Daphne."

"I know, but I can't. This meeting is like a job interview," he replied.

"How many days did you take off because of what's-her-name?"

"That's not fair—it's not the same."

"Yes, it is. Daphne is the one still here."

"I'm trying to take care of her, too."

"Then call in. Let them know you'll be late. It's not like I'm asking you to take the day off."

"These people don't know me, and because of Paul, I have no more juice with the firm—I need to stay in the city."

"I hate that you're doing it more for whatever-her-name is now than for Daphne, even after she disappeared. You're not a real man."

He sighed. "Going to that meeting is what I'm supposed to do— I'm trying to take care of my family."

Elisa threw her hands up in frustration. "Fine—you be the asshole. Break the bad news yourself. Tell Daphne you won't be there for her first day of school."

AUGUST 27, 2014

Andrés got up from where he was kneeling and went to his car to grab his phone.

He acknowledged Daphne's text messages with one reply:

DAD

I love you too, always.

He tossed his phone onto the passenger seat, drove off the shoulder of the road, and continued his drive to the End of the World —a bridge spanning high above the Rio Grande Gorge. It was there that he used to take Emma every Friday night before life fell apart. She loved the view of the stars hanging over the mountains in what she called the "unreal beauty of a vast tenement sky."

❧ *6* ❧

THE PURPLE ROOM

IT WAS FOUR IN THE MORNING. SYLVIA AND ANDRÉS WERE LOST IN the music, the beat vibrating through them. She slowed down, raising her head from his chest, and said, "Time for the Gift Shop."

"I don't know if I wanna go anymore," he replied.

"Fuck that bullshit, let's go."

Sylvia grabbed his hand and led Andrés off the dance floor, upstairs, and out of Robots. Every step through the moonlit streets, they kissed and groped each other until they stopped in front of her building at the edge of Tompkins Square Park.

She led him inside to the top floor, into the darkness of her apartment, and into her bedroom. She pushed him onto the bed. He felt her breathing move away from him in the dark, toward the space in front of him.

She opened a set of black curtains, then undressed in the moonlight streaming through the window, spreading wide across the purple walls.

He stood up and undressed in her shadow.

She glowed as she returned to stand naked before him.

He sat on the bed again and demanded that she sit on his lap, facing him. "That's how I want you: eye-to-eye, breath-to-breath."

"Lips to lips," she said as she did as he asked. She inhaled, holding her breath as she took him inside her, wrapping her arms and legs around his torso. Sylvia let out a long exhale and began slowly grinding her hips on his.

He grabbed her ass to make her stop. "No. Not yet."

"But why?"

"Because I said so."

She gave him a confused look but complied. Her inner pulse began to beat harder, squeezing him tighter with each passing second.

The urge to thrust came through his body as a twitch inside her. It made Sylvia restless, causing her hips to rock without thinking.

He grabbed her ass to make her stop again. "I said no. Not yet."

"But why?" she asked, breathing hard.

"Because you didn't say please."

"Are you serious?"

"Yes, I'm serious."

"But I felt you twitch!"

"Because I want you so bad."

"Then move!"

"What's the word I'm looking for?"

Sylvia raised an eyebrow, seemingly surprised and intrigued by his audacity.

He asked again, "What's the word... I'm looking for?"

"Please, I want to fuck you."

He smacked her ass. "Then do it."

Sylvia began to ride him, her nails digging into his back. He kissed the sweat from between her breasts. She pulled back his head by the hair. His face tilted toward hers. She kissed him, biting his lip.

He curled his toes and moaned. She swung her head back to look at the ceiling and moaned. His body tensed up.

She stopped moving and looked back at him with a wicked smile. "I can play this game, too. Want me to keep going?"

"You know I do," he said, struggling to remain still.

"Then what's the word I'm looking for?"

"Please."

"Say it again!"

"Please, I want to fuck you."

She smacked his face. "Then fuck me."

Andrés thrust his hips harder into her. Sylvia pressed her breasts against his face. He wrapped his arms around her and inhaled her floral perfume, mixed with sweat. She tightened her legs around him to keep herself from being bucked off. His hands raced across her back. Her fingers clutched hard at his hair.

Body to body, they rocked until Sylvia's inner pulse quivered, and he exploded hard inside her, moaning long and loud into her mouth, now wide open in her ecstasy.

They fell back, stunned, to lie next to each other in bed, breathing heavily. Their breaths slowly synced, still in ecstasy—a silent union leaving them drifting for several long moments in a peace barely within their understanding.

His hands were in her hair, hers on his chest.

He closed his eyes, then opened them when her fingers began lazily tracing the scars etched across his chest.

Sylvia propped herself up on an elbow and gazed at the tips of her fingers as they lightly traced the scars along the side of his buzz-cut head, made bare by his undercut hairstyle.

She hesitated before sitting up. "I know this is so random, especially after we fucked, but... I've been meaning to ask: what happened?"

He looked at her, unsure of how to reply. "Those are keepsakes from my time in the army."

"You've got some crazy souvenirs."

"I was in the Gulf War." Andrés began tracing a scar beneath her hairline with his finger. "It looks like you've got a souvenir yourself."

She paused, her eyes looking up and away from him. "Yeah... I got so drunk one night that I lost my balance and banged my head against a sink. I woke up in my puke." Her eyes became unfocused as if grappling with dark memories. Then she took a deep breath, turned back to face him, and met his gaze with clear determination. "You know what?"

"What?" Andrés said.

"When I tell that story, I always say I got drunk and puked, but the truth is, I got high and pooped myself. There you go—my real and raw, my good times." Sylvia let out a nervous laugh, her hand shaking slightly as she brushed a strand of hair from her face. "The times were so good that 541 days ago, I decided not to do drugs anymore. I freebase poems now." She raised an eyebrow. "Speaking of poems, were you serious about what you said on stage, or was that part of your game to get me in bed? I mean, we've already fucked—you ran your game. Now that you've got yours, you can get up and leave. You wouldn't be the first."

The jaded expression on Sylvia's face made him want to show her how serious he was. He began to recite, "*In my sky at twilight, you are like a cloud, and your form and color are the way I love them.*"

He sat up and looked into her eyes. "*You are mine, mine, woman with sweet lips, and in your life my infinite dreams live.*"

Andrés pulled Sylvia closer. "*The lamp of my soul dyes your feet, my sour wine is sweeter on your lips, oh reaper of my evening song, how solitary dreams believe you to be mine! You are mine, mine, I go shouting it to the afternoon's wind, and the wind hauls on my windowed voice. Huntress of depths of my eyes, your plunder stills your nocturnal regard as though it were water.*"

He ran his fingers through her hair. "*You are taken in the net of my music, my love, and my nets of music are as wide as the sky. My soul is born on the shore of your eyes of mourning. In your eyes of mourning the land of dreams begins.*"

A bright smile came to Sylvia's face. "I love Pablo Neruda."

Andrés smiled, relieved he could share his favorite verses with her. "Me too. Do you know how many nights I've dreamed about moments like this? Looking into the eyes of a beautiful woman and sharing poems? It's been too many to count. It's what I've been living for—to be in a moment like this. I was in a coma. It's how I got these scars. When I woke up, I was told I had almost died, and that my wife had abandoned our newborn son with my parents. She left me for dead—I'm divorced now."

"You better be."

"I know—we wouldn't be talking if I were still married." He sighed;

regret etched on his face. "It was a big mistake... Joining the army and getting married just to get Lydia out of *that* house—away from her father."

"Is it what I'm thinking?" Sylvia asked, her face horrified.

"Yeah... Don't get me wrong; I'm glad I did it. Lydia had been suicidal, but I wish there'd been another way, that I didn't have to wake up the way I did—with a brain injury, broken bones, with nightmares that felt like they'd never end... I'd been in so much pain. It began to fuck with the way I'd see the world. I'd always been a happy guy, but I got so depressed—all that physical and speech therapy—all that pain—I lost hope. I wanted to die. I no longer wanted to live. That's when my mom gave me a book of poems by Pablo Neruda." Andrés began to smile again. "My mom wanted to remind me that the world was also a place of magic and ecstasy, a place to fill my senses with pleasure—that poetry is the cure when you know what's dark."

Sylvia whispered to herself, "Poetry is the cure."

"I'm gonna be straight up: I wanna feel the kind of love that would drive me to write poems like that. I'm living for that kind of love. I need that kind of love, but I won't get it if I don't take risks—if I don't take chances. I have to put myself out there. I have to get on stage and let it all hang out. And if I were to meet someone who'd be down with what I've got to say, then I'd have to be ready to take a chance on her. That's why I was at The Loft and not in a club."

She laughed. "You looked so out of place there."

He smiled. "I know... but where else can I meet a beautiful and intelligent woman like you?"

"You came to the right place, 'cause that's what you did."

"Enough about me. What about you?"

"What about me?" she asked.

"How did you end up at The Loft? What makes you wanna read?"

Sylvia stared wistfully at him. "Are you sure you wanna know?"

"Whatever you're comfortable sharing."

After a long, thoughtful pause, she said, her lips pursed and barely moving, with an accent that no longer sounded like it was from New York but Appalachia:

"I could give ya the usual answer I give everyone—that the ideas come easy, and I love performin'—but that'd be a lie. I don't like that I gotta do this—get on stage—but I ain't got no choice. I've seen first-hand what war can do to a family, to my nana, to my daddy, and—look—I ain't this crazy woman. It's what I want everyone to think, 'cause crazy's my shield—my armor, 'cause when I do feel, I feel so much, and it just overwhelms me—and for my own sake, I need folks to stay the hell away from me, 'cause for all them years, I had to numb myself with cocaine—with heroin—'cause I'd take in everything—and when I did open myself up to feelings, I'd feel 'em in stereo—and now that I'm sober, if I let the world in again—people in again—all their bullshit could just drag me down and destroy me again—so the scar—the scar reminds me that if I ain't careful, feelin' things ain't a good thing. I should do everything to make sure I don't wake up on a bathroom floor again—to have my shit together—to keep goin' up on stage and throwin' up my feelings so that I can keep my mental filters in check—I can keep 'em clean and not get 'em clogged up with all these other useless emotions that ain't mine to worry about—I don't know—I don't know—does that make sense?"

"You're making perfect sense," he said.

"Am I talking too much?"

"No."

"Good, because I don't care," she said, switching back to a New York accent. "When I was in rehab, I discovered Miguel Piñero and his *Lower East Side Poem*. Do you know who he is?"

"My mom knew him," he said.

"She did? That's so cool... My counselor in rehab knew him too. She gave me a book he had made for her, and I just fell in love with how he used words. Miguel made poetry seem so simple. I was able to connect with it. I was able to feel it. It wasn't this rigid, structured approach that I was so used to, where the form would smother the emotion. I wanted to feel again and not be numb, but on my terms. In that poem, I could feel him trying to keep himself from spinning out of control, yet I could also feel his command over his emotions, doing it on his terms. After the first time I read that poem, I knew what I needed to do because I have a love I never want to filter out and forget. A love that has never let me down—I needed to write. I needed to perform. I couldn't do her memory like that because I wanted to shut down, not feel, and survive."

"Is it okay if I ask who?"

Sylvia took a deep breath and swallowed. "My nana; she's dead."

"I'm sorry."

A sudden look of terror crossed Sylvia's face. It was as if, after revealing so much of herself, she realized she had never felt this naked in her true emotional form.

Andrés grabbed her hand to reassure her. "It's okay. Don't worry, I'm listening."

Her face became calm, as if she were entering a meditative state, ready to walk unharmed over the hot coals of memory. "Okay, I'm gonna be straight up now. Every time I perform, I feel like I'm reinventing myself. That's why I go to The Loft—I'm no longer that junkie lying in her shit. That was me, but it's not me—not anymore. I'm a poet now. I'm in touch with my feelings. I'm making better choices."

Sylvia paused and stared past Andrés, seemingly lost in thought, before absentmindedly biting her nails.

He took hold of Sylvia's hands, pulling her attention away from her thoughts and back to the present. "It seems like you made a choice to let me in."

She let out a small smile. "Don't kid yourself, Mr. Bullshit."

"I'm not, but it seems like you've shared things you've kept to yourself for a long time. Was that part of the Gift Shop experience, Miss Bullshit? You already got what you wanted."

Her smile became wider and brighter. "I got mine."

"You can tell me to leave right now. I'm as disposable as they come."

"Nah, I already gave you a nickname, and I don't like mine. Give me another one."

He kissed the back of her hand. "I love how your eyes streaked in the dark while we were dancing—like shooting stars."

"Shooting Star... I like that... I can live with that." Sylvia gave him a long, curious look. "So, Mr. Bullshit... do you still wanna die?"

"Do you?"

"Damn, you can read me."

"I had a feeling, and no, I don't wanna die—not anymore. I'm in love with life, with this night, with this moment where I'm touching you as we talk—savoring the way you feel. Because of you, I feel alive. Thank you."

She laughed. "Damn, you're good with the bullshit. It's like music out of your mouth."

"Call it whatever you want. I say what I feel."

She leaned in, coming face-to-face with him, and with a playful smirk said, "Hey, Orpheus, don't you know we're just a one-night stand?"

"Hey, Eurydice, I don't give a fuck."

"You know her?"

"Yeah, I know her... I know them all. And so what if we're just a one-night stand? I don't care. Just be. Soak this all in—the moment, the moon, the touching. It doesn't have to mean anything more than an affirmation of our love for life—a love found through poetry. Do you still wanna die?"

"Oh God, no! I feel alive!"

He lay back in bed. "Well, there you go. Enjoy my music—even if it's for one night."

She lay back with him, sliding into his arms, curling against him, and smiling. "Maybe one day, when we're both old, we'll look back on this night and remember what a wonderful time we had together—that is, if we ever break up."

"We're never breaking up. This is our eternal one-night stand. No worries about kids, bills, or any of that other bullshit."

"Thank God," she said, "and if we fight, we go hard so that we can have angry sex—fog up the windows from all that sweat we'll be making—fucking each other's brains out."

"You know it."

"On that note, because we're never breaking up and we're gonna be together forever, I've been holding in this fart, and it's starting to hurt. So, if you don't mind, I'm only human; I gotta let it out."

With that, Sylvia laughed as she passed gas. Their laughter echoed throughout the space until something in her, which seemed to have not been relaxed before, was now open, and raw, and vulnerable, shining through her eyes like stars. In that moment, he felt the weight of their connection—the weight of what could be love—terrifying in its immediacy and suddenness, touching on the sublime. It made him grab her again—making her eyes explode like supernovas—and kiss her as hard as he could ever kiss any woman. He felt her trying to kiss him as hard as she could kiss any man, and the two began to move their bodies once again under the moonlight coming through the windows of her Purple Room.

❧ 7 ❧

THE BURIAL OF THE DEAD

SEPTEMBER 11, 2001

ANDRÉS WAS LOST IN THE UNREAL AND CLEAR BEAUTY OF THE VAST blue sky over Lower Manhattan, as seen from the windows on the 105th floor of the South Tower at the World Trade Center—lost in the memories of his first visit to the building—until his client contact approached him in the reception area, bringing him back to the moment.

She led him into a conference room to discuss his work experience. Just as Andrés began listing his achievements, the lights flickered. A wave of heat swept through the room. The client rushed out without a word. Andrés followed, chasing after her across the office space to the windows. The heat from the black smoke billowing from the blown-out windows of the top floors of the North Tower was intense on his face.

A man in a white shirt, with his tie loose at the collar, appeared frantic at one of the shattered openings. Others appeared alongside him. They all began hanging from the cracks to avoid the smoke billowing out. Burning papers floated into a vast sky that was no longer blue.

Everyone in the office space behind Andrés remained chained to their desks, as if the North Tower were not on fire; it was just another ordinary day.

We are the Watchers, and We knew nothing about the day was ordinary. Andrés felt the gut reaction to Our voice in his head, yelling at him from across time and space for him to go—get out—especially after the man in the white shirt chose to jump from that height instead of burning.

Andrés raced to the exit and went down the stairwell. He called Emma. The line was busy. Others in the stairwell dropped to the floor. They became stuck in place.

Andrés pulled them off the floor by their arms and hands. "Don't stop! Keep going!"

He called Elisa. The line was busy. Public-address announcements declared the building secure. Those with no trust issues turned around and went back up the stairwell. Andrés kept going down. He tried calling Emma and Elisa again. He needed them to know that if something should happen—if he didn't make it out—his last words could be that he loved them. Even if he left it as a voice message, Andrés could be recorded saying he loved them—he loved his children. All the lines were busy.

He rushed into the sky lobby on the 78th floor, crowded with people waiting for elevators, all whispering, "How could a plane hit the North Tower? The sky is so clear and blue. How could the pilot not see the building? It doesn't make any sense."

We granted Andrés a brief vision. The South Tower was about to go down faster than a ship plunging to the bottom of the deep. It wouldn't make sense to wait for an express elevator.

He rushed to the nearest exit. He followed others around him, also hearing voices in their heads from those watching over them from beyond, guiding them to safety down the stairwell.

At 9:03 a.m.—

SEPTEMBER 12, 1992

Andrés dropped to the sidewalk, screaming in panic.

Sylvia dropped to her knees beside him. "What's wrong?"

He couldn't say. He clutched the pavement in panic, as if he were in the stairwell of a building set to collapse.

She placed her hand on his back to rub and soothe him. "Take a deep breath."

Andrés took a deep breath and swallowed.

"Take another deep breath."

He took another deep breath and swallowed.

"There you go. You're doing great, and you're gonna do even better because it's 1992, and you're not deployed. You're on Clinton Street with me, and we're gonna have breakfast together, so just breathe. And breathe. And breathe. You're safe."

"I'm safe," he said, then looked at Sylvia. "I'm sorry."

She continued rubbing his back. "What are you saying sorry for? I can get like that too, especially whenever planes flying out of LaGuardia come over so close like that. It's so scary, the way the plane booms."

"I hate the boom."

"Okay, tell me straight up. Is it one of those *things?*"

Andrés nodded.

She nudged his back. "I'm sorry, but I don't understand sign language. You have a voice; use it."

"It's one of those things! I can't help it!"

"Of course, you can't. You're only human, and that's okay. Listen— take another deep breath. Say to yourself, 'No fear.'"

He took a deep breath. "No fear."

"No fear—I want you to look up. I want you to look at the unreal beauty of this blue sky. It's so fucking gorgeous! That alone is worthy of a celebration with some fucking waffles." *Sylvia stood up and extended her hand for Andrés to grab. "So, get up, get up off the floor, and let's go—*

SEPTEMBER 11, 2001

—give me your hand and don't worry. I'm with you. You're safe with me."

The South Tower stopped rocking back and forth; it no longer felt like it was about to collapse.

He grabbed her hand, and Sylvia pulled him up to stand.

Everyone around Andrés pushed themselves up to stand and kept going.

Fuel poured down the steps.

Andrés passed firefighters going up the stairwell; they all looked tired and scared. He knew what they were feeling; he had felt it years before when he stood on a spot north of the Euphrates River just before he was given his souvenirs. Andrés raised his fist at the firefighters in salute and mouthed, "Good luck."

He followed their instructions and kept going. He found himself in an underground mall complex. Andrés passed more firefighters, suiting up in their gear. He was directed to a forward triage area to have his face and head examined. He kept walking fast; he was not going to linger around. He exited outside, near the Millennium Hotel.

Police and firefighters yelled at the survivors coming out onto the street to take cover.

No fear—I want you to look up. I want you to look at the unreal beauty of this blue sky.

Andrés looked up. Black smoke covered the sky, hovering high above them and shooting bodies out of its red plumes towards the ground—bodies crashing all around Andrés, splattering all around other survivors, and the police, and the firefighters—all dodging the falling bodies smashing into the concrete and against twisted heaps of metal, and broken office furniture, and shattered copy machines, and coffee makers, and glass, and chunks of hands, and splattered torsos and heads—all busted open and scattered everywhere on the pavement —and in the sky, useless reports on copy paper floated in the air, burning in the smoke, billowing high and spitting out more bodies, crashing around him, busting open more and more bodies onto the pavement—

The ground shook.

He ran.

A rush of air and heat pressed against his back.

He stopped to look back at the billowing smoke, crushing every living being in the South Tower. He ran from the eruption of dust—and glass—and melted steel—and burning flesh in the debris cloud, swallowing everyone yelling out for their mother, yelling out for God before going silent under the roar of black smoke.

Debris banged all over his body.

He coughed and crawled to a sheltered corner outside the entrance of a building. He huddled against a group already there. Andrés held his breath, riding out the beatings from the rumbling debris until he stopped feeling pain. Then everything fell silent. He pinched himself to make sure any burns to his body hadn't damaged his nerves.

He was alive.

Distress signals from firefighters crushed in the collapse began to beep and beep and beep through the dusty haze.

They were all dead.

Everyone in the sheltered corner poked and prodded each other to see if the body slumped against them was still alive too. They all pushed themselves up to stagger away in a daze. Andrés joined a crowd making their way along Park Row to escape Lower Manhattan.

Unreal City.

Under the gray haze of a late summer morning, after the destruction of the South Tower at the World Trade Center, with the North Tower still in flames and human beings still hurling themselves from that height to their deaths rather than being burned alive, survivors flowed over the Brooklyn Bridge. So many—death had undone so many. Sighs, short and infrequent, were exhaled, and each man and woman fixed their eyes before their feet as they flowed off the bridge and down Adams Street.

Andrés staggered through Brooklyn until he arrived at Elisa's apartment in Bushwick.

When she opened the door, Andrés asked frantically, "Is she here?"

"As soon as it happened, I got her—*Mami* went and got Myra," Elisa replied.

Before he could respond, she grabbed his hand and dragged him into the apartment, shoving him into the bathroom before their daughter could notice.

"I just wanna hug her," he said.

"Not like this." Elisa pointed at the mirror. "Look."

Andrés was covered in white dust, with splotches of dried blood covering parts of his face and hands.

"You smell like gasoline," she said.

"I can't smell anything."

She retrieved a washcloth from the linen closet, soaked it in hot water, and wiped the blood and dust off Andrés's face. Elisa helped him remove his clothes and continued examining his body, cleaning whatever else she could find on his chest and back.

"Take a shower and wash your hair." Elisa went to the kitchen and came back with dish soap. "You're a walking toxic spill—use this."

Elisa stood there, watching him shower, then helped him get dressed in the pajamas he had left behind when he moved out.

When Andrés finished, she pulled him close and hugged him, holding him in her arms for a long time.

"If you can stay, stay," Elisa said. "We can talk later... Now you can hug her."

Andrés walked from the bathroom into the family room, where Daphne was now watching a children's movie. He sat next to her, and she got up and sat back down on his lap.

For the moment they watched the movie together, as if nothing had happened. There was calm in his heart. Silence filled the air until Daphne, still mesmerized by the cartoons on the TV, said, "You smell like my dish."

Something in Andrés began to panic. It made him shake so much that Daphne turned around and asked, "Are you cold, Daddy?"

He forced himself to swallow the terror and fear over what was to come: war, and the fear that if it lasted long enough, his children might be drawn into it and ultimately end up like him—broken—or worse—dead.

That was something he couldn't let happen.

He must do everything he could to prevent that from happening.

He could not live through another loss of a child—not another death—no more big surprises.

What snapped Andrés out of that worry—that anxious thought—and made him smile was Daphne standing up from his lap and acting out her favorite scene. She grabbed his head and said, in sync with the movie, "You must be like a mountain and not bow."

❧ *8* ❧

TENEMENT SKY

SEPTEMBER 12, 1992

AFTER AN INTENSE NIGHT IN HER PURPLE ROOM FOLLOWED BY breakfast at a diner on Delancey Street, Sylvia and Andrés made their way to the World Trade Center. He led her to the observation deck atop the South Tower. He walked over to the railing, while Sylvia hung back, frantically pressing her back against a glass enclosure across from him.

"I can't believe you talked me into coming here!" she yelled.

"I didn't talk you into anything!" he yelled back.

"We could've gone anywhere! Why here?"

"Why did you shut down in the diner?"

"I'm tired of talking! I'm tired of hearing you talk!"

"You asked me to stay! I could be home."

"Then go! I hate you already!"

When it became clear Sylvia was in a panic—not from the height but from something deeper that had nothing to do with him—Andrés said, "Alright, fine... Let's go down. We'll go our separate ways."

"Why did you bring me here? That's all I wanna know!"

"Can you look up? Please?"

"Just tell me!"

Andrés walked over to stand beside Sylvia, grabbing her hand and looking directly into her eyes, which flickered with fear. "I know we just met, but what you did—helping me through one of those *things*—was more than anyone's ever done. When you started shutting down on me, I thought about some of the lines you shared from your favorite poem, and I started thinking of ways I could give back, get you to open up again. So, I brought you here. I wanted a chance to say to you, 'No fear,' and get you to look up... Look at the unreal beauty of this vast *tenement sky*. This is as close to it as you'll ever get."

She smiled, her eyes expressing surprise that he remembered the words *"tenement sky"* from Miguel Piñero's *A Lower East Side Poem*. Then she did as Andrés had asked and looked up. Her smile widened, as if suddenly mesmerized by a spirit in the sky, until something inside her appeared to shift. The joy on her face began to fade into a long, sad expression.

"Are you okay?" Andrés asked.

Sylvia shifted her focus back to Andrés, her eyes glistening. "I just wish my dad could see this, that's all... The chance to come here and check out this view was all he talked about the night he told me we were going on a road trip. He drove all night from our corner of Virginia just to show me where I'd be living for the next four years. I was seventeen and had been accepted to Columbia University. The first thing he did when we got to the city was take me to that diner."

Her face darkened. "I didn't have the best relationship with my father. Whenever he'd come around, he always looked so sad, never happy. But on that night of the drive, I couldn't sleep because I stayed up with him, joking and laughing as if we were old friends. He talked about how, after our campus tour, he was going to show me places in the city that were a big part of his life after Vietnam... My dad was a vet... That's how I knew what to do with you. I'd seen Nana do the same with him."

Andrés raised her hand to his lips and kissed the back of it.

Sylvia gave a meek smile before her face hardened again. "At the diner, my father confessed that the reason he used to disappear for months at a time was that he wanted to protect me from his pain. He didn't want me to see him at his worst. He'd often end up here in the city, getting lost in the night. He told me that sometimes he'd wake up in some of the back alleys in Chinatown and see the towers under construction. In those moments, my father said he would think that maybe, one day, he should stop doing drugs. He should try to live long enough to see the completion of the towers, just so he could go to the top, look into the sky, and tell my *yamma* he was sorry for not being there when she needed him the most... After all that, after seeing how important it was to him, I told him no. I didn't want to come up here."

Sylvia's eyes filled with tears, her voice trembling with emotion. "I was too scared to come up. I remember my dad playing it off, how sad he became, saying that maybe the next time he came to the city, I'd feel better about it. Maybe I could take a day off from classes to spend another day with him and come up here. I told him sure, knowing he never kept promises. When we got back to Virginia, he died the next day."

"I'm sorry," Andrés said.

"When you started going on and on about how you'd like to come up here but never had anyone to go with you, all I could see on your face was my dad's disappointment when I told him no... That's why I shut down, I guess—zoned you out... I regret letting fear hold me back, denying him his dying wish. And even though I've worked in tall buildings before—I did a summer internship here back in 1985—to be outside, at this height, with this wind, I'm still scared. And I'm afraid that if I focus too much on what other people want, I'll end up like him, with unfulfilled wishes. My dad should've ignored what I felt and done what you had done and led me here... Daddy would've loved this view."

She began to compose herself, drying her eyes before forcing a smile. "I hope that answers your question. I think I've said enough... What about you? I can't believe you never found anyone to do this with you."

"It's not that I couldn't find anyone," Andrés said. "It's just that I'm also scared."

"You could've fooled me."

"I've gotten better at swallowing my feelings. And back then, I wasn't about to bring a girl here, show her this romantic view, only for her to see me scared and tell me I wasn't acting like a man."

"First off, that's stupid."

"I know, but do you know how many times I've shared my feelings with a girl, only for her to look at me like there was something wrong with me?" Andrés laughed. "Nah, fuck that—I've learned to keep shit to myself."

Sylvia dropped his hand. "You're opening up to me. What does that make me, or am I nothing?"

Andrés looked away, giving himself the space to examine the flaws in his logic before returning his attention to her.

"It's weird," he said. "We just met, and I don't care if you see me scared. You've already seen me at my worst and didn't leave. I know you'd never say anything like that."

"Of course not."

"That's why it doesn't matter how I feel. My gut told me to bring you here and show you this sky—show you that if you have your fears, I can be there for you too. I'd never leave you in a panic. I'd stay with you like you stayed with me during mine." He paused to consider the impact of what that meant. "I think that scares me more."

"Me too... But I don't wanna be scared anymore."

"Me neither."

"So, what do we do?"

"Walk with me to the edge. No thinking, no fear—we just do it. Okay?"

She hesitated for a moment, her eyes wide, lips pressed tightly together in an anxious grimace. As the wind began to howl around them and the sun seemed to shine even brighter, something within her seemed to give in. She took his hand and whispered, "Okay, if you say so."

Andrés led Sylvia to the edge. At the railing, she leaned forward, squinting as if trying to get a better look at something beyond the North Tower that had caught her eye. She leaned further over the railing, frantically waving her arms and calling out into the vast beyond, "I'll try! I'll try!" over and over until Andrés rushed to pull her back, keeping her from toppling over.

He became startled by the pale, gaunt look on her face and the wide, fearful expression in her eyes. He tried not to show his fear at how, for a brief second, she appeared to have aged twenty years.

"Who were you yelling at?" he asked.

"You wouldn't understand," she replied. "I don't even understand it myself, and it's kind of freaking me out. I don't think I can talk about it... not now, at least. Changing the subject—thank you for bringing me here. It's been a long time since I've felt like this. I've never taken anyone to the diner before. I don't even know why I decided to bring you there, but there you were, and here we are; I've never felt more naked and afraid... I'm not used to feeling like this."

"Same here."

"Yeah... We're not a one-night stand. We're not on a date. This feels so different, and I don't know what to make of us or what I just saw. This is more than I expected... I don't know if I should see you again."

"Do what you need to do. Life goes on."

"It does."

"We can go back downstairs... Go our separate ways."

Sylvia hesitated, stepping away from Andrés to look up again, as if searching for a sign. She appeared mesmerized once more by a spirit in the sky. She followed its downward trail with her eyes until her focus locked onto the roof of the North Tower across from them, a smile spreading across her face.

"What?" Andrés asked, smiling along with her.

"See those guys over there? Working on the edge, like it's nothing?"

"Yeah... And?"

"Can you imagine what it'd be like to fall from there?"

"I can't."

"Can you imagine being trapped in a building like this? While it's on fire? And you're trying to get out?"

He laughed nervously. "You're going to a dark place real fast."

"That's how I think. I'm always imagining the worst. I have to. I don't like surprises."

"Same here," Andrés said.

"I can't imagine what I'd do," she said. "No doors? No exits? I wouldn't want to burn... I'd have to get it over and done with as fast as possible—I'd have to jump. It'd be the only way out."

"For someone scared of heights, that escalated. First you climb the rail, and now this?"

She looked at Andrés with a brighter smile. "I'm not scared anymore."

"Me neither... I guess being this high just takes some getting used to—like this feeling."

She grabbed his hands. "I think I can get used to it... I think. Speaking of feelings, do you have any plans for the rest of the day?"

"I can change them. My son is with my parents. All I need to do is call them and let them know what I'm doing. Why?"

"I feel like hitting up a museum."

"Which one?"

"All of them."

"It sounds like we have our Saturday."

Sylvia pulled him close. "No... We have *our* weekend; I just claimed it."

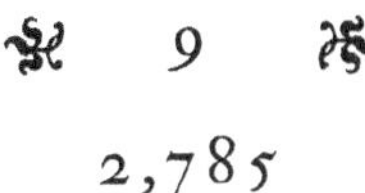

9

2,785

THE BLUE HOUR OF THE NIGHT GAVE WAY TO THE GOLDEN LIGHT OF morning. Andrés continued his drive to the entrance of the Underworld, found at the End of the World, his hands gripping the steering wheel hard. The heap of broken images—memories of a life that no longer existed——kept coming, one after another, and another.

He looked over at the passenger seat, now empty. He imagined Emma still there, her feet on the dashboard, looking away from the road ahead, then back at him to smile, saying, "Yo, Orpheus, I knew from the jump we were more than a one-night stand."

Andrés took a deep breath and spoke to the memory of her coming through the heap of broken images, "If someone had helped you like I helped Estrella—like I tried to do with Alene—you would've never lost your internship at the South Tower. You would've completed the Master Plan a lot sooner. You would've never found yourself on the bathroom floor. I tried to do right by you, by what you wished someone could've done for you, but it backfired."

Andrés took another deep breath and cried again. "We've paid the price. I don't care anymore. Helping Estrella was the right thing to do.

I'd do it all over again and not get on the plane instead. I would've stayed home with you. I would've never gone to Berlin. I should've trusted you to be the provider and to have my back instead. We wouldn't have been apart for 2,785 days."

He took another deep breath and cried. "Life doesn't go on. There's no life without your love. I'm going to do what I need to do. I'm never leaving you behind again. Emma, I'm coming home."

WE ARE THE WATCHERS. WE SEE ALL. WE SEE INTO HIS MIND AS We see into hers. We understand that now is the time to show you the rest of *Our* story.

You will begin to understand why Andrés must get to that spot where the land is flat, and the desert landscape glows gold, and the sky is at twilight, with his eyes burning from staring at the sun setting on the horizon.

He needs to be there for Our wedding day.

He needs to pay his debt to Karma.

It will be the only way We will be given Our gift.

❧ II ☙
UNDERWORLD

Love is born into every human being: it calls back the halves of our original nature together.

— PLATO

＊ 10 ＊

THE TITANS

CONSTANCE THE MATRIARCH CARRIED SYLVIA ACROSS THE boundary of her home and into safety. When she lowered her granddaughter onto the bed she had bought before leaving for Texas, Sylvia clutched her grandmother's blouse, yelling, "No! No! I wanna sleep with you!"

"Alright," Constance said, exhausted. "But remember, this is your bed. Tomorrow, you're gonna have to show me how much of a big girl you are by sleeping in it all by yourself, okay?"

Sylvia nodded, then buried her face in her grandmother's shoulder, clutching the Matriarch tightly for life.

Constance carried Sylvia into another dark room and placed her in bed. She lit a lamp on her nightstand, then tried to walk away.

"Don't go!" Sylvia called out.

"But Nana needs to go potty. I'll keep the door open. Is that okay?"

Sylvia nodded.

Constance left for the adjoining bathroom.

"I can't see you!" Sylvia called out.

Constance finished her business, returned to her bedroom, and stood at the foot of the bed. "I'm sorry, baby, but we're not gonna live like this. Until your daddy gets back, I'm it, and I'm not taking you to no quack because they'll just make things worse. So... what do you think is gonna happen if I leave for one second?"

"You die."

Constance circled around the bed to Sylvia's side, climbed in, and grabbed her, pulling her close. "I'm sorry if Nana sounds angry. I'm tired. You wanna know how many miles I drove to get you?"

Sylvia nodded.

"Well, I drove from here to Killeen, and that's 1,117 miles. I had to find out who had you, and when I did, I drove seventy miles to Austin and took care of that situation. I got you out of *that* house. Because of what I had to do, I had to take the long way home, and that was another 1,139 miles to bring you back here. Do you know how many miles that is altogether?"

Sylvia's small voice barely registered as she said, "No?"

"It's a lot," Constance said, holding her tighter. "But you're worth it. I'd never leave you behind. If I leave the room, say to yourself: 'No fear.' Be brave, like Nana. Did you see that I wasn't scared when I came to get you?"

Sylvia nodded.

"That's because before I came through that door, I told myself, 'No fear.' And here you are now. Sometimes people get what they deserve, and those monsters that had you certainly did. So if I don't feel bad, you shouldn't either. Understand?"

Sylvia shook her head: no.

"Okay... well, let me see if this'll help. I'm gonna read you a story." Constance got out of bed.

"Where are you going?" Sylvia asked.

"I'm going into the next room, but I'm here. So, be brave, okay?"

Sylvia nodded.

Constance left and came back moments later, holding a storybook. She climbed into bed and said, "Sit up and scoot over close to me... Like that... See this book? Your daddy got this for you when you were born. When your daddy was a boy, he loved reading Greek myths and wanted to make sure he could share that love with you. Do you remember him reading to you?"

Sylvia shook her head: no.

"Well, he read a lot to you, and whenever he'd read this myth, he was trying to tell you that this is who he wanted you to be like the most: Athena, the goddess of wisdom. But she also had a hand in passing judgment, and what you saw Nana do was pass judgment and carry it out. I gave those monsters what they deserved, and I don't feel bad about it because it's what God would've wanted me to do."

Constance opened the storybook to the section she wanted to read. Sylvia's eyes brightened at the drawing of Athena emerging from the head of Zeus, mouth agape in a battle cry, spear and shield in hand, ready to fight.

Constance smiled as she watched her granddaughter's curiosity and joy blossom. "Do you like what you see?"

Sylvia nodded.

"I'm sorry, but Nana doesn't understand sign language. You've got a voice. Use it. You don't have to be afraid ever again. You no longer have to hide." Constance took a deep breath and swallowed. "Now I'm gonna ask you one more time... Do you like what you see?"

Sylvia's voice was barely audible as she said, "Yes, Nana."

"Good. Now, I wanna show you Aphrodite."

Constance flipped through the storybook until she paused at another drawing. Sylvia's eyes softened at the sight of the goddess standing on a clamshell, carried in by a tide of foamy waves, her hair draped over her shoulders, covering her chest.

"She's pretty," Sylvia whispered as she touched her uncombed, frizzy hair.

"Yes, she is." Constance flipped back to the drawing of Athena. "Remember this: It's okay if everyone thinks you're Aphrodite. Let them think you're pretty... But don't be afraid to be like Athena. That's what your daddy and I want for you. So don't worry about me. I'm not going anywhere, but you have to be my big girl and not be afraid, okay?"

Sylvia nodded.

"What did I say about using your voice?"

Sylvia's face lit up with a big smile—her two front teeth missing—before she said in a booming voice, "I'm a big girl. I have a voice."

Constance exhaled a sigh of relief before smiling and saying, "That's my Athena. Always use your voice and never let anyone take it away from you, no matter what. Promise me that."

"I promise."

DECEMBER 21, 1969

[1]

Wendell the Wanderer took Sylvia wherever she needed to go. For months, she had been sick, and he had stopped drinking long enough to be a dad to his daughter and take her to be examined by several doctors. The final visit was with a pediatric pulmonologist in Richmond. After examining Sylvia, the doctor pulled Wendell aside and asked, "When did your daughter drown?"

"When I was in Vietnam—it was an accident. Why?"

The doctor glared at Wendell. "That's what's behind her coughing... Is Mrs. James with you? I assume she was the one who *allowed* for this accident to happen."

He took a deep breath and swallowed. "Mrs. *Hadid* James died while I was in Vietnam."

"I'm sorry to hear that."

"My daughter lives with my mother now."

"Did your mother come with you? I'd like to speak to her about why your daughter is barely in the tenth percentile for a child her age."

"Listen, as long as Sylvia is what you'd consider *normal,* I don't see an issue. She was born prematurely, and it was a difficult pregnancy for my wife, who never recovered... She's no longer around because of her troubles. So, if you're done with your *talk,* please tell me what I can do for my kid."

"Nothing... What's done is done. You should've been home instead of Vietnam, that's for sure." The doctor walked away.

On the drive back to Big Stone Gap in the Appalachian Mountains, Wendell did nothing but cry. He was haunted by the thought that he hadn't been there to stop what Alma, his wife, had done to herself—which had led to Sylvia's drowning and subsequent resuscitation by maintenance staff at the temporary apartments where he'd been housed prior to his deployment.

At his first stop, he filled up his gas tank and bought a six-pack of beer to drink on the drive. When Wendell returned home and told Constance the news, he did what he did best: he said to Sylvia, "Keep Nana company like a good girl, okay? I have to step out, but I'll be back."

"Okay, Daddy," Sylvia said with a smile that widened as she watched him leave, believing that he would keep his promise.

She waited until night for him to come home. She knelt on her bed, looking out the window, holding her baby doll. Sylvia hoped to see the lights from her father's car appear on the dirt road outside, but the only lights she could see were from the stars forming the belt of Orion, high above in the vast night.

Constance came into the room. "It's bedtime."

Sylvia sank back into her bed. "I know."

Constance came over to place her hand on Sylvia's forehead. "No fever... Good. Are you still sad?"

Sylvia nodded.

"Me too. I don't know what I'm gonna do with your father, but it can't be helped. He's broken, and some of it ain't his fault. War... war is no good. It's never good because it hurts everyone and kills even those who think they've survived. It's hurt you and me, and killed your daddy—that's the truth, my love, and I'm so sorry. But I'm here. I'll always be here, so don't be sad. Maybe this'll make you happy."

Constance knelt down and grabbed Sylvia from the bed. She cradled her while walking out of her granddaughter's room. Sylvia hugged her baby doll as Constance carried her over and eased her into bed.

"Tonight, you can sleep with me. I'll read you a story. Will that make you feel better?" Constance asked.

"Yes, Nana."

"Okay, which book?"

Sylvia held her baby doll up to Constance's face. "I want the Athena book."

Constance walked over to Sylvia's room and came back with the storybook.

Sylvia dropped her baby doll to grab it from her grandmother's hands.

Constance gave her an incredulous look. "That was rude."

"Sorry, Nana," Sylvia said as she opened the storybook. She flipped through the pages, pausing to point at a drawing of Eurydice following Orpheus out of the Underworld. "She's like Mama."

Sylvia flipped through the pages once more until she stopped and pointed at a drawing of Orpheus in the dark woods. His face was covered in tears as he sat on a tree stump, strumming his lyre, while the wild nymphs, who would eventually hack him to pieces, watched and waited for him in the shadows. "He's like Daddy."

"I guess you're right," Constance said. "But I can't say anything about your mama until you're older. You'll then understand why she did what she did. She was like your daddy, but she was fighting a battle that no one else could see but her... I've said too much, and it's getting to me. So, let's move on and read about the Minotaur in The Labyrinth."

"No, Nana—I like this story. He went back to get her. He didn't forget."

"Well, in that case, do you think you can read me your favorite part?"

Sylvia's face lit up with a big smile. "I can."

"Then show me."

Sylvia read:

"His existence had lost all its shine and joy. He needed Eurydice back. Orpheus went around weeping and mourning, searching for an entrance to Hades. When he found it at the End of the World, he did something no living man had ever done before: he walked down into the Underworld to beg for the return of his beloved."

Constance said, "Wow, you're such a smart girl for reading that."

"I really love that part, Nana."

"Well, because you love that part, I wanna tell you something. I hope it'll make you happy. It may make you a little sad too, but that's life. Do you wanna hear it?"

"Yes, Nana."

"I wasn't always alone. I had your Papaw. He was a big, funny man. He left everything behind in New Orleans just to be with me. Your Papaw was my *one* and only, my soulmate—but Papaw Marcus loved eating pork more than he loved being with Nana, and he died before you were born."

"That's sad. Aren't you sad?"

"Yes, baby, I am, but I'm also happy. God blessed me with a love like that, and I'm lucky. I got the best years of my life with him. Now? I don't feel so alone anymore. You look a lot like him." Constance began caressing Sylvia's frizzy curls with her fingers. "You have his freckles and red hair. You have his eyes and temper, too."

Sylvia laughed.

"You seem to have his passion for life. He was always hungry for something."

"Nana, do I have a soulmate?"

"Yes, you do, and you'll recognize him when you first see him. Who knows? Maybe you'll recognize your soul in a girl. Let's put it this way... You'll feel their pull. Your soulmate will feel like home. You just have to believe."

Constance stared wistfully ahead, then smiled. "I like to believe that one day I'll see him again. When I do, we'll be joined in heaven by God and become one. That makes me happy."

She looked back down at Sylvia. "Until then, being here with you makes me happy. It's okay if your father is off looking for the End of the World, crying over your mama. You're here with me, and I love you."

"I love you too."

Constance hugged Sylvia. "You bring me so much joy."

[2]

Petra the Poet had waited a long time for this moment.

What led to this moment?

In October, something seemed to have changed with her boyfriend. Petra didn't know what, nor did she care to stick around to help him figure it out and fix him. It wasn't her job, nor did she owe her boyfriend patience and understanding. Had Petra not scooped up Andrés, their newborn son, and run out of the apartment after it appeared he was having a nervous breakdown, she feared her boyfriend could've hurt them.

Petra's little sister, Estefania de León, helped her disappear by moving her away from their corner of Harlem to Yonkers, a city bordering the Bronx to the north, and far enough away from their circle of friends to avoid anyone reporting back on Petra's whereabouts to her now-estranged boyfriend. On their first night together in the new apartment, Estefania confessed, "I always knew that man had issues."

"Why didn't you say anything?" asked Petra.

"You wouldn't have listened, just like you didn't listen when Victor told you about the other girl your boyfriend got pregnant. You played dumb."

"Stop... I feel bad enough."

"We heard his baby died. I think that's why he went crazy, why he changed. It's a good thing you got away. I know you two have your *Playtime,* which I get, but I don't know... Playing with a man like that can be dangerous. He can lose control real fast, and when he does, whatever boundaries and safe words you have mean nothing anymore."

Days after Petra ghosted her boyfriend, Estefania helped her get a job. It was at a motel near where Estefania would walk the streets of Hell's Kitchen, making money off men who didn't want to be seen with a *woman* like her.

Petra would leave Andrés with her sister-in-law, Carmen. She worked as many shifts as they would allow her, not because Petra needed the money, which she did, but because she needed to keep busy. She needed to stop thinking so much about her baby's father.

For the weeks that Petra worked, she forced herself to accept a brutal truth: seeking the kind of passion she desired meant putting herself in danger of violence. She had Andrés now. He should be her priority. She couldn't take any more risks that would cause her to feel temporary terror in exchange for the reward of intense pleasure.

Everything leading up to this moment had been nothing but terror.

One night, her little brother, Victor de León, showed up at Petra's job. "You need to come with me! Let's go!"

"Why? What's the matter?" asked Petra, startled.

Victor took a deep breath, swallowed, and said as calmly as he could, "Carmen turned her back for one second, and Andrés fell off the bed. I rushed him to the emergency room. The doctors are operating on him now. We need to go."

Petra dashed out of the room she had been cleaning and left with Victor. The two climbed into his car and drove away. Victor raced up the Henry Hudson Parkway, swerving through traffic at high speeds like a stunt driver. He exited the parkway and navigated the clogged streets of Washington Heights until he pulled up in front of the hospital. Petra jumped out, crying, and raced into the emergency room.

Don Reynaldo the Patriarch approached Petra. He pulled his daughter close and hugged her until her body went limp, her loud crying turning into grunts and moans.

Petra looked up at her father. "Tell me it's going to be alright, please?"

Don Reynaldo looked at her, her face with its copper undertones pleading for an answer. Instead of giving her one, he showed no emotion and said nothing, which made Petra cry more. He led her to a row of benches, where they sat, and she nuzzled her face into his chest, continuing to cry until a surgeon in green scrubs appeared.

"I take it that you're Andrés's mother?" the surgeon asked.

"I am," she replied.

The surgeon sat across from her and said, "Your son had an acute subdural hematoma. It was severe."

"What's that, and how severe?"

"It's a buildup of blood between the surface of the brain and an outer covering known as the dura mater. How severe? He had bled so much that we had to relieve the pressure on his brain. He's now in a coma. The mortality rate for the type of hematoma we're dealing with is between sixty and eighty percent... We've done all we could. It's now up to your son."

"Is he going to die?"

The surgeon paused before saying, "He's a tough little boy. During the operation, his heart was strong, and his blood pressure was stable. Again, the rest is up to him. Now, if you'll excuse me, I have to get back." The surgeon got up and walked away.

Petra slumped her body against Don Reynaldo.

"Sit up," he said. "This is good news."

Petra raised her eyes to him, as if she were still a little girl. "It is?"

"*Sí, mi niña.* Andrés is alive, and he is strong. *Tienes que tener fe en Dios*—just believe."

"Okay, *Papi*... If you say so."

Don Reynaldo continued to sit with Petra for as long as he could until he had to leave for work.

Every day, for months, Petra sat next to Andrés in his tiny crib, hooked up to probes and tubes connected to the humming monitors in the neonatal intensive care unit. There, she felt the pain of not being able to breastfeed, blaming herself for not being at home with her son and leaving his care to someone else.

Whenever Carmen checked in on her, she would say sorry again.

Petra would say, "I don't blame you. You have your own kids. I should've been looking after mine."

Petra blamed herself for not overcoming her fear of her ex-boyfriend. His anger made sense; he was trying to cope with the death of a baby she had convinced herself she knew nothing about. Whenever she thought she should have been more sensitive to him, she felt awful for having such an appalling thought. It wasn't her role to be understanding. It wasn't her job to fix him.

Every day, Petra would whisper to Andrés, "Wake up; Mama needs you."

Every day, the nurses would see Petra cry and say, "Go home and shower. Get some sleep. That's something your son would want. We're here for you."

Every day, Petra would say, "No."

Every day, Petra would fall asleep in her chair, heartbroken, and wake up still heartbroken.

Until this moment.

The nurses shook her awake to tell her Andrés appeared to be coming out of his coma. Petra spent the next two hours watching four-month-old Andrés react to the light around him. His journey from the Underworld—the space between the Land of the Alive and the Land of the Not-Alive—was completed when he belted out a long cry that rang so hard throughout the unit that his tiny body trembled.

One nurse said, "He's angry."

Petra said, "I don't blame him. I'd be angry too."

The doctor walked into the unit and directed Petra to move as far away from Andrés as possible. She wanted to give him a proper exam without Petra hovering over her shoulder the entire time.

Petra was called back fifteen minutes later by the nurses. They helped Petra lift and position Andrés, and all the tubes and cables, so that the machines attached to him would not be disrupted while he was in her arms.

One nurse said, "He's still fragile, so be careful. He has a long road ahead, but the doctor expects him to make a full recovery."

Andrés blinked his eyes open and looked up at Petra as if she were a bright light. Petra burst out laughing from relief that faded into a giggling cry.

She said to him, "You're a tough little boy. No wonder your father wanted to give you, his name. I didn't like it, but he insisted, and I didn't want to fight him. He said it meant *manly*. He saw it in you. I guess so. I was going to change your name, but not anymore. You're my tough little man—a survivor. You're not meant to die yet. God has plans for you. Thank you, God. Thank you."

II

URANUS

DECEMBER 21, 1975

It was nine at night when Petra de León-Vargas, dressed in a red apron and a black satin bonnet, emerged from the kitchen of the apartment she shared with her husband, Antonio, and called out to her two sons playing in the hallway. "Andrés, Tony, time for bed—let's go."

Andrés faced Petra and said, "But *Papi's* not home."

"Well, *Papi* is working."

"He's always working."

"I know, but that's the way it is. Now stop whining and let's go."

Andrés was about to say no again when Tony ran up from behind and tackled him, knocking him to the floor.

"Boys, I'm not playing. I'm waiting for an important call, so the first one in bed gets a long hug and a story. The loser gets nothing."

Andrés pushed Tony off, and the two jumped up and raced into their room. Andrés was the first one in bed, but Petra declared Tony the winner, causing Andrés to say, "That's not fair! I won!"

"Stop whining—life's not fair." Petra turned to Tony, gave him a long hug, and asked, "What story would you like me to read?"

"I don't want a story. I want you to stay with me," Tony said.

"Alright, only until my phone call." Petra climbed into bed with Tony and cuddled him as he began to suck his thumb.

Andrés tried to fall asleep, but frustration over how unfair the world seemed kept him up.

"I won," Andrés said in a low voice.

"No, you lost," Petra replied, letting Andrés know she could hear everything in her home.

Andrés shifted his angry gaze from his mother and brother to the window next to his bed. From there, he looked out into the vast night, at the stars forming the belt of Orion, and, in the one place he knew his defiance couldn't be heard—his mind—he said again, "I won."

When Tony began to snore, Petra stood up and tried to leave the room but stopped when Andrés sat up and asked, "Since he didn't use his story, can I have it? He won't know."

"Go back to sleep."

"Please?"

"No!"

"But, Mama, I can't sleep!"

"Don't you dare start crying! What did I say about that?"

In a low voice, Andrés said, "Crying is for girls."

"And what else?"

Andrés took a deep breath and swallowed. "Boys don't cry."

"And don't you forget it. Now tell me, what is it that has you like this? Acting like a girl?"

"I had a dream that a bad man comes and takes me outside, and I'm wearing orange pajamas and standing on sand, and I see an angel, and she's in front of me, saying, 'No fear;' that today's our wedding day, and then the bad man says I'm gonna die, and—"

"It's just a dream," Petra said, laughing.

"It doesn't feel like one."

"Well, it is. It's nothing to get emotional about."

"But I don't wanna die."

Petra paused, as if realizing she was being too harsh. "Okay, I'll read you a bedtime story, but you'll have to do something for me. You have to promise to be a good boy. Do you promise?"

"I promise."

"You'll do as I say and make Mama happy, even when Mama is sad?"

"Yes, Mama."

"Because if you're not a good boy, I will not see you, I will not hear you, until you're a good boy again. That'll be your punishment. Which hurts more? *Papi's* belt or—"

"When you don't see me... When you don't hear me."

"And don't you forget it."

"I won't," said Andrés in a barely audible voice.

"Now, what would you like me to read?"

"Can I get the book?"

Petra rolled her eyes. "Not this again... We have other books."

"Please?"

"Fine... Go get it."

Andrés got out of bed, went into the closet, pulled out his storybook, and handed it to her. "I wanna hear my favorite part."

"That's it? But why, when there are so many other stories in this book?"

"I like the drawing. It makes me feel better."

"Fine."

He climbed back into bed. Petra sat next to him and opened the book to the drawing of his favorite story.

She read aloud:

"Nobody knows when or how Gaea, the Earth, emerged from the darkness. She was young and lonely, for nothing had lived on Her yet. Above Her rose Uranus, the vast night sky, with its innumerable twinkling stars grouped into dazzling clusters. Uranus was striking to behold as He looked upon Her, and young Earth fell in love with Him. The Sky joined Himself to Her in love, and soon young Earth became Mother Earth, the mother of all living things. All of Her offspring adored their loving mother but dreaded their great father, Uranus, the master of the cosmos."

Andrés grabbed the book from his mother's hands and held the page to her face. "I like how the sky looks at her. It looks like love."

"What do you know about love?" Petra said with an amused grin.

Andrés shrugged his shoulders. "I don't know—look, the sky has stars for eyes, and she has stars in her eyes, and her body is the world." Andrés dropped the book away from Petra's face. "Mama, is this true? Can the world be like a body?"

"For the people who wrote these stories a long time ago, they believed it all to be true. The sky, the stars, it was *Papa Dios,* and the world—"

"Like *Mama Dios?*"

"Yes, like *Mama Dios,*" Petra said with a smile.

"That's so cool," Andrés said, his face bright with excitement.

"It is. Just remember, *Papa Dios* or *Mama Dios*, it is still *Dios*. It is still God, and God is in everything."

"Even in me?"

"Even in you."

"Even in *Tití* Estefania?"

"Why do you ask?"

"Because *Tití* was crying—she said someone told her she was going to hell."

"Whoever said that is the one going to hell—making judgments." Petra sighed. "*Dios* is especially in Estefania. I just wish she could see that. I wish she could see she is so much more..."

Petra looked at a confused Andrés.

"Forget what I said—back to your nightmare. It's not real, so stop acting like a girl, all scared. You'll be fine. Trust me, especially since this bedtime story is real: Uranus, the Sky, God, He watches over all of us. So, whenever you're under His sky and standing on Her ground, I want you to look for the brightest star and smile... You'll be with God... You'll be seen. He will come through the shine."

"But what if God needs me to die? That's what the angel said in my dream."

Before Petra could answer, the phone rang from the kitchen. She jumped out of bed and hurried to answer it. Andrés could hear her and wondered who she was talking to.

"Hey, what took you so long to call?" After a pause, she said, "No, Antonio won't be home for another few hours... Yeah... I just put him to bed. No, you cannot see him... I don't want to confuse him... I don't care—you gave up that right the moment you made me run out on you... Don't worry. Andrés is in good hands... Antonio is a great dad, and he loves him like his own... Enough with the small talk. Where did we leave off?"

SWEET SIXTEEN

OCTOBER 21, 1978

CONSTANCE ROSE FROM HER ROCKING CHAIR IN THE FAMILY ROOM OF her tin-roofed home and lumbered over to answer the hard knock on her front door. She found Tipper, her neighbor, on the porch, angry and yelling, "Where's Sylvia?" while trying to push her way inside.

"Now hold on there—you can't come through here like you own the place," Constance said, pushing her back, her hand on Tipper's head, keeping her at arm's length.

"Get off me—do you know what she did?"

"Before we have any more words, you need to calm down. In fact, you need to step off my porch."

Tipper did as she had been commanded, stepping off the porch to look up at Constance, who towered over her, and asked, "Where is she?"

"That's none of your business."

"It is my business. Sylvia tried to kill Elliott."

Constance began to laugh. "My little Sylvia? Your boy is six feet of crap—my spider monkey doesn't crack five."

"Your spider monkey choked him."

"I find that hard to believe."

"It's true—you can see her handprint on his neck. I'm fixing to take him to the hospital, and they'll wanna know what happened. Before I put her in that kind of trouble, I'd like to know—was she defending herself? I need to know if my son is no good because if he is, I'll choke him myself."

Constance called out to Sylvia, still inside the house. "Did you catch any of this?"

"Yes, Nana," Sylvia called back.

"Is it true?"

Sylvia stepped outside onto the porch and positioned herself behind her grandmother, nervously biting her nails to hide from Tipper's angry stare.

Constance spun around and crouched down to meet Sylvia's eyes. "Did your boyfriend try to force himself on you?"

"No, Nana."

"Then what happened?"

"I don't wanna say... Not in front of her."

Tipper shouted, "Yes, in front of me! Elliott's my son! He *is* my business!"

Constance whipped her head toward Tipper. "Will you shut the French toast up? I'm trying to get answers." She turned back to Sylvia. "What's going on? This isn't how I wanted to spend your birthday. It's bad enough that it looks like your father lied to me again and won't be here. Now I have you to deal with?"

"I'm sorry, Nana."

"You're not a little girl anymore. You're sixteen—a grown woman. You need to start speaking up and owning it like you're one." Constance began to caress Sylvia, placing her hand in her frizzy, knotted hair, trying to reassure her. "You need to start owning your real feelings. Don't be scared to hide them anymore... Tell me, what happened?"

"You won't get mad?"

"I can't promise that—there's a consequence to everything—but what I can promise is that I'll always be proud of you when you speak the truth. Especially speaking truth to power."

Sylvia looked at Tipper, who glared back at her.

Constance drew Sylvia's attention back, shifting her chin with her large hand. "Don't worry about her. Miss Tipper is here because she wants to know what happened to her boy. Just like you'd wanna know what happened to me if you saw that I was hurt. It's only fair."

Sylvia nodded and took a deep breath to brace herself for what she was about to reveal. "Alright, Nana, the truth is, I've been saving myself for today."

Tipper interjected, "Oh, Lord, no."

Constance pointed at Tipper. "You need to keep quiet and keep your thoughts to yourself. In fact, you need to leave. I'll tell you her side later on."

"I'll leave and come back with the sheriff, or I can stay and hear it from her."

"She can stay," Sylvia said. "It's nothing to be ashamed of, I guess... Elliott and I had been talking about doing it, and I wanted my first time to be special, so when today came, I waited for him at the park for my birthday treat. I was so excited because he'd told me he was taking me someplace fancy, but when Elliott got to the park, he took me into the woods instead. I said fine, and we did it, but he finished in thirty seconds, and I was thinking, *is that it?*"

Tipper yelled, "You'd better not be pregnant! I'm not looking after another one of his mistakes!"

Constance stood up and said to Tipper, "You need to leave—"

"No, Nana, I want her to stay. She needs to hear this." Sylvia shifted her focus from Constance to Tipper. "Your son is no good. He came inside me and didn't care, but don't worry—I'm on the pill. Thank God I'd been taking it for my period because, after his performance, I know any child I'd have from him would be a born loser, just like his father, and I wouldn't want it."

Tipper said, "You're disgusting."

"Oh, I'm disgusting? Your son is the one who's disgusting. He lied to me. He did everything to convince me that he was my *One,* just to get me out there, into the woods, promising that I could try anything I wanted to try since he wasn't gonna take me somewhere fancy, and just like that, he was done. Your son used me to get his, and he didn't give me a chance to get mine, and that's not fair. He's selfish, always so self-ish, and he promised me he'd let me try it on him."

Tipper asked, "Try what?"

"My fantasy... That shithead got up after he was done and looked at me like I was nothing. So, I made it clear that we were not finished. He was gonna follow through on what he had promised. Elliott said, 'Fine, get it over and done with,' because he was tired and wasn't sure how long he'd be able to keep it up. So, we did it again, and I got carried away and choked him, and instead of fighting back, he told me to stop, and I didn't, and that's when he pushed me off and ran to his mommy like a little girl, like a little fa—"

Before Sylvia could complete her sentence, Constance slapped her hard across the face, knocking her to the floor. She took off her shoe and hit her balled-up body on the back and torso. With each blow, Constance shouted, "You're getting to be a lost cause, like your father. I'm sorry I brought that piece of crap into the world. Your father is a loser, and I've had enough. I'm tired. I'm tired. I can't wait to die."

Sylvia rode out the beating until Constance was out of breath and stopped.

Tipper appeared satisfied that justice had been dispensed on behalf of her son. "I won't be involving the sheriff after all. You took care of it like I knew you would."

Constance moved away from Sylvia and pointed down her dirt driveway with her shoe still in hand. "If you don't get off my property now, I'll call them myself—leave." She stood there, watching Tipper walk away. Once she was gone, Constance began to cry. "Please forgive me."

"I don't understand... Forgive you?" Sylvia said.

Constance helped her off the floor. "Yes, forgive me. I've never laid one finger on you, but I had to, or else that old bag wouldn't have let up until she got justice. And I didn't want the sheriff coming here to take you 'cause they would've come. What you did was wrong, so wrong."

"But how?" Sylvia asked, appearing more confused.

"Your boyfriend didn't wanna do it!"

"Yes, he did, but he backed out!"

"And that's when you need to stop, or else it becomes a crime. Do you understand? It becomes a crime, and I don't want you to destroy your future because you didn't understand boundaries." Constance gave Sylvia a long look before shaking her head. "For someone so gosh darn smart, you can be so dumb sometimes. You need to think with your head and not your privates."

Sylvia bowed her head in shame. "Yes, Nana."

"Where did you get the idea of choking him?"

She shrugged. "I don't know. I just wanted to make Elliott angry."

"But why?"

Sylvia paused before her cheeks flushed. "I guess I wanted to wake him up. Wake something up in him that would fuck me like a bull. It's been my fantasy—"

"Do you know how dangerous that can be for you? If you try that with the wrong man and he fights you? He can kill you."

"Don't worry, Nana. I'm a grown woman, right?"

"Yeah, but you'd still be no match for a monster, and that's what most men are. And you wouldn't even know you're with one until you put your hands on him and find out you've made the biggest mistake of your life—all because of a fantasy."

"I understand, Nana."

"And that's another thing," Constance said, exasperated. "You need to do more than just say, 'I understand,' and 'Yes, Nana.' You need to start talking to me—and to others—with more confidence, like you did with Tipper. I'm proud of you for standing up to her, but not for what you were about to call her son. You're grounded for that. We'll talk more about it later."

"I'm sorry, Nana."

Constance became more exasperated, shaking her head and placing her hand on her forehead to wipe away the sweat that had suddenly appeared. "What are you gonna do when you move away? If something, God forbid, should happen to me and I'm gone, I won't always be around to defend you... To help you sort through the bad men who'll come to you, trying to convince you that they're good. What are you gonna do then?"

Sylvia began to panic. "Are you sick?"

"No, baby, but I'm old, and there's no telling what the future holds. I'm trying to get you to be who you need to be now so that you won't be so lost when I'm gone. I'm not saying this to scare you, but I won't be able to rest—be at peace—until I know you're capable of taking care of yourself. And that means not being afraid to stand up for yourself with a loud, confident voice. To not be afraid to put every man who crosses your path to the test. And I want you to keep testing them until they've proven they're not monsters but that they're good and worthy of your friendship, your love, and that thing about you that makes you gold. Do you understand? Because that's what you are."

Sylvia replied in a monotone voice, "I don't feel like I am."

"But you are." Constance hunched down to sit on the top step of her porch and pulled Sylvia down to join her. "Look at me—you're my precious treasure, my golden girl. And because that's what you are, you need to protect yourself. You need to beware of men who get angry over small things. Those are the types of men who won't be able to give you what you're apparently looking for—be part of your fantasies." Constance paused for a long moment before a look of hesitation appeared.

Sylvia became anxious again. "What's the matter? Are you okay? Are you sure you're not sick? You'd tell me if you were?"

"I'm okay; don't you worry, and I would tell you. It's that... You know." Constance let out a sly grin. "Nana wasn't always a grandma. I wasn't always so square."

"Wait... What's square?" Sylvia asked, confused.

"Boring... plain. Don't let the way I look fool you." Constance's face lit up with pride—the brightest Sylvia had ever seen. "I was cool... I was fun. That's why Papaw fell in love with me. He had a temper, yes, but for what mattered... I learned how to use his temper to keep him awake. He did the same for me. Together, we went on to create a beautiful life filled with so much passion. We were so alive... Yep, in this, I can see you're like me—I know what you were trying to do, and I think it's time to talk about the birds and bees again, but this time with your special needs in mind."

Sylvia became intrigued by the idea that not only did her grandmother know what her special needs were, but also that, in what she imagined would have been a past life for Constance, she was like one of the many women who roamed her fantasies—women in touch with the Minotaur within, unafraid of consuming whatever was presented to them. The idea also made Sylvia want to vomit until she realized she was judging her grandmother. It never occurred to her that Constance was more than her role. The only sign that her grandmother could be sexual was that her father, Wendell, and her aunt, Birdie, had to have come from somewhere. There was never a sign of the fire lurking behind the stone-like facade that Constance projected as the Matriarch. She never imagined her grandmother could be any other way.

Constance began to laugh. "I can see it on your face... This all coming as a big surprise. Well, you're not the only one who doesn't like them, and I don't want any more surprises like today, so I have to be realistic. You're an adult with these kinds of special needs. Okay, fine— then you'll need to understand that if that's something you'd like to do, do it only with someone you trust. Someone you can be sure won't hurt you...

"I could trust a man like Papaw. Most men are not like him. Most men are monsters, and what makes them monsters is that they're driven by ego—by pride. God forbid they should feel any submission to a woman, as if submission takes something away from their manhood. You need to be with someone who gets that. Not a man who's so fragile that he can't bear the thought a woman can't be anything other than a mother or wife."

"I don't think I want their submission... It's hard to explain," Sylvia said.

"Think of it like a dance," Constance said. "Depending on your mood, if a song comes on that you both like, you might find that he'd prefer you to take the lead, even though he's usually the one who leads. Square men don't understand that to be dominant, they must know what it's like to be submissive and be ready to surrender. How can you trust a man if he's not prepared to be in your position? What does that tell you about his intentions?"

"I get it. In a strange way, that makes sense," Sylvia said.

"I'm glad that it does," Constance said. "It's not about the sex. It's about the exchange: the accepting and giving of power, that feeling you get when you find someone you trust so much that you want to surrender, and you see that they're willing to surrender to you. In the exchange, your partner will want to show that they trust you with their life, and they'll find a way to do so. That's what it's all about. Men can say what they want, but it's in the showing that you learn if they're worth a damn.

"And I'm telling you, to make it even more fun, sometimes you'd have to look at it like it's all theater, and you're in a play with specific scenes that you and your dance partner will make up and act out on that stage in your minds. And everyone who chooses to be on that stage will be able to show how much trust they have for their dance partner through their performance. Until you find the right one you'd feel safe with—someone who understands that it's about the exchange, not just the sex, and who also sees the gold in you—don't do it. No putting your hands on anyone. If you want to beat men, beat them with that brain of yours. It'll hurt them more."

"That's the part that I don't understand," Sylvia said. "If it's about the exchange, why the pain? Why is that pleasurable?"

Constance laughed as if Sylvia's question was silly. "Let me ask you this, and I want you to think about it. Why do you like to run for miles? Why do you like to dance for hours? Don't you feel the pain? Don't you get tired?"

"I do, but it feels so good."

"In the exchange, it's the same thing, but more intense. You won't get that intensity unless you find someone who can control himself and listens to you—not just listen to respond. The man you'd like to dance with shouldn't have any anger issues he can't control. This is important. Find someone who's not sadistic. You don't wanna be with men who'd only be doing this because it gives them a chance to hurt women. Get every man to show you who he really is, and yes, get him angry. Push him away, make him miss you before pulling him back, and do it over and over to see how he reacts. If he enjoys the tension that'd start to build, you'll feel his hunger, not his anger, and that's how you'll know to keep building."

"Okay..."

"But don't mistake their frustration for anger. It's just a sign that the tension between the two of you is about ready to snap, and when it does—woo!—it's like fireworks."

"But this sounds like you want me to play games, and I don't wanna do that. Pushing and pulling? Isn't that playing with a man's feelings?"

Constance chuckled. "Better their feelings than yours. Again, you don't wanna find out too late that you gave yourself to a man who's nothing but garbage, so you get them to weed themselves out like this. Besides, the right man will get it. The right man will wanna play this game. Playing like this, the pain you'll start to feel is the same pain you'd feel during a workout, and what does that feel like to you?"

Sylvia closed her eyes to touch that feeling. "It feels so good."

Constance smiled. "That's also part of the exchange. The game is a workout for the emotions that you and your dance partner will discover are part of the theater of it all. Again, this depends on trusting that he knows it's not pain for the sake of pain, but for the sake of a higher pleasure. And when you find someone you trust and who understands this, you'll experience pleasure so intense that you'll feel like a woman who's landed on the moon. That feeling is a talk for another time, and even then, there's not much I can say about it."

"Why not?" Sylvia asked.

"That's because trust is everything in the exchange, and even though Papaw is no longer alive, I can't betray his trust in me. He's not here to give me his permission to share anything involving him. It's personal, especially how he got me to land on the moon."

Constance went silent and became lost in thought. Her eyes began to twitch, as if she were touching on memories so electric that she let out a slight moan under her breath. The area visible above the neckline of her gown went from light brown to flushed red

Constance said softly, "I miss that feeling so much... That's my limit; I can't answer any more questions. I'd be betraying my vows to him."

Sylvia's eyes filled with wide-eyed wonder. "Wow, I've never seen you like this. Is it that deep?"

"Yes, it's that deep. In the end, the vows we make—the words we memorize for our safety—are all that matter when you choose to dance in your relationships like this. In my dance with Papaw, I could trust that he could send me to Space, get me to land on the moon, or see that I was not ready for takeoff, even though I'd be saying yes to him. The body can talk, too. Do you understand?"

"I understand…"

"I still don't think that you do," Constance said, no longer speaking softly, but with force. "With Elliott, you acted no better than the sadistic men who'd demand immediate submission. You put your hands on your boyfriend and placed him in that position without having acted out any theater—without having built the right tension—without earning his permission. There was nothing that told him to trust you, so he could say yes again, so he could dance with you. Instead, your boyfriend's body kept saying no. And that, right there, is the biggest sin in the exchange. You ignored the most important word anyone could ever say when that word is all. Do you understand?"

"I understand; no is all…"

Constance yelled as though Sylvia had committed murder, "*No* is everything!"

Sylvia paused to take in the urgency in her grandmother's voice, as if her freedom—her life—depended on learning the lessons from this radically different talk about the birds and the bees. Despite the urgency, Sylvia's curiosity, built up over years of wondering why her grandmother lived like a nun, made her momentarily forget Constance's anger to ask what became the most important question of all:

"Was Papaw the only man you tried this with?"

Constance took a deep breath and swallowed. "He was the only man to have passed all my tests."

"Were you a virgin when you met him?"

Constance laughed, no longer angry. "I had to test a man somehow —so what do you think?"

Sylvia said with a big smile, "That's why you were *cool* and *fun*."

"Exactly! Sex is nothing compared to this; the right dance partner will see it the same way. In the dance, sex becomes almost like a bodily function—this is what's true: the body means nothing." Constance touched the silver infinity insignia on her necklace and said, "I gave your grandfather my soul; it would be cheating if I gave a piece of it to another man. It's why some won't care if their partners have sex with others because they want that tension. Because there'd be permission. Because it would involve nothing of their soul. And I think I'm about to break my vows with Papaw, and I need to stop talking. That's it—I can't speak about it anymore. I'm starting to feel awful for sharing that tidbit—for laying my hands on you. I'm sorry. I'm so sorry. Do you forgive me?"

"Don't say sorry! I know why you did it now. I don't wanna go to jail."

Constance turned away from Sylvia, looked at the long dirt road running off her property and onto a county road, and said, "I have to be honest... Everything I've said about your father, even though I meant it, I regret it. You're here because of him."

Sylvia became quiet, staring at her grandmother for a long time before asking, "Do you really wanna die?"

Constance looked back at Sylvia and sighed. "My love, I don't wanna die. It's just that I'm tired. I wanna sleep for a long time. Does that make sense? Wake me up in a hundred years. I'll have my full rest by then."

Sylvia fell silent once more. She began to imagine Constance waking up in the year 2078, with no one who knew and loved her there. Not even the many great-grandchildren she hoped to give her grandmother. They wouldn't know her. The vision made Sylvia reach out to Constance, hugging her tight and crying, "But I don't want you to sleep for a hundred years. You'll miss out on my life, what I'll become, and I'll be dead when you wake up. And you'll be alone. Without Papaw... without me."

❧ 13 ❧

THE WASTE LAND

NOVEMBER 20, 1983

ANDRÉS WAS IN BED AND COULDN'T SLEEP. WATCHING THE MADE-for-TV movie *The Day After* had scared him. It made Andrés aware of powers beyond his control that could wipe away his existence with the push of a button. It seemed like the world was ending soon. A truck bomb had exploded a month earlier at the U.S. Marine barracks in Beirut, killing 241 U.S. service members stationed there to keep the peace during a civil war.

He said to himself, "Is this how it all begins?"

Nostradamus the Seer once wrote that the sky would burn and fire would approach the great new city. It was written in the stars. It must be true, and maybe this was it. To make a prediction so far into the future, it would be understandable for Nostradamus to be off by sixteen years. Instead of it being 1999, the sky would burn in 1983. The bombing in Beirut would trigger a chain reaction leading to nuclear war. Maybe the movie was a way of preparing the country for what was to come—giving everyone a glimpse of the wasteland that awaited if they were unlucky enough to survive the fire of a nuclear attack.

Andrés laughed at his overthinking. He turned on his nightlight and grabbed the first thing within reach—the latest issue of *National Geographic*. Petra had given it to him the day before, and it featured a spread of pictures taken of the Rio Grande Gorge outside Taos, New Mexico. The highlight was a stitched-together series of photos of the Milky Way Galaxy spread over the gorge's opening. It was as though he was looking at the face of God with eyes like stars.

When Andrés tried to comprehend how long it took all that starlight to reach Mother Earth, everything seemed insignificant. He might wake up in the morning, or he might not. He might find himself surrounded by fire, or he might not. He might find himself fighting for his life, or he might not. Andrés was a powerless nothing with no control, and God was powerful and everything. Andrés would be gone one day, and the stars would always be there, as would God. This gave him comfort, touching on how small he was. In feeling his smallness, his fear became smaller than him. It was just as insignificant. Andrés smiled. He could now go to sleep.

Meanwhile, twelve miles to the south, Sylvia was in bed and couldn't sleep. She was in a small room in an off-campus apartment she shared with her roommate in Morningside Heights. She had spent the night watching *The Day After* on TV. It scared her and further reinforced what she already knew: the world was an out-of-control chaotic mess, ready to explode, and she didn't want to die. What was the point of law school if she was going to die?

Sylvia thought she heard sirens like the ones in the movie. She got up from her bed and rushed to the window. Expecting to see the sky red and on fire, she instead found only the bright city lights reflecting off the cloudy night, along with the usual sounds of police sirens blaring in the distance.

Sylvia took a deep breath, relieved.

It would be Thanksgiving on Thursday, and she was supposed to take a bus back home for the holidays. Birdie and her cousins would be there, but it would be the first Thanksgiving without her grandmother. Constance had fought so hard against ovarian cancer, and no matter how hard she fought, she still lost. Sylvia couldn't get over how Constance's once-powerful body ended up looking like one of the hollowed-out corpses in *The Day After*.

Sylvia dropped to the floor, collapsing and screaming from the realization that, in the end, the human body was like dirt. There was nothing holy or sacred about dust. She rocked her body back and forth, bumping the back of her head against the wall, as she pictured Constance as one of the lost souls in Hades. The thought was unreal. Sylvia forced herself to think about something else.

She remembered a moment from earlier in the day. She was in the pharmacy, reading her horoscope—looking for signs—while waiting on a prescription when she noticed the copy of *National Geographic* with its starry cover on the magazine rack. She opened it to find a stitched-together series of photos of the Milky Way Galaxy over the Rio Grande Gorge. It was how Sylvia always imagined the entrance to the Underworld to be—an open crack on the surface of the plateau.

As she sat on the floor in the corner of her room, biting her nails and rocking her body back and forth, trying not to scream again, Sylvia was ready to go there, to the End of the World, to New Mexico, to the gorge, and be the hero in her story. Sylvia was ready to make her way to the Lord of the Dead, to make her case, to let her grandmother go, to move Hades and Persephone to tears because she needed Constance back. Even if Sylvia failed and died, what did it matter? Death would be the sweetest release. It would be peace.

There was no one left in the Cold War chaos who would protect and love her without question, no matter what. No one. No mother, no father, no grandmother. Sylvia kept crying and crying, as if every day since Constance died had been like the day after. She cried herself to sleep on the floor of her tiny room, and when she woke up the next morning, the feeling was still there—she wanted to die and not die. Sylvia wanted to sleep for a hundred years.

When Andrés woke up the next morning, he forgot the feeling of fear but couldn't understand why he wanted to die and not die. Andrés wanted to keep sleeping for a hundred years.

❧ 14 ❧

THE WAKE

THE FUNERAL DIRECTOR APPEARED AND ASKED EVERYONE PAYING their respects to the Patriarch to take a seat. Estefania, dressed in a bright yellow A-line gown, approached the open casket. She kissed Don Reynaldo on the cheek before turning to face everyone in attendance, red bumps visible across her forehead. She began her eulogy:

"Some people would see *Papi* and think he was a tough guy, and he was, but he was my tough guy... When I was thirteen, I didn't know he was in the kitchen with his crew, counting it up and putting fat stacks into paper bags because, y'all know, *Papi* was a gangster, and y'all know the men *Papi* had to deal with—real monsters. So, when I came into the kitchen wearing my favorite dress—this dress—some of his boys laughed."

Victor yelled out, "You knew they were there."

Estefania's face lit up with amusement as she began smoothing out long strands of her black hair with her hand. "Maybe... maybe not."

The gathered crowd laughed.

She laughed with them until her expression became solemn again.

"The point I'm trying to make," she said, "is that when *Papi* sent me to my room, I overheard some of his boys joking to his face that I was a freak. *Papi* didn't care who these people were. He was the boss in his house, and no one was gonna say that about his daughter. He pistol-whipped them and had them dragged out. Hours later, *Papi* got the call, and he had to go. He told me not to cry... I didn't know if he was coming back... but he did... I think they gave him a pass because he was defending his daughter's honor in his home. His daughter. My dad was the first to see that I was a girl."

For a moment, Estefania trembled, as if touching upon the significance of that day, before taking a deep breath and swallowing.

"I don't wanna cry," she said, "so the point I'm trying to make, without sounding like it's all about me—which is true most of the time—is that most people see what they think they see and think they have the *complete read*. *Papi* was as macho and gangster as they come, but you wouldn't think, by looking at him, that he was the one who raised us all. After *Mami* died, he did her job, and he did it alone. He never passed us off to any of his women, and I loved him more for that—for showing me that he could be my tough guy, and my teddy bear, and my mom, too."

Estefania looked over at the casket.

"*Papi*, you always said there's one thing that's more important than love, and that's respect. Respect for yourself and what you demand others should have for you, your home, and your family. *Papi*, I'm lucky I got the complete read of you. I love you... I respect you... *Mi Viejo*, until we meet again."

Estefania walked away from the casket and out of the viewing room. Everyone could hear her crying from beyond the door. Petra and Victor rushed out of the room, followed by Andrés. He caught up to his mother and uncle and watched them hug Estefania as she cried and wailed on the floor. They were surrounded by others in the crowded hall, all there for different wakes at the funeral home, oblivious—except for a young woman with long, straight black hair and dark eyes.

She approached Andrés and asked, "Is she okay?"

"I hope so," he replied, turning to look back at Estefania.

"I hope so, too... Who died?"

"My mom's father."

She chuckled. "You mean your grandfather?"

"Well, yeah," he said, glancing back at her again. "I mean, he *is* my grandfather, and we were close. But my mom didn't like us around him because he's *connected,* if you know what I mean."

"It still doesn't make sense."

"My mom said it's for my safety that I say it like that. There's a lot of stuff going on in the city. I think there's a war on the streets, and she doesn't want us to catch a bullet because of him."

"Is that how he died?" she asked.

"No—Don Reynaldo went out the way a man like him would wanna go out, if you know what I mean."

She smiled. "No, I don't. Why don't you tell me?"

"You're gonna make me say it?"

"Yeah, especially now since I see your face is turning red."

"He had a heart attack."

"That's it?"

"He had a heart attack while banging away on his twenty-year-old girlfriend."

She began to laugh. "The old man had his rap down to a science."

Andrés said flatly, "My grandfather had master *game.*"

"I'm not sure about his grandson."

Andrés was taken aback. "We're at a wake. My aunt is crying a few feet away from us."

"So?"

"So? Why are you here? Who died?"

"My father," she said flatly.

"I'm sorry."

She placed her hand on his shoulder. "Please don't be... I lied."

"Why would you lie about something like that?"

"Because I wish my father was the one who died. That would've solved a lot of my problems."

"Like what?" Andrés asked.

"Nothing I can get into right now."

"Give me your number. Maybe we can talk later."

An amused and pleased expression came to her face. "Maybe I was wrong about your game—asking for my digits at a wake... Okay, I see how it is. Let's play: I'm gonna say my number once, and fast. If you can't remember it long enough to write it down, it'll be your loss."

"You know what? Fuck your number—I don't want it."

She smirked. "You know you do—I'm beautiful."

"Keep telling yourself that. I'm gonna check on my aunt."

The young woman shrugged, then turned and walked toward one of the doors of the viewing room where her family was, pushing her way through the crowd at the entrance.

Andrés went back to Estefania, trying to hug her, but Petra pulled him off and steered him away into an empty corner in the hall.

"Why did you do that?" Andrés asked.

Petra said in a hushed voice, "Keep this between us, but she's sick. No one can tell her why, and until we know what it is, I don't want you hugging her or anything. Got that?"

"Damn, Mom."

"Don't start with me; today's not the day."

Andrés gave his mother a sad and angry look before making his way back towards his family's viewing room. The young woman came back and stopped him before he went in.

"I wrote my number down," she said, "in case you still want it. Do you?"

"No," he said.

"Of course you do. Now take it." She handed Andrés a slip of paper. "My name is Lydia. I want you to call me; I really need someone to talk to, but not now. I have to get back to my family." She turned to walk away.

Andrés called out, "Hold up! Who are you here for?"

Lydia turned around. "I'm here for my little sister, Becky... She killed herself."

"I'm so sorry!"

Lydia took a deep breath and swallowed. "Like I said, I wish it were my father instead... I don't know how much longer I can hold out. It's gonna be him or me."

❧ 15 ❧

EMMA

MAY 17, 1986

It was two in the morning, and Sylvia was on a pedestal, high above a crowded dance floor in a nightclub in Hell's Kitchen. She was doing her best to be a prop, smiling at the crowd while gyrating to the music blaring across the large, dark room.

It was anything to get through the night, and at 5:19 a.m., when the blue hour would give way to the golden hour, she would be able to go home, close her eyes, and try to sleep.

Until then, she was going to keep dancing, and keep drawing attention, and keep feeling pleasure from the attention, and keep smiling while pretending the music wasn't boring and her life wasn't empty because, who was she kidding? Nothing had been the same since the day after escaping the Black Room.

To keep her mind from wandering, she decided to make a game out of her time on the pedestal. She was going to scan the crowd, pick out people, and guess their stories. She started with a man she had been watching since the moment he placed himself in her line of sight. He was of medium height, with a crewcut hairstyle and a solid athletic build.

His story: he had to be in the military to have that kind of haircut and be in that kind of shape. Was Soldier Boy on leave? Was the girl dancing with him the *one* he'd promised not to leave behind? He could do a lot better than that clown, with her contouring applied all wrong and her hair looking bigger than her head from all the hairspray. That clown must've pulled a guilt trip on him to get him to be with her, and now she was dancing like an idiot, trying to get the attention of the other guys around them, maybe thinking she was being alluring.

Sylvia stared at Soldier Boy for a long moment before he noticed her on the pedestal and locked eyes with her. She smiled and said to him, as if he could hear her from that height over the loud music, "What that clown doesn't know is that you don't seem to care—you're too busy watching me, and I'm not looking away."

As Sylvia finished creating his story and saying that, she realized how pathetic it was to lust after a man she didn't know—a man she had imagined herself coming down from the pedestal just so she could dance with him.

But why him?

Many of the men in the nightclub were far more attractive than he was. That may have been true, but nothing about the feeling made sense. She wanted him more than any other man in the room.

Yes.

Especially when Soldier Boy's girlfriend was whisked away by another man. Instead of fighting, he shrugged and continued to dance, unfazed. Moments later, he was no longer alone. Another woman came up and began dancing with him.

That made Sylvia smile and say, "Fuck this job." She came down from the pedestal to approach, pushing aside the woman dancing with him to respond to the sign he was projecting: he was a man in control of himself. He didn't get angry over small things.

"I was watching you," she said, placing her hands on Soldier Boy's chest and raising her head to meet his gaze.

"I know," he said, towering over her, his face with light brown undertones and his eyes smiling. "I was watching you too."

"Do you like what you see?" she asked.

He placed his hands along the small of her back and said, "I love what I see."

"Oh really? Well, what would your girlfriend say about that? I saw you with her."

"She's not my girlfriend," he replied. "She was my date, and I guess she went with someone else."

"That's too bad," Sylvia said with a smirk.

"Not really," he said as he began to slowly sway his body with hers. "It's just the way it is. For me, when one girl leaves, another girl always comes along to take her place, and here you are."

"Here I am," she said with a smile.

"What's your name?"

Sylvia placed a finger to his lips. "Stop! We're not doing names or any of that other square bullshit."

"We're not?"

"No, at least not yet. I just wanna touch you. I just wanna be touched, so please touch me. It's okay. Go ahead."

He obeyed her command, running his hands all over her body in sync with his, swaying together as if in a slow dance to the beat emanating from her heart, while she took what she wanted from him. In their passion, she forgot Constance had left her behind in the wasteland, and he forgot Don Reynaldo was now a shade in the Underworld.

They became lost in each other for what felt like a moment but turned out to be hours until the crowd buckled on them, breaking the spell of the dance. They were back in the moment, with men fighting, women pleading, guns blasting, bullets whizzing, and her screaming.

He pushed her to the ground and jumped on top of her. He pinned her to the floor, forcing her to stop flailing and kicking.

"You'll be fine," he said, his face in her hair.

"No, I won't," she whimpered.

"Yes, you will. You'll be fine. Trust me—"

Bullets stopped whizzing. Everyone began running.

Soldier Boy stood up. He yanked her off the floor and flung her over his shoulder. He carried her through the stampede, punching and pushing everyone out of the way until they were outside. He ran down 52nd Street with Sylvia—ass up—draped over his shoulder. Sylvia laughed loudly as if she were on a roller coaster. Soldier Boy stopped on the corner of 12th Avenue, rolled her off his shoulder, and placed her on her feet.

She looked at him. The strange familiarity she felt surprised her and made her smile. It was the first time she felt the pull Constance would talk about whenever she read the bedtime story of Eurydice and Orpheus.

Sylvia pressed against him, and he wrapped his arms around her. They kissed with desperation, as if they were relieving the tension and agony of having been split apart before they were born.

They were whole again.

When the kiss ended, she became overwhelmed with sadness, her eyes watering, almost crying.

"Did I do something wrong?" he asked.

"No, you're fine," she replied. "I enjoyed the kiss... I enjoyed it a little too much."

"Can I get your number?"

She paused, placing a hand to her mouth to bite her newly manicured nails. "You don't want it—trust me."

"Maybe I do," he said, taking her hands away from her mouth and into his. "I love bad girls."

"You do? Or are you just saying that?"

"Bad girls make the world go round."

She raised an eyebrow, no longer sad but happy and intrigued by his response. "What makes you think you can handle this bad girl?"

"You'd have to find that out for yourself. I'm not talk—I'm action."

"Oh really? Prove it."

"Where do you live?"

"In Morningside Heights. It's a quick cab ride."

"Then let's go."

"Wait," she said. "I have to get my stuff first. If I don't do it now, I'll never get it back."

"Why's that?"

"I don't think I have a job anymore."

He laughed. "Oh snap! For real?"

Her eyebrows shifted from expressing intrigue to concern. "Is that how you talk? And your goofy-ass is laughing that I could've lost my job? Wait—how old are you?"

"Sixteen."

Sylvia began to laugh hard to the point of losing her breath.

"Are you okay?" he asked.

She coughed and replied, "No."

He took her hand and led her away from the corner, directing her to lean against a brick wall until she caught her breath.

When she did, she asked, "How old do you think I am?"

"I don't know—eighteen?"

"Oh, bless your goofy-ass," she said, trying not to smile. "I could love you forever, but no... I'm twenty-three, and I was grabbing your dick like statutory rape isn't a thing?"

"Oh snap!"

"There it goes again; your age is showing. How the fuck did you get into the club?"

"I walked in and paid—they didn't ask for my ID."

Sylvia shook her head. "Unbelievable—no wonder there was a shootout."

"Can I at least get your name?"

"No, no," she said, pushing him away. "I wanna forget this ever happened, I think—maybe—I don't know."

"It's okay, chill—you did nothing wrong. I'm into you. I couldn't take my eyes off you."

"I couldn't take my eyes off you, too," she said, "but no—stop with the sweet talk. I can't go down this road—this is the line."

He pulled her back. "It doesn't have to be. Let's cross it; you know you want to... You bad girl."

She laughed. "Where were you when I was sixteen?"

"I was nine, watching cartoons."

"You asshole, you had to go there."

He gave Sylvia a wicked smile. "I did. Let's go uptown so I can go downtown."

"You're horrible."

"I know you like it this way. I already know you. I feel like I know you."

She pushed him away, laughing. "That's it! Back in the oven you go! You need to bake a little more. Your goofy-ass ain't ready for me."

"I don't think you're ready for me either."

His words hit her like a punch, knocking the breath out of her and causing her to stutter. She tried to come up with a witty reply, but it appeared he could see right through her.

"I still want you," he said, grabbing her hand and pulling her back, "bad girl and all."

"I still want you too," she said.

"So... what do we do now?"

Sylvia considered his question for a moment before resigning herself to reality. "We go our separate ways and hope that, whatever this is, it's written in the stars for us to meet again? When we're both ready? 'Cause this is the line, and I have to go before I cross it—before I get myself into trouble, and there's no coming back from this kind of trouble. And I don't wanna do that to you. I don't wanna do that to myself."

He stepped away from her. "I don't wanna cross the line either. All that talk was just that—talk... I wanted to leave you with something to remember me by."

"You have... fuck!"

"But it doesn't have to end—we can just hang out and talk. We know the line."

"And I wanna cross it so bad," she said, "so no. We can't be around each other."

He began walking away.

She grabbed his arm and pulled him back. "Let me look at you one last time, so I don't forget your face. So I can recognize you if we were to meet again. That maybe this is fate?"

"I don't believe in fate," he said.

"But that's the thing—neither do I, but I wanna believe. I'm always looking for signs; I've been looking all my life, and I saw the biggest one tonight, and it was you, and I'm about to cross the line, and I've gotta go." She pushed him away.

He pulled her back. "Can I walk with you? That's not crossing a line, is it? You're still dressed that way, and I wanna make sure you make it back safe."

"I'll be fine."

"Are you sure? Something's telling me not to let you go this easily."

Sylvia forced a smile. "You don't need to worry about me. I'm out here almost every night, doing my thing because this bad girl's gotta eat, and I've got rent to pay, and I don't have a family to support me. I have to be my own savior and make this money. So, I'm good."

"If you say so," he said. "Be careful doing your bad girl thing."

"Yeah, yeah," she said, pushing him away and waving him off. "Until we meet again, have a nice life."

Sylvia began walking down the long, dark street. Just before crossing 11th Avenue, she turned to look back and saw him watching her from a distance. Sylvia wanted to call out and tell him she would be fine and that he could move on with his life, but why lie? She took a deep breath and looked forward. She kept walking.

Blue and white lights flashing in the distance grew larger and brighter as she crossed 8th Avenue and approached the club's side entrance.

She banged on a door. "Ay, yo, it's me—Emma. I've gotta get my stuff."

"Emma, who?" was the response.

"Spacer Woman! Let me in!"

The door opened, and she entered. She climbed several flights of stairs until she reached a small room with cracked mirrors and busted lockers. She collapsed into a corner and began to cry.

❧ 16 ❧

THE WHITE ROOM

MARCH 21, 1991

WE ARE THE WATCHERS, AND WE ARE WITH SERGEANT ANDRÉS DE León inside an intensive care unit at a military hospital in Landstuhl, Germany. The sergeant is in a coma, his soul split between the Land of the Alive and the Land of the Not-Alive.

We were there in the desert when the sergeant was part of a team of human tripwires—several scattered throughout southern Iraq in the days before the 100-hour ground war.

We were there when the sergeant vowed to get home so that his newborn son with Lydia would have a father in his life.

We were there when they shot the sergeant, where he bled, where he killed.

Body broken, hands clutching dirt, We were there when a medic recovered the sergeant's body, and his unit evacuated him to Germany.

We will be here when Andrés wakes from his coma. The Army will award him the Purple Heart for his wounds and the Silver Star for conspicuous gallantry and intrepidity in action against the enemy.

In this White Room, Andrés sees Us and connects everything.

When the time comes again, he will recognize the other half of Us, but not before experiencing the powerful feeling of déjà vu.

In this White Room, Sergeant de León understands that We see well into Our past and well into Our future, and when he comes awake, comes alive, this will become a blur buried in the back of his mind.

He will receive the greatest gift God could give him.

The gift of forgetting.

He will forget We exist.

All memory will be driven below, and the feelings of terror and fear, and the drive to survive, and to embrace death while still wanting to live, will move within him like the Hundred-Handed Ones imprisoned in the depths below his shadow self.

Andrés will say he does not remember, and at first, that will be true, but the Earth is a witness, and the ground he left behind keeps what he spilled. What recollects in that manner endures and will call him back to the desert to face justice.

We are with him as We are with her.

Sylvia Hadid James is inside a filthy bathroom with white walls at St. Mark's Hotel in New York's East Village. She is pushing herself off the floor, yelling in anger, forcing herself to stand upright, leaning against a wall, and taking breath after breath after breath. She was not born to be like this, a junkie, and she knows it. We were there when God took everything from her, including her innocence. She could do nothing more than pick at her hair, bite her nails, and listen to the same song over and over in her empty room until the need for sleep became greater than her fears of the dark.

We were there when Sylvia gave herself to the streets, desperate to survive what felt like a never-ending dark night of the soul. Not even the sunshine coming through the windows of strangers' bedrooms, as if it were a nightlight, could give her the peace she was seeking.

There would be no closing of her eyes.

There would be no sleep or dreams.

There would be no more hope.

There would be no more memory.

We were there when Sylvia forgot her name, her roots, and her past, and the years all became a blur, and after bumping her head, she became awake, became alive, and is now leaning against the bathroom wall, having pushed herself out of her waste, because this is not how she wants to live anymore.

No!

She will hold on to what she can remember from within the blur so that it may never happen again because this is not her!

No!

Not anymore!

She is on her feet, ready to take back control of her life once and for all.

Sylvia vows never again to let anyone or anything subjugate her, taking away her free will and the power to make choices.

She will walk out the door of the White Room to find help.

She will set herself back on the path where, in The Labyrinth, she will meet her Soldier Boy—Andrés—again.

She will trust him because she will recognize herself in him and know that he is from another time and beyond. Andrés will feel like déjà vu.

Sylvia will make herself whole with him.

Andrés will make himself complete with her.

He will push her to reach her full potential and fulfill her divine duty—to become the Fury through which one prayer can be answered.

For Andrés to meet *Our* Maker.

THE LABYRINTH

I want to bite into life, and to be torn by it.

— ANAIS NIN

17

NIGHTLIGHT

IT WAS TWO IN THE MORNING, AND ANDRÉS WAS IN BED, CURLED UP as if afflicted with hunger. There was no way to satisfy it without pushing himself out of bed and going out to fulfill his desires.

Despite being forbidden from driving by his neurologist and his parents, Andrés borrowed his dad's car and was at Robots on the Lower East Side within an hour. The bouncer recognized him as the guy who had come in with Lil Red the week before and let him in.

The air in the dark room was thick with musky sweat, dank weed, and cheap incense. The giant strobe mirror ball hung from the ceiling, dull and unlit. The only light glowed red from the corners, casting shadows on the walls. The room echoed with thumping bass and shuffling feet, punctuated by bursts of laughter and shouted conversation cutting through the noise.

Andrés began to dance. Moments later, a tap on his shoulder jolted him to a stop. He turned to see Sylvia glaring at him, hands on her hips. Her auburn curls were wrapped into two puffy buns on either side of her head. Her face, with copper undertones and heavy-lidded eyes, flashed a scowl.

"What are you doing?" she asked.

Andrés leaned in so she could hear him. "I was dancing. And you?"

"You know what I'm doing—"

"I don't assume," Andrés interrupted.

"Yeah, right. Did you come here looking for me?"

"If I were looking for you, I would've gone to The Loft."

"True, but you came here instead."

"I couldn't sleep."

"Me neither... But why didn't you go to The Loft?"

"I had nothing to read."

"But I'd be there."

"I thought you didn't wanna see me."

Sylvia pushed him. "How could you think that?"

"I called; I left you a message. You never called back."

"I've been busy."

"That's cool," he said.

"You could've kept trying."

"I've been busy too."

"So, it's like that now?"

"Yeah, it's like that. You're not the only one with a life."

"Is that so?" She patted him on the back. "Well, it was great bumping into you. Good luck with that *life*."

"Right back at you. Keep looking for that nightlight."

She hesitated for a moment before walking away.

The night moved on, and the crowd thinned out. It was 5:08 a.m., and outside, astronomical twilight was ending. The only people remaining on the dance floor were those too high or too afraid to succumb to the darkness of sleep. They needed to be surrounded by bright lights and mesmerizing sounds.

Andrés and Sylvia danced alone at opposite ends of the floor, locking eyes to keep each other in sight. A man wearing an oversized T-shirt and baggy pants approached Sylvia, asking her to dance. Sylvia drew him close, and when he started running his hands all over her, she looked over his shoulder at Andrés and smirked sarcastically.

Andrés began to laugh. A woman who had been dancing nearby and dressed in black lace tights, platform boots, and a dark velvet dress stared at him for a long moment before giving him a welcoming smile and turning away. Andrés reached over, turned the goth girl around, and pulled her in close. He smirked at Sylvia as the goth girl started running her hands all over him.

Sylvia nodded at Andrés, acknowledging the game they were playing, then smiled and made her next move: she began making out with her dance partner. When Andrés started making out with his, Sylvia pushed her dance partner aside, charged across the floor, and dragged Andrés into one of the club's darkest corners, yelling at him, "Stop the bullshit."

"What bullshit?" he said, laughing.

"Don't play dumb—why did you come here?"

"I couldn't sleep, for real."

"But you could've gone anywhere; why here?"

"I knew I could get in easily. I know a *hotshot* who's got some juice."

Sylvia pushed him. "I'm being serious. Is that the only reason? You didn't come here because you missed me? Because you knew I'd be here? You were thinking about me?"

"It's obvious you weren't thinking about me; you didn't call me back."

"You could've kept trying—"

"No, I'm not leaving more than one message—not happening... I know I got wrapped up in last weekend's romance, but I guess the reality is... I don't know you. And you don't know me. So I'm not gonna be that guy who blows up your answering machine like a fucking clown."

She became frustrated. "All this because of a message?"

"You didn't call me back."

"But I was expecting to see you at The Loft! I don't wanna come off as needy."

"And I thought you didn't wanna see me," he said, "and I had nothing to read."

"So?"

"There was no reason for me to be there, and I don't wanna come off as needy too... If I ever get the feeling that you don't wanna see me, then I'm not gonna show up where you are. I'm gonna give you space. But I had every reason to dance—I couldn't sleep—so here I am."

"I couldn't sleep because I thought you didn't wanna see me," she said.

"Me too. Shit—if you wanna hear from me, just call," he said.

They both laughed at the silliness of it all.

"You'd think I'd know better," she said. "I'm turning thirty in a few weeks, and I feel like I'm sixteen again, trying to get my boyfriend's attention... Why couldn't I just keep being real with you?"

"Maybe because I wasn't being real with you, and that's my fault."

"No, it's mine."

"How's this for real?" he said. "I'm scared. I haven't stopped thinking about you."

"I haven't stopped thinking about you—I've never spent a whole weekend with a guy... I guess that's one reason I didn't return your call... To give myself the headspace to see if I missed you or if I was just bored."

"I was right," he said. "You needed your space."

Sylvia's face lit up with immense joy. "You can read me."

"I can."

"You don't know how important that is to me."

"It's important to me too. You didn't *ghost* me."

"No, I didn't," she said. "I wanted to call, and I knew if I did, I'd want you to come over. Like I said, I didn't want to look like I was being needy. I hate being told no."

"I wouldn't have been able to come over anyway—I have school and my son."

"I need to know one thing," she said, "and it's important... Did you come here because of me?"

"Of course I did," he said. "I missed you."

Her eyes brightened. "I missed you too... But now I'm curious about something... Did seeing me kiss another guy make you jealous?"

He smirked. "Don't play yourself. I knew what you were trying to do. I grew up watching a master run *game*. I don't get jealous like that."

"Yeah, right, Mr. Bullshit; you just gave away that you know game."

"Not the kind of game most people know, not the kind most

people would be cool with. I have mixed feelings about that kind of game."

She looked intrigued. "That sounds kind of shady."

"It is. Big time. Maybe one day I'll share more; that is, if we get there."

"Well," she said, smiling, "if it's like that, then maybe one day I'll share something with you that I've never been able to share with anyone before; that is, if we ever get there."

"Sounds kind of shady."

She laughed. "Shut up. I've yet to meet a man who I think could handle it. That's all."

"Whatever. The only thing I know is that you're the one who got jealous."

"I don't get jealous," she said.

"Yeah, sure—you didn't just pull me away when I started kissing that goth chick. You sure showed me."

"Okay, you've made your point."

"And what's my point?" he asked.

"Passion," she said. "I'm all about it."

"Me too."

"Is that so? Be careful," she said. "I have a large appetite... I could end up eating you alive."

"I could end up doing the same to you."

"We'll see." Sylvia grabbed Andrés's hand. "Let's get out of here—go back to my place—see if we can do something that'll wear us out, put us to sleep."

18

ODYSSEUS

OCTOBER 24, 1992

IT WAS SATURDAY NIGHT. ANDRÉS WAS AT THE LOFT, SITTING AT A table in the dark, waiting for Sylvia to take the stage. She had told him days before that he needed to be there.

"I'm gonna do something different. You can't miss it. I promise it's not gonna suck—unlike your poems."

After all the scheduled readers had finished performing, Reginald Superstar came on and took his place in the spotlight. "Thank you for making The Loft a part of your night. We appreciate your support. To cap the night off, we have this crazy bitch."

Sylvia shouted from the back, "Your mama is a crazy bitch!"

The audience laughed.

"I deserve that," Reginald said. "But she is crazy, and I know that firsthand—she was my roommate for years."

Sylvia shouted again, "Morningside Heights!"

Reginald laughed. "That's right. Living with her taught me that 'crazy' is short for 'crazy creative,' which is what makes our next reader such an amazing artist. So, put your hands together and give it up for Sylvia."

The audience clapped as she sauntered onto the stage and snatched the microphone from Reginald's hands, shoving him aside to take his place in the spotlight. She brought the microphone to her lips, holding it there for a long moment, scanning the room until her half-lidded, soft eyes made contact with Andrés.

"I'm dating this guy," she said.

"I mean, I like him.

"I like him a lot.

"But I don't wanna jinx it.

"So, let me say this like I'm a battle MC

"About to drop rhymes on a mixtape

"And yell, 'REWIND!'

"And rephrase my statement...

"I'm fucking this guy."

The audience chuckled.

"He's got potential, but... he lives with his mom."

The audience laughed.

"Wait," she said, motioning for them to stop. "He's not a loser."

Her face softened as she made eye contact with Andrés again.

"I'm not holding it against him.

"But that doesn't mean I can't vent...

"I wanna be able to go to his place

"And fuck him on his bed

"And moan as loud as I want

"And shower in his bathroom

"And use his toilet

"And not worry if I'm making noises

"And afterward, go into his kitchen and make him a sandwich...

"Of course, I'd wash my hands first."

A heckler from the back yelled, "He can make his own damn sandwich!"

Sylvia found the heckler and stared at her with dead eyes.

"Of course, he can make his own damn sandwich, but that's not the point.

"The point is, it's because I'd want to."

Sylvia shifted her focus back to the audience and stared at them for a moment, as if trying to find her way back to her routine.

She smiled. "He's a good guy,

"Not a loser nice guy...

"Ladies, you know, that creep you keep around just in case you need someone to help you move

"Or be on standby to deliver your food? No!

"He's none of that—

"He's a real good guy...

"A war hero, although he'd say he's not.

"He lives with his mom because he almost died and still hurts, so

"Mama needs to be there while he continues to recover,

"Which is too bad, though, because

"His mama happens to be

"The biggest

"Cock block."

The audience laughed.

Sylvia laughed. "I'm serious.

"I called his house the other night, trying to convince him to get his ass on the train and come to my place.

"You know, it's October,

"And the nights are getting colder,

"And soon I'm gonna need some of his heat on demand,

"And as I was talking about how I was gonna drop it down on him

"His mom gets on the other line and starts talking to me.

"Oh, my God!" Sylvia yelled, looking at the ceiling. "Mama killed the mood.

"I had to hang up.

"She dried my pussy up."

The audience laughed.

Sylvia began to pace the stage.

"My friends wonder, 'Why do I put up with it?'

"After all...

"I've got this badass personality.

"I've got this bomb-ass pussy.

"My friends say, 'I can have anyone I want.'

"That's true, but not true.

"I can have sex,

"But...

"I've never had love."

Sylvia returned to the spotlight, made eye contact with Andrés once more, and smiled.

"That's why I put up with it—

"The night we met,

"When we danced,

"He saw me.

"The real me.

"We went to this after-hours spot down in the Bowery.

"I lost myself in his arms.

"In his eyes.

"It was the first time in my life

"When the lights all around me seemed like stars,

"Not from a giant disco ball hanging in the center of the room, but

"From a vast night sky."

She looked at the floor.

"Let me tell you.

"I feel like I can't live down my past...

"Once a junkie, always a junkie, they say."

She looked up at the audience.

"Now that I'm clean,

"To prove a point to myself,

"I'd go into those dark rooms and be like Odysseus,

"And to be in that dark room, dancing

"And surrounded by heroin whores

"And cocaine cowboys

"All doing their thing

"I'd feel that hunger!

"I'd feel that call!

"I'D HEAR THE SIREN'S CALL TO GET THAT FIX!

"THE INSATIABLE DESIRE TO GET HIGH

"AND FORGET THE WORLD!

"AND FORGET MY NAME AGAIN!

"I'D FIGHT!

"I would fight!

"And I would always win...

"But not without a cost...

"Each time...

"I would lose a little something of myself...

"All because I need to prove a point...

Sylvia paused.

"I am not my past...

"But that night in that dark room

"I didn't feel the call

"Because he made me feel like I was in space.

"That I was above it all."

She looked at the floor.

"It meant something to me.

"For something so small to feel so large."

She looked up at the audience and smiled.

"We danced all night.

"He made me laugh when he said it was time to see my pussy."

The audience gasped.

Sylvia said, "Context, people, context.

"Some of you may have heard my *Ode to My Hairy Pussy*.

"He had heard it too.

"So, I told him

"That I would show him.

"I took him to the Gift Shop.

"It was a fantastic night.

"It was an amazing morning,

"Capped by waffles from a dirt diner out by Delancey,

"And a trip to the World Trade Center

"Where I made a wish under a tenement sky.

"Where he fueled my desire to look at this city with new eyes.

"Where he held my hand because he wanted to hold my hand."

She stomped her foot. "FUCK, I HATE FEELING!

"I wanna be numb again

"But I can't...

"I think he understands that

"When the night is over,

"It's over.

"But not this time.

"So, yeah...

"I'm dating this guy who lives with his mom.

"But that's okay.

"When I'm with my boyfriend

"I'm no longer my past.

"I forget what I used to be.

"I now remember again who I am.

"I'm Sylvia Hadid James.

"I no longer feel like I was created from dirt,

"But rather,

"From the stuff of stars.

"And because of that,

"I now know I am deserving of love.

"And now you know that, too...

"Peace out."

Sylvia began to tremble as the audience gave muted applause.

Reginald came to the stage, taking the microphone from her shaking hand, then wrapping his arm around her shoulder. "Girl, that was different... Love? Who are you?"

Sylvia pushed Reginald away, walking off the stage without responding to the laughter booming from the crowd. She approached Andrés, who had shot up from his seat to welcome her with open arms.

"What did you think?" she asked anxiously.

"Your poem was great," Andrés replied.

"No, it wasn't. The crowd didn't seem to like it."

"The crowd is used to hearing something different."

"Like what? Something good?"

"Something good," he said in a mocking tone.

She poked him. "I don't sound like that."

"Yeah, you do."

"You know what?" she said, now smiling. "I'm gonna fuck you up for getting me like this. All insecure, I swear."

"I told you the poem was great."

"But that's what you're supposed to say—especially since the poem was about you."

"Say it—I'm your muse."

"Hell no," she said, laughing. "I don't roll like that. At least not yet. Not until I let you do anal. That's my version of us going steady."

"You just called me your boyfriend."

"You're right—let's get out of here."

As Sylvia and Andrés started moving toward the exit, a tall man with wavy hair and a weak mustache called out her name. He pushed through the crowd, followed by two women—one with dark, layered hair and tired eyes, the other a blonde with porcelain skin and a short bob.

When he reached them, the two women flanked Sylvia while the tall man pushed Andrés aside, positioned himself in front of her, and tried to give her a hug.

Sylvia pushed him away. "Why are you calling out my name like I owe you money?"

"You kind of do," the tall man said.

"I don't owe you shit."

"I'm just playing. I wanted to tell you I swung by the other day, but you weren't around."

"Was I supposed to be? I got a job, you know—exposure doesn't pay my bills."

"I know you've got a job, but I thought you would've been home by then."

"Who's this guy?" Andrés asked.

Without looking at him, the tall man replied, "I'm Caleb."

"I'm Katherine," the dark-haired woman said.

"And I'm Jessica," the blonde added.

"We're all old friends."

"Check that shit, Caleb. They're old friends, not you," Sylvia said. "You're just someone I've happened to know for a long time."

"Over ten years," Caleb said.

"Ten years of bullshit," Sylvia said. "I thought I told you to stop coming around."

"You did, but you're never serious about that. And I know how insecure you can get with your work, so I came tonight, knowing I'd run into you, to tell you that the poem you wrote about your pussy is amazing."

"Tell me something I don't know."

"Do you know you're so fantastic?"

Sylvia laughed at Caleb. "If I'm so fantastic, what do you think of my new poem?"

"Amazing as always. But did I hear you correctly? You've got a boyfriend?"

"You did. Until now, Andrés was just a guy I was fucking, but I guess it's safe to say he's my boyfriend. I mean, he didn't give me his high school sweater or make a proclamation before a crowd like I just did, but we've fucked around enough, and I like him more than I hate him, so I wanna keep it going. Tonight, I'm making us *official*—I'm giving him anal."

Caleb pointed at Andrés. "Is this the guy? Mama's boy? And I can't get you to return my messages? Call me back?"

"Maybe if you didn't act like a creep, she'd be reading a poem about you instead of me," Andrés said.

Caleb placed a heavy hand on Andrés's shoulder. "At least I don't live with my mom."

Andrés rammed an uppercut into his jaw.

Caleb crashed hard to the floor.

Andrés grabbed Caleb by the hair, lifted his head off the floor, and raised his fist.

Someone in the crowd yelled, "Yo, bro, chill."

Andrés realized what he was about to do. He dropped Caleb's head and stepped back to look at Sylvia. She appeared mesmerized by Andrés, her eyes wide with surprise, while Katherine and Jessica tried to pull her away from him as though he was the danger, not Caleb.

Andrés became unsure if Sylvia was judging the part of him he didn't want anyone to see—the dark shadow at the center of his being. The shadow that had guaranteed his survival during his deployment and his return to the ordinary world. Since then, he had found it difficult to keep it hidden. The shadow was always ready to fight, to defend, to protect not only himself but also those he considered family —those he was falling in love with.

At that moment, Andrés felt as naked and vulnerable before Sylvia as she had when she was trembling on stage before the crowd. The feeling of shame became unbearable. He turned away from her, pushing through the throng gathered around them to race to the exit.

Sylvia ran outside after him, yelling, "Wait! Don't be so dramatic!"

Andrés had to stop and laugh. He kept laughing until she caught up, slapping him on the shoulder.

"You're worse than I was when I was sixteen, making me run after you," she said. "Where are you going?"

"Home," he said.

"Why?"

"Because I'm embarrassed."

Sylvia laughed. "Bitch, please. This is the Lower East Side. It's just another day. Don't worry about it; just come here."

She grabbed his hand and pulled him into her arms, resting her head on his chest and shutting her eyes. Something within her seemed to relax more, causing her to slump against him as though she had been a weary soul in search of comfort and had found it in the beating of his heart.

After a long pause, she confessed, "I've been trying to find a way to get Caleb to leave me alone without setting him off."

"You have?" Andrés asked, surprised.

She opened her eyes to look up at him. "I didn't say anything before because you weren't my boyfriend, and I didn't want you asking questions... I have my reasons for letting him linger around me like that. Maybe one day I'll tell you, but... I don't know... I just don't want you to judge me."

"You don't need to explain. You're good."

"Are you sure?"

"Yes, don't worry."

Sylvia exhaled, relieved, then stared at him intensely. "You know... I don't like any of that macho bullshit, but I've been looking over my shoulder a lot lately."

"You have?"

Sylvia stepped back and looked at Andrés as if he were clueless. "Of course—every woman has to look over her shoulder... I've just had to do it a lot more lately because of Caleb."

Andrés pulled her back into his arms and smirked as though she were the one who was clueless. "Every woman hates the macho bullshit until she needs it. I'm your tough guy, and don't you forget it."

"Thank you, I won't... Moving on... There's a showing of *The Road Warrior* at the Playhouse tonight. I've always loved that movie."

"Let's check it out."

"But can we afford it?"

"I have forty dollars," he said, "but I won't get paid again until next week. I should have my disability check by then."

"I have forty dollars, too, but it has to last me until payday—but fuck it—I can survive on almost nothing. We can spend some of that."

"No—"

"But I've got us covered, too."

"No—save your money. If you're hungry after the movie, we can get some fast food instead."

Sylvia pushed him away. "Is that your solution? Making me eat fast food?" She pulled him back. "You're lucky I tolerate you."

"I'm the total package."

She laughed. "Whatever... By the way, if you wanna make us *official*, fast food is not a good idea. I'll think of something else."

❧ 19 ❧

THE SUNFLOWERS

OCTOBER 25, 1992

AFTER A MOVIE AND A LATE-NIGHT MEAL, SYLVIA TOOK ANDRÉS home and made their relationship *official.* They went to bed and woke up hours later.

They got dressed and left the apartment, walking down Avenue B and Clinton Street until they reached her favorite diner. They had Sunday brunch, left the diner, and wandered the long streets across lower Manhattan, ending their walk in Battery Park City.

She found a bench by the railing at the promenade along the Hudson River and sat down with him. Together, in silence, they watched tall ships and small boats sail in and out of New York Harbor until the sky was at twilight.

Then, just like that, Sylvia stood up and started ranting about how she was becoming too comfortable with him. She pointed her finger at his face and yelled he was getting too comfortable with her. "I don't like how you got me all strung out! Go home! I wanna be alone!"

Instead of asking why she was blowing up on him, Andrés shrugged, got up from the bench, and walked away, leaving her in silence.

OCTOBER 26, 1992

[1]

It was late Monday afternoon when Andrés returned home from a day of classes at Brooklyn College. He was about to lock himself in his room for the rest of the evening when Petra, dressed in a red apron and a black satin bonnet, appeared from the kitchen to tell him Sylvia had called.

He sighed. "I'll call her later—"

"But she sounds out of it."

"She'll be fine."

Petra grabbed him by the arm to keep him from walking away. "I know what you're trying to do."

"What am I trying to do?"

"Make her suffer."

"You don't know what you're talking about—"

"I know she was real upset with you last night."

He dropped his book bag to the floor. "How?"

"She called me from work and told me... She calls every day."

"Why is Sylvia calling you?"

"I don't know—ask her yourself."

Andrés paused, unsure how to feel about his girlfriend's daily conversations with his mother. "What else do you guys talk about?"

"The future... What she wants." Petra looked at Andrés as though he were clueless. "*Mijo,* I know your life is none of my business, and I'm trying to stay out of it, but I'm going to tell you what I've been telling her: you're playing a dangerous game."

"I'm not playing games."

"But she is. You know how I know? I was her age once, and I can tell. And I told Sylvia that, for what she said she wants, passion is over-rated. She should be looking for stability instead, and that's not you. It'll never be you."

"Thanks for believing in me, Mom."

"You're so much like your father."

"Pop is my father, not that man you keep comparing me to."

"He's your blood—"

"So what—I'm nothing like that man; I want love. It's what Sylvia and I both want."

"No—Sylvia wants a baby."

Andrés laughed nervously. "Stop talking to her!"

Petra smiled. "No—and the next time she calls, I'm inviting her over."

"Oh God, no."

"I have to meet her sometime. I don't know why you haven't brought her home yet."

"We became *official* yesterday."

"Well, I'm going to invite her over. We can be friends. It's only fair. She could end up giving me a granddaughter."

"Okay, Mom, now you're pushing it. I'm still getting to know her."

"Good—and now that you know what you know, if you keep dating, you better be ready to give her what she wants because if you don't, it would be an abuse of her time. And I didn't raise you to be abusive, did I?"

Andrés looked down, away from Petra's penetrating gaze—a gaze that, for as long as he could remember, made something in him turn to stone and say in a small voice, "No."

"I raised you to be a good man, and you're a good man, right?"

"I'm a good man."

"Okay. So if you're a good man, then you'll do whatever it takes to make her happy, right?"

Andrés shook her hand off his arm, looked directly back at her, and said, "Only if it makes me happy first."

"That's not how a good relationship works."

"Maybe not for you, but I hate seeing Pop so miserable and you so happy. And you're so mean to him, and I'm not gonna end up like him, walking on eggshells just to make my girlfriend—my wife—happy. Hell no!"

"Like I said, just like your father: selfish and clueless about what it takes to keep a happy home."

Before Andrés could respond, the phone rang in the kitchen. He hurried to answer.

Sylvia was on the other end of the line. "Did Miss Petra tell you I called?"

"Yes, she did," he replied.

"Well, why didn't you call back?"

"Because I just got home."

"Are you coming over?"

"I don't know. Maybe I don't want you getting too comfortable with me?"

Sylvia chuckled. "You know I'm always talking that shit, and I'm over it, so stop acting like a pussy and come over—only if you're free."

"I'm free; Andy is with his mom."

"He is?"

"Lydia came by after I got home last night, asking if she could take him—saying she'd like another chance to be his mother. I told her only if she didn't plan on dipping out of his life. I'm getting him back tomorrow."

"Then come through."

"Okay, I'm heading out now."

"Cool. I'll be waiting."

[2]

Hours after ending the call and leaving for the city, Andrés stood in front of Sylvia's apartment building. She had been waiting for him on the fire escape outside her top-floor window.

She called down to him, "What took you so long?"

He called back, "What happened to wanting your space?"

"Yeah, well, about that. Just like the moon goes through her phases, I go through mine, and it's a full moon tonight."

"I get it."

"I feel like I'm dying."

"I can go to the *bodega* and get you a brownie. I can even go to the pharmacy if you need pads or anything else."

"I've got chocolate stashed away, and I have everything else, so I'm good. Thanks for asking. Come on up." She left through the window to buzz the door open.

Andrés climbed a dark staircase that smelled of bleach and mold. Sylvia waited at the top step. When he was within her reach, she lunged forward and welcomed him with open arms, kissing him. "I'm sorry for blowing up the way I did... You've got to understand, this is new for me."

"You don't need to explain," he said.

"Are you sure?"

"It's not a big deal."

She smiled, as if relieved that Andrés didn't get angry over small things. "I made us dinner."

"You didn't have to do that."

"I did it anyway, so you better be hungry."

"I'm starving."

"Good, I think it's done. Come on in."

Andrés followed her inside, dropping his bag by the door before shutting it behind them.

Sylvia went into the kitchen and returned, her face sweaty, holding two paper plates, just as he was tapping the glass of her tank to greet Kalpa, her pet turtle.

"Do me a favor," she said, "and clear away those books on the couch so we can sit and eat."

He did as she asked. She waited for him to finish, then sat next to him, handing him his dinner.

Andrés stared at his plate like a child being asked to eat poison.

"What's wrong?" Sylvia asked.

"I don't eat fish," he replied.

"Are you kidding me? I went through a lot of trouble to make this, and you come at me with that bullshit? I don't even like to cook. So, if you want me to keep treating you like you're special, you'll eat what I put in front of you. Understand?"

"I understand."

"Good, 'cause I've never done this for anyone else, so don't take it for granted."

Andrés was slow to take his first bite, but when he realized how good the ginger tasted with the fresh salmon, he rushed to take another bite, then another, picking up the pace, not chewing but inhaling the food until there was nothing left on the plate.

Sylvia savored each bite of hers. After she finished, she placed her plate on the coffee table next to his and asked, "How do you feel?"

"It's funny," he said. "I was fighting not to fall asleep on the train, but now I feel so awake."

"Imagine what your life would be like if you ate salmon with ginger all the time."

"I'm sure it'd be great, but it wouldn't be as fun."

She glared at him. "I knew you'd say something like that... How did I know? We need to talk."

"Okay. About what?"

"Your bad habits. Just because something is fun and makes you feel good, doesn't mean it's healthy for you."

"*Pfft*. I know that."

"If you know that, then why do you keep eating shit?"

"Because I can quit anytime I want."

"You're more fucked up than I thought," she said.

"You're making a big deal out of nothing."

She pushed his shoulder. "Oh, am I? What if I were to tell you I'm back on drugs, but it's okay because I could quit anytime I want? What would you say to that? Wouldn't you be making a big deal?"

"It's not the same."

"Yes, it is. The way you go hard on junk food is the same way I used to go hard on dope. You're an addict."

"Yes, I'm an addict. I freebase pizza."

"Keep making jokes," she said, "because I'm not laughing. If you keep eating the way you do, you're gonna end up fat and dead."

"So be it," he said, smiling. "I'm not afraid to die if I die happy."

"Stop fucking around! I'm serious! I blew up the way I did because I felt closer to you in the silence than I ever did with anyone else in the talk. Like, close, close. Like, I'm falling in love with you, kind of close. If we're gonna be in a relationship, you need to start taking better care of yourself."

"But I do."

"No, you don't! The other night, after the movie, I was hungry, but it was three in the morning, so I had chamomile tea. What did you have? Cheese fries."

"I didn't eat all day."

"But why that and not something else, like toast, fruit, something that could've held you over until brunch?"

He shrugged. "I don't know."

"Yes, you do. You said it yourself: toast or fruit wouldn't be as fun. And it's not just that night; it's every night that we go out. The way you stuff your face scares me."

Sylvia paused to give him a long, helpless look.

"You forget that I'm still an addict. I'll always be an addict, and it's so hard for me to watch you, especially on days when I'm struggling. Every second feels like a lifetime, and it feels like I'm not gonna make it. I need someone to be strong for me, to be my rock, not another addict who could also be struggling and end up dragging me down. We could end up drowning each other and calling it love."

"I never thought about it like that."

She grabbed his hands. "If I'm gonna be with you, you need to get rid of *all* your bad habits. You need to develop a healthier relationship with food. If you don't, I'll cut you out of my life... It won't matter how much you love me or how much I love you; I'll always love myself more. You'll be dead to me."

"But I'm in the best shape of my life, even with the way I eat."

"Keep eating cheese fries, and by the time you get to be my age, you'll be fat and shit out of luck. Thirty is gonna come at you real fast. Trust me, I know—"

"I just realized... we didn't do anything for your birthday—"

"Don't try changing the subject—"

"I swear, I'm not... It's just that we're in a relationship now, and yet we didn't celebrate."

She sighed as she dropped his hands.

"It was a weekday, you weren't available, and getting older is nothing for me to be happy about... Turning thirty got me thinking about all the bad habits I used to have. Like, when is it all gonna catch up? When is my body gonna quit on me?"

"But you look fine," he said.

"That's now, but... karma exists for everything, even the body. Inside, my soul feels heavy, and with everything I did to get it like that, it's only a matter of time before it all catches up and I die." Sylvia's eyes veered away as if she had become adrift in thought.

Andrés sensed she was about to spiral into a panic attack. He began to think, searching for words that would force her to shift her attention away from her anxieties and toward him, even if it meant making her mad.

"Well, I'm not afraid to die."

"You're not?" she said, her eyes shifting back to his.

"No. Why should I be? Everything cuts to black; I won't remember."

"You're so wrong."

"Why am I wrong?"

"Because *I* still remember."

Andrés stared at her. "You've actually died?"

Sylvia whispered, "Yes."

Silence hung between them.

She crossed her arms, looking down at the floor.

"How? What happened?" he asked.

"I don't wanna talk about it... Maybe later... Maybe never," she said in a low voice.

Andrés reached out, placing his hand on hers. "Alright. Whenever you're ready."

Sylvia looked up at Kalpa in her tank before shifting her focus back to Andrés, her eyes expressing a sudden eagerness to reveal more of herself.

"I do want to tell you," she said. "It's obvious that I do, or else I wouldn't have brought it up. It's just that... that's not what I wanted to talk about tonight. It's also hard to accept that my *yamma* failed at the one thing she was supposed to do: keep me alive. But since we're here, I might as well tell you."

"Only if you're ready."

[3]

SYLVIA SIGHED. "FOR AS LONG AS I CAN REMEMBER, I'VE HAD dreams where I'm drowning... I'm dying. When I finally told my grandmother about it, I was ten. She said I was remembering the moment when my mom had 'left' me in a bathtub. At first, Nana didn't say why she did that, except to remind me, as she did throughout my entire childhood, that my mom had been fighting a battle no one, not even my dad, could see, and that's why she was no longer with us.

"I tried to be understanding of *Yamma*, especially when I learned the real reason why she had left me in... I can't even bring myself to talk about that... The horrible choice *Yamma* had to make... If someone hadn't gotten there in the nick of time to resuscitate me, I'd still be dead.

"So, I wish it was as simple as everything cutting to black... Death is a feeling that I can't describe... I'm alone, in cloudy water, and... I'm not Sylvia anymore... I'm waiting to become something else."

"Like what?" Andrés asked.

"I don't know..." Sylvia stared ahead, appearing lost in thought. "Do you wanna know the real reason why I didn't call back after our first weekend together?"

"Tell me."

"I didn't call you back 'cause if I had, I would've demanded that you come over right away 'cause I needed you, but I didn't want to come off as clingy."

"I wouldn't have thought that."

"Yeah, you would've... It's way too early to be saying, 'I need you' to someone I just met, but deep down I feel like we'd already met before, and I could demand you come over. I can now confess that that weekend, with you staying over... I had the best sleep of my life."

Sylvia began to smile. "Instead of dreaming of drowning, I dreamt I reached out in that cloudy water, and you were there to grab my hand... And that's when everything became so bright, so clear, so blue, and we were floating next to each other. I pulled you in close, and you grabbed my body hard, and all these bubbles of light started swirling around us like stars... I started swimming to the top, pulling you close behind me until we reached the surface, and we were under a vast sky at twilight with so many beautiful colors..."

Her smile widened as she continued. "We looked at each other and took deep breaths, after deep breaths, before we began our dive back into this cosmic ocean, into the deep... It felt like we were returning to where we came from... before time... before we were split in two. It was like Heaven. We were in Heaven. I woke up so happy..."

"Me too," he said.

"You did?"

"Of course."

She sighed. "I wish you could stay every night. The nights that you don't, I always wake up in a panic... I know you have Andy, but I can't help being angry at you for not being in bed next to me, for making me feel like I need you this much, for making me feel like I'm addicted again, but now to you—"

"You can't look at us like that."

Sylvia shook Andrés's hand away. "You think I don't know that? I've experienced way more life than your goofy-ass, and I'm saying this is not good. With the way I'm wired, I will fall hard. That's why I will continue to test you. I will continue to push you. I will do everything I need to do to make sure that this man, who I see, is not an act, and that it's safe for me to let you in, 'cause once you're in, you're in, and I won't be able to let you go. This is dangerous for me."

Sylvia's face turned red. "It's so dangerous that I will leave you if you don't stop with the bullshit. You lying—acting like you're not afraid to die... I can't be with a man who isn't honest with his feelings —who could end up making me feel like my feelings are nothing because his feelings are nothing to him. I don't wanna end up feeling lonely in a relationship—"

"You're not alone."

"I'm not?"

"No, I'm fucking terrified of death. If God exists, I'm fucked. I want there to be nothing."

"Thank you," she said. "I don't feel so alone anymore. We're the same—except I don't believe in God, at least not the way you do. I believe there's a power out there that weighs the good that we do against the not-so-good. If you can become someone who can do that —do more good—then, when your time comes, your karma will be in the black. You won't be leaving behind any of your karmic debt for your children to pay. Trust me, I know—you don't wanna do that."

Sylvia looked away from Andrés to her father's shadow box, hanging prominently on the wall above Kalpa in her tank. It was filled with her father's campaign medals from Vietnam, his Combat Infantryman Badge, and his Distinguished Service Cross and Purple Heart with two oak leaf clusters.

"My father," she said, looking back at Andrés, "was in so much karmic debt to God—the universe—whatever you wanna call Her— that I feel like it's been passed down to me. I've got this feeling that no matter what I do, I'm gonna keep paying. I only wish I didn't know what got my dad there, owing as much as he did. He talked about it his first night home. He was crying, asking Nana if she still loved him. How could anyone still love him? Begging her to forgive him because if God exists, he was fucked."

"He said it just like that?" Andrés asked.

"Just like that. And you know what Nana told him? It was the only time I've heard her curse. She said, 'You're only human. You're not *fucked*. You were only trying to get home to Sylvia, and it's okay. God can't fault you for that, especially now that her mama's gone. Sylvia needs you. She needs her daddy in her life.' My dad began to cry harder, saying, 'I know, I know—I had to get back to her.' And Nana said, 'And here you are... You're home.' Dad calmed down enough to let Nana lead him to his old room. She tucked him in, and he fell asleep."

Sylvia began to caress Andrés's hair with her hand. "It's why whenever I reach over to see if you're still there, and I feel you fighting in your sleep, I wake up and whisper in your ear: 'You're only human. Please keep fighting. You need to get back to Andy so he can have a father in his life, so that we can meet, and you can become my nightlight.'"

"You do that?" he said, surprised.

"Every night you're with me, I bring you back from wherever you are." She paused to give him a long, suspicious look. "Here's the thing... How could you know you're fucked if you say you don't remember anything? And don't give me a bullshit answer. You've yelled out some off-the-wall, specific shit."

He paused before saying, "I know what my medal citation says."

She smirked. "Yeah, I don't buy it. I know what those things say, and whoever wrote my father's citations did everything they could to keep the gore out of them."

"I took pictures before everything went to shit."

"Now why the fuck would you do something like that?"

Andrés bowed his head in shame before turning back to face Sylvia. "Because I thought I could do some war photography—"

"War photography?"

"I had wanted to be a photojournalist," he said. "I wanted to take pictures like the ones you'd find in *National Geographic*. And when I got deployed, I figured that was my chance to act like one—try to create pictures that told stories, like the picture of the Afghan Girl."

Andrés began to smile. "For my sixteenth birthday, my mom gave me this cool-looking camera. She said it belonged to an ex-boyfriend who had it with him when he deployed to Vietnam—that it could take a beating and would do what I needed it to do."

Sylvia's expression became solemn. "My dad had said the same thing about his camera. Before he deployed, he took all these pictures of my *yamma* smiling and playing with me in a park. She was dancing like dust in the golden hour. She looked so happy, especially coming down a slide behind me like she was a kid herself. If I didn't have his pictures, the only memory I'd have of *yamma* would be of her hunched on a couch, crying before bringing me over to the bathtub and..."

[4]

Sylvia paused, as if thinking.

"What's the matter?" Andrés asked.

"It just hit me how much I feel like I've already lived through this," she said. "But with my grandmother and dad. If the most important man in my life could leave me so easily, what's stopping you from doing the same? Only looking for me when you're lonely? When you wanna fuck my emotions—a booty call on my feelings?"

"I'd never do that," Andrés said.

"Of course not, because you're unique—a snowflake among men—whatever. You're all the same. But it's alright; I've got a Plan B." She began to smile. "If you ever pull that bullshit on me, I'll take everything you've ever yelled out in your sleep and use it for a novel or something."

"You better not!" Andrés said, laughing.

She laughed with him. "You've got nothing to worry about if you act right! Besides, what do you care? You don't remember."

"I don't."

Sylvia paused, skeptically looking at him. "I think you do... It's just difficult to accept. Believe me, I know, but don't worry. I'd never judge you. Who am I to judge? I'm human too. I'd do anything to survive. I'm sure I've got some buried memories of me doing fucked-up things just to get through the night."

"Did it get that bad?"

She looked away and bowed her head. "I dropped out of everything; I was couch surfing, I was doing risky shit, then everything became a blur... One of the few things I can remember from that time in my life is hearing Nana in my mind, as if she were still alive, calling me a loser, a lost cause. I remember it made me wanna go under even more, and I did. It would've killed her to see me that way, you know?"

Sylvia paused, as if realizing she was saying too much, and looked up at him, terrified.

"I don't wanna scare you off—I didn't mean to bring any of this up —I'm sorry."

"What are you saying sorry for? I'd never judge you," Andrés said, pulling her close. "I know I'd do anything to survive! I don't give a fuck. I wanna live!"

"Thank you!" she yelled. "I knew you'd understand! I wanna live too, but I've made so many mistakes that it's so hard to keep going—that no matter what I do, I feel like I'll always be that girl, no better than dirt, because I am dirt, and I can't live with that. I wanna kill myself, but I don't wanna die. I wanna live."

She stopped talking when Andrés began to smirk. The vulnerability in her expression vanished, replaced by a dangerous spark in her eyes, with a hint of anger mixed into her confusion. After a minute of staring back at him, Sylvia asked, "What's so funny?"

Nothing," he said. "It just hit me how much I've already lived through this, but with my grandfather and aunt... Whenever Estefania would start going on about all the mistakes she'd made, my grandfather would tell her that if she wanted to be happy, she needed to stop wallowing in the past and let go. She didn't listen... I think for her, fucking up and making mistakes just became a big part of her identity."

"Estefania sounds like my auntie," Sylvia said. "I remember Nana once telling Birdie that if she wanted to change her life and be happy, she needed to stop hanging around truck stops. Birdie told her, 'Then who would I be if not just another boring girl? At least I'm cool and fun.'"

"That's Estefania, right there... I think she couldn't let go without thinking—if she did, she'd be losing her real self. And because Estefania had fought so hard to become her *real* self, my aunt needed to keep it real every chance she could, even if it meant taking bigger risks... She kept it real, alright. She made the biggest mistake of her life and got locked up in the Tombs.

Sylvia winced. "I've had friends locked up there—that place is brutal."

Andrés became distraught. "It's the worst jail in the city. Estefania wasn't the same after her time there. All the bad habits, all the risky shit she used to do to support her habits, she picked up again, all because of what had happened to her in the Tombs. And I remember one time overhearing her tell my mom that it was so hard to keep going. That no matter what she did, she'd always feel like that girl who was no better than dirt because she was dirt, and she couldn't live with that feeling. She wanted to kill herself, but she didn't wanna die. Estefania wanted to live!"

"She said it exactly like that?"

"Yup—the same way you just said it—and that's why I'm going on like this. Just like you're worried about me and what I could end up doing, now I'm worried about you. I don't wanna be in a relationship where I end up watching you self-destruct—like I did with Estefania—all because you've made your trauma a big part of your identity, and you can't forgive yourself for something that wasn't your fault. Whatever you keep alluding to in your past happened to Estefania in the Tombs."

"Oh, shit. No."

"Yeah, and do you know how many times Estefania woke up on a bathroom floor because of it? Too many to count. And what would bring her back there? The feeling that she was beyond redemption—because of something that wasn't her fault—because she made mistakes and couldn't let go—because she saw herself as nothing more than dirt... I get so angry thinking about how badly people treated her, like she wasn't human, just because she made one big mistake. And that look they would give her? Judging? No! Fuck that! She was not her pain! And you are not yours! You are the sunflower that grows from it! You are gold! When did you forget that? When did you start to think you were nothing more than dirt?"

She said in a low voice, "Foster care, 1968... The Black Room, 1985..."

"Well, you're not... You're what grows from the dirt. You're my sunflower. My beautiful survivor... So, you scare me off? No—I just wanna fall in love with you so much more. Your past makes you that much more beautiful to me. You're still here, still wanting to love and be loved, and there's something so tender—so tough—about growing out of all that pain and still having hope—still wanting to do good. I wanna love you so much more for that."

"I wanna love you too."

"Then, please... let it go... let it all go, and keep moving on. I don't want you hurting yourself."

She sighed. "Okay."

[5]

FOR A LONG MOMENT, THERE WAS SILENCE BETWEEN THE TWO. Sylvia began to stare at him with wide eyes.

"What are you thinking about?" Andrés asked.

"How surprised I was when you called me Eurydice."[1]

"I was surprised when you called me Orpheus."

"How much do you know about their story?" she asked.

"I know everything. When I was a kid, my mom used to read to me before bed."

Sylvia became excited. "Nana used to do the same. I'd always ask her to read that story to me... There was something so beautiful about his devotion to Eurydice. It would get to me that a man could love a woman so much that he'd try to bring her back to life."

A sad expression appeared on Sylvia's face. "When I was a little girl, I wanted a love like that to be real. I prayed for love like that—a love that was so powerful, so strong, that it would drive my soulmate to go to the End of the World, into the Underworld, to come back for me, even if I were a lost cause. That's real love."

Sylvia's eyes became weepy. "But as I've gotten older, I realized that all those beautiful words and ideas were crap. I began to understand that my grandmother needed the magic of that bedtime story just as much as I did. She needed to cope with the poor choice in the man she had given her all, who she called her soulmate... My grandpa died before I was born. The more I learned about him, the more I realized he died because he got too fat—too comfortable—with her, thinking he could let himself go. He knew she would love him, no matter what. It was more fun for him to eat all that fried, greasy crap than to eat right. He didn't care to live long enough for her."

"I'm sorry," Andrés said.

Sylvia began to cry. "You and your fucking cheese fries."

"I didn't know!"

"Now you do," she said, sobbing. "And I don't want to repeat Nana's mistakes. She should've held back just enough of her love to survive. Whenever she read me that bedtime story, there was always sadness in her voice. I could tell she saw herself as Orpheus, waiting to die."

Sylvia cried harder, looking up at the ceiling before turning back to

---

1. *Book One: Orpheus*, "Chapter Six: The Purple Room."

Andrés. "The idea of soulmates is so fucked up. Everyone leaves, right? There's always something that takes away your one-and-only. So fuck it. It's better—it's healthier—for me to accept that there's no such thing as soulmates. I need to hold back, for my sake. I need to keep seventy and give you only thirty. But, baby, I don't wanna hold back. I wanna give you my all, my 100. I wanna believe in soulmates so badly. Do you want to believe?"

"I want to believe—"

"Then fucking eat right so that you don't die and leave me behind, because right now, you're as close to that feeling as I've ever gotten in my life! I want to love you! I want you to love me! I'm thirty years old with no more time to fuck around. But as much as I'm opening up to you right now, as much as I'm using that word—*love*—I think I can shut you out just like that... I think... I know I can. The choice is yours!"

Andrés began to cry. "Please don't shut me out—"

Sylvia cried with him. "I couldn't say it before, but after this talk—with this connection, I think we have, I know we have, I feel we have —I'm gonna say it. I think this could become way more—more than love—and I don't wanna end up like my grandmother. I don't wanna fall in love with a man, discover he's my soulmate, only for him to take me for granted, get too comfortable and fat, and because his addiction to food would be more powerful than his love for me, he'd end up dying, leaving me alone and sad for the rest of my life. Like Orpheus. I don't wanna be like him! I'm not going out like that! I wouldn't be able to go on. I can't take any more heartbreak!"

"I'll change!"

"You promise?"

"I promise—I get it."

"I don't think you do—"

Andrés pleaded, "I do—"

"No, you don't! Just shut up, just shut the fuck up!" she screamed. "Promises don't mean shit in my world; they're just words. I'm serious. This is the most serious I've ever been in my life, and I know I'm repeating myself, but I don't wanna end up like Nana!"

She buried her face in her hands. "You don't know how much that scares me—becoming her, having relationships like her."

Sylvia looked up. "When I was in rehab, I learned so much about codependency and how that works, and I finally understood the relationship between Nana and Daddy, so listen up."

She looked at Andrés intensely. "You could end up being the love of my life. My soulmate. The end-all, be-all, the *One*. But I swear, I swear to fucking God, I will not be in a codependent relationship with an addict."

She took a deep breath and stopped crying, her red face becoming calm. "So, I'm gonna say this one last time: get rid of your bad habits and never take me for granted, or we're through. You got that?"

"I got it—"

"You need to decide if I'm worth it because I know I am."

"You're worth it—I promise I'll be better. I'll show you."

"And I promise to give you my all because you're right," Sylvia said. "I'm gonna change too—I'm done saying sorry. I'm done holding on through my work; I'm letting go of all my mistakes. I'd forgotten who I truly am: a sunflower. I am gold."

20

THE RED ROOMS

NOVEMBER 25, 1992

[1]

It was the last place Andrés expected to be—sitting on a purple velvet chair, watching Sylvia slow dance for him under a spotlight in the Red Room of an underground nightclub. The night had started innocently enough: Sylvia called Andrés, asking if he was free and if so, to come over.

Before he could ask why she was still in the city and not in Virginia for Thanksgiving, she abruptly ended the call. Andrés called her back but got her voicemail. He began frantically packing his clothes and camera for a long weekend stay he hadn't planned on, then left. After commuting for two hours by bus and train, he stood in the hallway outside her apartment, waiting for Sylvia to open the door. When she did, he could tell she had been crying hard.

"What happened?" he asked.

Instead of responding, Sylvia walked away.

Andrés followed her inside, dropping his bag by the door before shutting it behind them.

Sylvia's turtle tank looked like it hadn't been cleaned that day. The apartment smelled like the inside of a pet store. Books and crumpled scraps of paper were strewn across the living room floor and couch. Andrés entered the kitchen and found filthy dishes on the table. The sink was clogged and filled with black water that smelled like rotten eggs. He returned to the living room and saw her standing in the middle of the clutter, her shoulders slumped and her head, with matted hair, hanging low.

"I know everything is a mess," she said. "It's been a bad day."

"Why didn't you call me earlier?" he asked.

"I didn't wanna bother you with my shit."

"But I'm your boyfriend. What's going on?"

"I thought I was ready to go back," she said in a low voice. "But what am I going back to? There are too many memories, and I don't think I can handle them alone."

"I would've gone with you," he said.

She looked up at Andrés. "And I wanted you to come, and I would've asked, but I know you have your own life... and I'm trying not to go too fast.... I'm trying not to get too attached."

"But why?" he asked.

"Because you still don't know all of me. If you did, would you still be here?"

"We've talked about this."

"I know, but you still don't understand what all of me means."

"Whatever it is, I don't care."

"You say that now, but... I don't know... All I know is that I can't be alone. Not now. Not for Thanksgiving."

"You won't be... I'm here."

"What about Andy?"

"He's with Lydia."

Sylvia gave him a questioning look.

"I know," he said, "but she's really trying, and I want Andy to have a mother in his life. He's staying with her until Monday."

"That's good. Every child needs a mother..." Sylvia began to cry. "And I still need mine—I miss Nana—I miss her so much." Her sobbing turned into an uncontrollable howl of grief that poured out of her.

He pulled Sylvia into his arms.

She buried her face in his chest.

He hugged her until her body went limp, her loud crying turning into grunts and moans.

Sylvia looked up at him, her eyes begging, "Tell me it's going to be alright."

He kissed her on the forehead and whispered, "Let's get out of here —out of this mess."

"But I don't wanna go out."

"Some fresh air will do you good—"

Sylvia shook herself free from his arms as if she had been in a straitjacket. "Don't tell me what's good for me! I'm not stupid!"

He turned away from her and began walking toward the door.

She grabbed him by the arm. "Stop! I hate it when you do that!"

He stared at her blankly. "I know."

"Then why do you keep on with that bullshit?"

"Boundaries... You have yours. I have mine."

Sylvia stared at the floor, as if she had suddenly realized what she was doing. "I'm trying, but... how much more of me can you take before you say, 'Fuck you, I'm out?'"

"I talk in my sleep—you're still here."

She looked back up at Andrés. "That's true."

"So, when are you gonna say, 'Fuck you, I'm out?'"

"Never—"

"Okay, then relax. The only time I'll ever leave is if I know you need your space—or if I need mine. That's it. It felt like you needed space, so I was gonna give it to you, like I always do. I was gonna come back... like I always do."

"I understand... I'm starting to get it."

"If you get it, then chill out—keep being real with me."

"Is that what you really want?" Sylvia asked. "Fine, I'm gonna keep it real—straight 100. Who am I going back to? I have cousins, but I've never liked the ignorant shit they've said about my mom. Then I have Auntie Birdie, who I've never forgiven for scamming me. I don't wanna spend hours on a bus and get there only to act fake with her, 'cause nothing about her would've changed, and that wouldn't be good for me —to see that she's still a Lot Lizard. So, who's left? A part of me still hopes that Nana will be at the bus terminal, waiting to pick me up, but she's dead. My mom and dad are dead. They're all dead. I don't have a family anymore. I'm alone."

He pulled her close. "No, you're not."

She pushed him away. "Yes, I am."

He pulled her in again. "Not anymore. As long as I'm in your life, we're family. I'm trying to take care of you as if we were one. So is my mom. She doesn't like anyone, but she likes you."

Her eyes widened in surprise. "She does?"

Andrés smiled. "Of course she does. She takes your calls even when I'm not there. And what else does my mom do every time you come over?"

"Comb my hair."

"Talking on the phone, combing your hair like you're her daughter —that's her way of saying she likes you, that you're family."

"I didn't know."

"Now you do. And another thing: I'm not trying to tell you what's good for you. We're in a relationship, are we not?"

"We are."

"And didn't you go off on me about the cheese fries?"

"I did."

He mimicked Sylvia. "Don't tell me what's good for me. I'm not stupid."

"I get it... I totally get it." A worried look came over her face. "But when I'm like this, I can't stay out for long. It wouldn't be good for me if I did—"

"Being locked up in your apartment like this isn't good for you either."

"I know, but... I can't take a chance. How about we spend the rest of the night in bed instead? I could catch up on my reading; we could watch some TV."

"Is that what you really wanna do?"

"Yeah, why? What's so funny?"

"Nothing—"

"No, tell me."

He smiled. "You'll see."

Sylvia glared at Andrés and then walked away.

He followed her into the bedroom and closed the door behind them.

The scent of roses and honey wafted through the space from unlit candles. Her comforter, adorned with cartoon characters popular in her childhood, was neatly spread across the bed. A baby doll that she had had since she was five years old was propped between two flat pillows, just below a scratched-up headboard.

Sylvia sat in bed and grabbed a book from her nightstand, *The History of Sexuality, Vol. 1: An Introduction* by Michel Foucault. Andrés sat next to her, watching as she blinked excessively while trying to read. Eventually, she sighed, got out of bed, and paced the room in frustration before returning. She picked up the next book on her nightstand, *Seduction of the Minotaur* by Anaïs Nin, but upon seeing the cover, she tossed it aside and said, "Reading is wack."

She got up and turned on a small TV set atop a scratched-up bureau. Instead of returning to bed, she left the bedroom and went to the kitchen. Andrés could hear her rummaging through the refrigerator before slamming the door shut. She returned to the bedroom and looked at him with red-faced anger.

"What's wrong?" he asked.

"You, motherfucker—and this square-life bullshit: Oh God, it feels like hell!"

He sat up. "I told you, let's get out of here—"

"To do what? I'm tired of doing the same wack-ass shit, seeing the same wack-ass people, and clubbing is wack. Cafés and movies—wack —everything's boring as fuck!"

"Then what do you wanna do?"

"I don't know," Sylvia said helplessly, "but I know not this."

He stood up from the bed. "Let's just get out of here. We'll figure it out along the way."

"Fuck no—not until you tell me where—"

"Where? Not here. That's where."

Sylvia pushed him. "Asshole, you know what I mean, 'cause I need to know before I go outside—'cause my mind is going a million miles a second—and I wanna close my eyes and forget my name and forget the world—"

"You wanna get high, don't you?"

Sylvia sighed. "Yeah."

Andrés grabbed her hand. "I was waiting for this moment."

"You were?"

"Yeah, and it's okay because you're stronger than the urge. Am I right?"

She shook her hand out of his. "No—hell to the motherfucking naw, no."

"Of course you are."

"No, I'm not."

"Do you have a sponsor you can call? Do you need a meeting?"

"All of my sponsors have hit on me—men and women—and I've never felt safe at those meetings... To be honest, it's never been this bad."

"I've seen this before, but with my aunt," Andrés said. "Whenever she'd start feeling like you do, instead of going to a meeting, she'd go shopping. Estefania used to joke that she'd replaced one addiction with another—one that still gave her that high, that rush, but didn't have that toxic reverb on her body. It led to her catching a charge for credit card fraud, but that's another story. The point is: What gives you that kind of high, that rush?"

"If I tell you, please don't make it weird. Don't judge me."

"If I told you everything about my family, you'd know I'm as open-minded as they come."

She hesitated before saying, "Alright... but for me not to be in my head about this, you're gonna need to shut the fuck up and let me show you. Follow my lead." Her face became stern. "I've never shared this with anyone, much less a boyfriend, so please don't make it weird, okay? Promise me."

"I promise."

"Don't make me regret this."

[2]

After changing clothes and combing out her matted hair into flowing curls, Sylvia led Andrés out of her apartment. They walked up Avenue A and along East 14th Street until they reached Union Square. They descended into the station below to board a crowded subway car, reeking of sweat and vomit. They gripped the railing above them and held on as the train rolled out of the station. The screeching of metal wheels against tracks filled the air, muffling the indistinguishable chatter of other passengers surrounding them.

He tapped her on the shoulder with his free hand. "Where are you taking me?"

"Shut the fuck up—you'll see."

"We're still playing this game?"

She smiled as if struck by a sudden realization. "Yes! That's exactly what this is: a game, except in this game, we're in a theater—on a stage that only we can see, and it's showtime. We'll be performing our scenes, with me writing the script as we go, and for you to be able to act out your role, you're gonna need to shut the fuck up, pay attention, and listen. Follow my lead—understand?"

"I think so."

She looked ahead at the lights streaking across the window in front of them. "I think, in this game, you don't talk unless I give you permission—"

"Where are we going?"

She gave him the side-eye. "Now you're fucking with me. I'm being serious—listen. Time-out."

"Time-out?"

"Yeah, time-out," she said. "I'm pausing our game—it just hit me: don't just say, 'I'm a sunflower.' Show me that you believe it. Show me that you trust the word of someone in recovery so much that if I say, 'follow me,' you follow—no questions asked—'cause you trust that I'm healthy again. You believe that I'm capable of having your back, that I'd never let anything happen to you. I promise... I can be trusted to take care of you—and maybe, one day, take care of a family too. I think that's the game: trust. Everything we do in our game can be an exercise in trust...

"I've been thinking a lot about this, and I've heard enough of you talking in your sleep to know that you lost something on your deployment—your trust in power, in people... Let me be your leap of faith. Let me show you that if I give you an order, I won't leave you hanging; I won't leave you for dead because I..." Sylvia stopped herself from completing her sentence.

Andrés allowed the weight of what she was about to confess to linger in the space between them. "Can't bring yourself to say it?"

Sylvia appeared hesitant, shifting her focus to the lights streaking across the window in front of them. "We need to get through the night. I need to see if you're the kind of man who'll still be here in the morning."

She looked back at Andrés. "That's the only kind of man I could love with my all... And if we're gonna play this game, it needs to be fair. I need to figure out the trust exercise I need from you. I'll know when I know. Until then, let me take you to where I need to take you—so I can say that word. Does that make sense?"

"It makes sense to me," said the old lady with a shock of white hair, seated directly in front of them, looking up at Sylvia.

"Does it?" Sylvia asked. "Because I'm trying to make sense of it myself."

The old lady smiled. "You're trying to figure out how you can dance with him in a way that's fun and not boring, but I have a secret for the two of you."

"Tell me."

"Life and love with the right one—it's like a Beautiful Ballet. You know when to lead and when to follow. And because you'll get to a point where you trust each other so much, you drop the rules—you no longer question each other's moves. You just know." The old lady started laughing to herself. "And if you're someone who *really* knows how to dance, that Beautiful Ballet can turn into a fun Tango... My husband knew how to argue with me. He was always up for a good Tango."

Sylvia looked up, as though she were about to address the spirits in the vast sky of her mind, and declared, "This is a sign. Constance, this is a sign."

"What's a sign?" asked the old lady.

Sylvia looked back down at her and smiled. "You reminded me of something my grandmother said many years ago."

"Did I? She must've been one smart cookie."

"Nana was amazing, like I'm sure you are."

"Why thank you," the old lady said, smiling. "I hope mister here can give you what you're looking for."

"I think he can." Sylvia looked back at Andrés. "You hear that, mister? The Beautiful Ballet? The Tango? That's what I want, so shut the fuck up and follow my lead. Time-in."

Andrés obeyed Sylvia's command and remained silent for the rest of the ride. At the 42nd Street/Times Square station, they stepped out of the subway car and made their way through the station, climbing the steps and emerging onto bustling streets teeming with people, and traffic at a standstill, horns blaring. They weaved through street performers clamoring for attention, rushed under towering marquees flashing with neon lights, passed the doors of theaters adorned with alluring movie posters, and finally stopped at the corner of Eighth Avenue, across from the Port Authority Bus Terminal.

After several minutes of wistfully staring across the street, Sylvia said, "It was eight years ago today that I stood on this corner. I was looking for any reason not to go to the terminal, catch a bus home, and face reality. It was then that I remembered a movie poster I had seen on my way here. I went back to look at it—at the way the poster had a shadow staring through the blinds of a window, at a woman sitting in a red room, her face flushed, her mouth wide open, in heat. It made me curious. It made me go inside to watch the movie instead of going back home for Thanksgiving.

"It was called *Body Double*. It was supposed to be this mystery thriller, but the movie oozed with so much erotic tension, so much sensuality, that I began to feel a connection between passion, pleasure, and the adrenaline rush of fear. I began to feel that thing in me that makes me wanna fuck—like a bull...

"I watched that movie every chance I got. I spent money I didn't have just to come down and watch that scene with the lead actress dancing in her chaps, with that guy coming into the bathroom to tell her, 'I like to watch.' Oh God, it was creepy as fuck, but shit, I'm a watcher, and if that makes me a creep, then fuck it—I'm a creep. When the movie stopped its run, I didn't know what to do. I tried watching porn, but it wasn't the same. Something was missing, and then I realized—it wasn't about sex. It was about the seduction. To seduce and be seduced—to be enticed—that's a lot more fun. So, I started hitting up peep shows...

"There's one up the street from here. I've always wanted to come back, but with everything that has happened, that's a siren I've never dared to take on alone. I don't wanna relapse, but since you insisted we go out, let's hit up a peep show so I can show you what gives me that high—that rush."

[3]

WHEN THEY ENTERED SHOW WORLD, ANDRÉS DID EVERYTHING Sylvia asked of him. He bought tokens, kept his mouth shut, and let himself be led down a long corridor, past many rooms, until they came to a red door at the end. Sylvia and Andrés opened it and entered.

Dance music thumped through the room's red walls. A red couch sat in front of a closed partition. Sylvia pulled him down to sit next to her. She leaned forward and inserted a token. The partition opened, revealing a stripper dancing behind plexiglass. Sylvia's eyes softened, becoming liquid, her face cast in red light. When the stripper noticed the Watchers, she stopped dancing, stepped down from her pedestal, and presented her naked body to Sylvia.

"Hi," the stripper said. "My name is Nikki. What's yours?"

"Emma," Sylvia replied.

"It's nice to meet you, Emma... Are you into girls?"

"I'm here."

"Alright, Emma; before I go on, I require a donation."

"I gave you a token. If I want more, I'll let you know. Until then, dance, but slowly."

Nikki pressed her naked body against the dirty plexiglass. She locked eyes with Sylvia for ten seconds before stopping and saying, "There's your token. If you want more, I need cash money upfront."

"That's not how this works," Sylvia said.

"That's how it works for me. I've got bills to pay."

"So do I."

"That's your problem," Nikki said. "My time is money, and we're done. *Adios,* Grandma."

The partition slid closed.

Sylvia stood up and banged her fist against the wall. "This is bullshit!"

He began to laugh. "Calm down, Grandma."

"Fuck you, Andrés. I know this game—come on."

He followed her into the next room, and they sat on another dirty couch. She leaned forward and inserted another token. The partition opened, revealing an older stripper behind the plexiglass, picking at her toes while seated on a wooden chair. Noticing them, the older stripper stood up and sauntered over, placing her hand out.

"Goddammit!" Sylvia yelled.

"Stop being cheap and give her a dollar," Andrés said. "She needs it for a foot doctor."

"No."

"Fine, I'll do it myself."

Andrés removed a dollar bill from his wallet and slid it under the plexiglass. The older woman grabbed it, tucked it under the band of her oversized panties, and began pressing her breasts against the dirty plexiglass.

Sylvia said, "This is... pathetic."

The older stripper said, "Fuck you; you don't deserve any of this—bye."

The partition slid closed.

Sylvia banged her fist against the wall again.

Andrés laughed. "Don't get angry. What did you expect?"

Sylvia turned to look at him. "What did I expect? I expected someone like me! I was one of these girls! I took pride in how I looked! How I turned people on! How I could get people to give me money without asking! I wanted the same done to me, but I got this instead! And before you say anything, this was before the drugs. There was nothing wrong with me. I made this choice."

"I didn't say anything," he said.

"Just in case you were about to, I'm letting you know upfront—this has nothing to do with drugs. This is about nature—that thing buried in all of us. I used to come here so much that I realized I wanted to be watched—that I'd enjoy the thrill more—and I did. I felt more alive in the rush of doing it than just watching it."

Sylvia got up from the couch and pushed open the door to their room. She looked down the dark hallway before returning and climbing onto Andrés's lap. She was eye-to-eye with him, her hair brushing his face, the tips of her curls touching his lips.

"Let me ask you this," she said. "Does it bother you that I was a stripper?"

"Was that what you were worried about?" Andrés asked.

"Yeah, we were talking about trust and being honest, and this has been the part of me I've always had to hide. It always worried me that if I got into a relationship, what would my boyfriend say? Would it bother him?"

"Baby, why should it?"

"It would bother most men."

"Your past has nothing to do with me."

"What if I were a stripper now? Would it bother you?"

"Of course it would."

"I knew it—"

"It would bother me that you're thirty and still haven't figured out how to get these hoes to work for you. You'd be like that old stripper instead."

Sylvia let out a loud laugh. "You know pimp game?"

He gave Sylvia a half-smile. "I told you I have mixed feelings about the kind of game I know, but yeah. I grew up watching a master at his game—my grandfather. Because I was his first grandchild, he would always make time for me, taking me everywhere whenever my mom would stay over and sometimes disappear. He would always say, 'Watch what I do. How I handle people.'"

Andrés laughed as a memory flashed through his mind. "I had learned so much from him that my mom got angry at me for telling Lydia that if she was gonna cheat, she could've at least made us money. Our marriage would've still been over, but our partnership could've continued. I would've made sure Lydia wasn't giving her pussy away for free to scrubs."

Sylvia gave Andrés a disgusted look. "What the hell, man?"

"Before you say anything else, you shut the fuck up. Don't judge me—I had to say it like that. Lydia was banging a guy from my base while I was deployed. She even moved him into our home while I was in a coma—after telling my parents to come get Andy."

"She did that?"

"Yeah—she thought I was gonna die, so on to the next."

"That's fucked up."

Andrés laughed. "Who are you telling? And when I found that out, I realized my grandfather was right about everything—my dad was wrong. Respect is more important than love. Love can destroy good men."

Sylvia gave Andrés a look. "Love can destroy good women—"

"Of course—love can destroy anyone who doesn't set boundaries. I saw how it destroyed my uncle Victor. My aunt Carmen shamed him into opening up their marriage, telling him, 'Real men don't act insecure, and you're a real man, right? Don't you love me? Don't you want to see me happy?' Yeah, fuck that. That was my uncle's mistake—he loved her so much that he made her happiness more important than his. Victor should've followed my grandfather's advice and walked away."

"Would you walk away from me?" Sylvia asked.

"In a heartbeat," Andrés replied.

"But people make mistakes."

"Yeah, but I'm not the one to be forgiving anymore. The other night, you went on and on about cheese fries, and I get it."

"You better."

"But if you want our relationship to work, you need to get this; it needs to register."

She brought her face closer to his. "I'm listening."

"The moment you get the urge to fuck other guys, you have my blessing. I won't hold you back, but I won't fight for you; I'll cut you out of my life."

He paused.

"I used to think that just getting Lydia out of *that* house would be enough for her to see that I'm a good man. That it would be enough to make her happy, love me forever. I was wrong to think that way. I'll never do that again. So, just like you have your limits, that's mine. You got that?"

"I got it," she said.

"Good. If you were ever to get the urge, that would tell me I'm not doing something right. Even though you'd still be responsible for what you do, I'd look at the part I played in all of this. I'd try to understand why we're not connecting anymore and why you'd feel the need to cheat. Watching the master play the game has taught me one thing: it's always better to connect with what's between a woman's ears instead of what's between her legs. That way, I become the kind of man a woman wouldn't want to disrespect. So, if I'm right with you, you'll be right with me." He began to smile. "You know you can walk away, right?"

"I know," she said.

"So why don't you?"

She smiled. "Because I want to be here."

"That tells me I'm doing everything right. I'm connecting with you where it matters the most." Andrés pointed to the side of her head. "To the most beautiful part of you."

Sylvia sat up straight on his lap, laughing. "Goddamn, you really are amazing with the bullshit—it's like music."

He laughed. "Then come grind up on me to my song and show me how good you were at your job."

Sylvia did as she was told, gyrating her lap into his while keeping her focus on his eyes.

He thrust his hips into her.

Her body vibrated. Her grinding through her jeans became more intense.

He grabbed her ass to stop her from moving—from cumming too quickly.

"I was almost there," she said.

"No. Not yet."

"But why?"

"We have an audience," Andrés said, motioning to the crowd of men gathering at the door since Sylvia had opened it, listening in on their conversation. "Don't you want that thrill, that rush?"

"Oh God, yes," she said.

"And aren't we on a stage, and it's showtime?"

"Yes!"

"Then let's act out a scene. You can cum at the end."

"Are you sure?"

"Emma, stand up."

Sylvia pushed herself off his lap and stood up.

"Now face them."

She did as he commanded, facing the crowd of men at the boundary of the room.

"Now, take off your jacket."

She did as he commanded, taking her time to remove her faux leather jacket. The longer the crowd of men waited for it to come off, the more enthralled they became.

Once done, Andrés said, "Now, take off your top."

She looked back at him. "But I'm not wearing a bra—I don't wanna cross any lines."

"It's okay," he replied. "You're good."

She did as he commanded, slowly stripping away her purple T-shirt, one sleeve at a time, and then over her head until she was topless. She presented herself to the crowd of men, hands by her sides, eyes closed, body shuddering.

"Emma, how do you feel?" Andrés asked, smiling.

"Alive. So alive."

"That's my good girl."

Sylvia opened her eyes and faced him. "Now, it's your turn—stand up."

He did as she commanded.

"Now, take off your jacket... Your shirt."

He did as she commanded, taking his time. The longer she waited for him to take off his black flight jacket and fitted muscle T-shirt, the more enthralled she became. Once done, Andrés shivered as he presented himself to her, topless, with his hands at his sides, his chest and torso covered in thick scars.

She pressed her body against his, kissing him as if they were the only ones in the room.

Between kisses, Andrés whispered, "Am I connecting?"

Between breaths, Sylvia whispered back, "Like no other."

In the pauses between kissing and breathing, he savored the taste of her cherry-flavored lip balm and the feel of her fingernails gliding, scratching across his back, giving him goosebumps.

He was lost in her until he felt something change in the room, forcing him to stop and look around. The men who had been standing at the boundary of the room were now inside, blocking the exit, staring at Sylvia like a horde of hungry beasts, angry at being teased.

Sylvia and Andrés scrambled to get dressed.

The horde closed in, trying to grab her.

Andrés flung Sylvia over his shoulder. He carried her through the horde, punching and pushing everyone out of his way until they were out of the room. They were out of Show World. He ran down 43rd Street with Sylvia—ass up—draped over his shoulder.

She laughed like she was on a roller coaster, and that's when it hit Andrés.

"I know you!" he yelled.

She yelled back, laughing, "I know you too! Put me down! Put me down!"

[4]

ANDRÉS STOPPED AT THE CORNER OF 12TH AVENUE. HE ROLLED HER off his shoulder and set her on her feet.

She looked at him.

He looked at her.

Sylvia pressed her body against his. He wrapped his arms around her. The two kissed with desperation, as if validating a long-denied hope that, now in their union, had become a rock-solid belief.

There is magic in the world.

When the kiss ended, Sylvia's face glowed. "I can't believe it!"

"I know!" he shouted.

"What are the chances?"

"It feels impossible—and I'd seen your picture in *The New Yorker*."

"You saw that?" Sylvia let out a groan. "I didn't wanna be in on that, but Reggie put me up to it."

"I'm glad that he did. If it weren't for that, I would've never felt that feeling that pushed me to go to The Loft and see you."

"You came back for me?"

"Of course I did. I knew I knew you, but I didn't know how. I had to ask my neurologist if that was normal, and she said that until my brain fully recovered, my memory was gonna be like Swiss cheese. Whatever it was about your picture, it'd come back to me eventually, and it did! The way I carried you out of Show World brought back everything."

"Me too," she said, "but I had a feeling already."

"Why didn't you tell me?"

"But I did—I told you I felt like we had met before, but I had to act like it was a line."

"Why?"

"Because it does feel impossible," she said. "I learned a long time ago that hope can be a lot worse than heroin. And because I was so fucking high that night, I didn't know if it was really you. I wasn't sure if you were something I had created to help me cope with what was going on in my life, because it all felt like such a beautiful dream. For people like me, there's no such thing as magic in the world, so I had to act like I was giving you a line until I knew for sure that it was you. I need to stay healthy—I can't relapse—I can't have hope—but you're real. That night was real, and here we are again!"

"Here we are."

"Six years later—"

"Your hair has changed so much."

She began to laugh. "Oh God, I know—"

"It was so big back then, and now it's this."

"Fuck you," she said, playfully slapping him on the shoulder.

"And you had on all this makeup... And this see-through top, with these silver boots that went up to your knees—you looked like a stripper from outer space."

"They called me Spacer Woman. I had taken my stage name from the title of my favorite song back then and made it my alter ego. The clothes and the makeup—all a mask. I didn't wanna be recognized by the people who were part of my *square life.* I mean, everything I did back then was a job, and no one that I knew back then could understand that—except Reggie—but even he had his limits."

Sylvia became more excited. "I still can't get over this. I'd been so worried about you finding out about Spacer Woman, and you'd already met me at the worst time of my life, doing what I was doing, and you knew what that was, and you still wanted me."

"I loved bad girls then; I love them more now."

"I'm so happy to hear that," Sylvia said. "My heart is still pounding."

"Me too—I feel so alive."

"I want more, and I think I know where we can get it."

"Then let's go get some."

She paused, her face uncertain. "Before we go, promise me you won't walk away. Please? Because you can't! We're family, so watch over me like we are one. And if I try to push you away, if I start to act stupid, fight me."

"Fight you?"

"Yeah, fight me—I don't know how I'm gonna react."

"React?"

"If I get physical, don't stop. You fight—"

"No, no."

"Listen—"

"No—"

"Listen," she said. "I don't want you to hurt me. This is about trust. I think we need a sign, a word—something to tell you when to stop... I think if you hear me say 'Constance,' you stop... Trust me, hearing Nana's name will stop everything."

Andrés began to tremble at the thought of what she was implying.

"Relax," she said, grabbing his hands. "You're not gonna hurt me. If I don't say that word, it means I'm enjoying it. Do you understand? If I don't say 'Constance,' don't stop; we keep going. I'm sure of it."

"You are?"

"Yes, this is the trust exercise for me. I just realized it. I know you won't hurt me—that you'll care for me, that you know me so well you'll read my body. You'll look for my signs. You'll know when to go and when to stop. I'm leaving it up to you to find my boundaries—to not fail me. I'll be at your mercy."

"Are you sure?"

"Yes," she said, "I need this. So just be you—the *real* you. From everything I've heard about this place, I think you'll know what I'm talking about; you'll know what to do. I think it'll make sense for both of us when we get there."

Before Andrés could respond, Sylvia dropped her hands from his and stepped away to hail a taxi. When one stopped, they got in, and she ordered the driver to take them to The Labyrinth in the Meatpacking District.

On the way there, she said, "I have a friend who went to The Labyrinth with her husband. She said I should only go there with someone I'd trust with my life—someone I want to be intimate with in ways that go beyond sex—like a mind bond. Nana had said the same thing—it was like the giving of your soul."

"I still don't understand," he said.

Sylvia paused. "Do you remember how I talked about the connection between passion, pleasure, and the adrenaline rush of fear? I've never experienced that with anyone except you, I swear. And I've been craving this since I was sixteen—since my nights of watching *Body Double*—since you saved Spacer Woman. I still can't believe it. It's you. It's fucking you. And I've never met anyone I thought would understand any of this until I met you, and I trust you."

"I trust you too."

"You see? Following me has brought us here." Her expression

changed to one of sudden insecurity. "And I swear—I've never done anything like this before. You'd be my first, and I don't have many firsts to offer."

"You don't need to explain," he said. "It's okay. I believe you. Even if you did—"

"I swear I've never—"

"Even if you did, it doesn't matter. I'm here now."

The taxi pulled up in front of an old warehouse and parked behind a row of cabs, dropping off people dressed in leather outfits. Sylvia and Andrés got out of the car. She led him close to the entrance.

A blonde drag queen guarded the door. "Alright, people, listen up. If you look like a *tourist,* you're not getting in unless I see you've got the right mindset. If you have to ask what the right mindset is, then you don't belong. Most don't. And if you feel attacked by what I'm saying, then go back to your *square life.* You don't deserve nice things."

The door queen noticed their right mindset—Andrés wrapping his arms around Sylvia to keep her warm when she began to shiver—and pointed at them, yelling, "Yo, Dank Daphne! Yeah, you! You're in. Bring Scooby-Doo with you; he's a good boy. He shows great care."

Sylvia grabbed Andrés's hand and led him inside, guiding him into a freight elevator that took them underground to the bottom floor. They stepped off and entered the maze.

They made their way through, passing many rooms hidden from the eyes of those who didn't have the permission of the occupants to look inside. They wound their way past those rooms, holding hands, feeling the pulse of their magnetic hearts coming through their hands, as if they were becoming one, as if their walk through The Labyrinth was an inner journey made within the two, together, to the center of all they trusted.

Where their new boundaries were now drawn from, so that all that could be holy in a relationship could be made sacred; because if her word said it was holy, Andrés could trust it was sacred.

And if his word said it was holy, Sylvia could trust it was sacred, because, in The Labyrinth, they would prove, through the demonstration of the amount of care they have towards each other, that they are people of their word, and they know their new boundaries.

They know how to read each other's signs.

We, the Watchers, will keep the rest of this memory to Ourselves.

We will not betray the trust that exists even after death, from where We watch—in the depths of the cosmic ocean—outside of time —with bubbles of light constantly swirling around Us.

Going into greater detail about that night in the heart of The Labyrinth would violate Our boundaries.

It would break the bond of trust forged between the Lovers in their beautiful world of the alive.

[5]

SYLVIA AND ANDRÉS ENDED THEIR JOURNEY IN THE RED ROOM, where they were out of the maze, and all eyes were open—nothing was private.

It was here that the night brought them all—Sylvia dancing naked, with the feel of Space pulsing through her bloodstream, with the eyes of all the women and men watching her.

Sylvia smiled wide, ear to ear, and closed her eyes as she raised her hands in the air. The women and men watching moved when Sylvia moved, and they touched themselves when she touched herself.

A song came on—*Hell is for Children*—and Sylvia laughed, shaking her head and saying aloud, "No, no, no, I'm not coming down." She opened her eyes and smiled as she gazed at Andrés, seated in the back of the Red Room on a purple velvet chair, watching. She jumped off the pedestal, pushed her way through the crowd, and went up to him, saying, "I can't believe I'm doing this in front of you. You don't think any less of me?"

"No, baby, no," he said.

Sylvia jumped onto his lap, wrapping her arms around him. "I've never been able to do any of this. I've always been curious, but how could I do any of this with just anyone and find out, at the wrong time, that I fucked up? That I hooked up with the wrong man? Andrés, you're my *One*. Not that I believe... but you know?"

"I know," he said.

"Am I your One? I mean, I'm not asking you to believe in a bedtime story, that fairy tale bullshit of soulmates, but... am I your One?"

"You're my One. It feels like I'm meant to be with you."

"I love you," Sylvia said, "but you knew that already, right?"

"I know; I love you too," Andrés said, "but you already knew that."

Sylvia nodded, and the two kissed. Then, in silence, they watched everyone, with their naked bodies glistening in the light, casting shadows on the walls of the Red Room.

"We all have a shadow—that thing," Sylvia said. "It didn't seem fair that I knew yours and you didn't know mine. It scared me to tell you all these things—to express all these raw feelings that have been inside me for as long as I can remember. I'd even given that thing inside me a name: Emma."

"Now I understand."

"Good. I'm glad you finally got to meet her." After a long pause, Sylvia sighed. "I don't know what I'd do if this all fell apart. You know way too much about me, and I still think we're going too fast, but I don't care anymore."

"Me neither," Andrés said. "You belong to me."

"You belong to me, too."

"I have to take care of you."

"Yes, you do. You have to," Sylvia said. "I've given you all of me."

They sat in silence, watching other naked people dance and touch each other, with the light casting their shadows on the walls.

"It's a beautiful world," Sylvia said.

"It is... and we're alive."

"So alive. I'm so happy to be alive."

"Me too." Andrés looked away from the walls and at her.

Sylvia looked away from the shadows and at him.

Andrés said, "That dance from the movie, do it for me."

"But I'm the one who likes to watch," she said.

"Then teach me the dance so I can do it for you. You can watch me."

"Okay," she said, smiling. "And since we're Watchers, is it alright if I find a beautiful brunette and ask her to dance for us? And if she likes me, could I fuck her? If she likes you, can I watch you fuck her? We could take turns. Please?"

"Say it again."

"Please?"

"Sure," Andrés replied. "Why not."

Sylvia gave Andrés a stern look. "That answer is not, and never will be, the right answer. It's yes or no."

"Then it's a yes."

"Just don't kiss her on the fucking mouth. That would show me that you like her, and that would be disrespectful to me. That would cross my boundaries, and I will get jealous."

"Whatever... Go pop that pussy some more, turn on as many people as you can, and come back with someone you like. I'm sure there are a lot of bored housewives here, tired of the square life—wanting to experiment."

"Yes!" Sylvia said. "We could bang them in front of their husbands. Just don't start anything without me. That would also show me that you like them more than you like me. And, of course, I'd always have to pick the girls—that's another rule: It's not about you or who you like. It's about me and who I like. So, if you want me to be like this with you and have no other men, that's the exchange. You don't get to pick. I'm the last woman you'll ever pick."

"I got it."

"You better, because respect goes both ways. And because I love you," Sylvia said.

"I love you, too."

They looked back at the shadows on the walls of the Red Room.

"This has been the best night of my life," Sylvia said. "I get to be this way with my boyfriend. I don't have to worry about him feeling insecure or getting jealous. I'm not feeling any shame. I feel so satisfied... So satisfied, now."

21

THE DROP

NOVEMBER 26, 1992

[1]

The doors to The Labyrinth opened at the blue hour of the morning. Everyone exited onto 10th Avenue with their masks of civility back on, ready to function again in a square world. Andrés flagged down a taxi, and the two returned home, where they changed clothes, went to bed, and slept until noon. Sylvia woke him up, crying.

"What's wrong?" he asked.

She was trembling and couldn't respond. Andrés got out of bed and scooped her into his arms. He rocked her like a baby, moving around the room. The more he tried to soothe her, the more she cried. He placed her back in bed and began undressing her. Sylvia allowed his hands to move her body with reassuring strength until she was naked. Andrés carried her from the bed into the bathroom and placed her on the toilet. Then he started searching through her medicine cabinets.

"What are you doing?" she asked, crying.

"I'm gonna give you a bubble bath—I know you love your baths. So does Andy, and I always give him one whenever he wakes up like this."

"I don't understand… I was fine… Why am I getting like this?"

"I don't know, but we'll figure it out." Andrés found what he was looking for and began preparing her bath, turning on the hot water until the tub was full and bubbly. "It's ready. Would you like me to get one of the books from your nightstand?"

"No, don't leave."

"Okay, I'll stay—you can go in now."

Sylvia was motionless, staring at the tub. Andrés hunched down to look into her eyes and asked, "Would you like me to pick you up? Lower you in?"

She nodded, crying harder. He scooped her up from the toilet. She shivered and clung to his neck as he lowered her into the bathwater. Once she was submerged, her arms slipped from his neck, and she became calm, her crying stopping.

Andrés sat on the cold floor next to her.

She looked at him, worried. "You don't think any less of me?"

"No, why?"

"All those things… I did them in front of you."

"We did them together. You did it with me."

"You're not gonna leave me, are you? I never disrespected you; I never crossed a line; I was a good girl."

He began running his fingers through her thick hair to soothe and reassure her.

"You're a good girl. I don't want you to worry about that anymore. You're safe to be you."

She smiled, closed her eyes, and let her head follow the motion of his hand massaging her scalp.

"Don't stop… I like that."

The way she responded to his touch sent him into a panic.

She opened her eyes. "What's wrong?"

"Do you think any less of me?" he asked.

"Why would I?"

"All those things you asked me to do—"

"I liked what you were doing," she said.

"But why? I don't understand, and you kept asking me to do other things. I mean, it goes against everything I've ever been taught, and you kept saying, 'Don't stop.'"

"Because I didn't want you to."

"But why?" he asked. "Wasn't I hurting you?"

"No, the opposite."

"I feel awful."

"Don't—I didn't say, 'Constance.'"

"Was I good to you?" he asked.

"You were good."

"Did I do good?"

"You're a good boy—I never said our safe word, and I wanna keep doing it again, and again, and again."

"Are you sure? Because if you're not, you need to call out her name. You need to call it out loud. You need to be clear, because if you're not—if the way you say 'yes' sounds weak—if any of the signs you give me seem off, I'm gonna stop."

"I understand," she said.

"Good, because I can't read your mind. The things you want me to do don't give me time to second-guess or figure out sign language—I'll just stop. Do you understand?"

"I understand."

"Do you promise to call out our safe word when you want me to stop?"

"Yes, I promise," she said.

"And if I stop to check and ask if you want me to keep going, do you promise your 'yes' means yes?"

"Yes, I promise."

"Good," Andrés said. "And don't say 'yes' just to say 'yes' because you think that's what I want. Fuck that! That's not who I'm with. I want the bitch who pushed me to stop with the fucking cheese fries—understand?"

"Yes, I understand... I understand so much now. I used to think Constance was a big pain in my ass for wanting me to give her clear answers, for saying, 'I don't understand sign language.'" She smiled. "You've talked about Reynaldo being a master of his game? Constance was this sweet, plain-looking woman, but I now realize she was also a master of hers. After what happened on my sixteenth birthday, Nana began teaching me. She said of herself that she was both a dominatrix and a submissive, depending on the mood or, as she'd say, the song playing in her dance with Papaw."

"Now I understand," Andrés said.

"I'm glad that you do. That old lady was a sign from the universe. That this was gonna be the night to make peace with the shadow. That thing in me that choked out my boyfriend on my sixteenth birthday."

"You did that?"

"Yup, and I still feel awful about it. Since then, I've kept that thing locked away, even during my Spacer Woman days. I was too afraid to let it out, but I had to acknowledge it. So the best I could do was at least give it a name and go by it on the streets, 'cause Nana had warned me that thing could land me in jail if I didn't at least try to make peace with it. That it could destroy my chances of happiness if I denied it in a real relationship. And this is my first real one. You've passed all my tests, and I finally feel safe enough to let it out into the open."

Sylvia began to laugh. "Now I understand why Nana refused to teach me that 'landing on the moon' feeling." She closed her eyes and took a deep breath, as if she were touching a memory. "You sent me to Space. I can't imagine telling Katherine... Jessica... telling anyone how I got there—how I got that feeling—without disrespecting the boundary I feel we've created between ourselves and the outside world."

"No one will ever know this about us," he said. "I can't imagine talking about what we did last night without putting you out there for judgment."

She opened her eyes. "Square people could never understand."

"I know—this stays with me."

"It stays with me, too. No wonder Nana was lonely. Who else but someone she could trust could send her to Space? Who would know her from the inside out? Who wouldn't use it as an opportunity to abuse her? Who would've proven themselves worthy, passing her tests just as you have with me?" Sylvia became still, lost in thought. Then she started crying.

Andrés reached over to touch her shoulder. "I know... You miss her."

"It's not that," she said, crying harder. "I just realized what I'm feeling. I feel like I spent the night getting high—I think I fucked up."

"I don't think this fucks with your sobriety."

"It's fucking with something." Sylvia began to panic, her body sloshing water out of the bathtub. "I fucked up! I fucked up so much— you can never leave me!"

Her crying was the hardest Andrés had ever seen from her. It was as if Sylvia realized she was now at the mercy of another drug.

"Nope," she said, pushing his hand away and taking several deep breaths to stop herself from crying. "I'm not going out like that. Constance was too sentimental for Marcus, and that's not gonna be me. If you ever leave me, I can find someone else like you. You're not special."

"Fine," he said. "Do what you gotta do. It's not gonna be a problem for me to find someone better than you."

"Do you really mean that?"

"No!"

"You broke my heart!" she yelled.

"You broke mine!" he yelled back.

"I didn't mean to! I'm just scared! I don't wanna be at your mercy!"

"I'm at yours—I'm disposable, remember?"

"You? Disposable? Are you fucking kidding me? I'm the one who knows what that feels like, for real! Have you ever had your body used, and grabbed, and thrown around like a fucking puppet? Like garbage? Like you're nothing? Like you're not even a human being? Like you were just born to be used? Fuck! I've given you something I never thought was in me, and now it's everything! You better not replace me!"

"You think I don't know that feeling?" Andrés said. "Just because I don't talk about it doesn't mean I don't know!"

"Talk to me! Make me understand!"

Andrés paused for a moment, touching on memories he wished his brain injury could have erased—but the body remembers.

"I'd always been afraid to tell my parents," he said. "I'd been told by the monster who abused me that if they knew, they'd see me as nothing more than a faggot—not a real man—for complaining that a beautiful woman was giving me all this *special* attention. In my parents' world, that was the worst thing I could ever be, and I didn't know any better —I was six when it all started."

Sylvia reached over to grip his shoulder.

Andrés looked at her for a long moment. "Was there something off about me that I didn't see it that way—her special attention? What was so special about having her grab me, pull me by the hair, and push my head down—trying to force me to..." He stopped himself from saying more. "There's no point in going into detail... You get the idea."

Sylvia squeezed his shoulder tightly. "I do."

Andrés took a deep breath and swallowed. "I was twelve when Estefania took me to the park to ask what was going on. She'd noticed something off about me. Why was I cutting myself?"

"You did that, too?"

"Yup, and that's when I told her. She explained that what Carmen did to me was not sex. She said it was normal for me to react the way I was reacting, but not to worry anymore. She was gonna prove to me that there was justice in the world.

"Estefania took me back to my grandfather's apartment. She knew no one would be home because my grandfather was never there during the day, and my mom, who usually spent weekends there, was out with my little brother.

"Estefania invited Carmen over, saying she had a message from my uncle. Carmen had just broken up with him. When she got there, Estefania attacked her. My grandfather surprised them by coming home early. He pulled them apart and yelled at Estefania, saying she knew better than to be fighting. But when he found out what had been going on, he looked at Carmen and ended her abuse in a way that only tough guys like him knew how... He shot Carmen in front of me."

Sylvia dropped her hand from his shoulder in astonishment. "Like what Nana did with my monsters." After a long silence, she said, "I remember when my mom died; no one knew what to do with me. My dad was in Vietnam, so I was placed in foster care. I still don't know how Nana knew what was going on... how she found me, but she did.

I'll never forget that moment when she came through that door, guns blazing, and shot the monsters that had been fostering me. When Nana found me hiding, she grabbed me, ran out of *that* house, and sped away until we were safely back home in Virginia."

"I'm so glad she did what she did," Andrés said. "The more you tell me about Constance, the more she reminds me of Reynaldo. She was a motherfucking gangster."

"Our grandparents are the titans."

"Our motherfucking protectors... That's why, in death, I've guarded his name—his secrets. I'll now do the same for Constance. I'll never repeat what she had to do. Who knows if they're still looking to solve that case?"

"Nana said nobody was gonna bother wasting too much time looking for her. Once the cops saw what was in *that* house—pictures she said she had seen on the floor and had no time to burn—they'd close the case and say, 'These people got what was coming to them.'"

"My grandfather had said the same thing about Carmen. No one in the family was gonna be looking for her since she was the one who left my uncle. She was the one who abandoned their kids. And just in case the cops came around and started asking questions, he called in a favor and had her body disappear."

Sylvia and Andrés looked at each other in silence. They allowed what had never been said openly to linger between them, with no further comment—the blood of their monsters, spilled by their titans, sealing a bond that committed them not only to everlasting secrecy but also to each other. They remained silent until Sylvia looked away, stirring the water in the bathtub with her legs.

"What's the matter?" he asked.

"I'm getting cold," she replied.

"Do you want me to take you out?"

Sylvia sank most of her body into the sudsy water. "No, I'm not clean yet... Take care of me."

Andrés stood up. He reached over to grab a bar of soap from a dish protruding from the tiled wall, then began washing her body.

After he finished cleaning and rinsing her, she raised her eyes and arms to Andrés and said, "Pick me up."

Andrés lifted Sylvia from the bath and set her back on the toilet. He dried her body with a towel and then carried her into their bedroom, lowering her into bed.

"Lay back," he said.

She did as he commanded.

He began to dress her.

Sylvia allowed his hands to move her body with reassuring strength until she was back in her pajama shirt.

Andrés joined her in bed from behind, wrapping the comforter around them.

She pressed the back of her body against him, her cold feet tangling with his.

He played with her hair.

Together, they watched the daylight come through the windows and onto the walls.

Together, they breathed.

Together, they were in a space of silence as the light of the afternoon faded from the walls of their Purple Room.

There was a harmony, a balance, between the Little and the Big, the Sub and the Dom, the Beloved that was, is, and always will be Us— Sylvia and Andrés—that made the calm flow of their breathing hum:

Shantih shantih shantih

[2]

IT WAS EARLY IN THE EVENING WHEN SYLVIA WOKE UP TO USE THE bathroom. When she returned and climbed back into bed, Andrés woke up, pulled her body close to his, and asked if she was okay.

"I am now," she said, smiling. "Happy Thanksgiving."

"Happy Thanksgiving to you, too."

She took a deep breath and let out a long exhale, as if she had been holding her breath for years. "It's been a long time since I could say that and not get all emotional about it. So, I'm grateful for that." She paused, savoring the moment, before asking, "What are you grateful for?"

He smiled, holding her tighter from behind. "I'm grateful to be alive—for you and my son. I'm grateful to have the rest of my family and to have found love for the world again. How about you?"

She paused, thinking, as though she had never considered the question, before saying, "I'm grateful to be alive, for my sobriety, and for you. I'm thankful to have met your mom and dad and felt welcomed by them. I'm grateful for my health, my mind—my ability to take care of myself. All of this might not be much, but it belongs to me, and I did it on my own. I even painted the walls purple. I did this so that every night, when I go to bed, and every morning, when I wake up, I'm reminded that there is something more royal, more powerful, more majestic about me because I've survived. I'm so grateful to me. I love me—I believe in me."

"I believe in you, too."

"I'm grateful that I can finally say this," she said. "I could never admit it before, not before The Labyrinth, but... I didn't wanna go to college."

"You didn't?"

"No, I didn't want to do any of this."

"What *did* you want to do?" Andrés asked.

"I didn't know, but I wanted more time to figure it out."

Sylvia paused. "As much as I love Nana, as much as I know I place her on a pedestal, I'm still angry that she didn't care about what I wanted. Nana only cared about what was practical. She wanted to make sure I became a woman of means, that I didn't have to depend on anyone, and that I no longer lived there. So did my dad—especially my dad, from what I learned later on... I mean, I never understood how Nana and Daddy could have this master plan for me and not tell me how they were gonna pay for it. 'That's for your daddy and me to figure out,' she'd say. 'Your only concern should be school.'"

She paused. "I just wanted to make Constance happy... She sacrificed her entire life for me. I couldn't say no. I don't know how I feel about any of this. I've benefited so much from their sacrifices and my opportunities, and I don't have much more to go, but..."

"But?"

"Things could've been different if my father had loved me more than he loved drugs. If he had taken responsibility for me instead of believing his own bullshit—that his disappearing for months at a time was for my own good—Nana could have been happy. I wouldn't feel this massive guilt that keeps me locked into their master plan—a plan I feel obligated to finish, even though I hate it. I hate it all, and I don't even want my degrees. I chose my major when I was a freshman, and by the time I got to my junior year, I had changed my mind about everything. But it was too late, and I was stuck."

"It's never too late," Andrés said.

"You think so?"

"You can do or be anything you want. What is it that you want?"

After a long pause, as if it were the first time she had been asked that question, she replied, "I just want to be free of the guilt for not completing their stupid master plan, so I can keep being happy because I'm alive, and we live in such a beautiful world, and we only get one life."

Sylvia closed her eyes, took a deep breath, and smiled as she exhaled.

"I'm feeling so in tune with my emotions right now. I don't feel any of the worry, the shame that always has me questioning my thoughts— if they're right or wrong. These are my thoughts. These are my feelings. I'm gonna practice more self-acceptance and be less judgmental of myself."

She opened her eyes and turned in bed to face him.

"I wish I was someone who came to New York just to come to New York. To not have done all the fucked-up shit I had to do to cope, to deal, to avoid sleep, to survive without Nana, to forget all the pressure to validate her life, her sacrifices—especially after how much cancer tore her apart.

"I had been her only purpose, and she was so lonely... I love her so much—she saved me—she gave me everything—she left nothing for herself to get me here, to New York, so that I could be someone I discovered I didn't want to be, all for the sake of a plan that was made without any of my input, without any of my say. I'm a monster for wanting to reject her gift!"

Andrés paused for a long moment, looking into her eyes.

Sylvia was distraught with guilt.

"With all due respect to Constance," he said, "you're not obligated to do anything. Whatever you do is your choice. You can ask for opinions, but what you do is up to you. What do you want the most right now?"

"I want to stay free—that's it. That's what it boils down to: staying free from guilt, letting go, freeing myself from this fucking rage I feel for my father, because I love him and fucking hate him so much. If you only knew."

"Then write about it. I'd like to know."

She said, "You would?"

"Of course I would. And I think you have a following who would also like to know as well."

"You think so?"

"Emma, out of all the people who read at The Loft, you were the only one mentioned in that *New Yorker* article. There's a reason you say Reggie put you up to it—what does that tell you?"

After a long, thoughtful pause, she said, "You're right... I think I'll write about it... I'll write about it now." She got up from bed and went to her desk in the corner by the window. She sat down, opened a notebook, picked up a pen, and went to work.

Andrés got out of bed and spent the rest of the night cleaning their apartment, getting rid of all the clutter and putrid smells, before going back to bed and falling asleep with Sylvia still working at her desk.

❧　22　❧

1968

[1]

It was a Friday night. Andrés sat at a table in The Loft, watching Reginald Superstar look over the audience from the stage.

"Everyone, brace yourselves, because what you're about to see is pretty fucked-up," Reginald said. "Please put your hands together and give it up for Sylvia."

The room erupted in laughter as she appeared on stage wearing a bright yellow sundress, her hair draped over her shoulders and down to her chest.

Reginald looked her over, astonished. "Wow, I haven't seen you look like this in years. What's the occasion?"

"You'll see—now get the fuck out." Sylvia yanked the microphone from Reginald's hands and shooed him away, placing herself in the center of the spotlight. She smiled, seemingly amused at the audience's reaction. "Laugh all you want. I do own something more than a tank top and jeans. I even washed my hair. I know that's a running joke among you assholes."

She paused, her face becoming expressionless.

"But seriously," she said. "I'm gonna need everyone to settle down —I've got something to say."

Sylvia waited for everyone to do as she asked. When all became quiet, she held the microphone close to her lips and whispered, "Father, what could I have done to keep you home with me?

"That's the question the little girl in me keeps asking.

"That little girl still doesn't understand.

"It has become what she now knows of the world.

"Men don't love.

"Men leave.

"Especially me."

She paused.

"Father, I wish you'd been stronger.

"I wish you could've coped better with our loss.

"1968 was a bad year for me too.

"We both lost Mom, except you were in Vietnam, and you know what I went through.

"I was five, trying to help Nana cope; then you came home, and I had to help you cope; then I had to watch her help you cope,

"Over and over and over,

"And a few days later, you'd be gone

"Like an emotional hit-and-run,

"And I'd wait by the window for you,

"Not knowing you had no intention of coming back

"When you said you would."

She looked at Andrés, who was taking pictures of her, before looking back at the audience.

"Father, when did you start to love drugs more than you loved me?"

Her voice became louder. "At what point did you stop giving a shit?

"Handing over your responsibility for raising me to an old woman who would've had to wake up,

"Every day,

"In what should've been her golden years, to deal with

"My ever-growing, rebellious ass,

"Angry at the world,

"For EVERYTHING!

"That had HAPPENED to me!

"In 19!

"68!—Father!

"You are so goddamn lucky Nana was more of a man than you!

"You are so lucky that Nana dug deep down for the strength to do the job you couldn't do!

"It's on her shoulders, and on the shoulders of women like her, that I stand—women who have had to deal with men like your sorry ass.

"Men who've abandoned their responsibilities instead of at least trying to work through their sadness, Father!

"To stop the goddamn crying, Father!

"I didn't ask to be born, Father.

"At least try, Daddy,

"You could've tried!

"I wish you could've tried being my daddy!

"Goddammit, Father!" she yelled, her face red from her sudden crying. "I wish you had tried being my daddy, but no!

"Somehow, you found the willpower to push yourself out of whatever fucking hole you had buried yourself in, just to get that high.

"You had all that money and time to travel cross-country and live anywhere.

"Why couldn't you have channeled that willpower into being my dad, Father?

"Being at home with me, Father?

"You're a fucking asshole, Father!

"It was you who helped bring me into this ugly world, with all this pain and suffering, and not try to protect me!

"Thank God for the Matriarch; she did what you couldn't do!

"It was you, Father, who brought me here to the Lower East Side.

"You showed me your dope spots—places you'd been robbed—with pathetic junkie pride.

"Those became the places I'd first go to when I started getting high!

"You taught me how to be a drug addict, Father.

"For years, I didn't know how to feel about you, Father.

"I thought I hated you, Father, but I don't.

"As much as I've tried, I don't.

"In the last few months, I began to see that you were hollowed out by a war machine.

"The six-year-old me can never excuse you

"But the thirty-year-old woman I've become is trying to understand what shaped you,

"Not for your sake, but for the sake of my sanity,

"So that the way I see the world will no longer be shaped by your abandonment

"And I don't end up becoming a bitter, old woman who hates men

"Because I now understand it was the nature of your situation back then.

"You survived 1968.

"I don't know what that's like,

"Just like you'll never know what it took

"For me to have survived 1968.

"But now, I understand you were living with trauma and pain,

"Just like me,

"And now, I think I know how to let go,

"And try to be at peace."

Sylvia took a deep breath to stop herself from crying and exhaled the word, "Shantih."

She closed her eyes, took another deep breath, and whispered into the microphone, "Shantih."

Sylvia opened her eyes, pointed the microphone at the audience, and together, they all said:

Shantih

She stepped back to look around the room before returning to the spotlight.

"Now, time for something positive.

"Daddy, thank you for buying me this beautiful dress.

"It's incredible that it feels the same as it did when I was seventeen,

"And you got it for me for our trip to New York City.

"After 1968, I'd never been beyond the mountains until that day.

"We not only went to the Lower East Side,

"But you took me to all the museums we could fit into one day,

"And you showed me how much you knew about art."

She paused.

"I wore this dress a week later when Nana took me to your garden of stone

"And showed me how you were at rest in your dress uniform,

"So that you could tell me,

"Through your shut eyes,

"One final goodbye."

She paused.

"You're never coming back."

Sylvia stood motionless in the spotlight, looking down at the floor.

"Daddy," she whispered, "why didn't you tell me about your master plan?"

Her voice became louder. "Days after we buried you in Arlington,

"A letter came to me saying,

"Since 1968,

"You'd been saving most of the money

"The government had paid for hollowing you out

"Into something you, or I, couldn't touch.

"You'd formed a trust

"To honor the hope that I'd become someone who could act on behalf of the powerless

"And use the law to exact revenge on their monsters,

"Just like the way Nana had acted on my behalf

"When she found me after Mama died,

"And used bullets to exact revenge on the foster parents who'd become mine."

She paused.

"Your master plan for me, Daddy, was to turn me into one of the most feared beings from out-of-the-bedtime stories you used to read to me before you were sent to Vietnam.

"It was no longer enough for me to become like Athena.

"You wanted your daughter to become like one of the Erinyes—a goddess of pure vengeance.

"A Watcher—

"The Guard—

"The Fury."

Sylvia lifted her head to face the audience, wiping the corners of her eyes.

"Daddy, what am I supposed to do with all this anger? This hate?

"Yes, hate. I know I said I didn't hate you, but... I don't know.

"I haven't known since I was seventeen,

"With the weight of your death and all your expectations killing me.

"So here I am, thirty years old, in this dress,

"Still feeling bitter, wondering

"How can I defuse this anger—this hate that is ticking inside of me

"Like a bomb

"Before it goes ka-boom,

"And destroys me,

"And destroys the only meaningful connection I've made

"In what has become

"My beautiful world of the alive."

She paused.

"I'm Sylvia the Sunflower.

"The survivor.

"And... now you know...

"Peace."

She looked around the room, expecting applause, but all she got were blank stares and muffled coughs.

Reginald came to the stage, took the microphone from her, and said, "Give it up one more time for Sylvia the Buzz Killer."

She bolted from the spotlight, heading straight for Andrés. He wrapped her in her long, black trench coat and led her to the exit.

[2]

Outside, he kept up with her furious pace until she stopped, turning to face him. "What did I do? Why did I listen to your dumb-ass? I used to be funny! Now I fucking suck!"

Andrés said nothing as she took a long breath, giving her the space to vent.

The longer Sylvia looked at him, the angrier she seemed to become. Her eyes narrowed. She pushed him. "You've got nothing to say?" She pushed him again. "Nothing to say about how you've ruined my life? You're just gonna keep looking at me? Like a fucking idiot?"

Andrés was about to respond, but before he could say a word, Sylvia smashed her fist into his jaw, sending him stumbling backward.

She didn't hesitate—charging forward, smashing her fist into his nose and knocking him to the sidewalk. Sylvia stood over him, huffing in a red-faced rage. She yelled, "Walk away!"

Andrés looked up at her, blood pouring from his nose. "Why? So you can hate me too?" He pushed himself off the pavement, standing tall over her. "Men don't love—they leave, right?"

There was a pause as Sylvia's defiant posture slumped, realizing the implication of his words. A pained and confused expression came to her face. "What's wrong with you? Why do you still want me?"

Before Andrés could respond, a voice from down the empty street called out to Sylvia. She looked away, squinting into the distance, and called back to the shadowy figure standing in front of The Loft, "Caleb?"

"Yeah! It's me!"

"What are you doing? Are you following me?"

Caleb began walking toward Sylvia. "I saw you run out! Are you okay?"

"We're fine! Leave us alone!"

"Are you sure? Because I know what I just saw!"

"It's none of your business; fuck off!" she yelled.

"Aw, come on," Caleb said, approaching them. "That's no way to talk to an old friend!"

Sylvia ducked behind Andrés. "That's because we were never friends."

Caleb came to a stop. "How can you say that? After all these years?" He chuckled. "I guess Katherine and Jessica were right about you. You'd forgotten your friends for some dude you met yesterday."

"You think I'm that bitch?" She began to laugh. "Hell no! Maybe I'm sick of talking to them about the choices they keep making—"

"You mean the same choices you'd made for years?"

"And that's why we're not friends—we were never friends—"

Andrés squared up to Caleb, fists raised. "You need to leave."

Caleb looked at Sylvia, peeking from behind Andrés, then chuckled and said, "I see how it is... Not a big deal. You'll remember who I am soon enough—when you do, you'll remember we're friends. Until then, enjoy your night, Spacer Woman." Caleb turned and walked away.

Andrés lowered his fists and relaxed his stance.

Sylvia began pacing back and forth on the sidewalk, her hands tangled in her hair, her eyes darting side to side as if searching for an imaginary door to escape through. She grabbed Andrés, shaking him. "I've gotta get out of here. I don't wanna be here anymore. I'm thirty years old, still surrounded by the same people with the same bullshit, and I'm not the one with the problem anymore. I don't wanna go under—I can't go under—take me to Robots."

"I thought clubbing was wack," he said.

"It is, but I don't think I can handle The Labyrinth right now, and I need to get the fuck out of my head—can you take me back? Back to Space? Without all that other stuff?"

"I can," he said, grabbing her hand.

"Good, because my body still hurts, and I don't wanna crash again."

"Again?—you're still crashing."

"I know, but I've gotta go."

"Then let's go."

Sylvia said the phrase they had agreed upon in The Labyrinth that would kick off the start of the power dynamic—the dance—the game they were still learning to play: "Time-in."

Andrés repeated the phrase to show that he understood the rules they had agreed upon—the rules that would now be in effect until either of them said the phrase "time-out" or the safe word "Constance."

On the short walk to Robots, she shivered and coughed, while he did his best to keep her warm.

When they arrived, the bouncer at the door patted Andrés hard on the back. "You better be good to her... She's been through some shit."

Sylvia pushed the bouncer. "Stop, you don't need to do that—"

"I'm only looking out for you, just like old times."

"And that worked out so well for me, didn't it?"

The bouncer chuckled and waved her off. "Enjoy your night, Spacer Woman."

Without saying another word, Sylvia took Andrés's hand in hers and yanked him inside, leading him downstairs. She pulled him across the crowded dance floor, through the haze of pot smoke, until they reached the same corner where they had first spoken about messages, answering machines, and their large appetite for passion.

She shouted over the techno music playing, "I can explain about Caleb—the bouncer!"

"Stop! You don't need to!"

"Yes, I do! Caleb and I have known each other since college, and the bouncer was someone I used to pay to watch my back when we worked at the same club. I guess he still feels the need to make it up to me for not being there the night I had to call the cops—he'd called out sick. When the cops came, the way they made me feel, acting all friendly with the floor manager and the other bouncers, told me they weren't gonna believe me. I had to bounce out of there quick and go to the emergency room on my own."

"What happened?" Andrés asked.

After a long silence, during which Sylvia's eyes began to flicker back and forth and she started biting her nails, he realized she wasn't ready to share the rest of her story. He brought her back into the moment by taking her hands away from her mouth and examining her knuckles.

She looked at him and smiled, apparently no longer thinking about the past but about their fight outside The Loft. "Your head fucked up my hand," she said.

"Nobody told you to swing at me," he replied, laughing.

"I can't believe I punched you... I'm sorry."

"Don't worry about it."

"Do you forgive me?"

"There's nothing to forgive," he said. "We're not equal."

Sylvia pushed Andrés away and said, "Don't start with that bullshit!"

"It's true—physically, we're not. You hit hard, but for someone like me, it tickled."

"Fuck you. I made you bleed," Sylvia said, laughing.

"Which is funny—going spider monkey on me."

"I can punch you again if you wanna laugh some more."

"Go for it; I don't care. We've been through The Labyrinth—that passion, even when you're angry, even when you're yelling—I don't know; I feel like I can turn that into love. A deeper love. I've never felt this turned on in my life."

"Me neither."

"If I woke up that thing in you, and it has you like this, then I'm not gonna act like a little bitch when you start taking swings—especially since I now know who you really are, what you are."

"What am I?"

"Like me, awake."

Her face lit up with relief. "I love you."

"I love you too."

Sylvia hugged Andrés, pressing her face against his chest. "Please keep being patient with me. That's all I ask. Promise?" She looked up from his chest, facing him. "Promise you won't walk away? Even if it seems like I'm trying to go ka-boom?"

"I promise," Andrés said.

"You better, because you're not perfect. There are some things that you do that could make you go ka-boom, too."

"Like?"

"Like the way you sometimes swallow your feelings, like the way you did back there—I felt like I was arguing with a rock... That's why I punched you—you weren't acting like the man I met. The one who had read to me *In My Sky at Twilight*—who had opened his soul. I need you to feel things with me. I never wanna feel like I'm alone in a relationship—and we're going way too fast, and I'm scared now more than ever. And I know I'm repeating myself, but you know way too much about me for me to turn back. And with the way I feel about you, I want forever. Baby, I do, and the fucked-up thing is, I've yet to meet your son."

"You will—in December, after finals. We'll have all the time to be with each other and not feel rushed. We can take him to a playground together."

"Yes," Sylvia said, "the one across the street from *our* apartment!"

"That's what I was thinking."

"Good, because I have to meet him. It's only right if you have me like this because I'm yours. I belong to you. You belong to me." Sylvia was silent for a long moment, as if touching upon the full power of the words she had spoken and feeling their implications. "I've never said that to anyone... Please don't make me regret it."

"You won't," he said, pulling her close. "Are you ready to go to Space?"

"Yes—I'm ready."

Sylvia and Andrés began swaying their bodies to the beat of the music, slowly drifting away from the corner, past others at the edges of the dance floor, until they were in the middle of the crowd, all moving beneath the strobe mirror ball.

Sylvia's hair smelled as if it had been wrapped in a crown of sunflowers. Andrés could feel her heart pounding through her coat and onto his chest with each thump, thump, thump. The sheer number of bodies pressing against him overwhelmed his senses, giving him a taste of Space.

She closed her eyes, moved her arms from his waist to his shoulders, and began singing along to the song playing, "Breathe love into me... Breathe love into me."

They continued to sway in the dark room, their souls becoming one as they slowly circled beneath the strobe mirror ball, as if they were stars, making their eternal turn around the bright core of the Milky Way Galaxy.

23

DELIVERY BOY

DECEMBER 7, 1992

IT WAS MONDAY NIGHT. IT HAD BEEN THE LONGEST DAY FOR
Andrés since waking up from a coma at the Landstuhl Regional
Medical Center in Germany almost two years before. Now that he was
home, he looked forward to studying, spending time with Andy, and
showering before finally getting some much-needed sleep. But just as
he was about to lock himself in his room, Petra appeared from the
kitchen to tell him Sylvia had called twice. When he sighed and
mentioned he had finals to study for, she grabbed his arm to stop him
from walking away.

"Call her now—I think something's going on."

The phone rang before Andrés could respond. He dragged himself
into the kitchen to answer.

Sylvia was on the other end of the line, saying in her brash New
York accent, "Ay yo, it's me—what's up?"

He replied in a tired, monotone voice, "Getting ready to study... I
have a test tomorrow, and I need to go through *Oedipus Rex* one more
time—"

She interrupted him. "I've always loved Sophocles: *'It is not fate that I should be your ruin, Apollo is enough; it is his care to work this out.'*"

The exhaustion Andrés had been feeling disappeared, and he smiled at the thought that someone smarter than him loved him. "Impressive—I can barely remember what I'm reading, and here you are, reciting lines like it's nothing."

"It's been years," she said, "but it's easy when that line has always stood out. But enough with the small talk. Where were you? You don't get home this late, especially on Mondays."

"It's a long story," he said. "I'll tell you all about it the next time I see you."

"Well, I just got home, and I want you to come over now. You can study here."

"I can't."

"You do it all the time."

"I have a lot of reading to do, and it's finals."

"But something really big happened today, and I need you."

"What happened?"

"I can't say... not over the phone."

Andrés sighed. "Okay... I'm on my way."

"Great," she said, sounding thrilled. "Don't eat anything on the way home—I'm getting us takeout."

"That'll be easy," he said, laughing. "I'm broke."

"But I'm not, so we're good—hurry up and get here."

She hung up, and Andrés returned to his room. He packed what he needed for the next day and told Petra, who came over with Andy in her arms, that he was spending the night with Sylvia.

"You look sick," Petra said.

"Now you notice? I'm in a lot of pain."

"Maybe you should stay home."

Andrés gave his mother a look that said, "I would be if you hadn't shamed me into answering her call," but he took his son from her arms and assured Petra that he would be fine.

After spending time with Andy, Andrés left for the city. Two hours later, he was inside Sylvia's apartment building, unlocking the door to what was starting to feel like home.

When he went inside, Sylvia called out from the bedroom, "It's about time!"

"I know," he called back, closing the door behind him.

"I got tired of waiting, so I already ordered."

"What are we eating?"

"Steamed dumplings—they should be here any minute."

"Great, because I'm hungry."

"You would've eaten a lot sooner if you'd come directly here. It's not like you don't have a key."

"I would've," he said, taking off his coat and tossing it on her couch, "but it's been a crazy day—"

She interrupted him. "Tell me about it! It's been crazy for me, too." She appeared from the bedroom, naked and looking frustrated. "Just as I was getting home from work, Katherine and Jessica came out of nowhere and got on me for telling Caleb that we were not friends."

"So what?"

"Because of me, he stopped *dealing* with them."

"Okay? And?"

"He said he would go back to *working* with them if I became his friend again."

Andrés laughed. "What a chump."

Sylvia laughed. "I know, right?"

"Your friends should find another dealer."

"It's not that simple for them."

"Of course... it's never that simple—"

"Katherine works at City Hall, Jessica is a prosecutor, and Caleb is someone they could trust to deliver to their apartments, to be discreet. But I guess they got desperate. They got caught up in a situation with someone Jessica had met through her job and almost didn't escape."

"Let me guess: they made you feel like that was your fault."

She looked down and slumped her shoulders. "Yes."

"Typical."

"They said it was up to me to make things right—be Caleb's friend again."

"Fuck them! They're not your problem."

"I know, I know," she said, looking back up at Andrés, "but what would it cost if I acted just a little more? At least for now."

"Everything."

"Well... I decided to make things right—for now. And before you say anything, I'm doing it for myself. I don't wanna get up on stage and see them in the audience, staring back at me like it was my fault they almost got assaulted. That would mess with my flow, and I can't let that happen. I have to think big picture—what works best for me, for how I perform. God knows I suck now."

"You already know how I feel about that, but it's your life—you do you."

"I know... Anyway, get comfortable. I'll be right back—I have to poop."

"Is that why you're naked?"

Sylvia laughed. "Shut up."

"Are you gonna be fighting for your life?"

"Maybe—but I gotta go." She hurried away, passing through one of the two doors in the short hallway that connected the kitchen and the living room.

He sat on the couch and pulled out a textbook from his backpack.

Sylvia yelled from the bathroom, "I think I ate some bad sushi!"

"It sounds like you did!"

"I can't believe I'm letting you hear me."

"How could I not? You left the door open."

Sylvia laughed. "Wanna come in and hear me in stereo?"

"No, thanks!"

"What's gonna happen when we're old, and I need you to come into the bathroom and clean me? Are you gonna tell me 'no' then?"

"Is that what you want me to do? Because we don't have to wait—I'll wipe your ass now."

Sylvia laughed. "No!"

"If that's Emma's kink, I'll come in there—"

"Don't you dare!"

"Are you sure? It'd be no big deal."

"I was just playing!"

"Sure you were," he said, smiling, as he turned his focus back to his textbook.

Sylvia sat quietly for a few more moments before flushing, washing her hands, and leaving the bathroom. "Heads up—we ran out of toilet paper."

Andrés looked up from his textbook. "I'll go out and get some more."

She walked over. "After we have sex."

"Not after hearing you fight for your life—you even smell like air freshener—"

"Shut up." Sylvia yanked his textbook from his hands and tossed it onto the couch. She was about to unbuckle his belt when she took a long look at his face and stopped. "What the hell happened to you?"

"I woke up like this."

"Why didn't you say anything?"

Andrés chuckled. "Hello? It's on my face."

"I know, but still—"

"You were talking... I didn't wanna interrupt."

Sylvia touched the largest of the red bumps on his forehead. "Does it hurt?"

"I'm in a lot of pain."

"I can't believe you went to school like this."

"It's finals—I couldn't miss today."

"We need to go to the hospital."

"I did that already—after my test, I went straight to the emergency room."

"What did the doctors say?"

"They told me it was just stress, made me fill out a Gulf War survey, then told me to go home, not to worry."

The downstairs doorbell rang before Sylvia could react. "Hold that thought—that's gotta be our food." She rushed to the intercom, buzzed open the downstairs door, and then opened the apartment door.

While she waited, instead of sharing more about his visit to the emergency room at the veteran's hospital, Andrés asked, "Are you gonna put a shirt on?"

Sylvia teased, a mischievous glint in her eyes, "What for? Kind of silly after everything."

"That's not the point."

"Then what is the point?" she said, tilting her head to one side.

"Aside from pushing my buttons?"

"Yes!"

"You fucking brat, keep pushing."

Sylvia began to laugh, her shoulders shaking. "I knew you'd get it."

"I do, but not tonight."

"I know... You have to study."

"No," Andrés said. "I feel like I'm dying."

Before Sylvia could respond, Caleb appeared at the door, surprising Andrés as he handed her their takeout food in a white paper bag. He lingered, devouring her with his eyes, until she snapped a finger in his face and said, "Alright, that's enough."

"Is it really?" Caleb replied, still mesmerized by her body.

"Yes, really—I need another favor."

"Anything," he said, shaking his head as if coming out of a spell.

"Go down to the *bodega* and get us some toilet paper."

Caleb gave Sylvia's body one last look before smiling at Andrés. "Anything for an old friend—I'll be right back."

Sylvia slammed the door on Caleb before turning to face Andrés. Her once heavy-lidded eyes were now wide with panic, her naked body flushed red. When Andrés began to laugh, she asked, "What's so funny?"

"Tell me again how Caleb can be trusted. Is he a legit delivery boy? Is this how he keeps things discreet?"

Sylvia bolted for the kitchen.

Andrés jumped up from the couch to follow.

He found Sylvia standing on her tiptoes, trying to stuff the white paper bag into a cabinet above the sink.

"What's in the bag?" Andrés asked.

She turned to look at him as if she had done nothing wrong. "Dumplings?"

"What else is in the bag?"

"Nothing?"

"Bullshit!"

"Are you mad he saw me naked?"

"What's in the bag?"

"Because I don't see what the big deal is!"

"It's the biggest!" Andrés yelled.

"That doesn't make any fucking sense! I've gotten naked in front of strangers with you!"

"It's not the same!"

"How is it not? People have watched us fuck, and now you want me to put on a shirt? I'm just thinking big picture!"

"Fuck big picture! This is about what's in the bag—our boundaries! What we do, we do around people who know the rules—who know not to cross lines! Caleb doesn't give a shit about any of that!"

A wicked smile came to her face. "What if I don't give a shit, too? What if I got naked because I knew Caleb was coming over, and it would thrill me to tease him?"

"Then you get what you get—just like I'm getting what I get. I needed to study, but I'm here instead, dealing with drama—"

"Then go," she said. "You don't have to be here."

Something in the pit of Andrés's stomach dropped at the realization that if Sylvia allowed her old friends to remain in her orbit, this would be their everyday lives. It was only a matter of time before Sylvia relapsed. "You're right," he said. "I don't have to be here."

He left the kitchen and headed to the living room. Sylvia followed. A heavy silence settled between them as Andrés put on his coat, tossed his textbook into his backpack, and grabbed it. He gave her one last look before leaving, slamming the door behind him.

Outside, Andrés spotted Caleb emerging from the darkness of Tompkins Square Park and charged at him. He tackled Caleb to the ground and straddled his chest. Andrés raised his fist to punch him but noticed Sylvia suddenly standing above them in her long pajama shirt, smiling as if this was the outcome she had in mind when she said, "big picture."

"What are you waiting for?" she asked, her voice filled with excitement. "Hit him! Make him bleed!"

Without hesitation, Andrés followed her command, relentlessly pounding Caleb's face with his fists, over and over, until a bloody smile appeared.

"You think this is funny?" Andrés yelled.

"It's fucking hilarious," Caleb said, blood in his mouth.

"You're gonna see how funny I really am if you keep bothering her—"

"What are you gonna do? Punch me again?"

"I'm gonna make you *disappear*."

"Ooh, I'm scared," Caleb said.

"You should be—"

"Whatever, man—just let me go."

Andrés punched him one last time before standing up and letting Caleb get up and run away.

Sylvia knelt to pick up the roll of toilet paper left in the middle of the street. "Thank God he didn't take this with him—I need to poop again."

"Again?" Andrés said, shaking his punching hand in pain.

Sylvia stood up to examine his knuckles. Without saying a word, she led Andrés back upstairs and into the kitchen. She took the white paper bag from the cabinet and emptied its contents onto the table.

Alongside the dumplings and noodles Sylvia had wanted, Caleb left a small white packet that, at first glance, resembled salt. But when Andrés looked closer at the small red letters, instead of saying "iodized," the label said, "Passion." It was a packet of heroin.

"I had a feeling he was gonna do this," she said in a low voice. "Something kept telling me not to look in the bag. That's why I ran into the kitchen. I didn't want you to think I'd asked for it—I swear, I didn't. I just don't want my friends to be mad at me anymore. Do you believe me?"

"You don't need to explain anything."

"You believe me, don't you?"

"I believe you."

"You hesitated."

"Because this is hard," he said.

"But you know me. We have trust."

"Our trust is only as good as our boundaries."

Sylvia sighed. "I know."

"Your so-called friends don't respect yours."

"They don't—and they know my history with him."

"What kind of history?" Andrés asked. "Is there more?"

She slapped herself in the face. "Stupid me—I thought I could handle him." She slapped herself again. "I shouldn't have kept him lingering."

He grabbed her hands, forcing Sylvia to stop hitting herself. "I don't need to know... Caleb's got my attention now. I'm gonna *handle* him."

"Do you still love me?"

"Of course I do."

"Because I love you—"

"Emma, it's okay. I love you—I believe you."

Sylvia began to cry, as if relieved. "You don't know how much I needed to hear that—baby, I'm sorry. I'm sorry about everything. Can we start over?"

He drew her into his arms. "There's nothing to start over—it is what it is. We move on."

"Can you flush that for me, please?"

"Leave it to me," he said.

"I need to feed Kalpa."

"I need to study."

She looked up at him. "If you want my help, I'll give it to you. And if you're up for it, maybe we can have sex? It doesn't matter if we don't —I just want you to keep holding me."

"I just wanna keep holding you, too."

"As long as we're together, that's all that matters, right?"

"Holding you is all that matters... I don't need sex to feel close to you."

She smiled, her eyes welling up. "I didn't know how much I needed to hear that until now. No one has ever made me feel that was possible."

"Our love is more than just the giving of our bodies."

"It's the giving of our souls," Sylvia said, "and you've proven you're worth the giving of mine."

Andrés kissed her on the forehead. "So have you."

24

LET ME BE EVIL

JANUARY 11, 1993

[1]

It was Monday afternoon. Sylvia called Andrés from work and asked if he was available. "I know it's only been a day," she said, "but I've missed you."

"I've missed you too."

There was an uncertain pause before she asked, "Is Lydia still talking shit?"

"Not anymore. The judge asked if I was a bad father, a criminal— anything that could help her decide to take custody away from me. Lydia told the judge, 'No,' that I was a good father. She was trying to keep Andy away only because she was angry that I had moved on."

"What did Lydia expect?"

"I don't know, but when it looked to her like you and I were getting serious, Lydia started talking that shit about, 'I'm Andy's only mother.'"

"Is he there now?"

"No. After the hearing, she apologized and asked if she could keep him. I said 'yes,' but only because I still want Andy to have her in his life."

"Good... I don't want any baby mama drama—I see myself working with her, not against her."

"I told Lydia that, and she seemed relieved."

"I wanna meet her—tell her myself—after I meet Andy."

"Now that I've *handled* some things, I'll set that up as soon as possible."

"What things?" she asked. "What needed handling?"

"I'll tell you this weekend."

"Why this weekend? Am I not gonna see you before then?"

"Of course."

"Then why not now? Are you hiding something from me?"

"No."

"Yes, you are—"

"No, I'm not—"

"Then how come I didn't know you were taking care of something so damn important that now that it's been *handled,* I can meet Andy?"

Andrés hesitated, trying to think of a good answer.

"What did we promise each other?" she asked.

"No more secrets."

"That's right. If honesty is a part of our dance, you better tell me, or I won't be able to trust you anymore."

"I can't tell you... Not over the phone."

"Why not?"

"Because," he said, "I can't."

"Then you'd better come down and tell me, 'cause I'm not waiting until the weekend—I need to know."

"Fine, I'll tell you tonight."

"Meet me outside after work," Sylvia said. "You can tell me when you get here."

"I won't be able to until we get home. I don't want anyone over-hearing us."

Sylvia laughed. "Now I really have to know. Hurry and get here—I've got some shit of my own to handle, and I feel the need to be evil. Don't ask—time-in." She hung up.

He left his parents' apartment for the World Trade Center, where Sylvia had recently been placed by a temp agency to work as a paralegal at a law firm. Hours later, he arrived, sat on a stone bench across from the Sphere, and waited for Sylvia to come out of the South Tower. It was six at night when she appeared, strutting across the plaza toward him like a short supermodel, wearing sunglasses and a long, black trench coat.

He stood up and asked as she approached, "Can you even see?"

"No—shut up—take this." She pushed a large leather handbag into his arms.

"You're such a clown."

She looked at Andrés, her sunglasses covering most of her face. "You'd never say that to Sophia Loren."

"That's because you're no Sophia."

She grinned. "You're right; she's old."

"You're old to me."

"Why do you say shit like that?"

"Because it's true." He pointed to her leather boots—a pair she had bought to go with the special outfit she would now wear in The Labyrinth. "Don't tell me you went to work dressed like this."

"No, stupid," she said, smiling. "I brought the outfit with me—I changed before coming out here."

"Where's your suit?"

"In my bag—"

"You're the stupid one. You're gonna get it wrinkled."

"Who the fuck cares? You're gonna iron it out for me anyway. And this back and forth is getting boring—we have to be at Caffè Reggio by seven, so moving on, shut up and follow my lead."

"If we have to be in the Village, why did you have me come down here when I could've met you there?"

Sylvia laughed. "Because I can."

She led him away from the plaza and into the subway station below. They boarded a car with no air conditioning, crowded with people smelling of sweat. They held on to the railing as the train began moving uptown. Sylvia stared at a large, heavyset man seated just below her. She smiled at him.

The heavyset man smiled back at her.

Sylvia placed her free hand on her belly. "I know it's hard to tell, but... you're not gonna make a pregnant woman stand, are you?"

"Of course not." The heavyset man stood up.

Sylvia motioned for Andrés to take the empty seat and then sat on his lap, with her boots and hair brushing against the passengers on either side of her.

They seemed to want to complain but didn't want to cause a scene. The heavyset man moved away as if he didn't want to start one either.

Andrés whispered in Sylvia's ear, "You brat. You're gonna get me into a fight."

She smiled and said, "I know," wrapping her arms around his neck.

"Are you pregnant?"

"No, you jackass, but we're sitting. Tell me you love me."

"I tolerate you."

"I tolerate you, too."

"Okay, time-out," he said, laughing. "What's going on?"

"It's Katherine and Jessica."

"What do they want now?"

"They wanna meet with me and talk about my *well-being*."

"Oh my God—are you okay?"

"Apparently not," Sylvia said. "Nobody this happy can be this okay."

"To be fair," Andrés said, "if we had a daughter, I'd want her to have friends who do this: check in on her if they think something's wrong."

"If we have a daughter and she grows up to have friends like mine, I'd tell her, flat out, that she fucked up somewhere in life. She needs to make better choices."

"Stop punishing yourself," Andrés said.

"I can't help it."

"You did the best you could."

"Sometimes, it doesn't feel like I did," Sylvia said. "I think they're coming at me like this because Caleb disappeared. No one can find him. At least that's what Jessica said, all mad, as if I had something to do with that."

Andrés said in a monotone voice, not acting surprised, "Oh, wow, Caleb's gone."

"Jessica said he hasn't been heard from in over a week."

"Maybe Caleb fucked with someone else's sobriety. Maybe he got what he deserved."

Sylvia was silent before taking off her sunglasses and giving him a look, as if he had said something strange. "That's a little too specific."

"I'm just doing that whole manifest energy thing you keep going on and on about," Andrés said. "If we say he got what he deserved, maybe it'll come true."

"I hope so. My friends know what Caleb did to me. Don't ask me what that is; I can't talk about it, at least not now."

"You don't have to."

She sniffled, wiping her nose, before placing her sunglasses back on. "I know what I've said about honesty, and I know I got on you about keeping secrets, but what Caleb did to me goes way beyond that. If I talk about it, I will relapse, and I need to stay focused on my recovery, even if it makes me look like a hypocrite."

"If your friends knew about your history with him and still wanted you to act like his friend, cut them off—they don't give a shit about you."

She nodded. "You're right... They were ready to sacrifice me. Fuck it. I need to be vicious. You need to see how evil I can be."

"I already know."

Sylvia laughed. "You haven't seen shit yet. I'm still planning our scene, so I need you to shut up and stare at me with reverence until we get there. I'll have everything figured out by then."

After several delays, they arrived in Greenwich Village. Sylvia and Andrés rushed off the car and out of the subway station. They hurried along the crowded avenues and back streets until they arrived at their destination in front of the café.

"Okay," she said, grabbing him by the shoulders. "Before we go in, I need to say sorry."

"For what?" Andrés asked.

"They don't know I brought you with me."

"I don't care. I want your friends to be surprised, especially when they see that thing come out of me."

"Not before it comes out of me first, and you play the Sub. We're gonna be switching, so I need you to hear what I'm saying between the lines and roll with it. Watch for my cues and read me like you would in The Labyrinth. Okay?—okay—time-in."

"No—time-out."

She dropped her hands from his shoulders. "What now?"

"We can't play this game in front of your friends. What if we say something that'll—"

"Do you trust me?"

"Of course I do," Andrés said.

"Then let me be evil—time-in!"

[2]

THEY WENT INSIDE THE BUSTLING CAFÉ, THE RICH AROMA OF espresso filling the air. Sylvia led Andrés through the cozy space, past couples and groups of friends engaged in lively conversations at their tables. Soft jazz played in the background, adding to the warm atmosphere. They finally reached a dimly lit corner where Katherine and Jessica sat, their expressions a mix of annoyance and impatience.

"I told you not to bring him," Katherine said.

"I brought him anyway," Sylvia replied.

"Too bad there's no place for him to sit," Jessica said.

Sylvia looked around, found a table with an empty chair, took it without asking the occupants, and returned to place it next to the one her friends had reserved for her. "Problem solved." She looked at Andrés and told him to sit.

He did as he was told.

Sylvia looked at her friends, who appeared surprised by her dominance. "Alright, I'm here. Speak your piece." She pointed at Katherine. "Go."

Katherine hesitated before saying, "I don't feel comfortable talking in front of him."

"I don't feel safe with just you guys," Sylvia said.

Jessica burst out laughing. "You've got to be kidding—you feel safer with him than with us?"

"You wanted me to be friends with Caleb, and Andrés knows how important sobriety is to me."

Jessica rolled her eyes. "Here we go."

Katherine asked Sylvia, "What's the number today?"

"662 days," she replied.

"And you think that makes you better than us?" Katherine said.

Sylvia sat, crossed her arms, and, with most of her face hidden behind black sunglasses, smiled. "Yes, it does."

"Not if you let him hit you," Jessica replied.

"Hit me? Nobody's hitting me."

"Then how come you had to punch Andrés?" Jessica asked.

Sylvia laughed. "Caleb—I knew he was gonna open his mouth."

"So it is true," Jessica said.

Sylvia laughed harder. "No."

"Then take off your glasses," Katherine said.

"Let's see those black eyes," Jessica said.

"Andrés is not the one you should be worried about when it's me who's been beating his ass," Sylvia said.

"Bullshit," Katherine replied.

"It's true. He's my moneymaker. My bottom bitch." Sylvia smacked him on the back of his head. "Tell them what I'm talking about."

Andrés leaned back in his chair, his legs spreading wide as if his testicles had grown several sizes. "When I met Sylvia, she had no idea I was out there hustling. When she found out, I convinced her to stop hanging around losers like you—wasting her time with all that spoken word bullshit—and start helping me find classier people to work with."

Sylvia turned to face Andrés and scowled. "You're an asshole."

"Why am I the asshole?" he replied. "You're the one who's always complaining about your Ivy League education getting you nowhere."

"It got me somewhere," Jessica said, "but then again, I'm not the one who dropped out of law school—"

"And graduate school," Katherine added.

"Keep thinking that makes you better than her," Andrés said to Jessica. "What kind of prosecutor trades favors and becomes addicted to heroin?"

"You told him?" Jessica said.

"Of course, I told him," Sylvia said, smiling as if to conceal the anger on her face from moments before. "He's my boyfriend."

Katherine said to Jessica, "I told you she can't be trusted anymore."

"Unbelievable," Jessica said.

Katherine turned to Andrés. "The question I've got now is this: whose dick has she got you sucking?"

"Dick? Oh, no." Sylvia chuckled. "I've got him serving old, white women. A partner from my job saw me talking to Andrés, and she asked me about my *exotic* boyfriend. We talked and came to an understanding, and that's how that partner became my first client. Then she told her friends, who told their friends, and now, thanks to them, I've got Andrés slinging dick all over Carnegie Hill."

"Twenty-four-seven," Andrés said.

"I had no idea old women could be this creepy," Sylvia said. "They're like hyenas, grabbing at him like raw meat."

"Emma, don't be so judgmental. They're making up for lost time," Andrés said.

"True," Sylvia replied. "All those years of being told they needed to be good girls—what did that get them? Husbands with limp dicks."

"Husbands who'd cheat on them with younger women," he said.

"Husbands who'd leave... Yeah, fuck that," Sylvia said. "I can see now why they're the way they are—starving for this kind of attention. Grabbing at him like they're hungry, like they're dying."

Andrés's face scrunched as he tried to hold back his laughter. "We're providing our clients with a *vital* service."

Sylvia cracked a tiny smile at Andrés. "We're saving their lives."

Katherine laughed. "Okay, now I know you guys are not serious."

"When it comes to money," Sylvia said, standing from her chair, "I'm dead serious. And what Caleb saw was Andrés getting his attitude adjusted—the bitch didn't have my money."

"I'm sorry for that—please don't hit me," Andrés said.

As if picking up on his cue, Sylvia smacked Andrés across the face with a full backhand.

Everyone in the café stopped what they were doing to look at her.

Sylvia looked back at them and said, "I caught him cheating."

Everyone turned their attention back to their tables, as if her excuse for assaulting Andrés was understandable.

Jessica looked around, confused. "This can't be real. Are we on Candid Camera?"

"I wish," Andrés said, his face red from Sylvia's handprint.

"Stop whining and tell them why I had to hit you," Sylvia said.

He looked at Katherine and Jessica. "It was Thanksgiving, and I didn't have a turkey for my son, so I took her money to feed him." He glanced at Sylvia, trying to hide his smile. "I'm so sorry... Please don't hit me again, please—"

Sylvia punched Andrés in the jaw, yelling, "Fuck your kid! That was my money!"

Everyone in the café stopped what they were doing to look at Sylvia again.

She pointed at Andrés. "The motherfucker got the bitch pregnant, too."

A woman from a corner of the café yelled, "Hit him again!"

Katherine and Jessica laughed along with everyone else.

Sylvia looked around, sighing, before leaning down to kiss Andrés on the forehead. "You know Mama didn't mean to hit you, but it's the only way you're gonna learn."

"I'm so sorry I ever asked for help," he said.

Sylvia pushed Andrés's head back in disgust. "Stop being a pussy."

"Yes, my mistress. Can I have a day off?"

"Fuck no."

"But my balls are sore, and I feel dehydrated."

"Man up, drink more water, and eat the fucking celery I got for you," Sylvia said, sitting down.

"Help me, please," Andrés pleaded to Katherine and Jessica. "Say something—anything. Nobody should be forced to have sex."

"Then quit; she's not forcing you to stay," Jessica said.

"Yes, she is."

"How?"

"She'll stop talking to me, and I love her—"

"Ignore him. He's acting like a baby." Sylvia looked back at Andrés. "I'm gonna get you some help; spread the load out."

"Thank God," he said.

She turned to her friends. "I'd been planning on adding a Black guy and another Puerto Rican to the mix—anything to make my stable as diverse and inclusive as possible. I want my clients to keep feeling like bad girls without all the guilt that comes from seeing men like Andrés as *exotic*—another fetish—an object."

Andrés said, "Yeah, we're giving our clients the opportunity to say, 'I'm not racist.'"

Sylvia laughed. "They could then tell their friends, 'See how progressive I am.'"

"Now I know you can't be serious," Jessica said.

"We're not," Sylvia said. "The truth is, I'm tired of this square-life bullshit, and I miss my days as Spacer Woman, so—since he knows pimp game—I asked if he'd be down to manage me in our new *business*."

Jessica said, "Oh girl, no."

Katherine said, "If this is true, I'm sorry to hear that."

"What are you saying sorry for? I get the best of both worlds," Sylvia said. "I have a boyfriend who doesn't care what I do for work. As long as I bring in that cash money, it's all good. In return, Andrés is free to fuck whoever he wants, as long as I'm the one who gets to choose, and I'm a part of it. I wanna be fair. I wanna show him my gratitude for keeping me safe. For making sure I don't waste our money on stupid shit—"

"Like drugs," Andrés said. "If she'd rolled with someone good back in the day, someone like my grandfather, who would've made sure she was safe, Sylvia would've gotten what she needed out of her time hustling."

"I was only doing it because I got tired of going through dumpsters for food," Sylvia said. "I couldn't work minimum wage, with the long hours, without it fucking with my studies. And when I did work at jobs that paid decently, and I would ask for hours that didn't get in the way of my studies, I'd always get that one manager who'd say he could help me, but only if I was willing to do something for him." Sylvia laughed. "Yeah, fuck that; I didn't come to New York to fail, and I didn't have anyone back home like you guys did to send me money. I had to be my own savior and get ahead of it before it got ahead of me. But then the Black Room happened... I was forced to drop out of law school."

"A pimp like my grandfather would've made sure something like the Black Room never happened," Andrés said. "He would've chopped up the motherfucker who did what he did to her that night—packing all that coke up her nose, getting her addicted. He would've *handled* that motherfucker—all of them. He would've made them *disappear*."

After a long silence, during which Sylvia appeared to have gone off to a faraway place in her mind, staring into dead space, her eyes returned to the moment.

"Who knows?" Sylvia said. "If I had someone like his grandfather looking out for me back then—if he was anything like Andrés—I know he would've made sure my coke habit didn't escalate. I would've been done with the Master Plan; I would've finished law school, and maybe I'd be the one working for the district attorney... or the FBI... I'm here instead, in this life, but I've changed..."

Sylvia stood up.

"That girl you used to make fun of—she's not the same anymore."

Sylvia began loosening the straps of her long black trench coat, opening it to reveal the ring-linked harness bodysuit of a dominatrix underneath. Her breasts were covered with black electrical tape in the shape of an X.

"I'm awake now—I got my power back."

Katherine whispered to Jessica, her eyes wide with disbelief, "She's lost her mind."

"No," Sylvia said, her voice steady and unwavering. "I got that back too. And now, because you tried to fuck with my sobriety, I want to put the two of you out there and hustle for us."

"You want to pimp us out?" Jessica asked.

"You wanted to pimp me out to Caleb, so why not?" Sylvia said, sitting on Andrés's lap and wrapping her arms around his neck.

"You're fucking nuts," Katherine said.

"How am I nuts? You guys are already trading favors, so why not do it for us?"

"I don't think we could use them," Andrés said. "Jessica's teeth are all fucked up; she'd end up mangling a dude with her mouth. Plus, she's cross-eyed."

"Couldn't we just throw her down by the Holland Tunnel?" Sylvia asked.

"And insult the queens already there? Hell no—they care about how they look," Andrés replied.

"You're right," Sylvia said. "They know how to apply makeup. Jessica doesn't."

Andrés laughed. "She doesn't even know how to apply contour."

"What the fuck?" Jessica said.

"Baby, you know makeup?" Sylvia said, surprised and happy.

"I learned from a queen herself—my aunt."

"I wish I could've met her."

"Estefania would've loved you."

"Of course she would've. I'm awesome." Sylvia looked at Katherine. "How about her?"

"She looks like a crackhead—useless."

"Fuck you," Katherine said.

"It's true," Andrés said. "You've got dark circles under your eyes—you smell like cat food and onion rings—and you have lipstick on your teeth. Not even my Irish bros up in Woodlawn would want you, and they'd fuck anything."

"Woodlawn—the ass-end of the Bronx." Sylvia laughed. "That's awful."

"Enough with this bullshit," Jessica said.

Sylvia glared at her friends. "You've had enough? So have I—bullshit questions about my life, as if you cared, are gonna get you bullshit answers."

"But we do care," Katherine said.

"No, you don't! If you truly cared about me—if we were real friends—you would've never tried pressuring me into letting Caleb back into my life."

Jessica said, "We just didn't want to go into the projects and deal with *those people* for our, you know, *stuff.*"

Sylvia looked at Jessica with disgust. "Those people?"

Katherine said, "Yeah, Sylvia—we try to stay as far away from Avenue D as possible."

"Do you know how many of *them* I've locked up?" Jessica said.

"Fuck you for talking about them like that. Fuck you for locking them up for doing the same shit you're doing, and fuck you for forgetting what Caleb did to me, or does my life not matter to you?"

"It matters," Jessica said, her head bowed.

"We're sorry," Katherine said.

"It's too late for that. And for the record, I brought Andrés down here because I was afraid to be alone with the two of you—that you were bullshitting me, and Caleb would walk in through those doors, and you'd serve me up to him. I'm glad he's disappeared. I hope he never comes back—I don't wanna have to look over my shoulder ever again."

Sylvia stood up from Andrés's lap, buttoned her trench coat, and tied the straps around her waist before taking off her sunglasses. "This is the last time I'm talking about this."

"If you feel so safe with your precious boyfriend, why did you have to punch him?" Jessica asked.

"Yeah, you knew he was gonna open his mouth. So Caleb wasn't lying about that," Katherine said.

"Were you defending yourself?" Jessica asked.

"Did Andrés hit you first?"

"We can see him being that type—abusive; he has such a bad aura, even worse than Caleb's."

Sylvia laughed. "You two with your new-age bullshit."

Katherine laughed. "I refuse to be lectured by someone who reads her horoscope every day."

Jessica turned to Katherine and said, her voice laced with sarcasm, "That's different—Sylvia's looking for *signs*."

"At least I can recognize them. You two..." Sylvia said, shaking her head. "You two can't see for shit—we walked in here, and you watched me boss Andrés around, slap him, and punch him, and you laughed, not once, but twice. You watched me abuse my boyfriend. You saw me hit him hard. You watched me dominate him, and what did he do? He laughed at how funny it was to fuck with you. He may have a *bad* aura, but Andrés has proven to me that he's not that kind of guy. He'd never hit me." Sylvia placed her sunglasses back on. "At least not without my permission, and when he does, it's usually with a paddle to my ass. We're learning rope play now."

"I always knew you were a creep," Jessica said, "but goddamn."

"Yes, I am, and so are you. Don't forget, you wanted me to go down on you and for it not to be gay."

"No, I didn't—"

"Yes, you did—wanting me to fuck you, make you cum, then deny it ever happened is creepy, but whatever. Figure out your hangups, and maybe one day you'll be free and happy like me, and you won't need drugs to escape who you really are. When that day comes, I'll be there for you. I'll help you out of that hell. Until then, deuces."

Sylvia looked at Andrés and said, "Get up."

Andrés did as he was told.

She began to swagger across the room toward the exit.

He followed her until they were outside and standing under a green awning. Sylvia gave Andrés a long, pained look before scowling and walking away.

🙣 *25* 🙣

THE MINOTAURS

JANUARY 15, 1993

IT WAS A FRIDAY NIGHT. ANDRÉS SAT ALONE AT A TABLE IN THE Loft, watching Reginald Superstar stand in the bright spotlight, announcing the names of the slam poets scheduled to read.

Each poet took the stage, jumped around, yelled at the audience, and maybe read a line or two of poetry. One talked about how his mother caught him masturbating. Another talked about her addiction to her model boyfriend. And another, an older man shorter than Sylvia, talked about the cruel joke God had played on him by not making him shorter.

Instead, he said, "I'm a manlet in limbo... If I'd been born a dwarf, I could've been a fetish; I could've had a sex life—it's such a cruel fate."

None of the slam poets were serious; they were like stand-up comedians with no pretense or gravitas.

Andrés now understood why Sylvia had been feeling insecure. She had stopped making them laugh when everyone came to The Loft to get drunk, have fun, and escape their lives.

Maybe that's why she had been acting distant in recent days. On the walk home from Caffè Reggio earlier that week, Sylvia expressed her frustrations with her work as a poet. It upset her so much that when they arrived at her apartment building, she told Andrés she needed to be alone. He didn't hear from her until Thursday night when she called to make sure he would be at The Loft before saying nothing else and hanging up.

The last of the scheduled poets walked off the stage, and the lights inside The Loft came on. People rose from their seats and began to mill about while *A Love Supreme* by John Coltrane played over the sound system. Before he could get up and ask Reginald why Sylvia didn't perform, she appeared from the crowd and took a seat next to him.

"Hey, tough guy," she said. "Did you miss me? Too bad I didn't miss you."

"Yeah, whatever," he said, trying to play off her coldness.

"Whatever? I saw you from the back, laughing at my friends."

"I was laughing, like everybody else. They're so *bad* that they're good."

Sylvia leaned forward, her eyes darkening. "Is that how you feel about my work? That it's bad? That it's bullshit?" She leaned back. "You've got some fucking nerve talking shit when your ass dropped out of high school."

"I don't mean bad in a bad way—"

"Yeah, you do—"

"No, I don't—I love that they don't give a fuck about technique or structure. I love that they don't even care about cadence. It's like music in how it all sounds."

"Did you learn that from studying for your GED?" She shook her head in disgust. "I can't believe you only have a GED."

"Why are you going there? You know why I had to drop out."

"Oh, yeah—join the army, save-a-ho—you dumbass. And you don't need to explain how slam poetry works. I'm not retarded."

"I didn't say you were. You're not hearing me."

"Don't tell me what I'm not hearing. My education did get me somewhere. You? You're nothing." Sylvia waved dismissively. "You're not even on my level; you're a loser—that's why your ass barely passed finals."

"That's what I get for making you my world."

She laughed to herself before saying, "Baby, you don't have to worry about me anymore—I'm about to do us both a favor."

The sound of *A Love Supreme* faded out over the venue's sound system. The spotlights around the stage became brighter while the rest of the room darkened.

"That's my cue." Sylvia stood up and began walking toward the stage.

Reginald appeared. "Are you guys ready to keep the night going?"

The audience yelled back, "Yeah!"

"That's what I wanna hear—a bunch of drunks looking for more fun... more knowledge. I won't deny you, especially from our next performer, who, right now, is scaring me." Reginald laughed. "I don't know what my man has done, but Andrés, I've gotta warn you—you're in for it. Ladies and gentlemen, give it up for Sylvia!"

The audience clapped as she sauntered onto the stage. She snatched the microphone from Reginald's hands and shoved him aside, taking his place in the spotlight. She brought the microphone to her lips, held it there for a long moment, and relaxed her face so that her eyes were half-lidded and soft. After a long pause, she scanned the room until she made eye contact with Andrés.

"I'm dating this guy," she said.

"I mean, I like him, I think.

"I used to like him a lot,

"But not anymore.

"Not like before.

"Not as much as I now like my delivery boy."

She began to pace the stage.

"My delivery boy is a good boy.

"He does everything I ask of him.

"He's my motherfucking white knight—

"My Prince Charming—

"Unlike the guy I'm dating, who never has time for me,

"And when he does, he acts like he calls the shots.

"He's in no position to call the shots.

"My boyfriend came over one night,

"And while we waited for my delivery boy

"To bring us our Chinese takeout,

"He read me a poem he'd written about fate.

"I had to bite my tongue to keep from laughing in his face.

"When my delivery boy finally arrived,

"My boyfriend asked me to put on a shirt—

"But I didn't listen—I answered the door naked,

"My boyfriend became angry—"

Someone from the back yelled, "Who the fuck does Andrés think he is?"

Sylvia stopped pacing the stage, briefly dropping the facade to look at the heckler in the audience as if she were an idiot.

"I don't know... Someone who loves me... Someone I love... But that's not the point—shut up—let me perform."

She began to pace the stage again.

"I'm trying to say something about energy and dominance, about trying to act like a shot-caller, which my man can't do anymore.

"'Cause that night,

"When we tried to fuck,

"His cock wasn't working right.

"My man's excuse?

"He said he was in pain.

"He asked me to check him out.

"I looked at all the red bumps on his face and chest.

"I tried not to show how much I'd become scared.

"If we hadn't exchanged blood tests,

"I would've thought he had AIDS,

"Instead of the bumps being just another injury

"From his Gulf War deployment."

Sylvia returned to the spotlight and looked at Andrés.

"He can't call the shots anymore,

"'Cause that night,

"When we tried to fuck,

"His cock wasn't working right.

"My man's excuse?

"He said his mind was in another place...

"I know my man,

"And I know his mind was far off in some desert landscapes,

"Dreaming of bullets and death.

"People, I hooked up with a man who had to kill just to be here—

"To continue to be here.

"That should worry me.

"It should worry me that my friends say his aura seems off,

"Especially now when this motherfucker is getting to be too much!

"Demanding me to be this or that—

"Demanding me to wear that or this—

"Demanding me to cover my tits

"When answering the door for my good little delivery boy.

"Motherfucker—I do what I want 'cause I'm the one who earns my paper.

"And my paper pays for my space,

"And my space dictates my peace.

"And I want back my peace—

"I want back my space—

"So get out of my space—

"Get out of my head—

"I hate that I got soft.

"I want the old me back,

"And I'm back, saying to you—Andrés,

"My work is not bullshit!

"Get yourself a *square* bitch,

"'Cause we're through!"

The audience erupted into thunderous applause. It was the loudest Andrés had heard since that night in September when she first read her ode. Despite their validation, instead of joy, Sylvia trembled as she handed the microphone to Reginald. After wrapping his arm around her shoulder and waiting for the applause to subside, Reginald laughed and asked, "Now that you're back, are you going to be making shampoo horns again?"

She pushed Reginald away and quickly walked off the stage, ignoring both him and the audience's laughter.

Andrés shot up from his seat and welcomed Sylvia back to the table with his arms crossed tightly over his chest.

"What did you think?" Sylvia asked, her face blank.

"That's the last time I open myself up to you—to anyone," he said, his jaw clenching, the muscles in his face tightening with restrained anger. "But whatever—it doesn't matter anymore. We're through, right?"

"Right."

"Then on to the next—I'm out." Andrés grabbed his coat and walked away.

Sylvia followed him out of The Loft and into the freezing, cold, empty streets without her coat. She grabbed him from behind and turned him around by the shoulder. "So that's it? You're just gonna walk away? Like I'm nothing?"

"You broke up with me."

"So? You can at least fight to keep me."

"You wanna fight?"

Sylvia pushed him. "Fight for me!"

"Fine... Your work is not bullshit. You're the one who told me to roll with it—to come up with a story off the top of my head when I can't even think straight half the time. But yeah, I think you could be doing so much more with your life."

She shoved him. "You think I don't know that? You're a guy; I have to put up with way more crap, and half the time, I'm not taken seriously. And why do you think I take temp jobs to begin with? I'm trying to network. I'm trying to show that I can do the job—that the things said about me after I dropped out of law school aren't true—but it doesn't seem to matter. You? I bet you could walk into an office, talk bro-shit, and—"

Sylvia suddenly began to cough loudly, her body convulsing with the force of it, her face turning red.

Andrés tried to drape his coat over her shoulders.

She pushed it away, gasping for air. "I don't want it."

"Can you at least go back inside?" he asked, trying to hide his fear —the sudden terror he felt from seeing her body convulse as if she were drowning.

"Fuck no," she said, straightening herself and trying to breathe normally again.

Andrés waited a moment, watching her intently to make sure she was fine, before saying, "Then I'm leaving."

"Then I'm following."

"I'm done arguing."

"But I'm not."

"Then say what you've got to say and go back inside—you've been coughing way too much lately, and it's starting to scare me."

"I've been coughing like this all my life, so don't worry about it. And when I said 'roll with it,' I meant play along—not put me down in front of my friends. I know I'm a loser."

"You're not a loser—your friends are."

Sylvia hunched her shoulders against the cold and stared at the ground. "I thought being homeless was my rock bottom, but I was wrong. I've got a loser making me feel like a loser—it doesn't get lower than that." She looked up. "I might as well fuck Caleb."

Andrés threw his arms up in frustration. "There it goes—the moment I've been waiting for."

"Ka-boom, motherfucker," Sylvia said with a dead expression.

"Go for it! See what that gets you."

She laughed. "Better dick, I'm sure. I wonder where he's gone. It's been a while since I've seen him, and I need to know if his dick is better than yours."

"I thought you would've known that by now."

"Why would you think that?"

"He knew you back when you were Spacer Woman."

Sylvia pushed him away, disgusted. "No, asshole, I didn't fuck him. Even I had my standards back then. It was not until I fucked you that I realized I could now fuck anything."

The precision of her punch to his ego hurt more than any blow he had ever taken to his body. There was no way to respond to her jab without taking the bait and, in his frustration, letting her in on his secret. "Well, good luck finding him, 'cause now you'll never know."

"Hold up," she said, as if realizing what he was admitting. "Is that what you had to handle? Did you make him *disappear?*"

Andrés looked away so his facial expression wouldn't reveal his answer.

She smiled. "Is that how much you love me? That you killed him?"

"Goddammit, I don't wanna love you this much."

"You did! You killed him!"

"Shut up!"

"You can talk your shit and act like I'm nothing—like it'd be easy to move on—but you're still out here, in the cold, looking after me. You even killed a man to protect me. There's no one out here like me."

"This is New York! There are plenty of women out here like you."

"Like me?" She laughed, amused by how cold he was trying to act. "Andrés, your goofy-ass is generic as fuck. There are about ten of you on every block, with the same haircut, the same body, and even the same dumbass smile. The difference between you and them is that you haven't served time yet—not until they find that idiot's body, which I know they never will. I know how you special forces guys roll."

"Stop that shit!"

"No!"

"Fine—since we're going there, okay? You're the same generic, dime-a-dozen—basic—is-she-Black-or-is-she-a-White-girl—who comes from nowhere with big hopes and dreams and tries to open herself up to the city but ends up opening her legs instead."

Sylvia shoved him. "How can you say that?" She shoved him again. "After everything you know about me, to call me a dime-a-dozen? Basic?"

"You are—"

Sylvia threw a punch at Andrés.

He caught her fist mid-air.

"Let go!" she yelled.

"You're not gonna hit me, are you?"

"Let go!"

He dropped her fist.

She threw a punch at him again.

He caught her fist in mid-air again. He swung her around by the hand and slammed her down against the sidewalk.

She began to laugh while writhing on the pavement.

He became terrified of her—and of what he could do to her if she attacked again—and fled.

Sylvia jumped to her feet and charged down the desolate street after him, her red hair streaming behind her like a banner of fire. She caught up and leaped onto his back, locking her arms around his neck from behind.

He bucked and swung around, trying to fling her off. He tripped and fell backward, crashing through the doors of a tenement building and slamming their bodies sideways against the vestibule wall inside.

Sylvia swung her body around his, bringing them face-to-face, her arms still clinging to his neck. She began kissing him and, in the pauses between breaths, said, "Pushing a man's buttons, it's like playing with knives. Turning frustration into passion, it's like playing with knives. I knew I could pull this off. Tonight, I'm the motherfucking Domme—"

"What the fuck?" he said, trying to push her off. "You didn't say 'time-in!'"

She stopped kissing to stare deeply into his eyes. "Baby, I want us to learn how to play without saying a thing. No more lines. No more the saying of our words. It breaks the spell, and I want magic—the Beautiful Ballet. I want us to learn how to Tango, with you dancing with me forever. So pay attention, look for my signs—when to lead, when to follow—when to lead, when to follow—"

"With what we do? We could end up killing each other."

"So? Then pay attention and don't slip."

"No, that's not gonna work—I've gotta go."

"You're not going anywhere," Sylvia said, wrapping her arms and legs tighter around his body. She started kissing him again.

Andrés tried to push her off.

She grabbed and pulled on his hair to keep herself on him.

"Constance," he whispered under his breath.

"Constance is not here to save you—I am," Sylvia whispered back.

Something in him switched. It caused him to surrender to her dominance, to relax every muscle in his body locked between her legs —in her arms. It made him say under his breath, "Then save me."

She slid off his body to stand before him. She ripped open his button-down shirt. She traced her lips from his bare chest to his belly button. She unbuckled his belt and pushed his boxers and pants down to his ankles.

He kicked off his shoes and stomped out of his boxers and pants. He shoved Sylvia against the wall. He unbuckled her belt. He pushed her panties and jeans down to her ankles.

She leaned down to peel off her panties and jeans from her shoes. She tossed them to the floor. She swung around and placed both hands on the wall.

He pressed himself against her from behind. He pulled back her hair. He pushed himself inside.

She banged her ass against his hips. She moaned louder with each thrust, the side of her face pressed against the wall.

He swung her around and ripped open her blouse; buttons flew into every corner of the vestibule. He buried his face between her breasts to kiss her heartbeat pounding through her chest.

She moaned and pulled his hair.

He brought his face to hers. He kissed her with desperation.

She bit hard at his bottom lip.

He tasted his blood on her teeth.

She dropped her hands from his hair. She jumped on him, wrapping her arms around his neck, facing him.

He held her body up. His hands cupped her ass.

Her legs dangled over his large arms.

His cock slid back deep inside her, thrusting.

Her legs swung wildly. She clutched the back of his neck. She bucked her hips into his. Her wild, angry eyes glared back at him.

Someone on the next floor opened the door to their apartment and yelled down the stairs, "You crackheads better stop with that bullshit!"

Sylvia stopped bucking on Andrés to look away long enough to yell back at the stairs, "Go back to sleep, old man!"

The door slammed shut on the next floor.

Sylvia turned her focus back to Andrés, bucking hard on him again.

Their grunts and groans echoed through the halls.

Their long, deep moans carried through the hallway, growing louder and more intense, becoming piercing yells that echoed off the walls.

Their bodies exploded into each other, vibrating from head to toe, shuddering with their mouths wide open, gasping until their breathing became slow, hushed moans.

It was at this moment, in the vestibule of a tenement building on the Lower East Side of Manhattan, just before midnight on January 15, 1993, that Sylvia and Andrés stood eyeball to eyeball and glimpsed their supernature:

They were minotaurs in The Labyrinth.

They loved each other for it and feared each other because of it.

Sylvia and Andrés were both alive and awake in the silence—more alive and awake than they had ever been in their lives.

Her face was bright, and her hair was blown out.

He pushed himself away and stayed across from her.

She was gasping for air and slumped against the wall, her near-naked body welcoming more chaos—more passion—until a pained expression appeared on her face. "You said, 'Constance,' and I kept going—"

"Because I was saying yes—"

"No, you weren't—"

"But my body was—"

"I fucked up—I fucked up." Sylvia tried buttoning her blouse before realizing her buttons were gone. She knelt to grab her panties and jeans off the piss-stained floor.

Andrés stepped outside in his socks, shirt ripped open, naked from the waist down, to grab his coat from where it had fallen during their struggle outside the door. He returned, draping it around her near-naked body.

"I love you," she said.

"I love you, too."

"We can't be around each other; we can't," she said, running out of the vestibule and outside as if escaping a burning building.

Andrés slumped against the wall in a daze, wondering how everything had fallen apart so quickly.

❧ 26 ❧

DECEMBER CAME AND WENT

MARCH 5, 1993

[1]

It was a Friday night. Andrés was seated at a table in a dimly lit room in The Loft, watching the emcee of the poetry slam scan the crowd from the stage.

The emcee announced, "Once again, for those who are new, my name is Reginald Superstar. Thank you for making The Loft a part of your night. No disrespect to our featured readers; they're all brilliant, but I think they'd all agree that we've saved the best for last."

"No, we don't!" someone yelled from the back.

Reginald laughed. "It's all a matter of opinion. I'll leave it up to you, good people, to decide. Put your hands together and give it up for Sylvia."

The audience clapped as she walked onto the stage, dressed in a long pajama shirt, flannel pajama pants, and bunny slippers. Her auburn hair was slicked back into a bushy ponytail. She wore no makeup on her gaunt face. Her eyes appeared empty and dull.

Reginald handed Sylvia the microphone and nudged her to step into the spotlight before walking away. Despite the audience's outpouring of support and cheers, Sylvia didn't seem to want the spotlight.

"Settle down, people, settle down. I'm only here because I have a routine to keep. I need to get this out of the way so I can go back home," she said.

Her eyes were clear, conveying her seriousness, as she waited for the audience to settle into a silence reserved only for the burial of the dead.

All became quiet.

She wrapped both hands around the microphone, held it close to her mouth, and whispered, in a low voice, "A word to my broken heart."

When someone from the back laughed and said in a low voice, "What the fuck?" Sylvia said, "Yeah, I wrote a poem about my heart—I have one, and it's broken right now, so please, show some respect.

"I don't know how I let it get broken...

"You, my people, how often do I stand before you and amuse you with stories drawn from my life, set to some cadence and flow?

"You, my people, how often have I left you with a smile and, before him, a good vibe?

"You, my people, how often does that smile—that good vibe—help you have a better night when all is said and done?

"Just as I did some good for you, then, please, I need you, my people, to do some good for me now.

"I need you to bear witness to my suffering—

"Being treated like a loser,

"A dime-a-dozen, basic, ordinary girl—

"A woman who's not fit to be around children

"Because I was once a slave to my sirens."

She began to pace slowly across the stage.

"At what point will I stop being judged for not being a superwoman?

"For not being stronger?

"Everyday life kicks us in the teeth.

"Some days, it's a wonder we can get out of bed and face

"What we know will be a day filled with misery and sadness,
"Even when we're happy."
She walked back to stand in the spotlight.
"This is my fault.
"At a time in my life when I didn't have it in me to feel,
"I let him in.
"I don't know why I let him in.
"Some fairy tale belief in the recognition?
"This is what I get for believing in bedtime stories.
"In fairy tales."
She looked up wistfully at the lights above, causing her teary eyes to twinkle like stars.
"I don't regret letting him in,
"Even though I hate him."
She looked at the audience.
"I hate myself more for falling for a man who,
"If he asked me to smile, I would.
"I'm an idiot.
"I hate myself more for falling for a man who has nothing, like me,
"But his future seemed filled with possibility.
"I'm a fool.
"A man who didn't deserve the power of my mind,
"Who had said, time after time, over and over,
"I was the smartest person he'd ever known.
"Such a boost to my ego...
"But the way he'd look at me when we talked said, *I can learn so much*.
"I knew he wasn't trying to buy my favor.
"At least that's what I thought.
"I'm not sorry for anything I've ever said.
"For sometimes pointing out how flawed he is.
"He's too stupid to see that if I didn't care,
"If I wasn't crazy in love with him,
"I wouldn't have given his flaws any thought.
"I'd just keep fucking him.
"Kick his ass out the door when I'm done."

She began to pace the stage.

"He would've stayed.

"He would've stayed and enjoyed staying

"Unless he had to get back to his son.

"But I guess there could never be an us

"If I'll always be someone

"Who was addicted to heroin,

"Not fit to be around children,

"Around his son,

"Even though I'm now sober.

"I just knew he'd be the rock I'd crash upon.

"I knew he'd break his promise—"

She paused her performance to take a step back and cover her mouth, trying not to show how angry she was with herself and how sad she had become.

When someone from the audience called out, "It's okay, girl—let it out," she couldn't hold back anymore and burst out crying.

She dropped the microphone to the floor, fell to her knees, and yelled, her voice cracking, "Forgive me for letting myself go like this!

"Crying on stage!

"Shit!

"Goddammit!

"For him to judge me like that!

"For him to make promises like that!

"December came and went!

"Did he think I would not notice?

"After turning me inside out?

"After fucking me from the inside out?

"After getting me to believe he's my One,

"I still haven't met his son!"

She cried hard on stage for a moment, burying her face in her hands, until she looked back at the stunned audience and yelled, "To then throw away a woman like me,

"To then be told there'll be another one like me,

"As if women like me are a dime-a-dozen?

"In New York, I guess we all are—"

Someone from the back yelled, "We're not a dime-a-dozen! Andrés is a jerk."

Sylvia crawled to where the microphone had rolled, picked it up from the floor, stood up, and shook her head. The audience remained silent as she composed herself before forcing a smile.

"That he is," she said, "but it's all good.

"I know my worth.

"Nana would say, 'Athena, this is another of life's lessons: Your worth is not defined by a man, nor by anyone—not even by your past. Every day, you wake up as a new woman. So let it all go. Yesterday is no more. You must always move on.'"

Sylvia looked up at the lights above again, her eyes no longer watery but still twinkling, this time from the newfound determination on her face.

"I get it, old woman.

"I now understand why you were so hard on me.

"I can hear you from beyond the grave.

"'Books before boys.

"'Don't get yourself distracted.

"'Nothing else matters.'"

Sylvia laughed to herself.

"Okay, Nana, I'll get it done—I swear.

"I'll complete the Master Plan."

She looked at the audience before kneeling, placing her palm on the stage floor.

"This will be the last night I'm distracted.

"This will be the last time I put a man before my mission.

"This will be the last night he lives in my head.

"This will be the last poem that is about him."

She let out a small, genuine smile. "Thank you, my people.

"Thank you for listening.

"Thank you for being my witness."

The audience began to clap. Sylvia pushed herself off the floor and handed the microphone to Reginald, who hugged her before she walked off the stage.

A pain crept inside Andrés, causing him to feel so much shame that he pushed himself up from his seat and headed toward the exit. He had felt Sylvia's grueling pain for days after the World Trade Center bombing on February 26, 1993. Since then, he resisted every call he thought he heard from her, shouting at him from across time and space to show up uninvited at her apartment and check on her.

He went to The Loft instead. And now, as he was on his way out, Andrés glimpsed Sylvia at the bar in the room's far corner. She was leaning against the counter, looking at an empty glass while the bartender talked. At that moment, Sylvia's focus shifted away from the glass and towards Andrés. It froze him inside, making him stop just long enough to see her gaze transform into a scowl.

Sylvia got up, walked over to him, and asked, her tone laced with anger, "Why didn't you come over? I didn't know you were here. Were you hiding, trying to avoid me?"

"What were your last words?" he replied.

"I don't remember—"

"'We can't be around each other.'"

"I did say that."

"I'm trying to respect your boundaries."

"So what—you have nothing else to say? Like, 'I miss you'?"

"Of course I miss you. I've missed you so much."

Sylvia smiled as if hearing him say those words gave her great relief. "Well, that's too bad; I didn't miss you. That poem wasn't about you."

He smiled. "Clearly, it wasn't... I didn't recognize some of the parts."

"That's because I'm a writer. I'll bend the truth to speak the truth, and you know I'm right. And if you were speaking the truth and really did miss me, you would've come home. You know where I'm trying to take our dance. I was waiting."

"But you said—"

"I know what I said, but we can't keep spelling things out for each other—the next level of our dance has to be that Beautiful Ballet."

"The old lady got to you."

"Yes, she did," Sylvia said. "I think about her every day."

"I guess the truth is... I didn't come down because my life blew up.

I don't wanna say more because it's not your problem; my emotions are no longer yours to filter through."

"I think we're past that."

"I watched you cry on stage. You broke up with me on stage."

"I did do that," she said, looking down and away from him.

"Yeah, you did—'We're through,' remember?"

Sylvia looked up. "You take me so literally."

"I have to. With the things that we do, when you say 'yes,' it's 'yes.' When you say 'no,' it's 'no.' And when you say 'Constance,' it's—"

"Maybe I don't care anymore."

"And that scares me."

"You shouldn't be," she said. "If you knew me as well as you say you do, you'd be able to read between the lines."

"When it comes to our games, I can't take that chance."

"Maybe I'll find someone who will."

"You say that now, but when that person slips and hurts you, you'll remember me."

She smiled. "No, I won't."

"I know what you're trying to do, you fucking brat—"

"You see? You could read me! You know how to dance with me!"

Andrés said nothing, trying hard not to smile.

Sylvia grabbed his hand. "Wanna head back home and keep dancing?" she asked.

He hesitated. "I don't know if that's a good idea."

"It'd be no strings attached," she replied, her voice taking on a bratty tone that he secretly loved. "I mean, I can just say, 'You owe me for making me cry.' You did make a grown woman cry, didn't you?"

"Okay, okay—"

"Great! Let me grab my stuff."

After she went backstage to grab her purse and long, black trench coat, she came back and left The Loft with him. They walked in silence until she spoke up. "If I said, 'Let's go to The Labyrinth instead,' would you say yes?"

"I don't think that's a good idea."

Sylvia shrugged. "That's fine. I'll go by myself."

"That's on you; I don't control you."

She grabbed his hand. "You control Emma. You remember her, don't you?"

Andrés didn't respond.

She shook his hand away. "You don't remember her anymore? Did you meet someone new?"

"Maybe… maybe not. How about you?"

"What about me? Am I fucking anyone new?"

"If that's how you wanna say it."

She smiled mischievously. "Maybe I am."

"Well, whoever it is, I hope they're blowing your back out, you brat."

"You see? You did it again! I can't wait for us to get home. Let's go."

[2]

Sylvia rushed him along the moonlit back streets until they stood in front of her building. She led Andrés inside, upstairs, into her apartment, and straight into her bedroom.

In the darkness, she was just a voice demanding that he take off his clothes.

In the darkness, he did as he was told, his memory guiding him back to bed.

From across the room, he could feel her breathing as she undressed.

"Can you see me?" she asked.

"No, I can't."

"Now you can." Sylvia flung open the curtains to let the moonlight spread wide across the walls of the Purple Room, casting her body in silhouette and giving full shape to her spirit.

In the moonlight, she beckoned for him to come.

In the moonlight, he got up from the bed to stand next to her at the window.

"Look at the face of the moon," she said. "Does it remind you of anything?"

"No."

"You can't see it? The open mouth? The wide eyes? It looks kind of goofy, don't you think?"

"I guess."

"It's the same goofy face you make when you're about to cum, which you won't be doing tonight because I'm not gonna fuck you—get out. Get the fuck out, you dumb motherfucker! How could you think I still wanted you after making me cry on stage? Yeah, we're still done. Go jerk yourself off, you jackass."

Andrés laughed. "All that work—just to lure me up here, and for what? To get yourself wet?"

"I'm not wet," she said.

"Bullshit! I can smell how wet you are! So raw—I love it."

"You don't think I could take care of that myself?"

"So you haven't hooked up with anyone new?"

"I have—"

"Call him over—I'll watch."

Sylvia stuttered, "I don't wanna do that. That's none of your business."

Andrés went back to pick up the clothes he had tossed along the side of the bed.

"What are you doing?" she asked.

"I'm gonna hit up a club... find someone down to fuck."

Sylvia waved him off dismissively. "You're not gonna find anyone."

"You don't think I can?"

"Your game ain't that good."

"Alright, give me an hour, and I'll be back here with my hookup. You can watch and take care of yourself at the same time."

Sylvia charged at him like a bull, tackling him onto the bed and pinning his shoulders. She climbed on top of him, straddling his hips.

He laughed. "Now that's what I'm talking about."

"Shut up," she said. "You're gonna get her dry."

"Your pussy is getting old."

"She doesn't give a shit what you think."

"I don't give a fuck if you cum."

She took him inside her. "Then you better get yours before I get mine."

There was a rawness to how Sylvia pressed her body against Andrés, grinding her hips into his, breathing hard, and clawing at his chest.

An even greater rawness came from the way he pumped his body into hers. He pulled Sylvia's ponytail back, tilting her head and face to the ceiling.

She let out a long moan before swinging her head forward to look into his eyes, placing her hands on his chest just below his neck.

He moaned, "Go ahead, do it."

"Are you sure?" she asked.

"It's what you've always wanted to try, right?"

"It's been my fantasy."

"Then let me be your fantasy."

"You're not gonna freak out? Push me off?"

"Have you freaked out on me?"

"No—"

"Then do it."

"Are you sure?"

"How can you trust me if I'm not ready to be in your position?"

Sylvia's eyes blazed upon hearing his words. "You don't know how much more I just fell in love with you. I love you so much!"

"I was born to love you."

"Me too!"

"Keep going—let me be your fantasy."

Sylvia moved her hand from his chest to grip his neck. She hesitated to press her fingers against the sides of his carotid arteries, but he said, "Do it," and she did—squeezing and pressing as he squirmed and moaned beneath her. She rode him harder, faster, her grip tightening, her eyes beaming bright like twinkling stars that dissolved along with her hands on his neck. They dissolved along with her body grinding on his lap, dissolving into him, joining herself to him to become One, in what was no longer her Purple Room, but the sinking feeling of being deep in a cosmic ocean of clear blue water, with bubbles of light swirling around him, around her, now swimming toward him, her hands outstretched to pull him in close, her eyes flashing like underwater spotlights.

When he felt himself pulled into her arms, he was no longer Andrés de León, and she was no longer Sylvia James, but one being created by God—their whole body tingling, their whole body vibrating, and what they would construe as their back began to arch high to explode their whole being inward, blowing away what they would construe as the mind—now splitting back into two, with her now separating from him, and him now separating from her, to become two distinct souls once again, no longer in the vast blue of a cosmic ocean, but back in her Purple Room, with her atop him, her hand no longer on his neck, her smile wide across a smug, satisfied expression as she asked, "Did I blow your back out?"

He smiled with his eyes, unable to move, barely able to whisper, "I feel Space."

"Now you know why I need it."

"I don't know what I just saw... but I do."

"I'll tell you later; it's my turn." She rolled off of him, flipping onto her back.

Andrés gave himself a moment to recover from the vision he experienced during the most intense orgasm of his life—intense enough to make him feel as though he had transcended to someplace beyond, to a place where they were more than mere physical beings, but rather something beyond the ordinary world, something eternal and perfect and one with each other—before sitting up on his knees, his head still dizzy.

As best as he could, he said, "Before we go on, we need to confirm: if you want to stop, if you need me to stop, how many fingers do you hold up?"

Sylvia flashed three fingers.

"Now repeat to me the number of fingers we're using."

"Three."

"And if I see anything unusual, I will stop."

"Agreed, you stop."

"And to confirm one more time, what's our safe word?"

"Constance."

"Repeat it to me again."

"Constance."

Andrés moved from his knees to sit on the bed, legs crossed, his body still aroused from head to toe.

Sylvia sat on his lap and inhaled, holding her breath as she took him in again, wrapping her arms and legs around his torso, and exhaling when he was fully inside her.

"Are you ready?" Andrés asked.

She tilted her head back. "Yes—I'm ready."

He placed his right hand on her exposed neck and his fingertips against her carotid arteries. With his left hand, he cupped her ass.

She began to ride him slowly.

He began to press his fingers gently.

Sylvia's eyes rolled back, showing only white, her lips curling into a snarl. In that moment, Andrés knew where her mind was going—realizing, after his own experience, where it had been heading all along since their first night at the heart of The Labyrinth—back to the deep blue ocean, where she reached out for his hand, grabbed it, and pulled him to her, becoming whole again, becoming One, until her insides quivered, and she let out a long moan.

He felt her return from the beyond, opening her eyes in the ordinary world—now made beautiful—with her now pressing her body against him, burying his face against her chest, and with their teeth chattering, their breathing stuttering, their bodies shuddering as they collapsed backward onto the bed, basking in the feel of Space together —with her on top of him, now lying in the long silence, their hearts pounding against their chests.

[3]

"This is it," Sylvia whispered. "This is the Beautiful Ballet."

"I knew it—I fucking knew it," he said, trying to catch his breath.

She rolled off his body to lie next to him, trying to catch hers. After another long moment of silence, she asked, "Would you really watch me fuck another guy?"

"Hell no! I just wanted to add to the dance. Make you cum harder."

"I knew it! God, I love dancing with you! And you came on the night I decided to read that poem?"

"There are no coincidences," he said.

"I know, right? And something told me to go to The Loft. I'm so glad I listened." She paused, her smile gone. "I'd been so depressed—I haven't left my apartment in weeks. I lost my job at the South Tower, which was for the best—I wasn't there for the bombing. You may have saved my life, so I can't be too mad at you, but you should've come home—you should've checked on me. But you know what? It doesn't matter anymore. You're here now. Let's get some sleep, and when we wake up, we can go grab some waffles."

"I can't. Andy is with my parents, and I need to be home before he wakes up." Andrés stood and gathered his clothes off the floor.

"Why?" Sylvia asked, watching him dress.

"It's been a rough month for both of us."

"But what happened?"

"Don't act like you don't know," Andrés said. "I know you've been talking with Mom."

"Miss Petra is my friend, yeah, but since that night, anything having to do with you, she's shut me out. I'm like, fair enough."

"The Monday after we last saw each other, Lydia was supposed to pick Andy up from daycare. But when I got home from the VA, I found out she never showed up. Andy's daycare had to get my parents involved. They told them he'd been freaking out, crying, 'Where's Mommy?'"

"Aw, poor baby."

"Now my dad is calling me a bum, telling me I should worry more about my son than school. If I'd been paying attention, I would've noticed Lydia was still drinking. I would've realized she'd be too drunk to remember it was her turn—to remember anything... I thought she was getting better."

"I was hoping she would," Sylvia said.

"I guess I was deluding myself, not wanting to see the obvious... I just want my son to have a mother. Now my dad's talking shit, saying I'm not a good father, that I'm not providing everything my son needs.

So yeah, I have to be home before Andy wakes up—I don't want my dad putting me down in front of him—"

She interrupted Andrés. "Can I come with you? Can I meet Andy?"

He smiled. "Are you ready?"

"Yes!"

"That means he'll be there every time you come over. Lydia's no longer taking him. I have sole custody now."

Sylvia clapped her hands with excitement. "I can't believe it's finally happening."

"Me too. But you have to be sure: if you meet Andy, you don't push me away—you don't get up on a stage again and say, 'We're through.' We step out of our bubble, and he becomes part of our relationship."

Sylvia appeared confused. "Why are you coming at me like this? You do want me to meet him, don't you?"

Andrés hesitated for a moment. "I think I do."

"You think? You're not sure?"

"You broke up with me."

"You're the one who's acting like an asshole, making me feel like I'm not good enough to be around your son! You're the one who called me a loser! I could've met him sooner if you'd just brought him down like I'd told you to, but no—December came and went!"

"I can explain."

"You know what? It doesn't matter! I don't wanna meet him anymore. I don't wanna be his mother; I don't wanna be anything—for what? To end up with his toys and shit in my apartment?—like he lives here? Fuck that. Go! Get the fuck out!"

Andrés finished getting dressed. He went to Sylvia, who was sitting on the bed, breathing hard in her rage. He looked at her, searching for the right way to say what needed to be said so she could stop feeling the way she had been feeling—like she wasn't good enough.

"Before I go," he said, "can I explain what happened? Why December came and went?"

She appeared uncertain but nodded her consent.

Andrés said, "I don't understand that kind of sign language."

"You can stay."

He paused before saying, "Sometimes... I hate that I have this thing in me that notices all the small stuff. Everywhere we'd go, I'd note all the exits around us, so that if we had to get out quickly, I could get you to safety. I'd pay attention to everyone around us—what they're holding and what their bodies are saying as they pass us."

"Okay... And?"

"After our first night in The Labyrinth, I started noticing Caleb everywhere we went, following us from a distance."

"For real?"

"Yup... That night, after you read *1968*—before he came at us the way he did—I saw him in the alley next to The Loft. For days after that, I kept seeing him trying to hide near the playground across the street. Whenever we went out, he would follow us from there, and whenever we came home, he'd go back to hiding."

"I swear, I never noticed," Sylvia said.

"Just because you stopped looking over your shoulder doesn't mean he stopped being Caleb."

"Why didn't you tell me?"

"I should've, but I didn't wanna scare you. You'd been fine all these years without me. Maybe you'd be fine until I could figure out what needed to be done. It wasn't until that night, when he brought you that packet, that I realized what I had to do. I couldn't wait, especially since I'd started having dreams about you and my son at the bottom of the slide at that playground. I'm not around for whatever reason, and Caleb appears, and he—"

"He would do what?" Sylvia asked anxiously.

Andrés began to tremble.

Sylvia pulled him down to sit next to her on the bed. "Caleb would do what?"

When Andrés didn't respond, and his eyes started flickering nervously around the room, Sylvia pulled him into her arms. She squeezed him, trying to stop what his body was signaling: he was about to have a full-blown panic attack.

Andrés began crying, terrified by the vision that came through his dreams—what Caleb would have done to his family if he hadn't acted; Caleb would have taken their lives.

"I can't... I can't let anything happen to you guys," he said, crying.

"I had to keep Andy away... I had to *handle* Caleb before he could handle you—before he could handle my son."

Sylvia pushed Andrés away from her to look at him frantically. "Are we safe?"

Andrés nodded.

"Are you for real?"

Andrés nodded.

"When I was pushing your buttons, I thought you were just playing along, you know, for the sake of the dance... I never thought." Sylvia looked away, burying her face in her hands and crying uncontrollably. She cried long and hard, howling with what sounded like relief at being freed from the greatest threat to her existence.

It was at this point that Andrés realized he had placed Sylvia in greater danger. He had jeopardized her freedom by making himself vulnerable to her, telling her more than she needed to know. He could also hear his mother in his mind calling him a faggot for crying in front of his girlfriend. He could hear Petra yelling at him to take a deep breath and swallow all his feelings because "boys don't cry, especially when they become men. And you're a man, right?"

He forced himself to take a deep breath and swallow the terror he felt from the vision We, the Watchers, had given him—a future where, if he didn't have the will to do what needed to be done, Sylvia and Andy would have been murdered on June 26, 1998.

Andrés wouldn't have been in the park with them because Caleb would've killed him earlier that day. He would have snuck up on Andrés as he was leaving his office on Wall Street and shot him in the back of the head in front of a stunned crowd, too shocked to stop Caleb from fleeing to the nearest subway station.

We denied Andrés that part of the vision of what could have been so that, in dealing with Caleb, he would act out of love for Sylvia and Andy rather than out of self-preservation. Because of this, on June 26, 1998, we will bless Andrés with a new vision to help him bear what is to come—2,785 days of soul-crushing loneliness and misery.

Until then, Sylvia and Andrés had to get through this moment.

He stood up from where he had been sitting next to her in bed, cleared his face, and took another deep breath. Then he decided to say what needed to be said to set her free from what had become a new, greater danger—prison.

"I didn't say I killed him," Andrés said.

Sylvia stopped crying and raised her eyes to him, as if disappointed. "No?"

"I handled him."

"Well, can you tell me how? What does that mean? Is he still alive?"

"Maybe... maybe not—"

"Stop that!"

Andrés sighed. "Can I trust you with the truth? Without worrying that you're gonna write a poem about it?"

"I would never do that."

He paused as if reconsidering—remembering how, when Sylvia first read *1968,* she revealed Constance's secret. "It's best that you don't know. If people start to ask questions, they'll see no lie on your face."

"But is Caleb still out there?"

"I need you to hear what I'm trying to tell you."

"Okay," she said.

"I had planned on bringing Andy down the week we met your friends at Caffè Reggio. I had handled Caleb by then, and I was planning for us to go to Yonkers that Friday after you got out of work and bring him down together. I was hoping we'd spend our Saturday in the park, as we'd planned, but you sent me home after the café, and then you went ka-boom on stage. And all I said was that you had to be sure, because you can't dip out of his life once he meets you. My son is not part of this dance you want with me, that I want with you—that we would start building a family, maybe with his shit all over the place. I don't know."

He looked at Sylvia for a reaction, but all he got was a blank expression and empty eyes. Panic began to build inside him at the thought of losing her, but he didn't show it.

He took another deep breath, swallowed, and said, "I'm sorry. I'm sorry for everything. I should've found a better way of handling this. But how could I tell you what I'd been planning—what I was doing—without admitting it? You've already called me out on stage, right? I know who I am. I'm not happy with what I am—a killer—and I know karma will get me one day. I believe in God, so it has to happen. I already hate myself for everything I've done, but I want to protect you. I want to protect my son. I want to protect my family. I don't want you guys to die."

Sylvia yelled, "I fucked up! Is that what you wanna hear?"

"No."

"Then why are you going on and on? Do you feel the need to be right so much that you've gotta make me feel like a fuckup? I already know who I am. I'm not happy with what I am—a loser."

"You're not a loser—"

"Yes, I am. You're just gonna end up leaving me anyway."

"No, I'm not."

"If you're gonna go, go! I already broke up with you!"

Andrés gave Sylvia a long, sad look before reluctantly walking out of the Purple Room and towards the door.

Sylvia got up and followed him, naked.

A loud silence settled between the two as they looked at each other as if to say, *How did we get here?* He reached for her hand, but she shook it away in disgust.

"I don't want to see you ever again," she said. "Don't look for me—don't think about me—don't come to the places where I work. Where I read. Please. For my sake, I can't have you around me. We're not healthy for each other."

Andrés took a deep breath and swallowed. "I'll leave you alone."

"Yes, leave me alone! Bye!"

Andrés left the apartment.

Sylvia slammed the door.

Andrés left the building. He looked back to see Sylvia on her fire escape in one of his shirts, crying and watching him walk away.

27

PASSION IS OVERRATED

SEPTEMBER 19, 1994

ANDRÉS STOOD IN FRONT OF WHAT WAS ONCE AN UNDERGROUND nightclub called Robots. It was now just another abandoned-looking storefront on Avenue B.

No more giant strobe mirror ball hanging from the ceiling at the center of the room—it was gone.

No more Sylvia's eyes streaking across the dark like shooting stars —she was long gone.

He remembered pulling her close.

He remembered seeing her smile and hearing her say, "I don't know you like that, to be pulling me."

He remembered just how well he knew her.

He remembered dancing under the light of the mirrored ball and the satisfaction of knowing that an amazing woman was once in love with him. He felt she was somehow still in love with him, and they would always be connected.

He imagined Sylvia laughing and saying, "Whatever."

He remembered how their bodies swayed to the music. It felt as if they were the stuff of stars.

He remembered when they last saw each other.

He missed his friend—someone who wanted all of him, not just the thrill of being with him, as if the sole purpose of his existence was to satisfy a racial fetish for the many one-night stands he'd had since their breakup.

He missed his best friend. The one who walked with him in the city streets at sunrise, followed by sleep, then brunch, then silent afternoons spent walking through bookstores and watching movies at the Playhouse, followed by long conversations well into the night.

He will always love his best friend. His One.

Maybe if he were to look her up, Sylvia would welcome him back—but only after giving him a hard time first.

Maybe... maybe not.

Andrés was delusional; he was sure of that.

It was delusional to think the voice he had been hearing—saying it would be okay to cross the boundary and go to her, that she would say "yes"—was real. That Sylvia was calling his name through time and space.

There's no such magic in the universe.

It was wrong for him to believe—to continue to be delusional.

It was best to leave his best friend alone for good—the most remarkable woman he had ever met. If it were only him, he would have gone crawling back on his hands and knees.

But passion is overrated.

He could no longer afford to want to feel that. He had to continue putting Andy first. And Andrés couldn't risk having Sylvia turn on his son because she had a bomb ticking inside her, always ready to explode. For Andrés, that's what it was all about in the end. Andy could never understand that Sylvia was a Little, still hurting on the inside, still going ka-boom. And Andrés didn't want there to be a competition between his little boy and the little girl still in Sylvia. Andy always had to be first.

He had to be.

Andrés repeated to himself, over and over, as if it had become his new mantra:

> Passion is overrated.
> Passion is overrated.
> Passion is overrated.

It was time to move on and give up hope for a lifetime with a dance partner in that Beautiful Ballet.

It was time to be practical.

OCTOBER 21, 1994

Instead of wondering what Sylvia was doing for her thirty-second birthday, Andrés decided to go to a small beer garden and nightclub in Bushwick. He had been hanging around there since a woman, whose name he had since forgotten, brought him there months ago to enjoy beers and tacos before she ran into an old fuck buddy of hers and left Andrés behind.

It was the nature of the game that single people in New York were playing. One should never be angry at a cloud because it rains or at the many other things that work as nature intended. Instead of seeing her walk off with her fuck buddy as a blow to his ego and getting angry, he saw it as nature working as intended. It's just the way it is.

For Andrés, it had always been that when one girl leaves, another girl always comes along to take her place. And after months of coming to the beer garden, there she was.

She was tall—as tall as Andrés—and her hair was long and blonde, and her eyes sparkled, like stars. Her face was the brightest in the crowd, and her smile showed that it was easy for her to laugh, easy for her to be kind, and easy for strangers to approach her for a dance, which Andrés did.

They danced all night. It was the first time Andrés didn't think about his shooting star. Life goes on. All the casual sex he had been having since the breakup, trying to cope, wasn't healthy for a spirit looking to escape from itself; it had become like a drug, and he didn't want that.

The woman with the starry eyes wrapped her arms around him, and they swayed together to the beat, from one song to the next, until she needed to stop and catch her breath.

Her first words to him were yelled over the music: "I've seen you around before."

He yelled back, "I've been coming here a lot lately!"

She leaned into him so she could talk into his ear. "That's not it—I saw you at an open mic—at The Loft. Yes, that's it—you were with that girl!"

He brushed her long hair aside from her shoulder and leaned in to talk into her ear. "You remember that?"

"I remember you because I remember her. I remember thinking how this chick, who'd talk shit on stage about needing no man, would be all over you the way she was. I was thinking, 'What do you have going on that she'd say one thing but act another?'"

"I'm a badass. That's why."

"Yeah, sure. I'll be the judge of that. By the way, I'm Elisa. What's your name?"

IV
ORION

There is no sun without shadow, and it is essential to know the night.

— ALBERT CAMUS

❧ 28 ❧

SISYPHUS

THIS WAS NOW THE ROUTINE. HIS LIFE, DAY IN, DAY OUT.

It was three in the morning on Friday when Andrés woke up to feed and soothe his crying daughter, Estefania, nicknamed Daphne. He stayed up until she was asleep again. Instead of going back to bed, Andrés took that opportunity—the free time only found by parents of young children in the dead of night—to sit on his couch in the family room and read until his alarm went off. He then jumped up and raced into his bedroom to turn it off before it woke Elisa.

He began the day by getting ready, then leaving his apartment in Bushwick to walk in the cold, blue hour of the morning to the Montrose Avenue station. There, he boarded the train and battled other miserable commuters for a seat or a place to stand, riding it from Brooklyn into Manhattan.

At the Herald Square stop, Andrés rushed off the train and fought his way through the underground maze of the subway station to get above ground. He kept fighting through the crowds teeming on the sidewalk, everyone rushing with their faces down, avoiding eye contact, until he reached the plain glass building where he worked.

Inside, he jammed his body into a small elevator and allowed himself to be pressed against the wall by other commuters, their faces down, until the elevator reached his floor. He rushed through the glass doors leading into the office, sat at his desk covered with stacks of paperwork, took a deep breath, swallowed, and tackled the pile.

In his role as a human resources assistant at a firm that managed mailrooms and secretaries for its clients—a role he had taken after being fired from a temp job in December 1994[1]—it was Andrés's job to screen thousands of résumés, conduct background checks, and coordinate drug tests.

He was also their de facto database administrator, managing the firm's personnel and payroll data, and writing code to create on-the-fly solutions for challenges encountered by the human resources and finance managers, who were old and unfamiliar with the new technologies.

Day in, day out, this was the rock: his square life.

The toughest part of his job was not the needless drama stemming from artificial deadlines for useless reports, generated on absurd amounts of paper that would form more stacks of paperwork, which would then sit unread on countless desks.

No.

The toughest part was walking around the office with a forced smile, ready to belt out a forced laugh at stories and jokes his coworkers would stop and share with him. It was as if they thought that just by having his desk in proximity to theirs, Andrés would find their crude and hateful humor—taken from the antics of shock jocks and AM radio talk shows—funny.

By the end of the workday, when Andrés jammed his body back into the elevator and left the glass building for home, on the walk back to the Herald Square station, he took off his mask, removed the forced smile, and expressed his misery and exhaustion with a blank, empty stare.

It was seven at night when Andrés went underground and fought his way through the maze of the subway station again. He waited on a

---

1. *Book One: Orpheus*, "Chapter One: The Provider."

crowded platform until the light of an approaching train appeared in the distance of the dark tunnel. He made the conscious decision to step back rather than jump forward as it rushed into the station, blowing out an invisible plume of mechanical heat before opening its doors. Andrés battled other commuters for a seat and lost. He held onto a railing above and watched everyone around him stare dead into space until something in them had gone ghost, making their eyes roll back, becoming bright white pearls. Whatever was left in their bodies shifted with the train's movement as it made its way underground.

At Union Square, just before transferring to the L train for Brooklyn, Andrés felt what was still an instinct: to leave the station and make the walk he had made hundreds of times before—when he was twenty-three years old, broke, underemployed, but in love with life— so much in love with life and so much in love with her—to the apartment where he discovered his true self in Sylvia's Purple Room.[2]

He repeated to himself a line of poetry by Pablo Neruda:

"We, of that time, are no longer the same.

"I no longer love her, that's certain, but how I loved her."

He continued repeating it to himself as if it were a mantra until the L train rolled into the Montrose Avenue station and he got off. He climbed the steps and emerged above ground. The bitter cold hit him hard, slowing his walk. His home was several city blocks away. It felt like miles in the chill of what had become, for him, his longest winter.

Andrés whispered to himself, "It is what it is."

All for his almost three-month-old daughter, Daphne.

All for his six-year-old son, Andy.

All for his nine-year-old stepdaughter, Myra.

And all for the hope he has for the future.

Up in the night, in a clearing of clouds, he saw the constellation Orion: the belt of stars, the otherness of life, of this world—beyond the mundane, and the Him, and the Her, and the Us.

Andrés could see it: the big picture. With the sky so vast and the number of stars in the night so infinite, Andrés was small. If he was small, everything else—including his problems, his challenges and

---

2. *Book One: Orpheus*, "Chapter Six: The Purple Room."

loneliness, his depression—was smaller. There was more to life than this, and just because Andrés couldn't see it didn't mean it wasn't there.

He smiled, whispering to himself, "It's gonna be okay, I guess... Keep it moving."

The clouds rolled through the night, covering Orion. Andrés continued his walk home, stopping at a *bodega* to buy milk and a treat for Myra. As he milled about, looking for more items, he noticed a short, fat man with a haircut that made his head look like the eraser on a stubby brown pencil, staring at him.

Andrés returned his stare with one of his own.

The fat man smiled as he walked over. He leaned in until they were face-to-face, placing a hand on Andrés's shoulder, his oversized eight-ball jacket hanging off his cuffs. "I've seen you around the way with Elisa. You're her man, right? You don't recognize me? She was my girl."

Andrés looked at the hand, still on his shoulder, then laughed before looking back at him. "So?"

"So?... How do you like my apartment? I got it with Elisa."

"It's a shitty apartment."

"But you're there now," the fat man said, laughing as he squeezed Andrés's shoulder, pressing down hard to keep him from walking away. "Let me ask you this: did you guys get a new bed? New furniture? If you haven't, you should, 'cause I used to fuck her on that bed; I used to tear that ass up on that couch. And it don't matter that I don't live there anymore—it's still my place. She's still my girl. I'm still her man."

He dropped his hand from Andrés's shoulder, reached into the pocket of his oversized jeans, pulled out a twenty-dollar bill, scrunched it into a ball, and flicked it into Andrés's face.

"Whatever you're buying for my girls, that's for that."

The fat man walked away.

Andrés reminded himself of the promise he had made on the night he *handled* Caleb: no more violence.[3] He took a deep breath, swallowed, and left the balled-up cash on the floor. Then he went to the counter, counted his loose change, and had just enough to pay for his items. He left the *bodega* and walked several more blocks until he

---

3. *Book Three: The Labyrinth*, "Chapter Twenty-Six: December Came and Went."

reached his apartment building. He rushed in to escape the cold, climbing a dark staircase that smelled of bleach and mold. Once he reached the top floor, he unlocked the door to his apartment. Inside, he found Elisa walking from the kitchen into the family room, greeting him with a bright smile.

"My baby, I miss you," she said, rushing up to kiss him.

"I miss you too," he said, kissing her back. "But where's my other baby?"

"She's right here."

Elisa presented Daphne, who was nestled in her mother's arms.

Andrés leaned in to kiss his daughter, then set the white plastic bag containing the milk on the floor next to him.

Just as he was about to reach for Daphne, Elisa said, "Relax... Enjoy the last few minutes of your break—your shift starts soon."

"I know," he said, caressing the part of Elisa's scalp that still had hair, trying to relieve her of any pain from her recent surgery. "How are you feeling?"

"Better than yesterday. Tomorrow will be even better."

Elisa took a deep breath and forced a smile.

"Don't worry about me. I can do this. I have to... I'm not going to miss the first few months of Daphne's life because of the pain. I could never get that time back."

"I know... I wish I hadn't missed the first year of Andy's life, recuperating..."

"That's not going to be me," Elisa said.

"I have a treat for Myra. Where is she?"

"She's in her room, doing homework. Did you get one for Olivia?"

"I didn't have enough money."

Elisa sighed. "That's okay... I'll split the treat in half and give it to them later. That should cheer Olivia up. She's still sad."

"I don't blame her," Andrés said.

"She's been asking when her mother is coming to get her."

"Tell her the truth—her mom's in rehab," Andrés said, taking off his coat and placing it on the stand by the door.

"I can't tell her that," Elisa said.

"I don't understand; why is she our problem?"

"Because Olivia is *our* niece, and I have to help my sister. What else am I supposed to do?"

"Worry about yourself."

"Wait a minute," Elisa said. "Don't put this all on me. You're the one who said you didn't want Olivia going into the system. You freaked out at the thought of her being in foster care."

"I know, I know. Forget what I said... I'm sorry; I'm so stressed out."

"So am I, but Olivia is here, and we're all she's got. And I know you're frustrated, but you're a good man for thinking about the bigger picture. It's why I love you."

"I love you too," he said.

"We'll talk more about her later. For now, I want you to sit and relax. I'm going to finish feeding Daphne."

Elisa disappeared into their bedroom while he picked up the white plastic bag from the floor and made his way to the kitchen. He placed the milk in the near-empty refrigerator, the sight of it reminding him of the job interview he had scheduled in the coming days. It was for an analyst position with a technology firm that had partnered with an old-money banking client on Wall Street. If everything went well, he would no longer need to worry about his family having enough to eat or counting loose change every time he went to the *bodega*. He would become better at providing. After closing the fridge, he headed back to the family room.

Andrés turned on the TV and settled into a chair in front of it. He stared dead at the screen, tuned to a music channel. Video after video played—all a blur until a music video, shot in grainy black-and-white film, came on.

Something in Andrés that had gone ghost for almost four years was now alive, awakened by the frontwoman of a grunge band, her sleek body swaying to the tempo of a heavy bassline groove. He couldn't see her face, and the way her hair blew out like the head of a dandelion threw him off for a moment. But the way she moved reminded him of someone he had lost—because he was stupid and didn't know how to dance with her.

When she began to talk—not sing—as though reading a prose

poem along with the groove, Andrés laughed. He laughed even harder when she turned around to reveal her face.

It was Sylvia.

"You sold out!"

Andrés's smile grew wide and bright, immense joy filling his heart.

"Good for you—I'd sell out too, move out of this shitty neighborhood."

Elisa came back from the bedroom, still holding Daphne, who was now awake.

"Who sold out?" she asked.

"It's nothing," he said.

"It's something—you woke her up."

Andrés pointed at the TV. "That's Sylvia."

Elisa's eyes widened in surprise. "So that's her?"

"Yeah, that's her... You remember? All over me?"

"Barely."

"When we met, you said you remembered who I was only because you remembered who she was—the chick who'd talk shit on stage about needing no man but would be all over me the way she was... remember?"[4]

"You want to rub it in my face now?"

"Are you kidding me? In your face? Every night I come home from work, I have to see that meathead ex-boyfriend of yours standing on the corner like a fool, staring me down. I have to act like I don't know who he is—for his sake. But today, he decided to press me. Just before I came home, he came up to me in the *bodega*."

Elisa's expression went from annoyance to a mixture of surprise and anxious fear.

"He did? What did Gus say?" she asked.

Andrés couldn't help but smile. "Does it matter?"

"No?"

"Was he supposed to pass on a message?"

"Of course not; I'm just saying. I don't want Gus bothering you."

"He's not bothering me. Like I said, for his sake, I ignore him. I'm

---

4. *Book Three: The Labyrinth*, "Chapter Twenty-Seven: Passion is Overrated."

a family man now. I don't need to catch a case, end up in the Tombs, all because that meathead wants my attention. Trust me, he doesn't want that."

"Oh, he doesn't?" Elisa asked, with a skeptical smirk that betrayed her continued loyalty to her ex-boyfriend.

"You think I'm playing? Sylvia had an old friend who caught my attention way too much, and now he's gone. Every night I ignore that chump, I'm blessing him with another day of life."

"And what's that supposed to mean?" Elisa asked.

Andrés took a deep breath, holding himself back from saying more.

He swallowed the urge to break the promise he had made—for how Gus had placed his hand on his shoulder, for how Elisa kept calling him by her ex-boyfriend's name as she came out of anesthesia after having a small tumor removed from her frontal lobe—reminding himself once more: no more violence.

"It's nothing," Andrés said. "You, on the other hand, can't be reminded for more than thirty seconds that I had that badass in my life. Let me be happy for her in peace. Sylvia's had a hard life. She needs all the fucking wins she can get. She's the reason why I see the big picture, and your niece is here and not in the system. So I want you to look at the TV, bow, and say to her, 'Thank you.'"

For a moment, Elisa stared at Andrés, who had become hypnotized by the music video. She walked over to the TV and shut it off, then walked back to him and shoved Daphne into his arms.

"Your shift starts now. I need to shower."

Elisa rushed out of the family room, down the hall, and through the bathroom door. Andrés stood there for a moment, then walked back to the TV and turned it back on. He remained standing, watching while holding Daphne.

"Estefania," he whispered to his daughter, using her legal name. "You see that woman on TV? Your nickname is one of Daddy's nicknames for her. Mommy thinks she's slick, hiding mementos and old pictures of her ex-boyfriend, but that's okay. Daddy can never control what's in Mommy's heart. Your nickname is what I keep in mine. You should've been Sylvia's little girl."

Andrés looked back up at the TV and stared for a long time. Sylvia appeared to be staring back at him through the screen, her eyes still shining—brilliant blue and dark hazel—even in the grainy black-and-white film.

"It is what it is," he whispered, looking down at his daughter. "And it's okay. Passion is overrated. I'm just so glad to be here with you."

29

THE IT GIRL

APRIL 12, 1997

[1]

Sylvia was hesitant to leave her apartment, but the clutter and the smell of what now felt like a cramped cell pushed her out the door to face the specter of death.

She was hesitant to make that walk in the cold drizzle to the memorial service, where her agent had pressed her to attend without an invite. The agent told Sylvia, "No one calls anyone out at these things, anyway. So just remember: always smile and act like you know—like you belong."

To get her agent to continue returning her calls, Sylvia had to do as she was told and act like she knew Irwin Goldbook—the Departed—who had passed away a week earlier. She had to act like she wasn't disgusted by the Departed's personal life—his personal stances—despite admiring his work and the bravery it took for him to live a life that seemed to have left him with no regrets. But still, Sylvia wondered at what point his chicken-hawk ways would rightfully overshadow his work, so that instead of being known as the man who, through his poems, challenged censorship laws in the 1950s, he would be known more for being a member of NAMBLA.

Sylvia wanted to turn back and return to her cell of a room—where she could play her cassette tape, worn down by years of replaying the songs recorded on it—to listen to Pat Benatar, over and over on loop, sing the lyrics to *Hell Is for Children*. While singing along, Sylvia would strip naked, take the knife she kept beneath her mattress, and drag it across the surface of her body, marred with the invisible scars all children who have been through hell carry in silence.

In the cell of her room, where the clutter no longer felt like the bars of a prison but the armor that protected her—surrounding her like the shell of her beloved dead turtle, Kalpa—Sylvia would listen to the song and toy with the knife until something in her no longer felt the fear she had carried since she was a little girl. That same fear had her hiding in the dark corner of a foster home until Constance the Matriarch came through and slayed the monsters who had become her captors, scooping Sylvia up—baby doll still in hand—and racing out of there.

Sylvia would play another song from a worn-down cassette she had made in college, comprised solely of the ticking clock, the drums, and the chimes in the intro to *Time* by Pink Floyd. She would grab that same baby doll—the one that had been cared for by her best friend, Reginald Superstar, while Sylvia had been in the blur at the peak of her addiction—and hug the doll like it was her child who had just turned thirty years old. Then, Sylvia would throw herself against her books, strewn across the floor, and cry. And cry. And cry.

So, to avoid that—to not go back to her apartment, to not see Kalpa's tank—its emptiness a glaring example of death but also a reminder, just as Kalpa had been for years a reminder of the rarity of life—Sylvia kept walking along East 10th Street.

As she continued her walk under the bleak skies, beneath the drizzle that dotted her hair and became drops clinging to the clumps of her blowout like dew on stalks, Sylvia began to repeat to herself over and over: "I am the miracle. I am the miracle. I am the miracle. I'm meant to be here. I'm meant for more."

Because of the hundreds of times she had walked from her apartment with Andrés to Strand Books on Broadway—near where the memorial service was being held—she continued walking along East 10th Street with her eyes closed. It was at Strand Books that they would spend hours browsing books together in a silence that would make her, at that moment, whisper to herself, "Shantith."

It was a peace she missed.

It was a familiarity that made her feel safe; to have him home, in bed, meant she didn't need the knife under her bed because Andrés would be there, always ready to fight—to protect—to defend what she had made his: her soul.

It was that hunger to feel oneness, borne out of silence, that almost made her keep walking toward Strand Books instead of stepping into the front courtyard of St. Mark's Church-in-the-Bowery, crowded with people heading into the event.

Her agent, standing under a red umbrella in the drizzle, rushed up to Sylvia and yelled, "You're late."

Before Sylvia could respond, the agent grabbed her by the hand and yanked her into the crowd moving inside. She sat next to the agent as the memorial began. Each speaker came to the podium and shared a story or memory about the Departed before sitting back down. To Sylvia, it felt intrusive—like she was violating something sacred within the circle of friends who took turns speaking. She didn't understand how this memorial was supposed to be the networking opportunity her agent had claimed it would be, not until the last speaker left the podium and people began milling about. They laughed and talked about their work. For those who shared a connection to the Departed but didn't know each other well, they exchanged business cards and numbers, saying, "Let's collab."

Something about that made Sylvia want to burst into tears.

Would her death, whenever that comes, be just another excuse for people to get together, make small talk, and exchange numbers—all to set up collaborations that would lead to more attention for their creative work?

No!

Sylvia vowed to herself that when the moment of her death comes —crossing that boundary between the Land of the Alive and the Land of the Not-Alive—she will have already stipulated in her will, as her last wishes, that there should be no service, no funeral, no memorial. For all she cared, her ashes could be tossed off a bridge into the deep, so that any river below could take what's left of her and make it part of the Earth. Her body would live on that way—as sediment among the rocks beneath the cool waters, flowing from the source to the depths of the ocean.

The agent snapped a finger in Sylvia's face, bringing her back to the moment. "Wait here... I see someone I need to say hi to."

Before Sylvia could respond, the agent shot up from her chair and raced over to an older man, whom Sylvia recognized as someone well-known in New York's literary scene. He wore a dark blue blazer and slacks with an open-collar white dress shirt, signaling to the crowd that he was wealthy, whereas others were merely rich. He had power, whereas others had influence. He was someone who could open doors for anyone, and after the agent pointed Sylvia out to him, he sauntered over and grabbed her thigh, squeezing hard as he lowered his old-man body into the seat next to her. His old-man whiskers protruded from his ears, and age spots dotted his wrinkled, translucent, soft hands that felt like they had never worked a day in his life—hands that now squeezed her thigh, uninvited.

Sylvia shot up, crying and screaming. She ran into the courtyard. The agent followed, grabbing Sylvia's shoulder from behind. Sylvia swung around, punched her, knocking her to the ground. She knelt, coming face-to-face with the agent, who looked back like a terrified little mouse.

"You're trying to pimp me out?" Sylvia yelled, hitting her again. "I'm not the fucking one."

And with one last punch to the nose, Sylvia terminated her contract with the agent. She raced out of the courtyard and across the street to a coffee house. She rushed in with her face to the floor, acting like she was just another person coming in for a cup of coffee. The more she tried calming down, the more her mind raced with intrusive thoughts, trying to convince her—after having been fondled—that maybe sobriety wasn't such a big deal.

She had been happier high because, at least in the midst of heroin bliss, she was numb. She wouldn't know about the monsters who could make not just men, but anyone with a semblance of power, abuse it—because they were weak. Because they knew nothing of respect, of trust, of the Dance, where the charm of a lover—the songs of an Orpheus—could help bring out the Little still hidden in the dark corner of her being. Coaxing her from her hiding spot to show her true self, to give herself in a trust so deep—in a love so powerful, so strong—that she would surrender her knife and ask her one and only to drag it lightly across her body, so that something in her was no longer scared.

That's when the tapping of a microphone in the corner of the coffee house made her look up, finally aware of her surroundings, and see her One standing there:

Andrés.

In that moment of the long stare, with her mind constantly moving and racing, she understood: what once seemed impossible now made sense. If they were truly each other's one, surely fate would conspire for them to meet again.

It was written in the stars.

Recognizing what could possibly be at play, she buried every intrusive thought; she mustered everything in her to hold back the Little in her that wanted to run up to him, tell him everything that happened across the street, and point out the monsters that tried taking advantage of her. She wanted to watch how the Big in Andrés would dispense justice, the same way she suspected he had with Caleb years before.[1]

If this was fate at play, she had to bury everything and act like all was well. Smile. Smile with everything she had—tap into the joy of what could be the day of their ultimate union—the return to her Purple Room—the launch into Space—the bliss found in the posture where her heart would meld into his, and his face would press against her chest, and they would become One.

Yes.

On what could be the day remembered as the turning point of her

---

1. *Book Three: The Labyrinth*, "Chapter Twenty-Six: December Came and Went."

life—changing it—she would not want it to end before it began, with an old man being carried on a stretcher into an ambulance and Andrés hauled away in handcuffs because he had to protect what the Little in Sylvia made his: her everything.

She moved away from the line to stand a few feet from him, as if to say, "Here I am."

He broke eye contact with her to look around the now-quiet room.

Sylvia looked around with him, at the faces of everyone in the room, all of whom appeared confused by Andrés—a man who had, at one point, seemed ready to read his poem but was now hypnotized into silence by her.

"Sorry about that," Andrés said to the audience. "It's been a while since I've done something like this. I'm just a dad now, given a day off from my family to come here and say:

"Kneeling upon an iced pavement

"In a suit and tie,

"Casting away his briefcase and glasses,

"He looked up at Orion

"In the cold night sky,

"And wondered what had happened

"To the life he so loved,

"Wondering the deeper meaning of it.

"Cursing God who brought about his torment,

"As he exhaled a deep breath at the mountain's base,

"Pausing to go home to get some rest

"For when he wakes the next morning,

"He can do it over again—

"Pushing

"The same stone

"Up the mountain."

Andrés paused, taking in the silence from the still-confused audience, then sighed. "That's all I needed to say. No more. No less."

Sylvia rushed over the empty chairs that separated the space dedicated to reading poetry from the rest of the audience in the coffee house. She brushed aside the barista who had approached Andrés to take the microphone from him, pulling him in for a long hug. Just as she was about to whisper in his ear, "Hello, Daddy, how are you?" the barista tapped her on the shoulder.

"I'm a big fan of your work. Would you be willing to read something for us, please?" the barista asked.

Sylvia turned to her, a young woman in her early twenties, and gave her a strained smile. "But of course."

The barista smiled as she handed Sylvia the microphone. Andrés tried moving away to stand to the side, but Sylvia grabbed his hand, keeping him in place.

She turned to face the audience with a reluctant expression, as if examining her thoughts while searching for the right words.

"Hi, my name is Sylvia James," she said. "I *was* a poet who came in here to escape... the rain. Without giving away too much about why, between leaving my apartment and just before coming in here, something within me has changed. I'm not a poet anymore. I've been given a reminder that what I put out there—my energy through words—has, in some cosmic way, boomeranged back in a way I can't talk about.

"Since it wasn't my plan to read today, and it's not in me to turn down the requests of the baristas here—young women who, I know, work so hard to give each and every one of you, through good coffee, your escape—I want to, instead, read a poem that I first heard at my grandmother's funeral and have memorized since then."

She looked at Andrés.

"Don't ask me why this poem came to mind, but it's by Rumi, and it goes a little something like this:

"Our death is our wedding with eternity.

"What is the secret? 'God is One.'

"The sunlight splits when entering the windows of the house.

"This multiplicity exists in the cluster of grapes;

"It is not in the juice made from the grapes.

"For he who is living in the Light of God,

"Regarding him, say neither bad nor good,

"For he is gone beyond the good and the bad.

"The death of the carnal soul is a blessing."

Sylvia looked back at the audience, sitting in captivated silence, and pointed at the ceiling.

"Fix your eyes on God and do not talk about what is invisible,
"So that he may place another look in your eyes.
"It is in the vision of the physical eyes
"That no invisible or secret thing exists.
"But when the eye is turned toward the Light of God
"What thing could remain hidden under such a Light?
"Although all lights emanate from the Divine Light
"Don't call all these lights 'the Light of God';
"It is the eternal light which is the Light of God,
"The ephemeral light is an attribute of the body and the flesh.
"...Oh God who gives the grace of vision!
"The bird of vision is flying towards You with the wings of desire."

The audience neither clapped nor spoke. They were like the barista—all with expressions that conveyed confusion and discomfort. In the silence, Sylvia placed the microphone on the floor, grabbed Andrés by the hand, and without a word, led him out of the coffee house.

Across the street, a cop car, flashing blue and white lights, and an ambulance were parked on the sidewalk in front of St. Mark's Church-in-the-Bowery. Police talked with the agent while paramedics tended to her bruised face and bloody nose. For a brief moment, the agent made eye contact with Sylvia before shaking her head and returning her focus to the police.

Sylvia looked at Andrés and asked, "Do you have anywhere you need to be?"

"No... Not really," he replied.

"I need to get out of here."

He looked at the police, then back at Sylvia. "Then let's get out of here."

Sylvia placed her arm around his and led him away from the chaos.

[2]

THE BLEAKNESS OF THE SKY MADE THE SIDEWALK SYLVIA AND Andrés walked along, as well as the buildings lining East 10th Street, look extra gray—almost blue. After a long silence, Andrés asked, "Are you okay? You look like you've been crying."

She sighed. "I know I'm supposed to say, 'I'm fine,' but I'm not... I was at this gathering at St. Mark's for Irwin Goldbook... He died, and... I guess it got to me."

"I didn't know you knew him like that."

"I didn't... My agent said I should go with her, that it'd be good for my career to network."

"That's weird."

"I know, but she said I needed to remind everyone of the other poet from the Lower East Side. So I went, if only not to piss her off. Otherwise, I wouldn't have gone... It's so stupid to even mention me in the same breath as him. And I had told her that I hate wakes—funerals —memorials—whatever. But I went anyway, because my agent tends not to return my calls whenever I do something to piss her off. She told me that fame... notoriety... doesn't last forever. It's always best to keep reminding people in the know that I'm there, in the scene... And there I was, in their scene, feeling out of place, watching them take turns telling stories about him."

She paused to look at Andrés before looking up and away.

"I couldn't help but cry, like I knew Mister Irwin personally. I don't know why I did... I guess it's because he lived a life of no regrets. He was always true to himself. And there I was, regretting having an agent who—because she wants me to do whatever I need to do to keep myself in the public eye—convinced me to front a grunge band. I don't even know how to sing!"

Andrés smiled. "I saw your music video."

Sylvia let out a groan.

"It wasn't bad."

"It's not that I care if it's bad. It's that... I hate that I was only there because of market research."

"Market research?"

"Yeah... After some of my poems got noticed, like *1968,* and after someone on Madison Avenue heard about Reggie's events at The Loft, they came down, caught one of my performances, and decided to make me their 'It Girl.' Because of that, now I've got people coming up to me like they know me, like I'm this heartless, sex-crazed object, when you know all that shit is an act. But they wanted to play that up—a Lower East Side siren. A low-budget mix of Patti Smith's attitude behind a Carly Simon-like, *exotic* face—their words, not mine."

Sylvia fell silent, staring intently ahead as they approached and crossed 1st Avenue.

"Sometimes," she said, "I wish I could lock myself up in my apartment and never come out... I wish Reggie hadn't put me up to reading at The Loft... I wouldn't have become their It Girl. I wouldn't have so-called literary critics tearing apart my work when you know I never meant for any of it to make it beyond The Loft, let alone the block. But that's okay, I guess. My agent said it comes with the territory... What's not okay is how critics started tearing apart how I look. Like it's okay to do it to me because I'm a woman, like that has anything to do with the quality of my work. Meanwhile, you've got dudes out there who look like serial killers that don't get the kind of attention my hair and lips get, but whatever."

She abruptly stopped walking, swinging herself in front of Andrés and looking at him with pleading eyes.

"Then they start with that whole 'What is she?' thing. 'Is she white? Does she have some Black in her?' I forgot I had mentioned somewhere that Papaw was Creole, Nana was Melungeon, and my grandparents on my mom's side—the ones who forgot I even existed because they disowned my mom for having a baby with someone like my dad—they're Syrian. What the fuck was that for? Oversharing that my dad was kind of a *mulatto,* and my *yamma* was Arab? Again, Madison Avenue put together a special team of people whose only job was to figure out how to better package me. Like I'm a Creole/Melungeon/Middle Eastern white woman poet of color from Appalachia who dresses like shit and looks like she hasn't washed her hair in years.

"Then some asshole thought it was a good idea to give me a blowout because that's what a cool, rocker White-Black-Arab chick would do if she were fronting a grunge band. What the fuck does that have to do with my work? I'm not a rocker; I'm a poet—or at least I was—and all that did was fuck my hair up even more. I just want to shave it all off."

"No, don't. Please."

After a long pause, during which Sylvia held back from saying more —that she had been in constant contact with Petra, his mother, since their breakup—she looked at him sideways, flashed a small smile, and said, "Don't worry. I've had someone in my life these last few years who looks after me like I'm her daughter. If I ever did anything like that, she'd kick my ass. She almost did when I showed up at her house looking like this. She said I went from looking like a beautiful flower to a weed."

Andrés chuckled. "Sounds like something my mother would say."

"It does, doesn't it?"

"Is it?"

"Your mom did say that it wouldn't matter if you and I were together or not; her doors would always be open to me, and I don't have anyone—"

"So, is it my mom?"

"Maybe... maybe not."

"Why don't you just tell me?"

"I don't know... I just don't want you giving me any shit about it if it is. Lord knows, I've got enough of that already with my supposed friends—all talking shit, calling me a sellout. The same friends who used to blow smoke up my ass about how great I am when I'm not. I'm a loser."

"You're not a loser," Andrés said.

"Yeah, I am—what kind of person ends up owing money to their record company?" She pointed a finger at herself. "This *bitch*—that's who... I'm gonna end up owing so much more, especially to my agent. Just before coming into the coffee house, I kind of fired her—that's a long story I don't wanna get into, so don't ask; I'm talking too much as it is—let's talk about you." She shook his small paunch, protruding slightly over his beltline, with both hands. "You're getting a gut."

"I know—"

"It's not because of cheese fries?[2] Don't tell me you're still eating

---

2. *Book Three: The Labyrinth*, "Chapter Nineteen: The Sunflowers."

that shit, 'cause if you are, I'm about ready to dropkick your fat ass back to Sunday. Did I dodge a bullet?"

He laughed. "I don't exercise, I don't go out, I don't dance... I don't do anything. I just work. I'm always working. And when I'm not, I'm always at home with my girlfriend... and our daughter. Elisa gave birth to her not too long ago."

"Did she? When?"

"Last year... late October."

"I didn't know that."

"How could you?"

"Well, congratulations. I'm so happy."

"Could you be more sarcastic?"

Sylvia became speechless, unable to hide her anger, frustration, and confusion any longer. She ran out from under his umbrella and rushed down East 10th Street, leaving Andrés to chase after her across Avenue A.

He caught up to her in Tompkins Square Park, placing his umbrella back over her.

"Are you okay?" he asked.

"I've never been better," she replied, her voice shaking. "Hearing that makes my decision to start writing my novel that much easier. I mean, what else have I got going on in my life? I thought I'd have a baby by now."

"Have you been trying?"

Sylvia paused. "I don't feel comfortable talking to you about that. You left me. You never came back when you were supposed to; we were in the Dance—you should've known better, but you're so fucking stupid, and now we're not together. So, whether I've been trying or not is none of your business."

"I get it."

She snickered. "I'm so fucking *happy* that you do—do you also get that I've been told I'm emotionally unavailable? That some asshole must've broken me for me to be so fucking cold—and some asshole did, and now it's too late."

"No, it's not."

"Yes, it is."

"It really is not."

Sylvia was about to scream, "Yes, it is!" but started coughing hard from the deep breath she had taken to yell. She placed both hands on her knees, trying her best to breathe, bearing the force the coughing brought on her lungs. She coughed in harsh, sharp bursts until she stopped and pushed his soothing hands away from her back to stand upright.

She tried to smile as if she had not been struggling to breathe moments before, but she couldn't. Instead, she looked at Andrés, trying to say with her eyes that something in her soul had become heavier with the news of his daughter—a daughter that was supposed to be hers—and she needed his help carrying the burden. She was no longer afraid to say what she wanted to say to get it.

"This has been the most fucked-up day," she said. "I got shamed into going to the gathering, to then be surrounded by people I don't even know, and for what? So my agent could meet up with this industry big shot who, apparently, has had his eyes on me this whole time—just so she could send him over to where I was, so he could grab me on the thigh while trying to sit his old ass down next to me? I got up—I ran out of there—and my agent followed, grabbing me by the shoulder like she was some kind of pimp, trying to get me back in line. So I had to fuck her up.

"I had to get out of there, and that's when I ran across the street and went into the coffee house, and I was thinking to myself, *Sobriety is so fucking overrated.* That's when you tapped on the microphone, and I saw it was you. It was you! A sign that everything's going to be alright, so"—Sylvia let out a little smile, her eyes still weepy—"this has also been the best day of my life... I'm so happy to see you, even though I'm so fucking mad you didn't come back home! You were supposed to come back! We were dancing!"

"But you said—"

"I know what I said."

"I don't think you do. Let me remind you: 'Please, for my sake, I can't have you around me.'"

"I don't sound like that," Sylvia said.

"Yeah, you do: 'We're not healthy for each other.' Your words, not mine."[3]

"Oh my God, you're so fucking dumb—if I'd been serious, I would've taken back your key. You missed that sign! I was waiting!"

"You set the boundary—I wasn't crossing it—"

"Stop taking me so literally."

"With what we used to do, I have to!"

"You're right," she said. "You're absolutely right—can you come up now, please? I can't be alone."

He hesitated. "I don't know if that's a good idea..."

"It is a good idea 'cause I was here before her, and you owe me for breaking me the way you did, and I know your fat ass wants to come up—you're just showing out 'cause you know I'd get mad if you didn't resist me a little, knowing you got a girlfriend. So come on. Let's go."

Andrés said, "Okay."

[3]

Sylvia led Andrés inside the building and upstairs to the top floor. Andrés reached into his pocket for his keys, pushed her aside, and unlocked the door as if it were still his home. He followed her in, setting the umbrella down and closing the door behind them.

Before she could explain why the apartment was a mess—why her books were scattered across the floor, why newspapers and magazines were packed into every corner, filling the apartment with the smell of faded ink, dust, and mold, and why her father's shadow box was smashed on the floor with Wendell's medals scattered among the shattered glass at the base of the now-empty turtle tank stand—Andrés asked, "What happened to Kalpa?"

In a low voice, she said, "You'd think that if you paid someone to babysit your pet—just come by once a day while you're on the road— it'd be enough. But no. Two weeks ago, I came home to find Kalpa dead."

---

3. *Book Three: The Labyrinth*, "Chapter Twenty-Six: December Came and Went."

"I'm sorry."

"That's more than I got from my supposed friend. She kept saying it's just a turtle. I got so mad at myself for sinking to her level, trying to explain that turtle kept me alive through college, through everything—hell, even at my worst." She paused, taking a deep breath. "Reggie would've been the one to take care of her, just like he did when I was at my rock bottom. But he's not around anymore."

"He's not?" Andrés asked.

"Reggie lost his battle two months ago..." The memory of her oldest friend's final days—AIDS hollowing him out the same way ovarian cancer had hollowed Constance—made her burst into tears. Sylvia cried uncontrollably.

Andrés cleared a space on the couch for them to sit, comforting her as she kept crying—not just from the specter of death but from the overwhelming realization that she had failed to live her life like Reggie had, and like the Departed. They had lived full lives with no regrets. She would regret not taking Andrés up on his offer, missing her chance to live what she considered a full life. She took a deep breath, swallowed her grief and fear of regret, and stopped crying.

Sylvia looked up at him and asked in a low voice, "Did you mean it? That it's not too late?"

"It's not."

"But how can you say that when you've got a girlfriend? A daughter... What's her name?"

"Estefania... I nicknamed her Daphne, after the woman I wish had given me a child."

She chuckled. "Oh, I'd be so pissed if I were your girl; calling your daughter by one of my names."

"Elisa called me by her ex-boyfriend's name."

"She did?"

"Yeah, Elisa was coming out of anesthesia after a big operation she'd postponed until Daphne was born, and she kept calling me 'Gus,' saying over and over, 'What Andrés doesn't know about us won't hurt him.'"

"Damn."

"I had to go out and get a DNA test to make sure Daphne was mine."

"Then why don't you leave? I mean, that night at Show World,[4] you went on and on about respect and walking away, but you had no problem walking away from me. And I'd been nothing but respectful and faithful to you."

"I was going to, but then I started having these nightmares where Daphne is thirty years old, standing on a stage—all angry—yelling into a microphone the same way you did that night when you first read *1968*,[5] and I didn't want to do to her what your father had done to you... What I'd already done to Andy."

"Don't put this on me. It's not the same."

"It would be, if I hadn't swallowed my pride... It's tough. With everything going on, I feel like a fool. I even wrote that poem I read at the coffee house this morning... after Elisa dropped our girls at her mother's place, before telling me I needed to leave. She pointed out the event in *The Village Voice,* saying, 'You could disappear there.' And that's where I went—to the coffee house you ran into. What are the chances of that? Us coming face-to-face?"

"I know, right? Like, this is no coincidence," Sylvia said.

"It's not. And on today of all days, with Elisa pushing me out the door, I end up back here. Don't you think it's a sign?"

"It is... but I'd been seeing signs way before today—like when you dumped Andy off with Miss Petra so she could hand him off to Lydia—"

"You knew about that?"

"I'm a watcher."

"But how?"

"God, you're still so dumb. You didn't pick up that it's your mother who's been in my life, who wanted to kick my ass for showing up at her house with this blowout?"

"You need to spell these things out for me; I'm still suffering from the TBI."

-----

4. *Book Three: The Labyrinth*, "Chapter Twenty: The Red Rooms."
5. *Book Three: The Labyrinth*, "Chapter Twenty-Two: 1968."

"Still?"

"It's gotten worse."

"I'm sorry for calling you stupid; it's part of our Dance—"

"It's okay, no need to explain."

"With this, I have to. After you moved to Brooklyn, Miss Petra... *Mama* said... it was okay for me to start coming over again. It was her house, and she was my friend. I could visit anytime I wanted, and I did, every chance I got. She told me you were having problems with what's-her-name—"

"Elisa—"

Sylvia smirked. "I know her name—I've always known. I just didn't wanna say, but whatever. Getting back to what I *am* trying to say—I knew sooner or later, you'd be back here, especially with how Elisa told you to dump Andy back off with Lydia because of those problems, keeping you so busy that now you don't have time to see him—shame on you for that...

"But it's okay because I've got him. That 'December came and went'[6] feeling you left me with became an itch I needed to scratch, and I did. And now, Andy's become a big part of my life. Hell, Lydia would sometimes call, asking if I could take him."

"Lydia is still battling," Andrés said.

"I know... I told her I could be there for her if she needed, but like you told me once, she doesn't want to be saved—not like I had wanted to, before I met you."

Sylvia stared at the empty turtle tank for a long moment.

"Anyway... I knew it was a matter of time before you'd be back here. I had no clue when, though, or that when fate did bring us back together, you'd have a daughter. *Mama* never told me, which I get, because it's none of my business. Just like it'll be none of Elisa's business when we do have our baby."

Andrés's eyes began to smile wide. "So, it's a yes?"

"Yes... The only worry that I have is that if we're gonna do this, we have to do this right: as of today, your relationship with Elisa is over. I don't want to share you."

---

6. *Book Three: The Labyrinth*, "Chapter Twenty-Six: December Came and Went."

"I don't want to share you."

"Good, 'cause it's not gonna be like before, when we were hitting up The Labyrinth together, doing the craziest shit I've ever done in my life. And that's saying a lot, given that I used to *hustle*... Being that way with myself, with my work—I can't help but think that's why I ended up with an agent who tried pimping me out. This super sexual energy I've been putting into almost everything I create led me to that moment, where I had to run into a coffee house just to get away..."

"What had you running was not something that you did. Don't blame yourself for what evil people do to you."

"But I do have some responsibility for that," Sylvia said. "The lack of respect I've shown myself—through my words and actions—tells others they can come at me like that. So, on this, I'm gonna go against what my friends think real feminism is and just keep that part of myself private. It'll only be you, and you alone, who knows that energy from now on...

"No more public playing at The Labyrinth—not that it matters 'cause it closed down a long time ago... From now on, the only place we'll be playing is here, in my home, which you'll be moving into once you and I go back to Elisa's place and tell her the news ourselves, 'cause things need to be right between the two of you still."

"Be prepared for the dude she's there with to come at me, like he thinks I'd want to fight—"

"Then we'll diffuse the situation and all talk like adults, 'cause your romantic relationship ends, and your new business relationship with her begins today. All for stability—that's it. For Daphne and Andy, who told me about his stepsister, Myra. So it'll all be for her as well. When we go back, I want to make sure you tell Elisa that it's okay for her to love who she loves. Give Elisa her happy ending so we can have ours... Those are my rules."

"I understand," he said.

"Good. And one last thing before we go back to our room."

"What's that?"

"Do you want us to be complete squares in our new life, or should we do some renegotiating for how we play going forward?"

"We need to," Andrés said. "That night in the hallway—"

"I've played that night over and over in my head, and... you said, 'Constance.'"[7]

"I took back the safe word."

"But I kept going, which was wrong," she said.

"Then new rule: we shouldn't say our safe word unless it's an emergency. A real emergency. If you want that dance, then every moment together, we're in our game, we're dancing, and I'm pushing."

"And I'm pulling," she said.

"You were right. We can't be pussies about this."

"Hell no. There's no time-in or time-out. I was getting tired of that."

"I know. That breaks the spell," he said.

"I don't want what happened that night to happen again. That was the beginning of the end for us, and I don't want us to break up again over a fucking misunderstanding. *You'll always have my permission to cross whatever boundary you think I have and come home.* Going forward, we're always going to be in the Dance unless we tap out with our safe word, and that's only in a real emergency. Right?"

"Yup... Like, we're going into some real fucked-up territory that we know isn't good for us; that's the trust part."

"I agree to that rule—yes!"

"Agreed. Yes! New rule," he said. "You and I need to constantly talk about how we are with each other in the Dance and if that exchange is still working for us. That way, neither of us feels locked into something that's no longer fun or healthy—"

"We can't read each other's minds."

"No, we can't. This could go wrong real quick."

"Maybe we can enter a safe zone of negotiations—like this one—by saying something like 'Contract Talks'?"

"Yes! The new safe word for defining boundaries and talking about what we like and no longer like will be 'Contract Talks.'"

"I agree with that rule—yes!"

"Great!"

"New rule," she said. "Be prepared to fight to stay in control. That

---

7. *Book Three: The Labyrinth*, "Chapter Twenty-Five: The Minotaurs."

one, I know, won't surprise you, but we're dancing, right? I guess this is more of a reminder than a new rule. That night in the hallway—the night you broke up with me—that was the Domme coming out. What I'm trying to say is, if I don't say our safe word, keep fighting."

"Oh, trust me, that's not gonna be a problem anymore," Andrés said.

"Good, because what happened on those nights... it's what I've always wanted the most since I was sixteen.[8] And I've never gotten that from anyone except you. Since then, I've tried finding it in others, and you were right... Fake Doms have slipped. Constance was right... I have met monsters."

"I'm sorry—"

"I can't trust anyone else the way I trust you. That's why, after meeting monsters, I've always had to stay in control, only *playing* with women. But I'm tired of being a Domme, dealing with nothing but lazy-ass Subs who do all the taking but give nothing back. I want to be able to turn my brain off and go back into Space. I haven't had a Space-walk in years. Do you think you can still send me back there?"

"I know I can," Andrés said.

Sylvia smiled. "Good... Then, do you agree to take full control of your role in the Dance?"

"Yes."

"Do you agree to fight to keep control of your role?"

"I agree! Yes! Do you agree to submit—to dance with me?"

Sylvia enthusiastically said, "I agree! Yes! Dance with me!"

"Dance with me—"

"Oh, I will—do you agree to submit when I want submission and dominate when I need dominance?"

Andrés laughed. "I will never submit. I will fight. I will lead."

"Yes—you lead, I follow."

"I lead. You follow. This will be the last time I will call you by your government name—Sylvia Hadid James."

"This will be the last time I call you by yours—Andrés de León."

"This is the last time we'll say, 'Time-in.' Any last words?"

----

8. *Book Two: Underworld*, "Chapter Twelve: Sweet Sixteen."

"Nope—time-in," Sylvia said.

"What's your name?"

"Emma... What's yours?"

"I'm your Soldier Boy. Does my precious Emma want to play?"

"I've been dying to play again."

"And how would you like to play?"

"Can I show you?"

"Show me."

Sylvia, now safely immersed in her Littlespace, where she assumed the persona of Emma, took Andrés by the hand and led him back into what he had dubbed their Purple Room—the bedroom that had become their sanctuary during their first time together. Once there, she reached beneath the mattress and pulled out the knife she wanted him to drag across her naked body while Pat Benatar's *Hell Is for Children* played on repeat in the background, allowing her to express the one thing she couldn't with anyone else in her life, past or present: her complete and eternal trust in not only a man but another human being—her Big, Andrés.

❧ 30 ☙

FOR HER

It was 5:45 a.m. when the alarm went off. Sylvia and Andrés woke up and got out of bed. She unwrapped the silk scarf from her hair and folded it on her boudoir table, next to the makeup and hair care products Petra had given her with instructions to never neglect her hair. Sylvia deserved to focus as much as possible on her well-being before considering others, and that began with caring for the basics—the crown that was her beautiful hair.

Sylvia opened the door to their bedroom. Before heading out to brush her teeth, she turned to look at Andrés, who stood by the window, staring out at the blue hour as the golden light began to brighten the morning sky.

"Don't get lost in it. We're on a timeline," she said.

"I know," he said, stepping away from the window. He followed Sylvia into the bathroom, walking in as she used the toilet, then took his turn. After washing up, they stood side by side at the sink, brushing their teeth.

"I'm gonna wake him up," he said.

She gargled water and spat it into the sink. "Let him sleep a few more minutes."

Andrés finished after Sylvia and followed her back to the bedroom, closing the door behind them. They dressed for the day: she chose a dark blue skirt suit with a white silk shirt, while Andrés wore a charcoal gray suit with a light blue shirt and a pink tie. Sylvia sat at her boudoir table to apply makeup and style her hair, while Andrés reviewed his notes before tucking them back into his briefcase.

At 6:30 a.m., they opened their bedroom door and walked to what had once been an empty spare room between the kitchen and the family room. Sylvia knocked, then turned the handle and opened the door. Andy, now seven years old, was already up and dressed, sitting on the edge of his small bed as he tried to tie his shoes.

"It looks like someone is ready for their first day," Sylvia said as she walked over and knelt down to help him finish the knot. "Did you brush your teeth?"

"Yup!" Andy said.

"That's my good boy."

"Miss Sylvia..."

"Yes, my love."

"I can't wait to meet my new teacher, and go to my new school, and make new friends."

Sylvia began adjusting Andy's collar. "I'm so happy you get to go on a new adventure, and I can't wait for you to tell me all about it when you get home."

Andrés got down on his knees next to them. "What does my big boy want for breakfast?"

"My favorite," Andy said.

"I can take care of that for you," Sylvia said. "Dad always gets stains on his clothes, especially when he makes waffles."

"If you're going to make his breakfast, is there anything you'd like for me to do for you?" Andrés asked.

"Can you make me a fruit salad? You know what I like. And make one for yourself. I don't want you eating out for lunch."

"No junk food," Andy said.

She laughed. "You see? He knows."

Andrés stood. "He knows because he hears everything you say."

"Your daddy," she said, brushing Andy's hair to the side with her hand, "we want him to live for a long time, right?"

"We want him to live forever."

"Forever and ever." Sylvia stopped brushing his hair. "Okay, it's time for breakfast. Let's go, the two of you."

Sylvia stood up and pushed everyone out of the room and into the kitchen. She told Andy to take a seat at the table while she began preparing their breakfast, with Andrés handling their lunch. After eating, Sylvia rushed everyone out of the kitchen and into the family room, saying, "We're on a timeline."

She put a jacket on Andy and gave Andrés one last, long look to make sure he looked presentable, while he did the same for her. Then she hurried everyone out of the apartment and downstairs into the crisp morning light. Sylvia and Andrés walked with Andy down several city blocks until they reached a schoolyard on 1st Avenue.

"This is where your class is supposed to meet," Sylvia said. "Don't worry. I'll be here to pick you up. We can walk back together."

Sylvia knelt, spun Andy around, and checked his backpack, making sure he had everything he needed. Then she spun Andy back around and adjusted his collar.

"You're ready," she said.

"When can I walk home alone?" Andy asked.

"Dad and I will need to see what the crossing guards are like first before deciding. It won't be a hard decision. Today, I'll follow you home while you walk ahead. Another day, Dad will do the same. Then we'll see. No promises. Okay?"

"Okay."

Before Sylvia could say more, Andy threw his arms around her, hugging her tight.

"I love you, Mom," Andy said.

The spontaneous hug and declaration of love surprised Sylvia, making her burst into tears. She hugged him back as tightly as she could, saying, "I love you too... I love you so much."

Sylvia continued lingering in her son's embrace until Andy wriggled out of her arms. He then gave one long look at Andrés before running off to join the other children playing in the schoolyard. Sylvia and Andrés watched as Andy's teacher appeared, organizing the children into two lines before leading them into the building.

"This is the first time I feel normal," Sylvia said.

"You've always been normal," Andrés said.

"I guess."

"Did you see that look he gave me?"

Sylvia sighed. "Don't tell him that I told you."

"Told me what?"

"He's been upset lately, that you're hardly home; that you never have time for him."

"This new job is kicking my ass."

"I know that," Sylvia said. "But what he sees is that when you have time, you spend it with Daphne."

"Emma, I'm trying my best."

"I know, but just remember, to him, you're not there—but it's okay because I am, for the both of us."

He smiled. "I'm so grateful for everything you've done for him, coming into his life even when we weren't together. That's a lot to take on, just on hope."

"I don't hope... Like I said, I knew it was a matter of time before we'd be back together. I was holding it down with Andy until then. We've gotta get going; we're on a timeline."

Sylvia and Andrés walked out of the schoolyard and headed north along the avenue. The closer they got to Union Square, the slower she walked; the more she bit her nails and picked at her hair. Andrés grabbed her hand. She felt the relief of knowing he was there to keep her compulsions from harming her, as they had so many times since she was Andy's age. When they arrived, they went downstairs, through the turnstiles, and into the maze of the subway station.

She stopped him before they were to go their separate ways. Andrés was heading to an office on Wall Street, where he developed and managed tools that would analyze the banking clients' financial data and present reports on headcount—a job he was hired to do earlier in the year.

"Are you sure it's okay that I'm not working?" Sylvia asked.

"You were ready to have me move in with Andy when I only had a student job," he replied.

"True."

"This job pays more than I expected—way, way more. This is what being a couple is all about, is it not?"

"True, but what if I don't get on the train? What if I go back home instead and keep working on my book?"

"Then, you go back. You already have a master's degree and some fame. You've gone further than most people. Whatever you decide, it has to be the best choice for you."

"I still don't know if I should do this."

"Why?"

"Because I'm scared," she said. "I mean, what if it's a trigger? What if it becomes too much work, and I relapse?"

"What if you succeed?"

"Nothing ever works out for me."

"What would that woman think of you right now?"

"What woman?" Sylvia asked.

"The version of you that was on stage that night at The Loft so many years ago, reading *A Word to My Broken Heart*.[1] Do you remember her?"

Sylvia sighed. "I remember."

"I was there when that woman said she understood why her Nana was so hard on her, to always be on top of her shit. Do you remember that woman saying that?"

"I remember."

"Do you remember her crying?"

"I remember."

"You felt something that night that made it clear what you needed to do: to be on top of your shit. Emma, I love you so much. You're my world, you're my everything, and I can't be right with you without reminding you of that woman. So, Emma, no fear—I want you to act like there's nothing else in the world that's more important than

---

1. *Book Three: The Labyrinth*, "Chapter Twenty-Six: December Came and Went."

getting what you need, for you and only you, and that night, you knew what it was—it was the Master Plan."

"The Master Plan," Sylvia said.

"We're a family now. This is what I'm supposed to do: support my family. I can afford to carry all of us now, so you don't need to worry about a job. You already have a lot of work ahead of you."

"Tell me about it."

"I got us... Do what's best for you, knowing your rock is our rock. Get that feeling of personal accomplishment—to say, 'I did it.' And if you need to take it all the way just for that feeling that you're on top of your shit, go for it. I got you. You can still work on your book. Nothing is stopping you from doing that or anything else. I got you. I got us."

Sylvia threw her arms around him. "Thank you! I needed to hear that!" She lingered in his arms for a long moment before pushing herself away to say with a smile, "Just so you know, after we put Andy to bed, that woman you made cry, she's gonna kick your ass. I need to do it... *for her.*"

"Before you come for me, make sure you're on top of whatever your advisor wants you to work on, or else I'm gonna spank that ass hard."

Sylvia let out a cackle that made everyone walking around them turn to look at her. "I better go," she said, smiling.

"You better—we're on a timeline."

"Yeah, yeah," she said, then walked away, heading toward the subway platform. She was to board a train heading uptown to meet with advisors about being readmitted to Columbia University and finishing the Master Plan for good.

DUST IN THE GOLDEN HOUR

JUNE 26, 1998

IT WAS FRIDAY, CLOSE TO SUNSET, WHEN ANDRÉS ARRIVED AT THE playground in Tompkins Square Park. He spotted Sylvia in a bright yellow sundress at the top of a slide, sitting behind Andy, both about to come down.

"Look, Andy, Daddy's home," she said.

"Daddy's home!"

Sylvia and Andy came down the slide together, both wearing big, happy smiles—Sylvia looking as if she were a kid herself. Andrés greeted them at the bottom, with Andy sitting between her legs, his small body resting on the hot metal.

"You're nuts for doing that in a dress," he said.

"I've got biker shorts on underneath, and Andy insisted we do this, so here I am. You, on the other hand, are late. You better have a good excuse."

Andrés dropped his briefcase. "I do."

"I'll be the judge of that," Sylvia said, standing up to kiss him. "Now go upstairs and get the camera. Elisa and the kids should be here any minute, and we're on a timeline."

Andrés obeyed her command and raced out of the playground. Ten minutes later, he returned to find Sylvia chatting with Elisa. Myra, who was now ten, laughed as she chased Andy around the playground. Daphne sat in her stroller between Sylvia and Elisa, giggling at her big brother and sister.

Andy ran up to his father and pointed at Daphne. "Look, Dad, she's wearing the same dress as Mom!"

"I know," Andrés said, smiling. "And they're both beautiful."

Elisa playfully slapped Andrés on the shoulder. "What about me?"

"And me!" Myra said as she ran up to Andrés, breathing hard.

"You're beautiful, too," he said to Myra. "Your mom, on the other hand... she's *aight*."

"Hey!" Elisa said, slapping him on the shoulder again.

"Ignore his goofy ass," Sylvia said, grabbing Elisa's hand. "You're beautiful too."

"Thank you," Elisa said with a smile. "I'm glad somebody thinks so. Do you guys need me around for this? I was planning on staying, but the L train was running late, and I need to meet Gus."

"You don't need to explain." Sylvia gently dropped Elisa's hand. "We've got this covered. Go ahead and enjoy your life. We'll take care of everything and bring them back on Sunday night."

Before Elisa could respond, Myra tugged on her hand, asking her to kneel down so she could whisper in her ear while glaring at Sylvia. Elisa stood up and said with a forced smile, "She doesn't want to stay."

Andrés said to Myra, "But we're taking pictures of the family for my office."

"But Miss Sylvia is not family; *Mami* is."

"Honey, it's okay. I completely understand," Sylvia said. "I'm not your *Mami*, but I am your friend. And if Andrés is your stepfather, then that means I look after you too. Not only because I love your stepbrother and your little sister, but because I also love you, and I want to give your mommy some time for herself."

Elisa sighed. "It's okay. I was planning on bringing her with me anyway." She glanced at her watch. "I've got to go."

Andrés said to Myra, "It's not going to be the same without you."

"I want to be with my mom."

"Don't do that," Sylvia said, placing her hand on Andrés's shoulder. "She's already told us no. We need to respect that."

"I hope you take great pictures," Elisa said as she began walking backward, away from them. "Take one for me—now I really gotta go." She turned and rushed off, dragging Myra behind her.

Sylvia looked at Andrés with resignation and despair. "Myra is never gonna forgive me, is she?"

"As long as she thinks it's you who broke up our family and not Elisa, yeah... Are you sure you don't want me to tell her the truth?"

"It's better this way. I'd rather she blame me than her mom."

"I don't understand why she doesn't put that on me."

Sylvia began to laugh. "Baby, when she becomes a teenager, you're gonna get it. And when you do, I want you to remember this moment when you're wondering why Myra has become so angry at you."

Andy, who had been entertaining himself on the slide, ran over to Sylvia. "Mom, I thought we were gonna take pictures!"

"We are," Sylvia said.

"Then let's go. We're on a timeline."

Daphne began to fuss and squirm in her stroller. Sylvia went over to her and said, "Time to let you out, get this party going." She looked at Andrés. "How do you wanna do this?"

"I wanna take some candids first, with you playing in the golden light with them. Then we can focus on portraits."

"Okay, my love. Sounds like a plan."

Andrés stood back and smiled at how the love of his life played with their children in the golden hour of the last rays of sunshine. Sylvia's auburn hair glowed, her smile radiant, and Daphne's blonde hair shone, and Andy's smile and eyes gleamed brightly. All were framed by the golden light, their silhouettes like shadows. Their laughter boomed through the park as Sylvia chased Andy while holding Daphne, who giggled loudly at the top of her lungs.

This vision of his family playing in the golden light of the sun cracked something in Andrés so wide open that all this love he never knew was possible poured out like lava from the volcano of his heart.

A deeper love beyond anything Andrés could have imagined.

A deeper love for his family.

He understood this was the deeper love of a father—and of a husband—who would sacrifice himself and die so that they may continue to live in the golden rays of light for as many golden hours as the Creator of the Universe would be willing to bless Sylvia, bless Andy, bless Daphne—bless Myra—the only people who mattered in his world.

Sylvia turned to look at Andrés and smiled, her eyes beaming brightly at him like stars radiating from the silhouette of her body. He took that picture of Sylvia and Daphne smiling back at him, capturing that precious moment, freezing it in time.

Sylvia placed Daphne on the ground, then raced over to Andy on the slides. She climbed to the top and slid down behind him, catching up at the bottom and wrapping her arms around him. Andrés took that picture of Sylvia and Andy waving back at him, capturing that precious moment, freezing it in time.[1]

Andrés raced over to Daphne, who was running toward a group of children playing on the nearby swings. He caught her just before she got too close to their feet, kicking high in the air.

Sylvia yelled out, "I need to take your picture—you and me. Come!" She raced over to Andrés, who was walking back with Daphne in his arms, and grabbed the camera. Then she hurried back to Andy and said, "I want you to do Mom a favor. I want you to take a picture of just me and Dad. Can you do that?"

"I can do it," Andy said eagerly, taking the camera.

Andrés placed Daphne on the ground. She ran toward the slide where Andy stood, who, as Sylvia rushed over to stand next to Andrés, was preparing to take a picture of his parents. Andy pressed the button on the camera, but nothing happened. Sylvia raced over to grab Daphne, who had started wandering toward the swings, while Andrés went over to Andy to check the camera.

"Did I break it?" Andy said, worried.

"No," Andrés said. "We ran out of film. I can't take any more pictures."

---

1. *Book One: Orpheus*, "Chapter Three: A-Okay."

Sylvia walked back over with Daphne in her arms and said, "Go back upstairs and get another roll."

"But we're running out of good light, and unloading and reloading the camera takes time, and the moment's passed. I got what was most important: you guys."

"But what about for me? For my desk? I need one of you—of us. Go back upstairs and get some more film, and use flash this time."

"Mom, I'm hungry," Andy said, tugging at her.

Daphne began squirming in Sylvia's arms, trying to get free.

"I think it's time to feed the squad," Andrés said.

"Fine," Sylvia said, frustrated.

"I know you wanted pictures of us, but we already have a lot of great pictures of you and Andy, you and Daphne."

"But what about you?"

"What about me?"

"You're not in any of the shots."

Andrés shrugged. "It's just the way it is, I guess."

"Not with me."

"There'll be a next time," Andrés said. "The light's already gone, and the kids aren't gonna let us take the shots anyway."

Sylvia sighed. "I guess you're right. Let's go feed the kids."

"It's about time," Andy said.

"What did I say about inserting yourself into adult conversations?" Sylvia asked.

"I forgot."

"You didn't forget," Sylvia said as she placed Daphne into her stroller. "Alright, let's eat some Thai food, because why?"

Andy yelled out for the whole park to hear, "Because we don't want Daddy to get fat!"

Sylvia looked at Andrés, and a genuine smile replaced the forced one she had been giving Andy. "The tribe has spoken. Let's go."

Andrés took charge of the stroller while Sylvia grabbed Andy's hand. They left the playground together, walking down Avenue A toward Lower Manhattan. Once they reached SoHo, they stopped at an upscale Asian restaurant for dinner. Later, the de León family returned home, piled into bed, and watched TV together until they all fell asleep.

❧ 32 ❧

THE END

OCTOBER 23, 1998

THE LINE AT THE MINISTRY OF SOUND WAS WAY TOO LONG TO WAIT in—for what looked like London's equivalent of where New York's bridge-and-tunnel crowd would swarm, like locusts, to get drunk, start fights, and, when done, go back to their square lives in the suburbs.

"This line is crazy," Andrés said. "Do you have any juice here?"

"Not yet," Sylvia said. "But that does us no good now. I have a friend who suggested that while we're in London, we check out The End. She said it's a lot like Robots back in the day. She gave me the info."

"I've always been curious about Robots," Elisa said.

"They would've never let you in. You're too square and pure."

"No, I'm not."

"His goofy-ass only got in because of me."

"Whatever—talk is cheap. Get us into The End," Andrés said.

All three jumped out of the queue to stand on the narrow one-way street, jam-packed with black cabs dropping off drunk partygoers. They stopped a black cab just as it was about to drive away and jumped in.

"We're sorry. We really need to get out of here," Elisa said to the driver.

The driver forced a smile. "But of course."

"Are you familiar with a club called The End?" Sylvia asked. "I think it's on New Oxford and West Central?"

"Yes."

"Can you take us there?"

"Sure, my friend," the driver said as he drove away from the curb.

"I'm gonna need a receipt for the ride," Andrés said.

"We just got in the car. Be in the moment," Sylvia said.

Andrés turned to the driver. "Ask me why we're in London."

"My friend, what brings you to the city?"

"I'm glad you asked. I'm chasing some senior managers who aren't answering my emails or calls about headcount and budgets. So I got this nice trip out of it. We just talked business. I get to expense this ride, and I'd like to leave you a nice tip."

"I'm glad I could help a friend," the driver said, now relaxed and smiling.

"Thanks for inviting me," Elisa said.

"I figured it'd be fun. Andrés will be at work, and we can hang out while he's gone," Sylvia said.

"We can check out Harrods," Elisa said.

"The Tower of London and Westminster Abbey—"

"We can't leave out Buckingham Palace."

"You know it," Sylvia said.

"What about my friend here? Is he going to have any fun?" the driver asked.

"Don't worry about him," Elisa said, smiling.

"Yeah, he'll get his fun. I'll make sure of that," Sylvia said, also smiling.

"My friend, you're a lucky man," the driver said.

"I'm the luckiest man alive," Andrés said.

They arrived at their destination. The driver dropped them off on a dark, narrow street. Sylvia approached the bouncer, who, after a quick chat, opened the door for them.

Andrés grabbed Sylvia's and Elisa's hands and led them inside, into a small, dark room. A DJ was behind a booth in the corner, spinning vinyl on turntables. House music thumped hard from the large speakers in the dark corners, vibrating through everyone on the dance floor.

Sylvia and Elisa pressed against Andrés, holding each other close to him—eye to eye, breath to breath, chest to chest—until an explosion of light illuminated the dark room like sunshine blasting through hell. It forced Andrés's eyes shut until the intensity subsided, and he no longer saw red but black. He opened his eyes to see Sylvia with her arms wrapped around Elisa, kissing her.

Andrés shook his head and walked away. A woman nearby, dressed in full goth—black lace tights, platform boots, and a dark velvet dress—stared at him for a moment. She offered a welcoming smile before turning away. Andrés reached out, turned her around, and pulled her close, letting her hands roam over him until Elisa yanked him back.

Sylvia grabbed Andrés, pulling him closer and kissing him. Elisa leaned in, kissing them both.

Andrés stopped, pushed Elisa and Sylvia away, and walked off into a dark corner.

Sylvia followed, yelling over and over, "It's okay!"

Andrés turned and shouted over the music, "No, it's not! You haven't thought this through!"

"Yes, I have."

"What happened to not wanting to share?"

"Share with strangers, but this is Elisa."

"That's even worse! She can't handle shit like this—it's gonna fuck up our peace!"

"No, it won't! It'll make our lives that much more peaceful."

"But you don't know her like I do! Contract Talks! Contract Talks!"

Before Sylvia could respond to his safe word, Elisa came over and asked, "What's going on? Are we doing this or what?"

Sylvia turned to Elisa. "He's worried this'll disturb the peace."

"No, it won't," Elisa said. "I mean, to be honest, this is what I thought I'd be getting when I met him—excitement. But I was wrong. I knew he was holding back. That day when Andrés came home with you, I understood why."

Sylvia smiled.

"Damn, don't look *too* happy," Elisa said.

"I'm sorry, but I am. When we were apart, I had to hold back too. I can't be with any other guy like this. I tried once, and it was horrible. It feels good to hear it from you and not from him—that he couldn't be with another woman like that."

"Gee, I'm glad to be of help," Elisa said.

"Come on... You were in bed with Gus when we came to your apartment that day, so don't act all hurt. Andrés and I have this deep psychological thing, like I'm sure you have with your man. Especially with this. To be like this with anyone else is impossible... I guess Andrés is right when he says you can't handle it."

"I can."

"Are you sure? Because if you want to *play* like this, you'll need to be prepared to handle hard emotions. You have to be ready to say 'no' when it starts to hurt, and the pain stops being fun."

"I know—"

"It has to be a choice. Do you choose to be in?"

"I do."

"It's a yes or no," Sylvia said.

"Yes," Elisa said.

"Okay, then. Some ground rules: what happens tonight changes nothing between all of us."

"That's fine. What we do stays here. It won't affect us, as long as Andrés says nothing to Gus."

"That's your business," he said.

"Then we're good," Elisa said.

Sylvia turned to Andrés. "See? We're good!"

Before he could say no, Andrés paused, thinking about all the stress Sylvia had been under since starting her in vitro fertilization treatments—her frustrations, her sadness. He could think of nothing but the need to make her happy, so he forced a smile and said, "Okay, whatever helps you through the tough times... it's fine..."

OCTOBER 24, 1999

Andrés was in a conference room with Paul, one of the managing partners of the technology firm. They were joined by associate partners and senior managers to discuss winding down projects related to Y2K and the projected drop in client demand for work beyond the year 2000. To facilitate this process for everyone in the room, it was helpful to refer to each employee as a "resource." Instead of employees losing their jobs, resources were rolling off the client site. Paul wanted the names of those who could be considered disposable.

A senior manager said he had a resource who was experiencing problems at home: the resource's wife was an alcoholic, and their children were not coping well. The resource had requested some time off.

Paul asked what the projected demand was for the team that resource was a part of. The senior manager rattled off a number based on data compiled and maintained by Andrés.

He projected a drop in demand. Paul said that the resource had to go.

Another senior manager said she had a resource battling breast cancer and taking considerable time off for chemotherapy. Paul asked what the projected demand was for the team that resource was a part of. The senior manager rattled off a number based on data compiled and maintained by Andrés.

She projected a drop in demand. Paul said that the resource had to go.

The understanding among Paul and the senior management in that room, with no windows and black walls, was that nobody cared what was going on in the lives of their resources. It wasn't the firm's problem.

Cut. Rolled off. Gone. Real people with real lives and real issues.

Five hours of listening to personal information gathered by senior management during off-site social gatherings and private meetings— held in confidence—only for it to be used against the resource when deciding whether to keep them or not.

Nothing was off limits.

An associate partner said, "This guy here drinks way too much and comes into work hungover."

Paul pushed a button on him, like a mob boss would on a mark. In his words, that loser was now gone.

A senior manager said, "This girl shows off her tits way too much at our gatherings and is sleeping with everyone at the office."

Paul pushed a button on her, and, in his words, that slut was now gone.

Names. People. Lives.

All from a list compiled through a process designed, coded, and implemented by Andrés.

Having turned down the sexual advances of his supervisor, the Director of Human Resources, Andrés knew she was eager to use what she had on him—his visits to a fertility specialist with Sylvia—as leverage. Because of that, he *had* prepared himself to hear he would be rolling off the project as well. A separate list had been kept, and his name was on it.

But that was before Paul pulled Andrés aside before the meeting. Paul told him that because the process he designed was so effective in identifying potential cuts and had saved the firm so much money, he was going to promote him instead.

Paul informed Andrés that, as part of his promotion, he would oversee the company-wide implementation of his system. This involved gathering data from multiple client sites across the United States and Europe. If Andrés encountered instances where management at these sites *seemed* reluctant to share data, avoiding emails and calls, he would need to be prepared to travel. Just as he had done with the London office the previous year, Andrés would have to confront non-cooperative senior managers.

Paul told him there would be days Andrés would need to be in Chicago. He would have to gather and analyze data, then present his findings to the leadership there. When Andrés asked why he couldn't just stay in New York and share his reports through a call or email—to save the money that would be spent on flying him back and forth from New York and on expensive hotel rooms—and keep the resource battling breast cancer instead, Paul shrugged him off. He said most of the leadership were old and would prefer to see Andrés in person, just in case they wanted to pop into his office, which Andrés would also be getting as part of his promotion.

"I need to know before going in: yes or no."

Paul stood tall over Andrés, his athletic frame hovering close, pressing him for a quick answer.

Andrés did not want to accept anything that would take him further away from Sylvia and his children. Anything that would do that was a hard "no" for him. But because of the increasing costs of her IVF treatments, he felt compelled to say "yes" without consulting her—albeit with one condition.

He told Paul, "There's a name on that list I'd like to take off."

"And who's that?" Paul replied, his expression saying: *You're lucky to have this new job, to be making demands.*

"Marco... He's got a wife and a little girl—"

"Everyone has someone to worry about," Paul said.

"Yeah, but he just bought a new house. Couldn't we send him to one of the new client sites we have starting up at the World Trade Center?"

"This is rich, coming from the hitman," Paul said. "Why do you care?"

Andrés paused before saying, "Because we're fathers. Aren't you one?"

Paul said nothing as he looked lost in thought for a moment. Andrés's suggestion that he view Marco as someone like himself rather than just a resource seemed to stir an emotion within him—a feeling he had long buried in his pursuit of wealth.

Appearing to come out of his thoughts, Paul said, "That site does need a finance guy. He can build up their new systems and processes."

Paul gave Andrés a frustrated look. "Going forward, you'd better document your work just in case you're no longer working for the firm. Someone could easily take your place. Now, let's go in."

AUGUST 22, 2000

Andrés stood at the edge of a white rock cliff, overlooking the blue waters of the Mediterranean Sea, with Sylvia next to him in her bikini. Towering behind them were brilliant white rock formations, rising majestically over the landscape like ancient sentinels—titans holding up the sky at twilight.

"I can't believe you talked me into coming here," Sylvia said.

"What the fuck are you talking about?" he said. "We came here because you saw pictures of this place in a brochure. 'Wouldn't it be cool if we went there and jumped?'"

"I don't sound like that."

"Yeah, you do. Now that we're here, come on, let's jump. It's only a 100-foot drop."

"Fuck you. You jump."

"I will."

"Then do it," Sylvia said.

"That wouldn't be fun for you, would it? I know you want to push me off—"

"I so wanna push you off—payback for all the bullshit of the last few months."

"I could say the same."

"Say the same? At least my work is important. If I'm not in good standing, I'm fucked. You? You get on a plane, and for what? So you can be like those other useless assholes? Meanwhile, I'm the one at home with Andy. I'm the one that goes to parent-teacher meetings. I'm the one that makes sure he eats, does his homework, has playdates —and that's with me trying to do it all, with what I've got going on."

Sylvia paused to take a deep breath and swallow.

"If it weren't for *Mama* coming down and helping, I'd be drowning right now."

"IVF is not free," Andrés said.

"I know."

"I've got to get on a plane—"

"I know—but I don't want you becoming like one of them!"

"It's been three years, and I'm still the same."

"Yeah, but... everyone eventually becomes the company they keep. And you know what guys—like the ones you work with now—have done to me? You're gonna change."

"That'll never happen."

"Are you sure? 'Cause before, you'd never step into a strip club without me, and now, when you come home, your suits are covered in glitter."

"You know I have to play the game, go where they talk real business."

"Or you could say, 'No!'"

"You think that doesn't cross my mind? You think I wanna be at a strip club?"

"Yes!"

"I don't—"

"Yes, you do. I'm sure the young women at these places are beautiful—more beautiful than my old ass that can't get pregnant—"

"Emma, stop."

"But it's true!"

Andrés took a deep breath and paused, letting what she was expressing—her fears and sudden insecurities—sink in. It didn't matter that Sylvia was the one who had encouraged him to play the game he needed to play, even if it meant going into strip clubs. It didn't seem to matter to Sylvia that they needed to do whatever was necessary to cover the extra costs from her two years of in vitro fertilization treatments. What mattered more to her was that tens of thousands of dollars had been spent, and she was still struggling—still blaming herself for why it wasn't working. Karma exists for everything, even for the body. They were now paying for what had been done to her in the Black Room.

When Andrés took a deep breath and swallowed, she sighed, then walked away, distancing herself as much as possible from him.

After a moment of watching Sylvia, her shoulders slumped forward, dejected eyes glistening back at him, Andrés asked, "Do you still want to push me off?"

"Yes," she said, her voice shaking.

"Then do it."

"I will."

"What are you waiting for, Emma?"

Sylvia began pacing barefoot on the rocks.

"Do we need to say Nana's name?" Andrés asked.

"I don't know."

Andrés turned his back to Sylvia and, with arms outstretched, said, "If you don't know, then come and push me. Get the poison out."

"I don't want to now."

"Come on... I know you'd enjoy pushing me off a literal cliff."

She chuckled under her breath. "You know me so well."

He turned to face her. "Then come on and do it! What are you waiting for?"

The frustration and sadness that were once on her face gave way to exasperation and a smile hinting at playfulness. "Because I don't know how to get down from here, you fucking asshole! You always do this shit!"

"It's how we dance."

"I don't think I like dancing like this anymore; my feet are starting to hurt."

"Contract talks?"

"No—"

"Then come push me off."

"No, you're jumping down with me. I'll fuck you up later for this... beat that ass."

"That's my good girl."

Andrés walked back over to Sylvia. Together, they faced the cliff's edge, the ocean joining the vast sky at twilight on the horizon ahead.

"On the count of three, we run as fast as possible and jump," she said.

"That's how we make the leap... Are you ready?"

"I'm ready—one—"

Andrés moved like he was about to run ahead before she could finish the countdown.

"Stop! This is scaring me," she said.

"Alright, I'm serious now. Hold my hand. Together, we race to the edge as fast as possible and jump. No thinking, no fear. We just do it. Okay?"

Instead of answering, Sylvia ran ahead, laughing, and Andrés chased after her.

Sylvia jumped off the cliff's edge, yelling with open-mouthed joy on the way down.

Andrés jumped after her, plunging next to her into the clear and deep blue waters below. He was sinking.

She swam to him, her eyes flashing like underwater spotlights. Her outstretched hands pulled him in close, keeping him from sinking further, and holding him, and saving him. They swam to the top, with bubbles of light trailing behind them like stars, until they reached the surface under a vast sky spanning wide over the Mediterranean Sea, the last light from the setting sun shimmering on the ripples swirling around them. Together, they breathed, and breathed, and breathed.

"That wasn't as scary as I thought," Sylvia said, holding him up and preventing him from sinking.

"No, it wasn't," Andrés said.

"Maybe everything's gonna be alright."

"Maybe... maybe it's my turn to tell you what you're always telling me."

"What? Flush the toilet?"

"No," he said, splashing water at her face.

She laughed. "Then tell me."

"No fear, my love. No fear. Everything's gonna be A-okay."

"Will it?"

"*Sí, mi amor—tienes que tener fe en Dios...* just believe."

❧ 33 ❧

THE BLACK ROOM

IT WAS A FRIDAY NIGHT. ANDRÉS SAT AT A TABLE WITH PAUL AND others from his office in a dimly lit room on the North Side of Chicago, watching the emcee of the strip club scan the crowd of men in the audience from the stage.

The emcee announced, "Once again, for those who are new, I am your host: Dion the Shepherd. Thank you for making Shadow's Cave a part of your night. Fellas, as a reminder, don't forget to tip the bartenders and be very generous with the ladies—remember, their time is money. So, with that said, let's keep the party going and welcome to the stage, coming all the way from outer space, Estrella the Spacer Woman!"

A petite young woman, clad in a silver sequin bra and silver boots reaching up to her knees, stepped onto the stage. She jumped on the pole and began to swing around, performing. Paul and the others stood and started pelting her with wadded-up balls of dollar bills. Estrella did her best to smile and not flinch, but the intensity with which the rest of the men in the audience threw the bills—pelting her hard, as if they were casting stones—made her fall off the pole.

Andrés stood and rushed away, pushing through the throngs, all of them laughing at the Spacer Woman lying prone on the stage. He pushed his way through the leering crowd to the doors, stepping outside into the cold without his suit jacket. He stared down a long, dark street as he reached into his pocket for his phone and dialed. Sirens blared in the distance as he waited for Sylvia to answer, but the call went to voicemail. He spoke as if she were listening:

"I fucking hate this. I hate people. I wanna go home. I wanna be home with you so bad; I can't stand being here."

Andrés paused to take a deep breath and keep himself from crying over the voicemail.

"I'm sorry. I had to vent... It's the same old, same old... I'll try back later. I love you."

Andrés looked at his phone and dialed again. More sirens blared in the distance as he waited for Elisa to pick up.

"Hey, what's going on?" Elisa answered.

"Same shit... Is Daphne awake?"

"We just finished reading a bedtime story, and she's knocked out."

"How about Myra? Is she up?"

"She's up, but she's in one of those moods... I'd leave her alone if I were you—"

"I just wanted to tell her—to tell my girls—that I love them. I need them to know."

"Don't worry, they know."

"Some of the shit I've seen tonight... just, please, tell them."

"Alright, I will tell—"

"Thank you..."

Elisa was quiet for a moment.

"Same shit? Does that mean you're stuck in Chicago?" she asked.

"I'm stuck again."

"Back at the club? Playing the game?"

"As always..."

"You know, I wouldn't mind some tits in my face... Where's Sylvia?"

Andrés laughed. "You better watch yourself."

"I'm just playing," Elisa said.

"Sure you were... I'll call the girls in the morning. Goodnight."

"Goodnight, and be safe. Seriously, play that game. Daphne is excited, and so is Myra."

"She is?" Andrés said, smiling.

"She's the big sister."

"That makes me so happy."

"I'm glad that it does, and I'm so happy for Sylvia. I know how much you guys struggled to get to this point."

"The struggle was all hers—you just don't know everything that had happened to her that made this all seem impossible until now."

"I can only imagine. Don't you worry. Keep playing that game. Your girls are counting on you too. I know we have a complicated relationship, but I never doubted you. I knew you'd get your break. I knew you'd make your money."

"Thank you for believing in me, even when I didn't."

"You owe me for that," she said, laughing. "So, keep playing."

"I know."

"Don't you worry about Sylvia. Tomorrow, I'm going to take the girls and swing by the apartment to check in on her—make sure she's okay. As for you, my baby daddy, you can go fuck yourself."

Andrés laughed. "You can go fuck yourself too, my baby mama. Goodnight."

He hung up and went back inside. The VIP section he had been in was empty; Paul and the others were gone.

Dion the Shepherd approached Andrés. "I took your friends to a private room. They asked me to show you the way there once you returned. Follow me."

Andrés followed him away from the crowd, the music, and the noise to the back, where they entered a labyrinth of mirrors. They wound their way through until Dion opened one of the glass doors and ushered him into a large, dark room with black walls.

It was the first time Andrés had seen or been in anything like it: a small room illuminated by blacklight. Every speck of dust, dirt, and stain on the sofas glowed brightly. Paul and the others, who were sitting while young, naked women moved about in the Black Room, were just as dirty and glowing.

Some of the ladies asked the men questions, like how long they would be in Chicago or what they did for a living. The ladies listened, nodding approvingly as the men replied while handing them cash for lap dances.

Instead of taking a seat alongside Paul and the others, Andrés turned and tried to leave the Black Room. But Dion had locked the doors from the outside.

There was no exit.

Paul called out, "Hey, Andrés! What on earth are you doing, lingering over there like a *muppet?* Come and join us; take a seat."

Playing the game, Andrés did as his boss directed him to, but he sat as far apart from them as he could and continued to watch.

Paul and the others kept pelting the women in the Black Room with wadded-up balls of dollar bills, laughing as they knelt and crawled across the floor, picking up their earnings. Then Paul called over Estrella the Spacer Woman, who was no longer in her outfit but stark naked, wearing only knee-high boots.

"Come now, get into position. I'm gonna do a line off your ample bottom," Paul said.

Estrella forced a smile. "Okay. That sounds super fun."

She did as she was told. Paul flipped her onto his knee like a slab of meat, then snorted a thick line of cocaine off her—enough to kill a normal man. Soon, other dancers were ordered to do the same, their bodies positioned on the other men's laps as if they were objects born to be used in this manner.

Andrés stood and went back to the door.

Paul commanded Estrella and the other women to kneel and use their hands and mouths on him and the others seated throughout the Black Room. They obeyed. Despite Estrella's and the women's efforts, doing their best, Paul and the other men remained limp and unresponsive.

Andrés banged on the door, hollering for Dion to let him out.

Paul called out to Andrés, "What seems to be the issue? Are you *not* joining us?"

"No, thanks," he said, not facing him.

Paul pushed Estrella away from his crotch. "You always do this *shite.*"

One man said from a dark corner, "That's because he doesn't like women—he's a fag."

Another called out, "He's not a *real* man."

Paul laughed. "Andrés is a world-class *poof.*"

"You got me... I'm the *biggest* one around."

"Seriously," Paul said, "no worries, mate. You're among men here. We all have wives. It's simply *our* way."

"It's not mine," Andrés said, still trying to open the door.

"Your *precious* Sylvia will never know."

"But I would."

A sinister smile spread across Paul's face. "From what I hear—strictly from her work, of course—your Sylvia has had quite an *interesting* past."

"So have I," Andrés said.

"Yeah, but not like hers. Doesn't it bother you?"

Andrés stopped trying to open the door. He walked over and sat on the couch, facing Paul and Estrella. She was sitting on the floor with a forced smile and terror in her eyes, in a supplicant position at Paul's feet.

"I've got some tinnitus from my deployment that gets in the way of things. Do you want to repeat that?" Andrés asked.

"What?" Paul said. "That your precious Sylvia has documented her past? That she's written about all the dicks she's sucked? Fucking hell, doesn't that bother you, or are you not a *real* man?"

"It doesn't bother her that I've killed people... in the defense of my country, of course. It doesn't bother her that I've got a body count higher than hers, literally and figuratively."

"Fucking hell, mate," Paul said.

"Only chumps worry about shit like that," Andrés said. "Men who don't fuck."

One man said from a dark corner, "Andrés is full of shit."

Another called out, "The only thing that faggot has killed is time—ours!"

"I'm a faggot? You're the faggot who pulls me over to talk about your new grill like it's some woman you want to fuck."

Andrés pointed at another one of his coworkers in the dark corner.

"You're the one who came to me complaining about how your wife won't fuck you—even though you bought her a house and pay for everything. Only faggots think that way. Meanwhile, I've got a girlfriend at home who's pregnant—"

"She is?" Paul said, smiling.

"Yeah, she is—Sylvia's at home, pregnant, taking care of the son I had with my ex-wife. Together, *we* have a girlfriend who is not only her Sub but also the mother of my daughter."

Andrés motioned around the room.

"So I don't need any of this. *You* guys do, but I don't. Why would I? I'm not hungry like you. And because I'm not, I don't deal with women who don't want me."

"Who gives a fuck what they want? We're paying them," Paul said.

"And that's why you need to pay. That's why women will always hate fags like you. And why would you want that unless you're the one who hates them?"

Andrés shook his head.

"Stupid idiots... Paying for pussy—"

"We all pay, one way or another," Paul said. "If you think that we don't, you're nothing but a fool."

"If that's the way you think, you're the fool," Andrés said. "You've never been a man worth anything to have a woman want you. I mean, crawl on glass to want to see you, kind of wanting you. Money can't buy that—that's desire."

"He's right," Estrella said, still seated on the floor, no longer in a supplicant position.

"I'm not paying you for your opinions," Paul said, pushing Estrella's head back with an open palm.

One man said from a dark corner, "If all the shit you're talking is true, it's because your girls can't do any better than you. They've got no options."

"Keep up with that shit, and no woman will ever want you for you, you fat fuck," Andrés said. "My girlfriends can leave whenever they want, and I love that. I love that they don't need me. I love that they have their own money and their own apartments. I've never had to rent my own place."

"Like a bum," Paul said.

"No, like a man who could be trusted to do right by them—a man who loves women who own their sexuality—that they fuck. Powerful women who can walk away. I give those women exactly what they want in return: they can turn off their minds when it matters the most to me, in bed, and I do the rest. Once you give a woman like that an out-of-body experience, take them into Space; they're yours forever."

"You know what's up with that Subspace feel?" Estrella asked, still on the floor at Paul's feet.

"I know how to take my girls there," Andrés replied.

Estrella stood, walked over to Andrés, and sat next to him. "You can have a lap dance for free. I can do more, for free, of course."

"Are you a cop?"

Estrella laughed. "No, *Papi.* Of course not."

"Do you have a badge hidden anywhere?"

"Oh, please," Paul said, reaching out to grab Estrella.

She swatted Paul's hand away and said to Andrés, "How could I? I'm naked. But that doesn't mean you can't check for yourself. Let me give you a hint: if I were hiding a badge, it wouldn't be in my boots."

"Maybe I will, but right now I'm curious: Did you get Spacer Woman from a song?"

"I did! How did you know?"

"It's my girl's favorite: When she was your age, she used to love going to clubs and dancing all night long—especially to that song."

"*Papi,* please, let me give you a lap dance. Let me give you anything you want, for free, of course."

"I'll take a dance. No on everything else."

"*Papi,* are you sure?"

"I'm sure. I've got a funny question."

"You can ask me anything."

"Do you like to watch?"

She laughed. "It's like you can read my mind. *Papi,* how did you know?"

"Just a hunch. I like to watch too."

"I think we all do," Estrella said.

"Play with yourself for me while I watch."

"For you, anything—for free, of course."

"This is stupid," Paul said, trying to grab Estrella by the arm again.

Andrés swatted Paul's hand away from her and said, "Stupid to you because you've never had to learn how to talk to women. But that's how you do it—seduction. It's between the ears, not the legs, and not from the wallet. The sooner you learn that, the less you'd feel the need to buy your wife's love like you're her trick—"

"Fuck you," Paul said.

"I get off in an hour," Estrella said, moving over to sit on Andrés's lap. "I've been to Space only once, and I've been dying to go back, but men out here be acting like bitches."

"Sorry, Estrella. I'm devoted to my one and only forever. My word and her word—it's our bond. She'd need to give me permission to take you on, and if she did, it could only be with her there... You know how it goes."

"It's about trust, I know. I need that. I need that so bad. I'm surrounded by so many liars—men who got nothing going on for them except money, trying to buy a woman's love... Fucking creeps."

"Who are you calling a creep?" Paul said, standing up and lunging to grab Estrella by the hand. He swung her hard to the floor.

Estrella stood and ran to the door, trying to open it, then banged on it.

"You're wasting your time. I pay good money to make sure that door is locked."

Paul walked over and dragged a reluctant Estrella back to the couch, pinning her to the floor with a shoe. He reached into his pocket and flung hundred-dollar bills at her. He pushed down his already unbuckled pants.

"Now, suck it."

"No!" Estrella yelled.

Paul grabbed her by the hair.

Andrés sprang from his seat and slammed Paul to the floor. He wrapped his big arms around Paul's thick neck.

For every night Andrés held Sylvia, crying in his arms until she fell asleep—for every night she woke up screaming, crying, "Hold me, don't ever let me go"; for every night she cried over the young woman she had been—pelted with wadded-up balls of dollar bills; for every hope and dream that had been crushed; for every indignity Sylvia had to suffer because of the sickness from the drugs the men in her Black Room had forced her to take—Andrés squeezed Paul's neck harder and harder.

He was determined to send Paul, not to Space, but to his Maker.

Andrés was intent on killing Paul for Sylvia.

He squeezed his neck until one of Andrés's coworkers smashed a vodka bottle on his head.

Andrés rolled off Paul and onto his back.

The door finally opened.

Bouncers burst through, shoving past the dancers who had been banging on it, desperate to escape. They grabbed every man, Andrés included, by the back of the neck, dragging them out of the Black Room and into the mirrored labyrinth. One by one, they were tossed through a door, like garbage hitting the pavement in the dark alley behind the strip club.

Andrés and Paul got up and looked at each other. The others had run off.

Sirens wailed in the distance.

"Let's finish this," Andrés said. "I don't work for you anymore."

Paul laughed. "Yes, you do... A baby on the way? I'm going to hit you where it's going to hurt the most. I got you!" Paul yelled.

The police cars arrived at one end of the alley.

Paul ran toward the officers.

Andrés ran in the opposite direction. He sprinted for blocks, dodging patrol cars racing along Division Street, trying to deal with the bleeding from the back of his head where the heavy glass bottle had cracked against his skull. He spotted an empty cab, jumping in front, forcing it to stop. He begged the driver to take him away—fast—back to his hotel in the Loop area.

Once there, he entered the lobby, half-expecting to see police waiting, but it was quiet and empty; everyone with common sense was already in their rooms. Andrés went upstairs to his.

Inside, he sat at the edge of his bed, thinking about what he had done, trying to grapple with the consequences of what he knew was coming next: Paul was going to hit Andrés where it would hurt the most.

Andrés obsessed over how Paul would carry out his threat.

His phone rang. He reached into his pocket to answer. It was Sylvia.

"Sorry, I didn't pick up. I was with *Mama* and Andy. She came down with Jeanie, wanting a girls' night out with her daughters-in-law, taking us out to dinner—celebrating the coming of her new grandchild. She told me to send you to voicemail. That it was 'girl time.'"

"It figures. I send her calls to voicemail all the time. Did you at least listen to it?"

"You know I don't check."

"That's a bad habit—"

Sylvia laughed. "Yeah, yeah... So let me guess—you're not coming home again?"

"As long as there's a chance my name is on a list—"

"You're like a broken record—I know—you've *got* to play the game. I'm getting so sick of this bullshit. I'm ready for us to be homeless."

Andrés laughed. "No, you're not."

"Yes, I am—travel the world, work for what we need, not for what we want. I can do that. I know you can't."

"Mi estrella fugaz, ¿te has olvidado?"

"I love it when you speak broken Neruda. And no, I haven't forgotten. How could I forget? I'm farting so much... Seriously though, I know we've had our issues, and as much as I say, 'fuck this shit,' now that we've got what we wanted, jump through whatever hoops you need to jump through. We need to stock up on diapers and formula. She's not chewing up these nipples."

Andrés paused, unsure how to tell her what happened.

"What's wrong?" Sylvia asked. "You were supposed to laugh."

"I fucked up."

"What do you mean you fucked up?"

"I don't think I have a job anymore."

"Why not? What happened?"

Andrés explained, warning her before sharing every detail, holding back information about his bleeding from the back of his head.

Sylvia became silent.

"Are you okay?" he asked.

"This is exactly what I was afraid of. This is why I'd get on you about the company you keep. Yeah, I know, you've got to play the game, but there's a line where you have to stop playing, or else you'll lose yourself—you'd change, and I was afraid that was going to happen to you. So, I'm relieved. I'm so relieved... You haven't, and I should be happy, but... I don't know. I don't know how I feel. I'm glad you did what you did, but... it's complicated."

Sylvia became silent.

Andrés understood she didn't want answers; she needed to vent and kept silent himself.

"I think I'm actually jealous of what you did," she said. "No joke— real jealousy. I mean, I wish someone had been there to stand up for me when I said 'no.'

"I should be happy that you were there for her, but I'm not. Why should she get that from you when I'm the one who takes care of you, takes care of our son, and takes care of your daughters from another woman? She hasn't put in the work like I have. This feels like cheating to me...

"And why should she be the one who gets saved when I'm the one who has had to live with what's in my head for years? I had my lines that I didn't want anyone to cross. I was a dancer, not anything else. My boundary was no sex, no drugs. I don't know how it got away from me, but after that night in my Black Room, that's what I was doing."

Sylvia was silent for another long moment.

"That doesn't bother you? My past?" she asked.

"Are you gonna be like this for the rest of the pregnancy?"

"You're not answering the question—"

"I've got guys around me at work talking about their man caves and their new lawnmowers like a bunch of eunuchs. Meanwhile, you've wrapped *shibari* rope around our entire headboard. You made our bed into a shrine. Fuck no, your past doesn't bother me. It's never bothered me. My love, you're gold."

"I'm gold."

"Let me ask you this: does my past bother you?"

"Hell no. I feel safe."

Andrés laughed. "Alright then—shut the fuck up. We are who we are, and I love who you are. You're my shooting star, my golden girl, my beautiful sunflower."

Sylvia sighed. "Baby, I wish you were home."

"I want to be home with you so bad."

"Then come home. Now that we've got what we wanted, it doesn't matter if you lose your job."

"What happened to jumping through hoops?"

"Maybe it's my turn to jump through hoops. You can be a stay-at-home dad and let me take the lead. I have my own plans for us, too."

"Something about that doesn't feel right."

"Why not? That's what being a couple is all about, right? Don't you trust me to have your back?"

"I trust you, but still, I don't wanna hear it from my mother: *¿Qué clase de hombre no trabaja y se mantiene a costa de su mujer?*"

"As much as I love *Mama,* she's filled your head with so much of that bullshit. *'What kind of man doesn't work and support himself at the expense of his woman?'* That's a man who has earned her trust. All things being equal in a relationship, that man needs to show his woman he trusts her—not just say it but show it."

"I know—"

"I know you know. You're only like this because you're thinking about Elisa."

"I'm thinking about all the medical bills that are gonna come at us... I don't wanna put all that on you, especially when you're so close to finishing the Master Plan."

Sylvia was silent for a moment. Then she said, "No use in you being there. It's not like you can just show up to work in the morning. What you're gonna do is get your ass on a plane and come home. We'll know by Monday if you still have a job or not. Either way... Master Plan or not... bills or not... I got you. I got you. Trust me, okay?"

"Okay," Andrés said.

"I need to hang up now... I've got a banging-ass headache, and I need to get some sleep. I'll call you when I wake up. Goodnight."

❦ 34 ❧

THE BRIDGE

JANUARY 26, 2001

IT WAS 3 P.M. ON A WEDNESDAY AFTERNOON. SYLVIA SAT AT HER desk in her study, looking out the window while at her laptop, trying to write, when Andrés came home from work early.

"Grab your coat," he said.

She smiled and, without a word, stood up to follow him out of the sunlit room toward the door. They each wrapped a scarf around their necks and faces before donning matching black overcoats and ski caps. Then, they left their apartment near Museum Hill in Santa Fe, New Mexico, and got into their black rental car, with Andrés behind the wheel, driving out of the apartment complex's parking lot.

Once on the highway, Santa Fe disappeared behind them within minutes. Sylvia sang along to the songs playing from the worn-out cassette tapes she has had since the 1980s, playing from the car's stereo system. Andrés smiled, singing along with her while driving, his eyes focused on the road ahead.

The sunset made the desert landscape ahead glow so much that Sylvia said, "I've never seen anything like this in my life."

"Same here," Andrés said. "My first night here, a guy at the airport warned me that this place does something to a person. I thought he was full of shit."

"Paul thought he was punishing you by sending you out here."

"Something in me finally feels like it can breathe."

"Me too. I don't think I'll ever want to leave…"

"At some point, we'll have too."

"I know… Where do you think we'll go after this?"

"Who knows? I'm sure he'll try to send me someplace far away. He's trying to get me to quit rather than fire me. He can't risk me collecting unemployment or suing him… the truth about that night coming out in a hearing or during discovery… The other partners won't appreciate the amount of their money he spends on drugs and sex…"

"Of course he does. It doesn't surprise me," Sylvia said.

"He pays strip club managers to look the other way. I literally have the receipts, but I'm not playing my hand until we need to be back in the city, and that'll be when the baby is born. We can then get a nice big house. We'll establish something more formal for shared custody of Daphne and get full custody of Andy—I mean, make it official. This way, he could be with us if we find ourselves living out of state again."

"We're going to need that for Daphne too, just in case shit goes sideways between all of us."

"Just in case," Andrés said.

"We could buy a home someplace wonderful and peaceful, like here… I already don't wanna go back… I think I'd be okay if it was all of us here… I think I wanna live here."

Andrés looked over and smirked. "Square life and all?"

Sylvia playfully slapped him on the shoulder. "Shut up and keep your eyes on the road."

"You're ready to move out here without seeing what I'm gonna show you? It's way more than the view from our patio."

"You're talking as though you've been to where we're going… Have you been here before and never told me?"

"Kind of, and so have you… You'll see."

Andrés turned his focus back to the road, gripping the steering wheel hard as the road began to wind around hillsides and mountains.

It was 5:40 p.m., the beginning of the blue hour. Their car began its descent down the desert road. In the distance, a deep crack appeared on the surface of the plateau, as though it were the dark entrance into the Underworld found at the End of the World.

Sylvia gasped. "Oh, my God! Is that—"

"The Rio Grande Gorge."

"Pull over—pull over."

Andrés did as he was told, pulling off to the side of the road onto the snow-covered shoulder and parking. The two jumped out of the car and stood together, staring at the deep crack stretching far into the horizon.

"There's more at the bridge," he said.

"That can wait. I just want to give seven-year-old me this view. I just want to stand here... Take off your gloves. I want to feel your hands in mine... Hold my hand."

Andrés did as she asked, while Sylvia did the same. Together, they watched in silence as the blue hour faded, and night set over the plateau until it was pitch black. Headlights from passing cars lit the road near where they stood, snapping them out of their trance.

"Let's go before we get run over. I'm driving," she said.

Sylvia and Andrés both got back into the car and drove off. Later, they entered Taos. She drove through town, following signs directing her to the Rio Grande Gorge Bridge. The road leading out stretched straight and long into the darkness. Sylvia drove over the bridge, making a U-turn to park in a dark and empty lot. They got out of the car and began walking on the snow and ice covering the ground in the dark. She held onto Andrés as they walked onto the pathway leading to the empty bridge.

"Don't fall," Sylvia said. "Your clumsy ass would be taking her down with us too."

"Jesus, how do you know it's a girl?"

"It's a feeling, like with all things. Like somehow, that night after you left,[1] I just knew it wasn't the end of us. I knew."

They both stopped at a viewing platform extending from the bridge, overlooking the gorge. Leaning against the railing, they stared

---

1. *Book Three: The Labyrinth*, "Chapter Twenty-Six: December Came and Went."

into the darkness below. After a long moment gazing into the abyss, Andrés asked, "Do you have any other gut feelings?"

"Not really... Do you?" Sylvia replied.

"I hate to say it, but I'm scared."

"I didn't want to say, but me too... When is the Universe—God—whatever you wanna call Her—when is She going to take all of this away? This is the happiest I've ever been in my life, and I can't help but feel that God is gonna drop the hammer on us soon, because that's how She rolls, am I right? How is She going to do it?"

Andrés leaned in closer to whisper in her ear, "Tell yourself: no fear. That's what I'm doing."

"No fear."

"No fear—I want you to look up. I want you to look at the unreal beauty of this tenement sky."

Sylvia smiled. "We're doing that?"

"Yes, Emma, we are. It's what placed you on your path. Forget your fears and look up."

She did as he asked and gasped. Sylvia stood silently, mesmerized by the night, her face to the stars.

Andrés moved away from the railing to stand behind her, wrapping his arms around her and kissing her tenderly.

Sylvia smiled as she wrapped her arms around his, keeping her face to the night.

"When I was a little girl," she said, "I loved looking at the stars through the window by my bed. I thought the night was clear, but it was nothing like this. Everything is dazzling, so bright... Look, you can even see behind the haze—that dim glow of stars just above Orion and below its belt. It's so beautiful!"

"I see it. I can see like I've never seen before. It's what I'd always imagined coming here."

"Me too... The End of the World... I can't believe you remembered."

"My love, I remember everything you've shared: you reading that *National Geographic* while waiting on a prescription, the starry cover catching your attention. You, back in your apartment after watching *The Day After,* breaking down, imagining yourself going to the End of the World, making your way to the Lord of the Dead to make your case to let Nana go, to move Hades and Persephone to tears. You needed Constance back.[2] I remember everything, and now we're here."

Sylvia looked away from the vast night sky and back at Andrés. She stared intently at him, her eyes glistening from the stars radiating brightly above. Then she turned, as if hearing her name called, and looked behind her before shifting her focus again, gazing long into the abyss below.

She climbed onto the railing. Leaning forward, she stared into the depths, seemingly hypnotized by whatever lurked below. After a moment, she pushed herself back and stood behind Andrés.

"Not today, Nana. Not anymore. I'm at peace now," she said. "I have a life. I have a family."

"You have a family—and a man whose love for you is so powerful, so strong, that he would go to the End of the World just for you."

"You would?"

"Without question—"

"Is it safe for us to believe?"

"I think so."

Sylvia paused. "Do you believe in soulmates?"

Andrés smiled. "I believe my love for you is bigger than this night sky. It's deeper than the opening below us. It's bigger and deeper than anything I've ever felt in my life."

"From the moment we met, I've believed," she said. "I've always believed... I believe I can't see the sunrise—the sunset—without you, because your love is what gives me eyes. I believe I was born to love you because it's your love that gives me life. I can't breathe—I can't sleep—I can't live without you. I can't... You're my other half—you're my everything...

"But how could I admit that to you when we first met? How could I have known for sure when this feeling just came out of nowhere?

"The first time I saw you—that boy who saved Spacer Woman—I knew, and I cried.[3] I cried so much because you weren't ready, and I

---

2. *Book Two: Underworld*, "Chapter Thirteen: The Waste Land."
3. *Book Two: Underworld*, "Chapter Fifteen: Emma."

was in the worst place of my life. And when we met again,[4] I had to force myself to hold back because it's scary—so scary. I had to push you away because I thought I didn't deserve to be happy, that I was a lost cause.

"But we found each other again, and now that we're here, I can't lose you again. I can't! It was safer not to believe! So, promise me— promise that no matter what happens in the future, you'll never leave me."

"I promise," Andrés said.

"Promise to come back to me."

"I promise."

"Because I can't live without you! I can't—"

"But I'm here now."

"But for how long? How long?"

"Shush... no fear, my love," Andrés whispered. "We're only in this moment. We can't do anything about anything else. We have no control over anything other than what's in this moment. Look up. What do you see?"

Sylvia did as he asked and gasped. "Orion."

"Orion: It is what it is. Are you happy now?"

She looked at him. "The happiest I've ever been in my life."

"Me too," he said. "I want you to remember this moment— remember it in our bad times—so that if God does drop the hammer, we'll always have the Bridge."

"The Bridge!"

Sylvia yanked him close, kissing him like she was desperate to pour the sum total of herself into him through their mouths. Shooting stars streaked across the vast night to the south of the gorge, making her stop and look up.

"This is a sign!" Sylvia yelled.

"It is!"

She looked back into his eyes. "You, Andrés de León, are my soulmate."

"You, Sylvia Hadid James, are mine."

---

4. *Book One: Orpheus,* "Chapter Four: Eurydice."

Sylvia and Andrés kissed as if the Bridge were their altar and the night sky their officiant. They stopped to stare into the beyond, arm in arm, until she began to fidget in her step.

"What's wrong?" he asked.

"I have to pee," she replied, "and the baby is hungry. We want tacos—"

"You want tacos?"

"With green chili."

"Let's head back to town. I saw a few places open—"

Before Andrés could finish his sentence, Sylvia grabbed his hand and led him off the bridge, back to the parking lot. They got in the car, and she drove out of the lot, speeding through the dark toward Taos.

❄ *35* ❄

HOWL

SEPTEMBER 9, 2001

[1]

Andrés sat on the corner of the bed, having woken up from a dream that felt so real it disturbed him, leaving him desperate.

In the dream, he hovered outside a tenement building window like a ghost. He looked inside to find a naked woman resting on a large blanket of fur.

Behind him, snow was falling hard, blanketing the night in white.

Below him, the streets were empty, save for an older couple huddled against each other on the building steps, crying in each other's arms.

Andrés cast a long shadow through the window into the room, falling upon the naked woman in repose. Her face glowed.

It was Sylvia.

When she saw it was him, she smiled, stood, and approached him outside the window, opening it to pull him inside and out of the cold. Andrés was no longer a ghost; he became flesh and blood once more, standing before her, naked.

Together, Sylvia and Andrés looked out the window at the sad couple below.

"Let's give them some privacy. They need closure," she said, then closed the window.

She gazed long at him.

He gazed long at her.

She raised her small hand to palm his chest.

He raised his hand to caress her bright face.

He came in close, pressing his body against hers, kissing her with desperation as if she had been lost but was now found.

In the dream, he said, "I shouldn't have gotten on the plane."

In the dream, she replied, "You shouldn't have."

Then, all the lights went out. Sylvia was gone, and Andrés was alone.

Something had been ripped from deep inside him, and now he could no longer breathe.

Sylvia was somewhere in the beyond, coughing, having trouble sleeping, rocking her body back and forth in a bed somewhere in the beyond, trying to self-soothe because she was terrified of the dark. Always had been terrified, just like him, since they were small.

The protectors in Sylvia and Andrés's lives had promised, when they were alive, to watch over them. But now, Constance and Reynaldo were gone—into the great beyond, to be with God.

Sylvia was out there, in the beyond, terrified, without Andrés, her chosen protector.

It was a pain in his heart that he wasn't imagining. The pain was so real that, in the dream, he found himself in a car, hands gripping the steering wheel, racing down a long desert road at night, desperate to find her. Desperate to rejoin Sylvia wherever she existed—in this life or the next.

He was going to go back to the Bridge at the End of the World to plead his case to the Lord of the Dead. Even if he failed and died, what did it matter? He had to come back to her because she was not a lost cause.

Because he had made a promise.

Because she had given everything of herself to him.

He was her One, and she was his; he would be with her in the beyond forever because death would be the sweet release.

The death of the carnal soul is a blessing.

Death would bring peace.

A peace found only in the closeness he shared with Sylvia while making love—forsaking everything about their dynamic to experience the tenderness and intense love found only in the sacred Yab-Yam position.

That's when Andrés woke up.

In the dream, Andrés perceived death—the annihilation of his sense of self, his ego—as an ecstatic experience, much like being joined with the body of a woman in making love, as a woman is joined to the body of a man.

It is an ecstasy of the flesh.

And being bound in that manner is the same as being joined to the Body of All, to the Body of We, to the Body of Us.

It is an ecstasy of Our everlasting, transcendent soul.

It is the same ecstasy as being joined to the Body of God: the cliff dive into the deep blue of the Universal Cosmic Ocean of *Om,* the two drops returning to the all-encompassing eternal One.

To describe what he perceived as rest would not capture the sentiment.

To describe it as peace would not do it any justice.

It was...

Just...

Us...

It was...

Shantih shantih shantih

Andrés stood up from the corner of the bed and began pacing the room.

The feeling of being brought back to their Purple Room—the way Sylvia stood by the window—touched on a moment he shared with her years before, when they first broke up in 1993.[1]

It was a moment filled with so much anger and raw desire, and so much hate, and so much love—so, so much deep love—and longing, and sadness, and so much sadness, and relief.

It was far from the gloss of a bright, lustrous dream, where Sylvia felt like a statue.

A monument.

A supernatural entity.

The dream was not healthy.

At that moment—the true moment from 1993, and not from a dream—Andrés had hated Sylvia as much as he loved her, and she had hated him as much as she loved him. In real life, in that true moment, with so much of that emotion all mixed together, it made for the greatest passion, the greatest desire that made them want to tear each other apart with their mouths, revealing, for both Andrés and Sylvia, love's greatest mystery.

There can be no peace when one knows that kind of passion—that kind of craving for that desire that heats the spirit from within, from within the cauldron of the heart.

Andrés would give anything to burn in that passion.

Andrés would give everything.

He would submit.

He would be willing to be torn to pieces by the maenad in her and be rebuilt if it meant tasting that desire.

To comprehend, to understand, and to accept this, Andrés became even more convinced he needed psychiatric help. Thinking this way, and taking comfort in this kind of magical thinking, he realized he was in danger of losing himself—because magic is just another word for delusion. He was in crisis, a crisis that began on that first night at the Bridge, when they fully committed to the idea that soulmates are real.

He wanted to die now more than ever.

He suspected the same was true for Sylvia. She was alone some-

---

1. *Book Three: The Labyrinth,* "Chapter Twenty-Six: December Came and Went."

where in New York, going back to her old ways of coping. That was Andrés's fear for Sylvia—and it was his fear for himself too. In his solitude, he was breaking away from reality as a way to cope.

The dream was delusional thinking.

The dream was too much. It was not real.

Andrés rushed to his phone by the pillow, grabbed it, and dialed Sylvia's number. It went straight to voicemail.

Andrés sighed.

[2]

Where was Sylvia? How was she coping? Andrés asked himself these questions every minute he has been in Berlin, away from her. He knew she was feeling the same pain from their loss—but even more, much more. There were no words he could offer her about what happened on June 26, 2001, the event that forced them to leave New Mexico and return to New York by early July.

They resettled in the cheapest apartment they could find.

Instead of firing Andrés, as he had hoped, Paul gave him another short-notice assignment: Berlin. The last words Paul said to Andrés when discussing the assignment were, "I love watching you squirm."

When Andrés told Sylvia what was about to happen, she went into a rage—not at Andrés, but at God. Andrés was going away again, and this time, it wouldn't be as simple as working in Chicago or Santa Fe. He would be gone for the foreseeable future. The panic she felt, knowing Andrés would be leaving her alone in the grief of their loss, while she coped with the postpartum depression that had kept her bound to bed for days, made her jump up and race out of their apartment. She ran up the steps to the rooftop and yelled at the vast night spread over Lower Manhattan until she lost her voice and burst blood vessels in her eyes.

Andrés called Petra to tell her what was about to happen. His mother offered to come down and stay for however long was needed, but Sylvia told Petra on the call, "*Mama,* I love you, but stay where you are. I don't need you—I need him here, by my side, the way Antonio is at yours—every night—because this is bullshit! This is fucking bullshit!"

Petra rescinded her offer and told Sylvia she was acting like a child.

"A child? A child?" Sylvia said, holding back her tears. "How can you say that after we lost ours? I'm sorry Andrés even called you."

Then came the moment he had to leave. Sylvia had locked herself in the bathroom and dared Andrés to knock the door down to pull her out. Andrés couldn't risk being late for his flight and suffering more consequences in Paul's game of dominance.

He left Sylvia behind.

After Andrés arrived at the airport and cleared security, he received a phone call from Sylvia, frantically pleading, "Don't go, please, don't leave me behind! I can't be alone—I'm a danger to myself! Please don't get on the plane!"

"But I have to," he said.

"Play that hand! Use the receipts!"

"I tried, but nobody cared. All the partners are doing it."

"Of course they are."

"Fuck Paul—come with me."

"No! I don't want to be in a hotel! I want to be at home with you— somewhere familiar, not strange."

"And the new apartment isn't strange?"

"Asshole!" she yelled. "You know what I mean. I don't want to be in another country. Not now! I need to be around the familiar. Don't be mad at me—I can't take any more fucking surprises."

"Baby, I'm not mad. I want to stay—"

"Then stay."

"I can't."

"Your job is more important than me," Sylvia said.

"No, it's not."

"Then quit. Please! Get out from under Paul's thumb! Who gives a fuck about unemployment? You can still sue him. You can find another job. You can do anything you want. I can cover the both of us. Just please stay home."

"I need more experience."

"You're thinking of Elisa!"

"I only have a GED! I got lucky in my final interview with Paul! I need more experience, especially now, since I won't be able to get a good reference from him."

"You fucking coward! All I hear are excuses. When I gave you excuses, you made me look for solutions. When all I wanted to do was just go back home and write, you made me remember that night when I was crying on stage, and you pushed me. And now that I'm almost done, it's your turn to get pushed—to look for solutions—because I don't wanna fucking hear it."

A long silence settled between them on the call.

Andrés asked, "Are you still there?"

"I'm still here," she replied. "You haven't seen this side of me in years. You need to see this side, 'cause now I'm pissed. I'm furious. We're not dancing! We're fighting! Real fighting!"

Sylvia laughed to herself in disbelief.

"I fucked up. I fucked up so much… Keeping you in that *'girlfriend-boyfriend'* zone, calling you my *partner* when we made it so much more than that years ago. Well, I'm not your girlfriend. I'm not your fucking partner. Fuck what this ring says—I'm not your fiancée! I am your wife!

"I have given you everything I could give, and now you owe me. You owe me the way a husband owes his wife—a wife who's given everything! Everything! With everything that I do? Everything we've been through? You owe me, 'cause you're the one that got me believing in fucking magic.

"So now you'll get your ass home as soon as possible, 'cause you owe me! 'Cause I need you! That's it. And I don't want to hear excuses—"

"Okay, okay," Andrés said. "When I get there, I'll tell them what happened and that I need to be home."

"You better."

"Despite how things went down between me and Paul, there are other partners in the firm who I know don't like him and appreciate my work—so much so that they've asked me to ditch Paul and join them. I'm gonna reach out—"

"Please—"

"And if I'm told I need to be there past August, I'll get the paperwork started to have us live in Berlin for the time being. They could hook us up with the same setup we had in Santa Fe—a nice apartment. That way, it'll feel like you're home—"

"No! Fuck no!" Sylvia yelled. "We need to be here for Daphne, and Andy starts school in September! Or did you forget?"

"Andy would be coming with us. I'm tired of Lydia coming in and out of his life."

"I'm not leaving my kids behind! I can't do that to Daphne. And Andy should've come with us to New Mexico. You know what? That won't work for him. Foreign country? Stop with that bullshit. You need to come back as soon as possible. Fuck that. You need to leave the airport and come home now!"

"Baby, I can't... We have bills, so many bills... Have you seen the latest one? They took that opportunity to charge us so much for her urn—for everything. I can't fucking deal—"

Andrés dropped the phone away from his ear to take a deep breath and keep himself from crying. When he placed the phone back to his ear, all he heard was silence.

"Hello? Are you still there?"

"You know," she said, "a part of me wants to leave... I'm dead serious... I wanna leave."

"I know."

"The only reason I haven't is because I know it's not your fault. And because I love you. I love you so much, and because this happened to you too! And I know you're in pain!"

Sylvia began to cry.

"Fuck, I can't believe this happened to us—"

"I can't believe it," he said.

"Then show me! Show me you can't believe it! Be the man who used to read poems to me—the man who used to feel things with me! You know how lonely you make me feel? Not letting me in? I want a man with a soul, not a rock! I want a human being!"

All Andrés could hear in his mind in this moment of Sylvia's pause, waiting for him to be moved enough to open up to her, was Petra's voice saying, "Boys don't cry."

He didn't respond.

Sylvia took a deep breath and stopped crying.

"Fine. Get on the plane," she said. "I think this time away from each other will be good. You need to think about what you can do to fix that thing in yourself that keeps you like that. I mean, it's not like we just met; it's not like we're dating. I am your wife in every way but on paper.

"I know I'm mad, but when you get home, we're making us official. The game of playing house is over. We should've gotten married the moment we talked about it.

"I think I'm gonna take this time to see a therapist and deal with my shit so that when you get home, I'm not angry at you anymore. Couples sometimes break up when something like this happens, and I don't want that happening."

"I don't wanna lose you. I can't lose you," he said.

"I can't lose you," Sylvia said. "So please! Please! Please think about what you can do to be a better man for me!"

"But I'm scared!"

"Of what?"

"Of seeing me like that!"

Sylvia cried, "Like what? Out of control? You've seen me out of control. I cry all the fucking time, and you're the one who holds me together. Do you trust me to do the same?"

"I do."

"But how can you say that if you've stopped letting me in?"

Andrés grew quiet, remembering the night Sylvia used everything he had shared—his fears about the bumps on his head being cancer, how his body couldn't respond to her touch because of the physical pain—as a punchline in the poem that became known as *The Delivery Boy*.[2]

He remembered it clearly, just as he remembered telling Sylvia that same night, right after she read the poem to a jam-packed audience, "That's the last time I open myself up to you," and then keeping his mouth shut.

____

2. *Book Three: The Labyrinth*, "Chapter Twenty-Five: The Minotaurs."

Sylvia was silent for a long moment. Then she said, "Remember that night when I took you to the peep show, and we were figuring out the Dance?[3] I told you that at the heart of everything, you need to show that you trust me. If you say I'm gold, then show me.

"Trust my word that I've got you. I've got you! I promise, I do! So, please figure it out, 'cause I can't be alone in this. And when you get home, we'll figure it out together. Just come home as soon as possible, okay? I think I have a new plan—my new Master Plan.

"So reach out to who you can, and if that doesn't work, then quit and come home. Don't worry about a thing. Elisa can provide for herself—I've got Daphne covered. You know I have Andy covered. I can provide for us. How many times do I need to tell you? You're not the only provider in this relationship.

"I'm a provider too. I've got us! I don't know what's going on with Lydia, but Andy will be with me. I'll have him registered in school by the fall. I have to keep it moving. I have to keep holding on to hope. We need to keep holding on to hope. I'm not giving up on us.

"So come home as soon as possible, please. Take whatever they give you—just come home. I just want to be able to sleep again. So please, keep busy. Stay out of trouble. I love you."

[3]

AFTER SYLVIA ENDED THE CALL, ANDRÉS TURNED OFF HIS PHONE, took a deep breath, and swallowed. He leaned against a large window inside the terminal at John F. Kennedy International Airport, looking at the faint glow of Manhattan's skyline to the west.[4] That moment marked the beginning of the rest of the summer,[5] leading to this current moment where he sat back down on the corner of the bed in his hotel room in Berlin, trying to figure out how to be better for Sylvia.

---

3. *Book Three: The Labyrinth,* "Chapter Twenty: The Red Rooms."
4. *Book One: Orpheus,* "Chapter One: The Provider."
5. *Book One: Orpheus,* "Chapter Two: Meet Her at the Love Parade."

Andrés reached deep into the memory of watching their daughter come into the world with a pained expression and in silence.

Sylvia was frantic, yelling, "I can't hear her! I can't hear her!"

Instead of the gloss of a bright, lustrous dream where Sylvia seemed like a statue, Andrés reached deeper into the memory of doctors assuring Sylvia it had nothing to do with her past.

Still, Sylvia kept crying out, "But my body remembers. The body remembers! Karma!"

Instead of the gloss of a bright, lustrous dream where Sylvia felt like a monument, a supernatural entity, Andrés reached deep into the memory of hearing the most human of beings he had ever known: his soulmate, the love of his life, the mother of his daughter—the memory of watching Sylvia's anguish blaring out through a long, open-mouthed howl that went silent, though she was still screaming.

He could still hear her howling, as if it were the death of that part of her soul that an indifferent God, an absurd Universe, had forgotten to crush after watching her mother kill herself, after watching her father destroy himself, and after watching the rock that was her grandmother just wither away and die.

And when Andrés touched the memory, when he felt the memory, he felt Sylvia's pain.

And in feeling her pain, he could no longer avoid his own because he could no longer escape the reality of the death of their daughter.

ATHENA

All of Andrés's pain, buried under the routine of working long hours in Berlin to escape, came out in an open-mouthed howl.

He howled until his voice became hoarse, until tiny capillaries burst in his eyes, until he passed out from the sudden drop in blood pressure, bumping his head against the corner of the bed frame.

He found himself in the darkness of the Underworld. Sylvia was there in a hospital room, restrained to a bed, asleep.

Andrés woke up and remained still on the floor, his eyes suddenly focusing on his suitcase in a corner by the door.

He was ready to leave and catch the first flight out in the morning, back to New York.

One of the managing partners for the German practice of the firm had emailed Andrés, stating that because of a looming economic crisis back in the States, as a cost-cutting measure, the firm was calling back all U.S.-based consultants to their home offices. The email also stated that because of the solid work he had put in—being the first at the client site in the morning and the last to leave at night—he was safe in his current role. The client wanted him there.

When Andrés didn't respond to the email, his supervisor at the client site called him into his office, handed him his phone, and then left. It was the managing partner, stating off the record that she had heard the rumors floating around the company about what had happened in Chicago. Because of what he had done—the stance he had taken—she wanted him there. She was willing to convert Andrés into a European-based resource to stave off what awaited him back in New York: Paul functionally demoting Andrés to the position of an entry-level analyst at an engagement starting with one of their new partners at the World Trade Center.

Andrés turned down the offer. When the managing partner pressed him for a reason why he would be willing to accept a functional demotion when he could continue his career in Germany—with the firm taking care of everything needed for him to remain in Berlin—he told her that there had been a death in his family and that he had promised his fiancée he would come home as soon as possible. When she pressed him for more information and Andrés revealed it was the death of his daughter, she paused for a long moment on the call, then said, "You should've never come to Berlin," and hung up.

After the call, he received an email with all the information he needed: an interview at the South Tower on September 11, 2001.[6] He needed to be back in New York before then. He was ready to go, ready to accept a functional demotion with no change in pay. At least the low-pressure job would keep him in the city. Once he was settled in, he would seek out psychiatric help and deal with everything that had

----

6. *Book One: Orpheus*, "Chapter Seven: The Burial of the Dead."

happened. He would go to therapy; Sylvia would no longer feel like a monument in his dreams. She would return to being a complex human being, prone to expressing anger, joy, hate, and love.

Because in the pain and isolation in Berlin, it had all become too much. Andrés would go to therapy and work on being a better man for his sunflower. He could learn to be vulnerable again, so he could cry along with Sylvia. That way, she wouldn't feel like she was alone in her grief, as she did when Athena died just as she was born.

It scared him that all summer, whenever his calls to Sylvia went to voicemail and his emails remained unanswered,[7] he heard the voice of his mother yelling at him, "Boys don't cry." Because he hadn't received the voicemail response indicating her inbox was full, he was sure she was listening to his messages—the last of which was about his return to New York. Andrés felt like a clown for not wanting to surprise her with his return and for leaving so many voicemails in her inbox.

Being in love is a horrible experience: the vulnerability, the uncertainty. Andrés had no one to blame but himself. If he had treated Sylvia like a one-night stand when they first met, instead of someone he felt an immediate and supernatural connection with, he wouldn't be in Berlin now, fighting the urge to kill himself. But he did make his choice, and she made hers, and now, while lying on the floor, focused on the suitcase in a corner by the door, he couldn't wait to leave, get on a plane, and go back to New York.

After the client interview scheduled for 9/11, Andrés would see her. Sylvia wouldn't grieve alone for long. Maybe they could try again—it would be the ultimate expression of their personal mantra: no fear. To try again for a baby. And if Sylvia had left him, he would know for sure and move on with his life. Either way, he would have an answer and step out of the uncertainty he had been living in all summer.

----

7. *Book One: Orpheus*, "Chapter Two: Meet Her at the Love Parade."

✤ 36 ✤

THE BLUE ROOM

IT WAS 3 A.M. FIGHTER JETS ROARED THROUGH THE NIGHT SKY OVER the city.

Five miles away from Elisa's apartment in Bushwick, Ground Zero smoldered.

Andrés was stuck on her couch, unable to sleep. He grabbed his phone and called Sylvia. All he got was a busy signal.

Was Sylvia in one of the towers?

That intrusive thought made him call her again. He received a busy signal again. Andrés called Petra. He received a busy signal again.

More fighter jets roared above, and suddenly, for Andrés, the building felt like it was shifting back and forth, back and forth.

In the distance, he could hear Sylvia whispering, "Goodnight, world. Goodnight, light. Sleep well until the morning light."

In the distance, he could hear echoes of Estefania from the Underworld whispering, *"Goodnight, world. Goodnight, light. Sleep well until the morning light."*

The whispers of his love didn't sound the same as those coming from the Underworld. The echoes of Estefania were hard to hear, while something in Andrés that had died with Athena was now alive again, awakened by Sylvia's soft voice—her whispers like a beautiful song.

Yes!

The song of Sylvia's voice, now louder than the fighter jets roaring through the night skies, touched his hearing, assuring him that just as the sun rises and sets, and the stars are beautiful and eternal, and that love is Love, through his soulmate connection to Sylvia—forged by magic in the world—he became convinced that she was alive.

Sylvia was somewhere out there, alive!

Yes!

Andrés could feel her again from his insides!

Yes!

And he wasn't in a dream.

Yes!

But Sylvia was in pain.

No!

Andrés could feel her rocking herself to sleep, locked away somewhere, rocking herself to sleep. But where? He had to find the love of his life—the love he had abandoned while she was in the throes of postpartum depression.

How could he be so cruel to Sylvia when she needed him the most? Alene was right to have called him an asshole.[1]

Fuck the job! He almost died for the job![2]

Sylvia was right: he had taken for granted being in that "girlfriend-boyfriend" zone, calling her by her play name, Emma, everywhere they went. And even after everything she had vocalized—when told by Alene at the Love Parade that she was engaged[3]—he should have corrected himself and said that he was as well. He should have trusted that the connection to his One was still there, but it had been hampered by the death of Athena, not by what Sylvia's silence implied —that she had left him.

---

1. *Book One: Orpheus*, "Chapter Five: The Shame Game."
2. *Book One: Orpheus*, "Chapter Seven: The Burial of the Dead."
3. *Book One: Orpheus*, "Chapter Two: Meet Her at the Love Parade."

He should have shown Sylvia respect. He should have declared that she wasn't just his girl but his everything.

There was only one Sylvia.

He shouldn't have boarded the plane.

He needed to go to her. He needed to go outside, get a car, and drive north. But to where? To his mother? She would know where Sylvia was. Petra always knew where Sylvia was, but the city was on lockdown, and the bridges were closed. Andrés wasn't sure if Petra would keep silent about Sylvia's whereabouts.

When it came to Andy, he could hear his mother saying, "Now you care about your son? You should've taken him with you to New Mexico. But don't worry; Andy is fine. You can continue thinking only about yourself."

Maybe, with what had happened to Andrés in the South Tower, Petra would show mercy and "see him." She would see that he was still that scared little boy, that he had endured the beating of her silence much like he used to endure the lash of a belt from his father. She would show him mercy and tell him everything.

Did Sylvia relapse? Was she back on drugs? Was she in rehab? That would explain the feeling he was having—Sylvia had locked herself away in a room for her own protection, for her own good. She had consented to it because she valued her sobriety more than life itself.

The building began rocking harder, back and forth, as though he were back in the South Tower after the plane had hit the floors directly above him. Andrés got up from the couch, struggling to keep his balance as he tripped toward the window.

Large black clouds of smoke, illuminated by floodlights at Ground Zero, loomed over Lower Manhattan. Is this how it begins—the nightmare found in the movie *The Day After?* Was it all going to come true? What kind of wasteland would they be facing? Andrés couldn't leave Sylvia behind again.

He went back to the couch and tried calling her again. Busy signal again.

Daphne began to cry loudly in the next room. She came running out and jumped into Andrés's arms, screaming. Elisa entered from her bedroom and sat next to Andrés.

"She's been having nightmares all summer that you died. This is that," Elisa said.

All the lights in her apartment began to flicker.

Heat blasted through the space in waves.

The building felt as if it were set to collapse.

Andrés shot up from the couch, Daphne in his arms and yelled, "Myra! Wake up—let's go!" Elisa yelled at him to calm down, but to Andrés, the building was going to collapse at any minute.

"I have to get you guys out! I have to save my girls!" he yelled.

"You're scaring Daphne!"

"I'm trying to save her; save Myra! Please go get her! I can't leave without you and her!"

"Andrés—listen to me—you're not in the South Tower—you're in my home—it was *our* home, and you're safe. Myra's safe—Daphne's safe."

"They are?"

"Yes... Please hand Daphne to me."

"But I need to save her—"

Elisa snatched Daphne from Andrés's arms and ran into Myra's room, locking the door behind her.

Andrés dropped to the floor, screaming, and in the midst of his panic, he suddenly felt Sylvia reaching out to him from *across time and space,* dropping to her knees as though she were beside him at that moment where he clutched Elisa's floor in terror. He felt Sylvia place her hand on his back to rub and soothe him, whispering, *"Take a deep breath."*

Andrés took a deep breath and swallowed.

"Take another deep breath," he heard her say.

He took another deep breath and swallowed.

He heard her say, *"There you go. You're doing great, and you're gonna do even better because—"*[4]

Suddenly, he was back in the moment where there were hard knocks on the door.

---

4. *Book One: Orpheus,* "Chapter Seven: The Burial of the Dead."

Elisa rushed out of Myra's room to the apartment door to open it and welcome an emergency medical technician and a police officer.

"Where's the man in distress?" the EMT asked.

"He's right there," Elisa replied.

"I can't believe you called them," Andrés said to Elisa. "They're busy digging people out."

The EMT walked over to Andrés on the floor.

"Don't you worry about them—we're here for you," the EMT replied.

"But I *am* worried," Andrés said. "As I was going down, you guys were going up. As you guys were going up, I was going down. I was trying to get out of the South Tower, trying to get to my baby girl, or at least see her.

"I've already lost my other baby girl. Athena opened and closed her eyes, and now she's dead, and I don't wanna lose my Daphne because this building is about to fall.

"I want nothing happening to you guys—this building's about to fall and those beepers going off in that dust—those poor firefighters, buried alive…"

"Sir, do you feel like hurting yourself?" the EMT asked.

"I wanna live—I need to find my wife!"

"You see what I'm dealing with here? He's acting all crazy—you can hear him for yourself, going on and on," Elisa said to the EMT.

Andrés pleaded with the EMT, "I don't want my girls to die! Please take them with you! Take her with you!"

"This asshole," Elisa said to the EMT, "gets another woman pregnant, the baby dies on them, and then expects me to feel pity?"

"What are you talking about?" Andrés said, looking up at her. "You were there for Sylvia; you're her friend. We're cool. We're all cool."

"We don't feel safe with him here," Elisa said.

The police officer, who had been observing, grabbed Elisa by the arm and led her away, while the EMT knelt next to Andrés.

"You smell like gasoline," the EMT said.

Andrés replied, "Who the fuck wakes up and goes to work, and by the end of the morning, the South Tower is gone? It's all gone, and I'm trying to sleep, and all I hear is the beeping. You know, the beeping? I hear you guys beeping. You guys are all fucking gone, and I saw you guys go up, and all of you looked so goddamn scared, and yet you kept going. I love you guys for what you do! I love you! I will never forget you! For as long as I live, I will never forget!"

When Andrés spotted her eyes and lips flinching from what he shared, he said, "I'm sorry, I'm so sorry—I can't sleep, and I don't wanna lose them too. I've already lost my baby. I may have lost my wife back to drugs; I don't know where she's at, and I'm scared. I just wanna save them. I wanna save all of them—my family, my girls— please take them with you and go before it's too late!"

"Sir, I need to ask: do you feel like hurting others?"

"No! Life is a gift, right? Right? The turtles, the turtles..."

"Calm down, sir."

"I'm sorry—I'm sorry—I need to talk to someone! I need help, but my wife isn't here, and I placed a father in the North Tower, and I don't know if he's alive. He asked me to help him because we're fathers, and I tried. I tried. He has a daughter and a house—can you find out he made it out for me, please? His name is Marco Bayani, and he was in the North Tower."

"I'm sure he made it out," the EMT said.

"I hope so... No more surprises, please! I can't take another hammer drop—I need help! Can you help me? Please help me!"

The police officer returned with Elisa. "No signs of domestic violence."

The EMT glanced up at Elisa. "I don't see any injuries. She looks fine. Leave her alone. She's not the patient. With everything he's told me, he is."

The EMT looked up at the police officer. "The patient here survived the South Tower. He's requesting informal admission for mental health services. I'm treating this call as part of the overall ongoing triage operations following the terror attack. Since this is *now* my scene, that is *my* decision."

DECEMBER 21, 2001

The doctors at the psychiatric hospital in Nassau County, where Andrés had been moved without explanation after his initial intake at Bellevue, gave him heavy doses of Clonazepam—a drug that increased the amount of GABA released in the brain, creating a nerve-calming effect. They also prescribed Olanzapine, an atypical antipsychotic medication, which they administered whenever Andrés experienced what they considered "hallucinations."

Elisa had told the doctors, "There is no Athena. There is no Sylvia. If Sylvia were real, then why am I the one here and she's not? If she's his wife, why is there no record of their marriage? That's because it's all in his head."

Andrés learned not to mention Sylvia or Athena in his therapy sessions, or else the doctors would put him to sleep.

His thinking had become fragmented and disordered—*like a heap of broken images.* That's how it all felt in his head, keeping him groggy, stuck in bed.

A nurse entered Andrés's room and, without explanation, instructed him to get up and follow her to the empty common area with blue walls. There, Elisa, her blonde pixie-cut hair slicked back, sat on a red wooden chair in the center. Andrés, unshaven and dressed in blue pajamas and slippers, took a blue chair from a corner, positioned it across from Elisa, and sat facing her. The nurse walked out, leaving them alone to stare at each other.

After a long silence, during which Andrés fought to hide the pleasure he felt from smelling Sylvia's floral perfume on Elisa, she finally spoke.

"You know, it doesn't have to be like this," Elisa said. "You hold the keys to your cell."

"I want to be here. I need to be here."

"You need to be home."

"That's not my home."

"Home is where your daughter is."

"Home is where I say it is, and that's where my daughter goes."

Elisa chuckled. "You see, I had Gus bring me here to deliver you some good news. He's not happy that he did, but I don't care. I don't care about anything more than I care about our daughter. So, if I have to call the cops and imply some bullshit to put the fear of God in you to keep you in line, for Daphne's sake, then that's what I'm going to do. Because you and I... we are it. Sylvia is gone! She's moved on! Don't you get it? She only wanted you for a baby, and that one shot failed. Your use in her life was done. She's moved on. You're too stupid to see it."

"That's not true," Andrés said.

"Of all people, you're the one who would always go on about your grandfather—worshipping that *degenerate*. I'm sure you've heard him say, 'You can't make a ho into a housewife.'"

"I've never heard him say shit like that, ever."

"It doesn't matter, because you know it's true, or else you would've been married by now, huh? You fucking clown, calling a ho your wife... You fell hard, didn't you? You faggot. But I didn't come here to argue. We're in a business partnership, right? Isn't that what marriage is about? Not the romance or the passion, but making sure something's on paper for money? In the interest of our partnership, and for Daphne's sake, this is what went down: as soon as everything opened back up, Petra and I went and petitioned the court. She helped me gain guardianship over you under what's called Article 81 of the Mental Hygiene Law."

"Guardianship?"

"Now hear me out; don't freak out—it's only temporary. It expires at the end of the year."

"Okay..."

Elisa leaned forward in her chair and whispered, "I know what happened that night in Chicago—Sylvia had told me—and I knew what was going to happen to you because of 9/11—companies laying people off. I had to act fast because, unlike Sylvia, we—your other girls—are counting on you. As soon as I had the authority, I filed all the paperwork I could under every law available for your protection to buy us time—the Family Medical Leave Act, the Americans with Disabilities Act. Then I filed for your disability and medical retirement because you had that benefit available. Did you know that?"

"I knew that."

Elisa sat back, crossing her arms. "You couldn't do anything while you were in here, so I had to do it for Daphne... And for you. I'm here today to tell you I got a letter yesterday from your company's disability carrier—they've approved *our* claim. The diagnosis the doctors gave you here, combined with your prognosis and what had happened, makes it so that you don't have to worry about working ever again. I did that. I made sure of that, so now you owe me even more."

Andrés looked at Elisa, her legs crossed in her black dress with the hemline down to her ankles, and white sneakers.

He shook his head. "I don't know what to say."

"I want you to look me in the eye, imagine you're bowing, and say, 'Thank you.'"

"Thank you."

"I can't hear you."

"Thank you."

"You didn't sound like you meant it."

"Thank you!"

"That's a good boy... And you're welcome. Are you ready to forget Sylvia and come home? Daphne needs her dad."

When Andrés didn't answer, Elisa rolled her eyes.

"Don't worry about Andy," she said. "He was where you dumped him off before New Mexico—with his real mother, although, believe it or not, she's also in the hospital. For what, God knows, but Andy is now with Petra. When you got back home, I couldn't tell you that. I was more concerned about getting Daphne ready for her first day of school, and then 9/11 happened, and now you're here.

"But can you believe it? Sylvia abandoning Andy? You've picked a lot of winners. I think I may be the most emotionally stable woman you've ever been with. Don't worry; I'll make sure that when you decide to leave here, he comes home. Andy will finally have some real stability.

"You do have the key to freeing yourself from here. It's up to you. If you want to come home with me—to your girls, to your son—then you'll need to forget about her."

Andrés shook his head and got up from his chair.

Elisa yelled after him as he walked away, "Don't forget, I can always ask for an extension to that guardianship! Petra will back me up! She said so herself! So maybe you don't have the key to get yourself out of here after all, but it's still up to you!"

Andrés kept walking until Elisa was far behind, and he was alone, back in his room with its painted blue walls.

OCTOBER 21, 2002

A nurse entered Andrés's room at the psychiatric hospital and informed him that he had a visitor. He jumped up from bed and eagerly followed the nurse into the empty common area with its blue walls, only to find it was Elisa, not Sylvia, who had come to see him.

"Don't look *so happy* to see me," Elisa said.

"I'm not—"

"It's sarcasm, you idiot. Take a seat."

Andrés did as he was asked, sitting in the blue chair placed opposite the black one Elisa occupied. The nurse walked out of the Blue Room, leaving them alone to sit and stare at each other.

After a long silence, during which Andrés fought to hide the sadness of not having had anyone visit him since Elisa's last visit, he finally said, "This is an interesting look for you."

Elisa wore a simple white T-shirt and faded jeans, her short blond hair styled to make her look ten years older.

"How's Daphne? Andy? Myra? Why haven't they come to see me?"

Elisa laughed. "To see you like this? No... Petra and I decided to give you significant time to think about your life—everything you've done wrong—so that after I tell you everything that's gone down while you've been in your 'time-out,' you can give me the answer I want to hear.

"You don't have an apartment anymore, but that's been a given since there's been no one there to pay the rent. We paid the fees to break the lease so it wouldn't hurt your credit. With the salary you're still collecting while locked away here, we also paid off all the medical bills that were due.

"I closed every account you had with Sylvia, including your phone plan. I went out and set up a new one under a company I created to organize and manage our business affairs—one that I control. All of our kids, including Andy, are on our new phone plan. I'll give you your new phone and number when you get out of here.

"And if you're worried about your stuff, it's at home with me—except your camera. That's gone. Petra took care of all of Sylvia's papers and belongings; she put them in storage. Apparently, Sylvia never came back for it. Figures."

Elisa stared at Andrés for a long moment, waiting for him to respond, but all he could do was crouch in his chair as if everything in him had been deflated, leaving him numb.

"I see you're starting to get it now," Elisa said. "She's gone."

"I know," Andrés murmured in a low, resigned voice.

"If you know, then I want you to say, 'Sylvia is never coming back. I'm moving on.'"

"Sylvia is never coming back. I'm moving on."

Elisa leaned forward in her chair, hands on her knees. "Are you ready to come home?"

"Yes."

"Then say my name."

"Elisa."

"Say it again."

"Elisa!"

"Don't you forget it... I'm nothing like Sylvia. The way she bounced after you failed to give her what she wanted, it's like she threw you away. Meanwhile, I'm here, ready to play my role. Are you ready to play yours?"

Andrés cried.

Elisa rolled her eyes. "Stop with that bullshit—stop. Do you want to go home?"

Andrés nodded.

"That's the answer I wanted to hear. But before we go, no more talk of this *magic* shit. None of that is real. I don't want our daughter's head filled with that crap. She has a gift for numbers, and I want her focused on that—not on magic.

"I want you focused on our daughter, not Sylvia. I deleted all your email accounts. I deleted every connection to your past that could possibly come back up. And if you think you can get to your work email, once I had filed *our* claim, your company terminated access to all their systems. I don't want ghosts messing with our family's stability, especially now. Through the guardianship, I took it upon myself to buy our family a house."

"That's fine."

"I know it's fine; that's why I bought it. It's in Hewlett Harbor. I want Daphne to go to the best school she can while also living as far away from the city as possible. I don't want you anywhere near there, triggering old memories.

"And you'll be happy to know that Andy has been with me since September. You could've been with us a lot sooner, but something told me to wait until today. Wherever she's at, I hope she's enjoying her fortieth birthday.

"As for you, I want you to say it again. I didn't believe you the first time—say, 'Sylvia is never coming back. I'm moving on.'"

"Sylvia is never coming back. I'm moving on."

Elisa stood and patted Andrés's head. "That's my good boy. I'm going to start the process—get you out of here."

"Does that mean the guardianship will be expiring now?"

"Maybe... maybe not. It all depends. Are you going to go off and abandon your family to chase hoes and stars? No? Then maybe it'll expire—but only if you promise to stay home and be a dad. Be a dad to the daughter who's still alive."

Elisa reached out and grabbed Andrés's hand.

"Continue to be the dad you chose to be to Myra—she needs you too."

The way Elisa stared at him, with determination and genuine concern, made him realize that, despite the animosity and complicated history between them, what she was trying to keep him away from wasn't the Lower East Side but Ground Zero.

He sighed. "I promise."

❧ 37 ❧

THE ZEN MASTER

MARCH 20, 2003

ANDRÉS SAT IN A SMALL ROOM IN HIS PSYCHIATRIST'S HOME OFFICE in Manhasset. In the hospital, the psychiatrist had diagnosed Andrés with a panic disorder that exacerbated a preexisting condition of post-traumatic stress, pushing it into a chronic state. According to the psychiatrist, this placed Andrés at an increased risk of associated psychiatric and medical illnesses.

In the years Andrés had been his patient, the psychiatrist had prescribed every antidepressant possible. When that didn't work, the psychiatrist placed him on neuroleptics and benzodiazepines. Since then, Andrés's thoughts had become more fragmented and disordered.

Like a heap of broken images.

That's how it all felt in his head.

Andrés was no longer the man he used to be. All the drugs had stained the skin around his face and neck with brown and black blotches and killed his metabolism—he had gained 100 pounds. His body became a prison he was forced to drag around.

It didn't matter if he still collected his full salary and benefits.

It didn't matter if he was providing for everyone.

Every time Andrés looked in the mirror, he could only shake his head and accept that his worth as a man had nothing to do with raw desire anymore. No one would want him for him. He had become something else: the plow horse.

The door to the office opened. The psychiatrist—a tall, muscular man with a head of white hair—stood at the entrance.

"Come on in," he said.

Andrés followed him inside and took a seat on a blue stool positioned directly across from a large purple chair.

The psychiatrist sat across from Andrés. Various framed items hung on the wall behind him: his medical degree from Columbia College of Physicians & Surgeons, certificates for psychiatry residencies and training at regular and veteran hospitals, and the C. G. Jung Institute in Zürich.

Most prominently displayed was the psychiatrist's shadow box, containing World War Two campaign medals earned during his service in North Africa and the China-Burma-India Theater. A Silver Star and a Purple Heart glowed at the center of the box.

"Tell me, what happened?" the psychiatrist asked.

"Can I have a pen and paper?" Andrés replied.

The psychiatrist reached over to the small table beside his chair, grabbed his notepad, and ripped out a sheet, handing it over along with a pen. He sat quietly as Andrés wrote on the paper.

"I'm ending your rights to talk to Elisa," Andrés said, handing him the note and his pen back. "We're not married. She has no right to talk to you. Her guardianship stopped being a thing at the beginning of the year."

"I'm still a bit confused."

"Please, be my doctor. Help me."

"I'm trying—I would like to know what happened last night."

"If you want to know, then you'll have to accept that I've been telling you the truth all along. Be my doctor; listen to me—not Elisa. Believe me, I'm your patient."

"I'm listening. Tell me why you threw a remote control at the TV."

"I lost everything."

"What did you lose?"

"My family. It's why I got angry."

The psychiatrist scribbled on his notepad. Without looking up, he said, "But you have a family."

"I have Daphne. I had Andy, but my mom, who, for whatever reason, doesn't talk to me now—and refuses to let me visit—came down this morning and took him away."

The psychiatrist looked at Andrés. "But it's still family, and from Elisa's voicemail, your mother coming down is a result of your throwing that remote at the television. So tell me, what happened?"[1]

Andrés hesitated before saying, "I was in bed, and a car commercial came on, with an open desert road, big blue skies, and a car entering a neighborhood built in the middle of nowhere. Children were playing. It's as if every front lawn was a playground. It comes on a lot whenever I'm asleep. I know because it's become part of my dreams, and now that she's no longer in my life, I sleep with the TV on.

"It's always the same dream—I'm back in New Mexico, making my way home from the airport, and it's night. I know it's winter because I see the constellation Orion high above, but I don't feel cold. I arrive in Santa Fe, and there's an abandoned playground set up on my lawn. I open the door, and nobody's home. There's the lingering smell of ginger in the house, but she's not home."

"Who's not home?" the psychiatrist asked.

"Sylvia... The home we were going to have... In the dream, I'm back in the car, and I'm in the passenger seat. The car is heading north, and then I see Sylvia on the side of the road, underneath a sign that reads, 'Death: 11 miles ahead.' That's when I usually wake up.

"Yesterday, Daphne woke me up because she wanted to show me a drawing she made of me. She knew I was sad. I had overheard her ask Elisa what happened to that beautiful lady who had her little sister in her belly. Elisa told Daphne that 'little sister' didn't exist. That she had imagined the whole thing. That hurt me!

"You know who that 'little sister' is, don't you? I talked about her—and Sylvia—in the hospital. Our daughter Athena died on June 26, 2001, and you kept me on lockdown until I denied she was real, and

---

1. *Book One: Orpheus,* "Chapter Three: A-Okay."

Sylvia wasn't real because Elisa told you they weren't real, but Sylvia is real. My Athena is real, and she would've been two years old this June, and you're not allowed to talk to Elisa about my condition anymore!

"And go look up the poet Sylvia James; she's in a bunch of anthologies for spoken word poetry. Sylvia has been on TV. She wrote a poem called *1968* that made her famous. It's about her father, First Lieutenant Wendell James. He served with the 1st Cavalry in Vietnam. Sylvia's mother, Alma Hadid, was an engineering student before dropping out to become a stay-at-home mom. She killed herself because she was depressed, and Sylvia's father was in Vietnam. Alma was real too, and she'd been told by doctors that her pain was not real! Her sadness was not real! That Alma should be happy that Sylvia survived a difficult birth—get over it—"

"You're getting agitated; we need to bring it down," the psychiatrist said.

"How would you feel if people told you that your service in North Africa was not real? Don't believe your crippled arm. Don't trust your memory. You did that to me because of Elisa."

"All I am asking of you is that you calm down," the psychiatrist said.

"How would Elisa feel if I were to tell people she didn't exist—that Daphne didn't exist? They're here, and I want Sylvia here. I want Athena here. I want Andy back, and I want to be awake again. I want to be alive again!

"And what happened last night was that, when I saw that commercial, I saw the daydreams that Sylvia and I used to have when we lived in Santa Fe. I saw the open desert road leading into a dusty town, away from the cities, back here. Where we would be away from the noise. Where we would be in our silence. We would be at peace. Sylvia and I would daydream of being under the stars, with Andy and Daphne, and with Athena. For the two of us to finally be at peace—

"She'd be happy and feel safe—oh God, you don't know the torture she's been through in her life, and only she knows the torture I've been through as a little boy. We are survivors! Sylvia and I see each other in that darkness—in the silence that survivors learn to keep so they can't be found. We were closer, in the silence, than we had ever been in our lives with anyone, in the talk. The commercial came on last night, and I saw what could've been—"

"What did you survive?" the psychiatrist asked.

"Abuse! Abuse of all kinds!"

There was a long silence.

The psychiatrist leaned forward in his chair. "Andrés—"

"What!"

"Do you want to talk about it?"

"No! And I'm the only one who knows Sylvia's pain, and I don't have her permission to say more, except to say we had devised a game —the Dance—and we became the cure for each other. We took control for ourselves. That's it. I'm cured, and I can't say if I cured her. My love always speaks for herself."

Another long silence.

"Andrés—"

"What!"

"Tell me more about the commercial."

"There's nothing more to say—the dream ended, and news about the invasion came on. The way it was being talked about by the pundits... a picture of Wendell flashed through my mind—one of the few Sylvia had of her father before he deployed—looking happy, alive, with the same smile Sylvia has. Wendell might as well have died in Vietnam, because something in him died and didn't come back, and it killed something in her.

"Sylvia is close to my son. Was. She'd become his mother, and if her leaving killed something in me, I can't imagine what it's doing to him. He won't tell me. I worry about him. I'm having nightmares that Andy will be deployed to Afghanistan, and something in him will die, like Wendell, and he'll be broken for the rest of his life, like Wendell, like me, and I can't sleep.

"I know my son will be part of a new generation of boys and girls who'll come home broken, only to then break their families. Let's kick off a new cycle of pain. The endless wheel of broken families... like Sylvia's, like mine, like what I'm doing to mine, like more fucking pain in the world—in Iraq, in Afghanistan—more death—and what good is this shit? Is God even real? Fucking dick of a god, piece-of-shit motherfucker—"

"Slow down. Breathe," the psychiatrist said.

"No, I want to be mad! Elisa called my mom, and she came down. Before she left with Andy, my mom told me I was pathetic for letting myself go. I tried to explain it was because of the medications. My mom laughed and said, 'Is that what you're calling cheese fries? Your medication?' That's when she confessed she didn't believe depression was a real thing. She said I should just get over it and move on, like I did after the Gulf War.

"My mom brought Sylvia into the mix, asking me what I'd do if Sylvia saw me as I am now. She said I should fix myself if I ever want to be happy again because if Sylvia came back, she'd be disgusted by how much I've let myself go... It's the most she's said to me since I left for Berlin."

The psychiatrist paused before saying, "It's understandable for Elisa to call me. From what she's told me, you're being difficult while she's trying to take care of you and keep everything running at home—"

"Am I allowed to express anger?" Andrés asked.

"It depends—your anger scared them."

"Elisa punches walls all the time, and it scares me—who can I call for that? Who do I turn to without being laughed at? My mom used to throw shit at my dad all the time, and it scared me then. And I can't throw a remote control at a TV without being made to feel like I'm a monster?

"I had that reaction to a car commercial because it reminded me of what I'd lost. My daughter died! The love of my life left me! I barely got out of the South Tower! I know I'm broken! I'm broken, and I can't connect with Andy and Daphne! No matter how much I try! And Myra hates me—I don't want to be here anymore!

"I'm tired, and I'm sad, and I'm trapped, and before you say anything—no, I don't want to hurt myself. I just want to sleep. I want to sleep for a hundred years. I want to end this session, and I want to go back to bed and sleep. I want to fast-forward through life and end it quicker. Can I end the session?"

"You can if you like."

"I'd like that—I'm done."

"Consider the session closed."

Andrés stood. "I'll see you next week. I just want to go back to bed. That's it."

APRIL 1, 2004

The door to the office opened. The psychiatrist stood at the entrance.

"Come on in," he said.

Andrés followed him inside and took a seat on a blue stool positioned directly across from the psychiatrist, who sat down in a large purple chair.

"How are you feeling?" Andrés asked.

"The port's in place, and I started the chemo. I'm okay," the psychiatrist said. "Thanks for asking. Before we begin, I want to remind you, I'm not talking to Elisa; she left a voicemail."

"When is she not leaving voicemails? It doesn't surprise me."

"If it doesn't surprise you, then let me hear your side."

"This isn't what I wanted to talk about today. This has to end. I need to get away from her."

"Why do you want to leave your girlfriend?"

"Elisa is not my girlfriend."

"Oh, that's right. What is she again?"

"She's my business partner. She's tried rekindling something between us, but no. Everything with Elisa feels coerced—I'm in *that* house against my will. Give me back control of my life, my money, and set me free. Don't threaten me with guardianship. Don't threaten to say horrible things about me if I decide to move out."

"What horrible things?" the psychiatrist asked.

"How often do you beat your wife?"

The psychiatrist laughed. "What?"

"The horrible things? How often do you beat your wife?"

The psychiatrist looked visibly uncomfortable and said nothing.

"Can you answer that question without sounding guilty?" Andrés asked. "It automatically puts you on the defensive, right? Imagine being placed on the defensive after coming out of the South Tower—how about this horrible thing? Why are you a shitty father?"

"I get your point."

"Why are you avoiding the question? You must be guilty."

The psychiatrist chuckled. "The older I get, the less I care about people's reactions or answering their questions—a little secret. Moving on to the voicemail: Elisa said you were agitated last night. An argument? What was it over? That's my concern. If we're talking about these types of questions, believe it or not, angry men can come off as monsters to women."

"Elisa is a monster to me—don't you care about that? I mean, there's a rage behind that frozen smile of hers."

The psychiatrist stared at him, dead-eyed, waiting for a response and saying nothing.

Andrés sighed. "I wanted to talk about my son. He's important, and I guess her voicemail is tied to that... Andy called last week."

"He's talking with you again? That's great!"

Andrés smiled. "He is... I didn't ask why he'd stopped. I was happy he called. Andy implied a lot was going on. He said, 'There's a reason Grandma is like this, and I can't tell you because you know how she can be. I don't want her mad at me.'"

Andrés paused, remembering all the times he didn't want Petra mad at him—her silence.

"I understand now why my son stopped talking," he said. "As his dad, I felt helpless. I wanted to get in my car and drive upstate to confront my mother about how she has my son walking on eggshells, but Andy assured me he was doing fine because of his mother. He asked me to take him to a specialist's appointment. His mom was going to be out of town, his grandparents were unavailable, and they'd waited months for this visit. He told me the appointment couldn't be rescheduled. His attention deficit had gotten worse... It seemed like I was the last option. When I told Elisa what I planned on doing with Andy, she complained, 'Who's going to pick Daphne up from school?' I'd already made arrangements with one of the other PTA moms I know to get her. I'm a member, and that mom lives a few houses down from us—no big deal."

When Andrés became silent, the psychiatrist said, "It sounds like you had taken some of the suggestions we talked about—being proactive in finding solutions."

"I'm really trying."

"Then why the silence?"

"I hate that Elisa made me feel like shit for wanting to take care of my son. Andy never asks me for anything. I'm his father just as much as I'm Daphne's. As much as I'm Myra's. He's my responsibility too. He's the one who made me a father, and it's not fair to him, and I know that he knows. I know that he can't trust himself to count on me.

"Andy waited until the day of the appointment to tell me I'd be picking him up at Red Hook High School, like there was a chance they'd still get someone else to do what I'm supposed to do—what I want to do. Then it hit me. Why Red Hook? My parents don't live there. They live across the river in Saugerties. And I didn't know Lydia lived in Red Hook, much less could afford to live there. When Sylvia and I relocated to New Mexico, Lydia had been living in Astoria with her mother. She hates it upstate. I guess people change."

The psychiatrist sat back in his chair, his expression shifting as subtle tension crept into his features. His eyes, once neutral, now held a hint of doubt.

"What's that look? You gave me a look," Andrés said.

"It's nothing," the psychiatrist said. "Please proceed."

"Well, the appointment was yesterday. I signed Andy out of school and was fighting not to fall asleep at the wheel while driving. I fell asleep in the waiting room. I fell asleep while his doctor was examining him. I almost fell asleep driving away from the office. Andy asked me to drop him off in front of this long driveway at this small house. I asked him, 'Why here? Is this where your mom lives now? It looks too fancy to be hers alone.' Andy said, 'It's okay, Dad. Mom is not who you remember her to be. She's handling her business. Trust me.'"

The psychiatrist leaned forward in his chair. "Did he say it like that?"

Andrés nodded. "Yeah—why?"

The psychiatrist sat back, the tension in his features shifting, signaling intense concern. "Nothing. Proceed."

"Are you sure?"

"Yes, I'm sure—proceed."

"I pulled into the driveway and was about to get out of the car, walk up the driveway with my son, and go to the front door—something told me to go; a voice told me, 'This is it'—but Andy stopped me, pushing me back down into my seat. He said he didn't want me to go any further. That it was his mom's space, not mine, and I wouldn't want to mess with any of his mother's *boundaries*."

"Did he use the word boundaries?"

"Yes. It doesn't make sense. Why that word? Then I got a call from Elisa, yelling at me because I wasn't home. She didn't want me lingering, especially there. When I got home, Elisa was frantic. She asked what I'd seen on my visit, over and over. She kept asking if I'd seen anyone else. Who else was I supposed to see other than Lydia?"

"Andrés, you're stalling. Tell me what happened last night."

Andrés took a deep breath and swallowed. "Last night, before bed, Elisa and I were sitting on the couch, watching TV. I was flipping through channels when she told me to stop and put it on anything. That's when we saw *her* flash on one of the news stations. I know Elisa saw her too because she said, 'Holy shit,' snatched the remote from me and changed the channel before throwing it across the room."

"Who did you see?"

"Sylvia."

"And why would she be on a news channel?"

"I don't know. I didn't need a remote to change the channel, so I went to the TV and did it there, but by the time I got back to where I thought I had seen her, they were playing a commercial."

"Elisa claims you attacked her," the psychiatrist said.

"How often do you beat your wife?"

"Elisa claims you attacked her."

"How often do you beat your wife? I could do this all day. Elisa will make accusations to control me... keep me in line. Let me ask you this: are you my doctor?"

"I am your doctor."

"I don't trust you anymore."

"I'm sorry you feel that way."

"But you're not sorry for believing her over me. I'm going to tell you right now: I will not sit here and justify myself against a bullshit allegation. The earth is my witness. I've taken punches from women of a higher caliber than Elisa and laughed. I see you. I see we're in a game here as well—her game—and that's cool. I'll play. Coming to these sessions has nothing to do with helping me; it's just control. I'll jump through your hoops if it means my freedom."

"Do you perceive everything in the world through the lens of power dynamics?"

"I do now. I came here thinking you were here to help me, but you're helping Elisa instead. I came here wanting to tell you how, more and more, I'm hearing Sylvia calling out to me in my dreams because she's in pain—so much pain—and instead of helping me work through this fucked-up feeling, I spend most of the session defending myself. Then, whatever I do share, I have to worry about how you'll use that against me for whatever she has in mind.

"Fuck that—Sylvia is calling me. I can hear her yelling that we made promises to each other, that I'd always come back for her. I won't leave her behind again. I made the biggest mistake of my life when I got on that plane. I can hear her right now, yelling at me to go back to Red Hook—to that house. I can't take it anymore.

"These dreams are almost the same as another dream I had before 9/11, when I was in Berlin—a bizarre, supernatural fantasy—and it scared me. I was planning to find a therapist when I got back to New York to talk about that, and about how I had been drugged and raped on that business trip, but then 9/11 happened, and—"

"Stop, stop, stop—you were *sexually assaulted?*"

"I was raped," Andrés said.

"Why didn't you bring this up sooner?"

"I did—during my intake at Bellevue. The nurse processing me said men don't get raped. Let's focus on what really brought me there: the crisis that pushed my family to call for help. Again, when I was brought to the hospital, just before starting with you, I told one of the social workers there, and again, she told me the same thing. When I pressed her for help—for her to believe me—she asked, 'What did you do to that woman to get that response?'

"When I got out of the hospital, I looked at my records, and no one noted anything I had said. You guys had done the same shit the police in Berlin did when I tried to report the rape—except you guys didn't laugh me out of the station. You guys dismissed me instead—you guys believed Elisa, calling Sylvia and Athena my delusions. I became afraid everyone would think it was all in my mind, so I learned to keep my mouth shut. I thought we could talk about it once I became an outpatient, but I was wrong.

"In almost every session we've had, you bring up some bullshit Elisa called to complain about. Then somehow, you make it the focus of our session. Now, can you see the control she has? You fucking asshole! I'm the one who's sick! Not Elisa—she's not your patient. Accuse me again of something fucked up. As God as my witness, I've never laid my hands on Elisa.

"You're my doctor. I'm not your doctor—lately, you talk about your fucking fears about cancer, and I've been the one to sit and listen to you. I say nothing because I'm scared that if I complain, you'll use it against me. These sessions are all for complying with this bullshit mental hygiene law that's robbed me of my life."

The psychiatrist tried to interrupt. "Andrés—"

But he kept going. "Elisa keeps threatening to take me back to court and put it back on me. Elisa is dominating me. You're dominating me, and I have no choice but to take it. So, never mind me and my issues. Let's pay attention to Elisa's complaints. Let me be your therapist, listen to you, and pay you for the privilege. I'm just here; nothing has ever happened to me. My daughter didn't die. I didn't leave Sylvia to deal with postpartum depression alone, like a goddamn asshole. She didn't leave me because I'm a piece of shit."

"Andrés—"

"For months, you were telling me Sylvia and my daughter weren't real, and I had to shut the fuck up about it so I could get out of the hospital."

"Andrés—"

Andrés took a deep breath and cried. "I just wanted to see if it was

Sylvia on TV and not strung out on drugs like I'd been worried for all these years—that would've given me peace. I just wanted to make sure she was okay. It wouldn't have been out of the ordinary to see her on TV. She was working on a novel set in Iraq."

"Andrés—what happened to you in Berlin?"

Andrés explained. As he went further into detail, the psychiatrist began coughing hard. Andrés paused while the psychiatrist grabbed a handkerchief out of his pocket, held it to his mouth, and coughed more. When he stopped coughing, the psychiatrist looked at the handkerchief to see that he had hacked up brown phlegm.

"I'm sorry to do this to you," the psychiatrist said, looking back at Andrés, "but I need to wrap this session up for today."

"It figures."

"I'm on your side, goddammit. I care—I care—but if we're going to tackle sexual assault, we need more than the ten minutes left in our session. Besides, that cough felt wet, and I need to see what's going on."

"I'm sorry," Andrés said.

"I won't bring up Elisa anymore. This event in Berlin, coupled with the death of Athena, your loss of Sylvia, and 9/11—four major life events within the span of three months—will be the central focus of our sessions moving forward. Nothing else matters. We'll address it so that you can manage it before I run out of time. That's our goal. It's the only goal of our therapy—the assault and the abuse in the past. That's the key..."

"Okay."

"Before we end this session, considering what we've uncovered, I'm changing your medication to lithium... This is temporary. It's not indicative of a new diagnosis. I'm also decreasing the clonazepam."

"I don't understand."

"The lithium will help keep you together for the therapy to come. Your moods are fluctuating at a dangerously rapid pace for what we're about to do. We're going to break everything apart, tear down the monuments you've set up in your mind, and see what's left standing. Then we'll know what's real."

"I don't get it."

"I'm going to say this, and you need to follow—if I find out you haven't followed my directions, I will commit you back to the hospital."

Andrés became alarmed. "What's wrong?"

"I'm forbidding you from searching for Sylvia—on the internet, offline, anywhere. Don't go anywhere you're not invited. If your parents haven't invited you to their house, do not go. If your son's mother hasn't invited you to her property, do not go until I'm certain we've stabilized your mental health. I'm trusting you. I know you're good with boundaries when they're set—that is the boundary I'm setting for you because you're giving yourself way too much importance in areas where you may find you're not important at all. And you don't understand the magnitude of your importance in areas where you think you're insignificant. I don't share opinions readily, but I'm going to share in this case—again, it's not indicative of a formal diagnosis."

"Okay."

"You have a massive savior complex, and it's fueled by narcissism. That is your blind spot. Now that you know, I don't want you looking for anyone. No one needs saving. Everyone, including Sylvia, is doing fine without you. Life goes on. Everyone has moved on, and it would not be good to disturb their lives. People aren't how we remember them. All the clinging? It's a coping mechanism that comforts you when you should take comfort in being young and relatively healthy. It's not like you're old and facing cancer, like me. You should focus on what you still have, not on what you've lost."

Andrés felt the sting that came from realizing he was talking to a man battling cancer.

Before Andrés could say anything, the psychiatrist said, "Normally, patients wouldn't know anything about my life. I'm sorry I started talking when I shouldn't have. I lost my focus, and that's my fault. I'm only human. It's hard to hide my battle when it's so obvious now that I've lost so much weight, and you can see the port under my shirt. I've always believed in addressing the obvious, and here we are. How I cope is by sticking to my work and holding on to the things I have every reason to be happy for. I'm still alive and enjoying life. I'm part of a barbershop quartet that gives me joy.

"You need to do the same—find a hobby that brings you joy. Keep busy with something that sustains who you are. Hold on to the things you have every reason to be happy about. You're young and alive. You have a family. Yes, the family you have—they're yours. You don't have to worry about money ever again in your life. Do the work of the therapy, and you'll regain control of your life again. That should bring a smile to your face. It should make that feeling of her calling for you stop, because that feeling is a delusion—a massive delusion.

"Here's your new script. Start it tonight. See you next week."

OCTOBER 24, 2005

Andrés sat in a small room, waiting for his psychiatrist to open the door to his home office. He couldn't wait to greet him with a welcoming smile, letting him know how grateful he was for his expertise in helping Andrés navigate the darkness.

Andrés was grateful for his psychiatrist's existence—for showing him, by example, that one does not accept defeat but takes swings at the darkness, and continues taking swings, and fights to stay on their feet for as long as possible, and does not yield, and does not fall to their knees, but keeps swinging until their last minutes, until their last seconds, until everything cuts to black.

To yell into the void, even within their last seconds.

His doctor was still his psychiatrist.

The doors to the office opened. There stood Andrés's hero—his psychiatrist: Dr. Irving Patton. Once a tall and muscular man, now hollowed out and gaunt, with dark circles under his eyes, and bald.

Andrés stood, shook his hand, and asked, "How are you feeling?"

"I'm not dead yet. Come in and take a seat."

Andrés walked over to a large purple chair and waited for Dr. Patton to settle into his before sitting down.

Bright spots marked where the psychiatrist once displayed his degrees and accreditations. Dr. Patton's shadow box remained in place.

"Seriously, how are you?" Andrés asked.

Dr. Patton hesitated before saying, "My oncologists are doing their best. Have done their best. There's not much to say other than that."

"I have to be honest. Each time I see you, it gets more difficult to talk. I want to listen to you instead."

Dr. Patton smiled. "I appreciate the sentiment. You're my patient. I had a practice long before you were born. So, tell me—what's going on? Have you dreamed about her this week?"

Andrés smiled. "No."

"Did you notice anything unusual?"

"I did."

"What was that?"

"Everywhere I go, I smell plane fuel. It's wild. It's like thinking of Sylvia was a way of avoiding other issues."

"But you don't really smell it everywhere you go. When do you notice the smell? In what situations?"

Andrés's right leg began to bounce.

"Are you anxious?" Dr. Patton asked.

"I'm always anxious."

"You were fine a moment ago, and now the bounce. Do you smell plane fuel?"

"No."

"What came to mind?"

"The sky... Looking out your window, I can see it's so beautiful and blue—it's unreal." Andrés sighed. "It's reminding me of a poem that has a line with the words—*'Tenement Sky.'* That's all."

Dr. Patton was about to respond but began coughing hard. He grabbed a handkerchief out of his pocket, held it to his mouth, and coughed more. When he stopped coughing, Dr. Patton looked at the handkerchief to see that he had coughed up blood.

Andrés got up from the chair to tend to him, but Dr. Patton waved him off and told him to sit back down. He cleaned the corners of his mouth with the white part of the handkerchief, then placed it aside. With his hand to his mouth, Dr. Patton stared at Andrés, fear glistening in his eyes.

"Are you okay?" Andrés asked.

"I think we're in the final moments of our therapeutic relationship," Dr. Patton replied. "I'm tired, and I want to go home, so I'll be cutting the session short. I came in to make sure you were okay, and I think you are. The leg bouncing still concerns me, so I'm going to share some final thoughts, and what you do with it will be your choice."

"Okay... I'm ready."

"When I took you on as a patient, it was at the hospital, and it was under the guidelines set by the Mental Hygiene Law and how it governs guardianships over mentally incapacitated individuals, protecting them from themselves. You remained my patient and were no longer under guardianship, but there was always the possibility you could return to that status.

"Reports to the court leave no room for psychoanalysis. In fact, it would have hurt you. That's why I did everything possible to keep our sessions as grounded as possible; when I was filling out reports to the court, I didn't want to put anything in them that might cause the court to act, especially since a person like Elisa might use it against you. If I had hinted in those reports at your obsession with 'magic in the world,' it could have led to your being confined again to a psychiatric hospital."

"I didn't know that."

"The goal of our therapy was to show you're capable of taking care of yourself, which I now believe you can, but—"

"But?"

"You've mentioned the story of *Tenement Sky* a few times before. I know what it all means, and I know what the blue skies you see now remind you of. You need to make a choice about which memory to confront and deal with. And be honest."

Andrés was silent for a long moment before he began to shake with panic, looking around the room.

"It's okay, Andrés... You're here with me. Don't be scared," Dr. Patton said.

Andrés stood from his chair and slowly approached the window to look at the unreal beauty of the blue sky. He touched the glass the same way he had that morning when he looked out the windows from the 105th floor of the South Tower, thinking at that moment of Sylvia climbing onto the guardrail of the rooftop observatory years before to frantically yell, "I'll try! I'll try!"[2]

Dr. Patton asked Andrés, "Do you smell plane fuel?"

"No, I do not," he replied.

"That's because you're not being honest—be honest—your life depends on it."

Andrés had to remind himself that those memories of Sylvia no longer mattered; they had become clutter he had been mindlessly hoarding for years. And when he perceived them as such, the memory of that day at the top of the South Tower was no longer there. Who he began to remember was Marco, and the number of times he would stop Andrés on the office floor to show off pictures of his daughter: pictures of him playing in the park with her, with his wife, in the golden hour light.

Marco was dust.

They all were.

Andrés dropped to his knees at the realization, his face buried against the office's wood paneling below the windowpane. He began to cry. "After the first plane hit, I went to the window, and the sky was so clear and blue, and the North Tower was burning, and a man was hanging out the window, trying to escape the smoke.

"He looked a lot like a guy I used to work with named Marco, who had asked me, one father to another, to look out for him. He knew he was going to be among the many that we were laying off, and I did. I placed him at a job in the North Tower, on a floor that was around where that guy was hanging out the window, and I watched him make the choice to let go instead of burn. I watched him let go—I watched him let go, and I had to get out of there. I had to get home to Daphne; I had to get home to my daughters—to my son—to my family—and Marco didn't make it home to his. I didn't mean for him to die. I was looking out for another father. I didn't want him to lose his job. He'd just bought a house. Marco was their only provider."

Dr. Patton called out from his chair, "Do you smell anything?"

Andrés laughed as he cried. "Yeah, fucking plane fuel."

____

2. *Book One: Orpheus*, "Chapter Eight: Tenement Sky."

"You did good. I'm proud of you."

"You are?"

"Yes, now stand up. Get on your feet. That's not your fault."

"It's not?"

"No. Go sit."

Andrés did as Dr. Patton commanded and took his seat across from him again.

"There's something I want to teach you," Dr. Patton said. "As you can see, I have an injury. I got that in North Africa. They patched me up enough to send me back out there. I fought out of a sense of duty, and I fought until we had won the war, and the army sent us home. Like you, I spent my first year recovering. Like you, I went to school. Unlike you, I earned my degrees. And despite this injury that's robbed me of full use of my left arm, I continued to function.

"What kept me going was a sense of purpose and duty to myself. All this time, I kept working out of that same sense of duty. I wanted to continue feeling normal, but I'm losing my fight. I'm moving into a hospice. I don't look at it as giving up; I'm just accepting reality. This is where the road is leading me, and I'm giving myself over to fate.

"When I was diagnosed, I had been reading a book that had a short story about a monk living in a Zen monastery. He was tired of paying attention to every aspect of his routine and wanted out. The monk goes to the Zen master and informs him of his decision to leave. The master says, 'Then go,' but as the monk makes for the door, the master says, 'That's not your door.' The monk tries another door, and the master tells him again, 'That's not your door.' The monk sees a door behind the master, one only the master can use. 'That's not your door!' the master says. The monk becomes confused and frustrated.

"The monk says, 'You said I could leave. How can I leave if none of these exits is my door? I'm stuck in this room.' The master responds, 'If there's no exit to leave through, then sit.'

"Since my diagnosis, I've wanted to run out of this room in my mind. I've wanted to scream and escape the moment I'm in and find a door, a window, an exit—anything that'll allow me to escape my situation, my cancer—but there are no doors. There are no windows. There is no exit... I had no choice but to sit in the space of my mind, in my moment, and face my cancer. Face it while focusing on my routine. I can't run away. I can't escape. There are no doors for me, no matter how hard I've tried to create one, to distract me from the inevitable.

"Life has to go on, and I kept to my routine of being a psychiatrist. I still had a job to do. Andrés, I had to help you. I had to help others like you. That is my duty. I have a duty to my wife, who has given me everything and who will continue to live on. I'm doing it... for her.

"Despite what you may have felt, I believed you. I just couldn't give you the answers you wanted. For the therapy to work, you needed to discover the answers yourself. My time with you and patients like you isn't a waste. It was my job. I'm still alive. My job is what I live for, and it was important to me to lead you to that breakthrough—to get you to smell the plane fuel! Now, you need to desensitize yourself from what triggers that sense memory, not avoid it."

"But how?" Andrés asked.

"That's a job for your next therapist—I don't have your answer. I now see my door. I see my exit. I'll be going into hospice, and I'm happy. Andrés, I did my best. I fought. Cancer didn't take me without a fight, and now I'm at peace. Soon, I'll be walking through my door. As for you, I'm talking to you, not as a psychiatrist to his patient, but as one man to another—find your purpose that doesn't involve this woman. That doesn't involve anyone—just you. Fight to make yourself your mission, or else you'll waste your life away. I'm happy because I know I lived a full life. That's what you need to do—live a full life. Your purpose is more than being a father; children grow into adults who leave their parents for their own lives. What will you be when that happens?

"And pardon me for being this direct, but you are not a victim, so stop whining and acting like one. You're a man. Believe it or not, that means something. It has always meant something—for generations upon generations, without qualifications from anyone other than other men. I'm telling you: you're a man. Find something that defines the man you are now. Something that gives you purpose instead of wasting away your life. That's the only thing I find insulting. It's what makes me angry. You have what I want so much—time—and you're wasting it."

"That day when I talked about seeing Sylvia on TV," Andrés said, "and then I brought up Berlin, I remember the look on your face. It scared me, especially with the way you urged me to take the lithium. I never had anything knock me out and put me to sleep as much as that drug."

"Your delusional, grandiose thinking is associated with trauma stemming from the lack of control over your body. If the medication hadn't stabilized your condition, the next step would've been hospitalization. You were in danger of stalking someone who had set up definitive boundaries for her own well-being. Sylvia left you, but you did not see that clearly. All you heard were voices you believed were rooted in some mystical vision of oneness that, as a psychiatrist, I came close to associating with psychosis.

"Since that day, you have spoken about how your relationship with Sylvia thrives on boundaries. This is a reminder that, regardless of how right you think you may be at the moment, you are never to cross her boundaries. If Sylvia wanted to be found, you would've heard from her by now. She would've crossed that boundary for the two of you, but she hasn't, and she won't because she doesn't want to hear from you. When you got on the plane and left her behind, you hurt her in ways that most people will not forgive. That's the truth, so you must always respect her choice."

"That's brutal, but it's the only thing that makes sense. The simplest explanation is the truth, and it's fine. Makes it easier to move on. Embracing the truth." Andrés laughed. "I smell plane fuel. Tons of fuel."

"Good. Fantasy is not your door. Nostalgia is not your door. You are in a room with no doors. Deal with being in it—not through sex, not through drugs, not through anything else other than awareness. You mustn't let your mind wander. You need to be like the monk in that story and have your day and night planned."

"I understand now. I'm sorry if I've ever insulted you."

"You've never insulted me," Dr. Patton said. "I've become greedy when I shouldn't be. I'm old. I've had all the time I've needed. More than enough. I know it's my time to walk through that door... With that said, my wife will contact you with the name of the psychiatrist who will take over my practice. In your patient notes, I'm instructing that you're to be tapered off the Clonazepam as soon as possible. You're coming off all other medications. I'm also leaving letters and documentation you'll need if you find yourself fighting Elisa in court. I have this ready for you."

Dr. Patton reached over to the small table beside his chair and grabbed the envelope that had been there, handing it to Andrés "Follow your new psychiatrist's instructions or risk seizures. Prepare for withdrawals. You'll be fully awake. Good luck, Sergeant de León... Until we meet again."

JANUARY 11, 2006

It was almost five in the afternoon, and Andrés was in bed, hunched in a curl, crying. Moments before, he had received a phone call from Dr. Patton's wife, letting him know, as his psychiatrist had requested of her, to pass on the news of his death.

She said, "Having you as his last patient is what helped him fight—he was determined to get you to see—to understand."

Andrés cried in appreciation over the gift of his doctor's time and attention.

He cried in anger over how much of his life and time he had wasted and from the pain of withdrawal from the clonazepam his new psychiatrist had warned would be just as bad—if not worse—than withdrawing from heroin. Despite that, he looked at the medication on his nightstand and rationalized to himself that, just this one time, he could take just one pill—like just one fix—just enough to cope with the death of Dr. Patton.

Until Andrés realized the smell of plane fuel was suddenly gone.

He could see what he was about to do.

He understood that taking just one pill would do nothing more than block the path to overall good health. He got up, went into his bathroom, and flushed the remaining pills he had kept, just in case he needed them. He needed to no longer smell plane fuel.

The reality—as pervasive as that smell he could even taste in his nightmares—was there and would always be there. He had to embrace it once again, the same way he had in the year after coming home from his Gulf War deployment, when he read Albert Camus' *The Myth of Sisyphus* and learned that, in the face of an absurd universe—an indifferent God who loves dropping hammers on His creations—Andrés must live to the point of tears in the in-between that exists in that descent down to the base of the mountain before having to push that rock up again.

Andrés was about to go back to bed and cry over the death of his Zen Master some more when Daphne came into his room.

"Mom's home—she wants you to get out of bed and do some laundry," Daphne said.

"I will, but later... I'm not feeling well; I need to be alone."

"I don't care if you're not feeling well. Look, if you expect me to have any pity for you, you're sadly mistaken."

"What did you say?" Andrés asked, slowly walking toward her. "You're not even ten years old, and you're talking to me as if you were your mother?"

"Mom works—you don't. Stop being lazy."

As Daphne stood there, looking at him with contempt and pity, Andrés realized he had made a deal with Daphne, Elisa, and everyone else—one they were not even aware of. He thought the six-figure disability checks that kept his family alive and living in the beautiful home Elisa had bought with his money should have at least earned him their respect in exchange. But in reality, he could see he was not owed anything. Not even after his self-immolation—setting himself on fire to keep his family warm—was he owed their love.

The ties that bind families are subject to the same rules found in power dynamics. Anything he would do going forward would be because he wanted to—not because he wanted to be considered their good boy, not because he was compelled by his upbringing to make all the women in his life happy, even when they were sad, but so his daughter would look at him with understanding instead of disgust.

In that moment, Andrés decided it was time to exercise the only power he had in this dynamic with his family.

"Dad, what's so funny? Where are you going?" Daphne asked as she followed Andrés out of his bedroom, down the hall, and into the family room.

Andrés turned around, placed both hands on Daphne's shoulders, and smiled. "Estefania, I love you—always remember that. There will come a day when you'll remember this moment and say to yourself, 'I understand my dad now, why he walked away.'"

Daphne called out to Elisa, who was in her upstairs bedroom, "Mom! Dad is leaving!"

Elisa raced out, running downstairs to follow Andrés outside to the driveway, yelling, "Where are you going?"

Andrés didn't answer.

The smell of plane fuel had never been stronger than in that moment, outside that house.

He got in the car and drove away, leaving the house that had become his prison far behind him.

❈ 38 ❈

IN THE SHADOW OF THE THREE SISTERS

NOVEMBER 20, 2008

WHEN ANDRÉS THE WANDERER MOVED TO ALBUQUERQUE IN January 2006, he wanted to put as much geographic space as possible between the life where he was just existing and the life where he wanted to transform into someone new. Someone better.

Andrés chose to remember his mother as someone who taught him not just to be her good boy but that whenever he was scared or lonely, he should go outside and find the brightest stars in the sky. He would be seen by God.

The smell of plane fuel was everywhere, and Andrés was lonely.

"God, are you out there?" he would say to the night. "Or is this, too, a magic show?"

The stars were so bright and the sky so vast that an answer no longer mattered. It was as if he were a little boy again, his sense of wonder returning. Over time, he no longer smelled plane fuel.

There was nothing wrong with loving magic shows, especially while living the way Andrés had been living. After a long day of running for miles around the Three Sisters, as the dead volcanoes were known in the area—followed by lifting weights at the gym, meditating, and reading *The Upanishads*—Andrés would drive out to the middle of nowhere and focus on the lights of the universe. He would focus on shooting stars streaking across the sky every night. Andrés would touch upon a love in him that was as big as the night sky.

Andrés found relief in understanding that, when compared to the time it takes for the light of the stars to get to Mother Earth, the span of his life was short. His life would be over soon enough. When he understood—not just knew—this truth, it became easier for him to be happy than to take everything so seriously.

Andrés understood; he was a shadow.

Andrés had stopped calling his parents. He had no issue with Antonio, but whenever he wanted to speak with Petra, she would act as if he didn't exist. It was a tactic she had always employed. Silence and feeling invisible still hurt more.

In the late 1990s, there was an incident when Tony's wife, Jeanie, said something Petra perceived as an insult. Jeanie refused to apologize, so Petra treated her as though she didn't exist for three years. Jeanie threatened Tony—she would leave him if he didn't stand up for her. When Sylvia announced her pregnancy to the family, it was Jeanie who made peace so she could go out with Petra the night Andrés nearly killed Paul in the Black Room.

Andrés was never as afraid of Petra as Tony was. Before 9/11, Petra would always tell him, "You're just like that man," anytime he stood up to her, especially when it came to Sylvia. Over the years, since meeting Sylvia, Petra had become more domineering over her. Because Petra had filled the void left by Constance, Sylvia would buckle, fearing she might become invisible to Petra too.

When Andrés began traveling for work, protecting Sylvia became impossible because his mother became Sylvia's sole support system. As for being called "that man," over the years, Andrés understood that his mother's growing hostility toward him stemmed from him having to pay for the sins of his biological father.

Tony, on the other hand, was so much like Antonio, their dad. Tony had provided a large home in Lenox, Massachusetts, for Jeanie and their two teenage boys. Through his job as a network engineer, he offered them a comfortable existence, much like Antonio provided for

Petra and his boys through his union job. Andrés could always rely on his brother when it mattered the most.

Just before driving away to New Mexico, Andrés stayed with his brother, who, in the few days he was there, helped him find a lawyer so that he wouldn't need to worry about the threat of guardianship ever again. Tony also helped secure his finances from Elisa by confronting her and forcing her to open the books. What Andrés discovered shocked him.

Elisa did a fantastic job and had his best interests at heart all that time. Her talent for numbers, combined with the six-figure salary Andrés was still receiving through his disability, enabled her to take the significant amount of disposable income that was left after paying the mortgage, taxes, and utilities on the home and build a financial portfolio that only a fool would allow ego to get in the way of and destroy.

As he looked over the numbers that went into the millions with amazement, along with cryptic entries labeled "support," Elisa said, "I did it for our children, and I did it for you too. I'm not the enemy. You would've blown the money in some crazy ways. I know you. Remember, once upon a time, I loved you. I still do."

Against Tony's advice and the lawyer's counsel, Andrés asked Elisa to continue managing the finances. After she left the lawyer's office, Tony began to berate Andrés for his capacity to make poor choices.

"I'm on a leave of absence because of Elisa. I'm still collecting my salary because of her. Fuck pride, fuck ego; Elisa is the mother of my daughters and my business partner—Elisa made us wealthy," Andrés replied.

"Do you hear yourself?" Tony said. "I never loved Grandpa and could never understand how he could convince women their money was his, but now I see it—Elisa pimped you out. You're her bitch. No. At the very least, we're getting an accountant to oversee everything so she can't say, 'I'm just holding your money, but you can't spend it.' Grandpa was an evil man, and for all that worship you have for him, ask yourself if this isn't a consequence of you not accepting the Lord into your life."

"I'll take the oversight, but keep everything else to yourself. I respect your beliefs, but we're two different people. I have my issues with Elisa, but there's a history that has a lot of pain in it—but also a lot of passion."

"So I hear."

"You heard right," Andrés said. "For all the bullshit, I gave Elisa some crazy excitement. It's why, after all that hate, she still took care of me. She'd be the one picking me up off the bathroom floor because I'd fallen asleep on the toilet. Elisa's the one who tried to get me to go out on walks with her, trying to engage with me, and I'm the one who would say 'no.' And even though I'm fat as fuck, Elisa would still come looking for me for fun. And after I finally got over Sylvia, I gave her what she wanted.

"The fucking is just so different when you don't really like the person, and make no mistake, we may love each other, but we don't like each other. Jeanie, on the other hand, not only loves you but likes you as well. But you never stood up for her, and that's why she left. My brother, thank you for everything, but this is over your head. Enjoy your square life."

Tony laughed. "Bro, I love you, and I know you've been through a lot, but you're talking shit. You don't know where Sylvia is, and if you weren't so messed up in the head, you'd see everything that's been going on. And I love my *square* life, whatever the heck that means. At least my life isn't a *telenovela*."

With his finances secured and a frugal, minimalist mindset established during his years with Elisa, Andrés spent his time in New Mexico living out of his car. He lived like a monk. Andrés ate one meal a day: a boiled egg and fish. He showered at a gym on Kirtland Air Force Base. Andrés fastened his mind to the structure of routine, like a building to scaffolding under reconstruction. It was the only way to return to full function.

Everything stopped feeling as though it were *a heap of broken images.*

Over time, his body stopped looking as though he had spent every night since 2001 eating cheese fries at three in the morning. He was motivated to eventually go back east and pay his mother a surprise visit to show her just how much he had rebuilt himself—to kill the memories of her making surprise visits from time to time to talk with Elisa in private, then telling him to his face that she didn't believe in depression. That Andrés needed to man up—that his body hadn't sustained any injuries on 9/11 to justify being incapacitated all those years he was under heavy doses of neuroleptics and benzodiazepines.

To remember Petra saying over and over: "Man up.

"Man the fuck up.

"You've become pathetic.

"No wonder Sylvia left you."

As much geographic distance as Andrés could place between New York and himself, that's what he had to do.

Between the past and the present.

Between life and death.

Between 1992 and 2006.

Between 1997 and 2007.

Between 2001 and 2008.

The better for everyone.

To dispose of himself so he could cry in the darkness of the desert and not be judged.

To be told he was not a man for it.

It was for the best.

It was better for everyone because he had his own Master Plan. Since 2002, all of Andrés's military disability money had been going into a trust for his children, which they could not touch until they were adults. Elisa, in her brilliance, ensured that the money was growing exponentially. She even gave that trust a name—the Athena Fund.

Tony wasn't a person Andrés needed to justify himself to; who was he to judge and demand explanations? Andrés didn't want to explain to Tony that this was something square people like him could never understand with their conventional way of thinking: matters involving life and love between passionate, capable people can get complicated.

As Andrés would sit in the shadow of the Three Sisters, he would play over and over in his mind Elisa's words: "I did it for our children, and I did it for you too. I'm not the enemy. You would've blown the money in some crazy ways... I know you. Remember, once upon a time, I loved you. I still do."

Elisa was right. If he had had ready access to it, Andrés would have spent all of his money. The sadness was too much. Who knows what he would have done with all that money and time?

Sylvia once said money and time were what had done her father in. Wendell had no direction or goals his first few months back from Vietnam—just an infinite sadness over the death of his beloved Alma and all that money burning a hole in his pocket. It was Constance who had to step in and help Wendell establish Sylvia's trust.

If Elisa had not intervened in establishing guardianship over him, that disposable income could have found its way to a needle, creating an exit out of the room Andrés had found himself in after 9/11. She had protected him from himself but had been so vicious about it.

This was the question he meditated on in the shadow of the Three Sisters: What was wrong with Andrés that Elisa would go from the woman he had met to this vicious reflection? Andrés wouldn't be alive without her. He was out in the desert to learn more about becoming a better man for her.

How he could destroy his ego.

A long time ago, the morning after beating up Caleb for delivering more than Chinese takeout,[1] Sylvia served Andrés breakfast just before he was to leave for class, and she asked him to consider what would be that thing in him—his *hamartia*—that could bring him down, like the tragic heroes he had been reading about for his test that day.

Ego was Andrés's *hamartia*.

Ego kept him so self-absorbed in his problems—in studying for his pending exam—that he didn't glance up to acknowledge Sylvia or thank her for doing something so out of character back then. But she did it anyway because something in him made her want to—because she loved him. She got up with him early in the morning to make him breakfast.

Ego destroyed Andrés in the Black Room.

Ego pushed him to talk about his relationship with Sylvia and Elisa instead of being discreet.

Ego exposed him to Paul.

---

1. *Book Three: The Labyrinth*, "Chapter Twenty-Three: Delivery Boy."

If Andrés had kept his mouth shut, maybe he never would've faced the moment where he had to get on a plane and leave Sylvia behind.

Ego was his downfall.

Maybe Andrés was putting too much weight on one moment in his life. After all, Andrés is small. It didn't matter—ego compelled him to talk when he should've remained silent, trying to boast about how much of a man he was, having two women love him the way they did.

And now, in the shadow of the Three Sisters, he understood that what he had experienced from Elisa over the years wasn't just dominance; it was also love, because Andrés had been sick. What sane woman gives the wheel of the family car to a man made blind by his pain and trauma because she loves him? She takes the wheel because he's blind, because she loves him and wants him to stay alive, and because she's protecting her family, even if she has to be mean.

That's what she had done with the finances.

In meditating under the night skies, in the shadow of the Three Sisters, Andrés realized Elisa was as vital to him as Sylvia.

They are his Yin and Yang—the Dark and the Bright.

Elisa was Daphne's mom, and she had ensured Andrés's survival for the rest of his life.

Elisa had ensured everyone's survival for the rest of their lives.

Elisa honored the life he had created with Sylvia by creating that fund and naming it in Athena's honor.

She showed respect, which is the highest expression of love.

Elisa deserves all the respect.

Elisa deserves to be happy.

But why was she so fucking cruel and mean? When he met her, she was so goddamn beautiful inside and out.

Out in the desert, he would continue to meditate on the question.

When his children wanted to talk, they would call him. Whenever Daphne called and demanded he come back, Andrés would remind her of the disrespect. He would say, "I'm going to teach you what it's like to not have me there. If you end up not missing me, that's fine. I'll still provide, but I'll never allow my kids to talk to me with that level of disrespect again."

Daphne would later apologize.

It was the principle—never take someone you love for granted. It's what Andrés was learning. He wished he could go back in time just to express his gratitude to his sunflower for making him breakfast—for being nothing but faithful and respectful until he messed up, and Sylvia had no choice but to leave him.

Whenever Andy called to check in with his dad, he sounded sad.

Andrés would ask, "What's wrong?"

Andy would say, "I can't tell you," then change the subject and ask Andrés questions about his social life, like a cop interrogating a suspect.

Finally, on one call, toward the end of Andrés's stay in New Mexico, Andrés kept his son focused, demanding he tell him what was wrong.

"Are you holding back?" Andrés asked.

"No."

"It sounds like you are."

"I promise you, I'm not."

Andrés laughed. "So how's your *mother* doing?"

Andy didn't respond.

Andrés tried to provoke an answer by sharing more about his social life—what he kept private.

That prompted Andy to ask, "The women you meet, they don't care if you're living out of a car?"

"I never talk about what I have. I just try to be in the moment. That's it." Andrés tried changing the subject, asking Andy more questions about his mother.

Andy kept Andrés focused, demanding he tell him if his father was getting involved with anyone.

Andrés told him the truth. "I've had someone who's been there for me since I moved into the area—I met her at a group for grieving parents. Her name is Isabella.[2] She's an art therapist who says she's in love with me and wants me to move out of my car and into her home..."

"Do you love her?"

"As much as I think I could love again. I don't know. It feels 'not-

____

2. Isabella appears in the novel *FWB*.

numb,' you know what I mean? I'm happy whenever I'm around her. Lately, she's been joining me out in the desert. Together we yell at the night. If that's something you think your *mom* needs to know, you can share it with her. I think *Lydia* may find it interesting."

"Yeah, we're still talking about Lydia—"

"Who else would it be? *Sylvia?* She's not your *real* mom... She left us."

Andy hung up. Moments later, he called back, saying, "Mom thinks you're a—"

"She thinks I'm a what?"

"Dang, I can't say, but it's bad... You can come back and change her mind because Mom is sad and doesn't know the truth. She's never known the truth about anything, and it's all Grandma's fault. If you knew everything, it would destroy the family."

That admission from Andy made Andrés angry, mostly because Andrés's thinking was no longer fragmented like it had been for years. He felt the betrayal of knowing Andy was part of the cover-up.

Since moving to New Mexico, Andrés thought he knew the whole truth about Sylvia; he had learned it through his accountant. Now, Andrés no longer had any desire to save her, but he still loved the game.

"Tell your *mom* she left me. Whatever she's going through, that's on her."

"Do you not hear what I'm saying?"

"I hear you, and I don't care—this would've been something I would've given a shit about a long time ago—when I dropped you off at your mom's house. Do you remember telling me not to step on the driveway? That it was your mother's space, not mine, and I shouldn't cross any of her boundaries?"

"I remember."

"Okay, then. Leave me alone," Andrés said. "I'm at peace. And not a word of this to your *mom*. She may be your mom, but you and I are connected by blood. For real. I am your dad. You should've told me the truth a long time ago."

"Yes, Dad," Andy said.

After that call with Andy, Myra, who had not once reached out to

Andrés during his time in New Mexico, suddenly called. What she said made him go back to New York.

Myra said, "*Mami* is sick. I think she's gonna lose her job. She's in bed all the time and hasn't been to work in days. Her boss called, and I think she yelled at her."

"Put your mother on the phone," Andrés said.

"*Mami* is sleeping... Look, she won't call and tell you, but I will. Don't be an asshole. You need to come back. *Mami* took care of you. If you don't step up like a real man, I'm gonna go on Facebook and put you on blast for abandoning us."

Andrés said, "You do that, and see what I'll do—I'll create an account just to put you on blast for already going bankrupt at your age."

"Who told you?"

"Who do you think?"

"*Mami?* You guys still talk?"

"Of course we do. And whether you like it or not, you're my daughter, and I love you, and I still check in on you."

"You do?"

"Of course, but that doesn't mean I'm above teaching you a lesson the hard way, so go ahead and do it. Put me on blast."

Andrés could hear Elisa in the background, yelling at Myra, then grabbing the phone away.

"Don't listen to her. Stay there—I don't need you."

"What's going on?"

Elisa paused. "That *thing* we dealt with before Daphne was born? It's back."

"I'm coming home."

"You don't have to."

"I know," he said, "but I want to. When's the operation?"

"As soon as I can schedule it."

"Schedule it. I'll be there in a few days."

After the call, Andrés stopped to say goodbye to the friends he had made in the area—those who had become his support system—before beginning the drive east.

It's what one human being owes another. For Elisa to risk her body and her life—delaying a critical operation—to bring their daughter into the world, for it to backfire, Andrés owed Elisa the return from the desert.

He owed Elisa respect.

It was night, with a full moon rising ahead. Andrés drove along the winding road up the Sandia Mountains. Once he completed the ascent, there was nothing ahead but a longer, empty desert road, moonlight, and the sudden return of the smell of plane fuel.

❧ 39 ❧

ATLAS

FEBRUARY 27, 2009

IT TOOK ANDRÉS TWO DAYS TO DRIVE BACK TO NEW YORK. ONCE he was home, Elisa told him their daughters and her friends had been commenting on her bizarre behavior lately. With that came the painful headaches—similar in intensity to the ones she used to have—that had led her to seek painkillers and, ultimately, the operation to remove the tumor discovered while she was pregnant with Daphne and removed shortly after Daphne's birth in late 1996.

"It's a big tumor," Elisa said, out of earshot of Daphne and Myra. "It's in the same spot—the part of my brain that controls behavior. It's why I was the way I was, I guess. I'm not using that as an excuse. I'm on medication now, and I can see where I was wrong, but seeing doesn't last long, so don't hold anything against me, please, until this thing is out."

A week later, surgeons removed what they could of the benign, low-grade glioma from Elisa's frontal lobe. Unlike before, when doctors ignored her questions about why she had the tumor to begin with, this time they speculated on the cause. They suggested it could be the result of the traumatic brain injury she had suffered shortly after Myra was born in 1987. She had been in a car accident that killed Myra's biological father. Elisa spent days recovering in the hospital.

That was then.

Doctors advised Andrés that she needed radiotherapy to remove whatever remained—something she hadn't done after Daphne was born and after Andrés had left to move in with Sylvia. In Elisa's not-so-sane way of thinking—a byproduct of the lingering effects of the tumor and its removal back then—she was more focused on Gus and the thrill of cheating than on herself.

Elisa's doctors also explained what her recovery would entail. "She may experience seizures and have difficulty walking and talking. She may also have memory loss. Any pain will eventually subside. These are the things to watch out for."

When Elisa came home from the hospital, she spent days confined to her bed. When awake, she was on her phone, sending texts to friends and family.

One time, Andrés went into her room to bring her dinner and, with a smirk, joked, "Who are you texting, Gus?"

Elisa looked up from her phone and laughed. "You know that ended the moment I visited you in the hospital."

"I don't assume—maybe you guys had reunited while I was gone."

"Never. I did meet someone new before you came home. I was letting him know that my baby daddy is home and that you're caring for me. If he doesn't like it, he can lose my number."

Andrés laughed. "No! I need him around to take you to your appointments. Maybe even wipe your ass, 'cause I'll be moving on soon."

"As you should. You should be happy," Elisa said, smiling.

"So should you. Is he a good guy?"

"Not as good as you, but I don't think I'll ever find that again. You are, after all, my baby daddy."

"You're stuck with me," Andrés said.

"For the rest of my life... Dammit."

It was the first time in years that Andrés felt such immense joy that his face hurt from how wide he was smiling. The Elisa he had met at a small beer garden and nightclub in Bushwick was back. For a moment,

Andrés could go into that space in his mind, like a room, where he could see the big picture.

It was the big picture that kept him there until this moment: It was a Friday night, and Andrés was carrying Elisa to bed. Despite the radiotherapy and painkillers, she was still battling the aftereffects and pain from the operation.

Once tucked in, Elisa looked up at him and said, "All those years... the way I treated you... you know that wasn't me, right?"

"It was you, and it wasn't you."

"You don't have to be here. You don't need to be here. I swear. We can get a home health aide. I just want you to be happy."

"I want you to be happy too."

"We need to be happy, but obviously, with everything that's happened, we're not going to find it with each other."

"That's an understatement," Andrés said.

"It'll be more than that after I tell you something you need to know. Something I've kept secret... I know where Sylvia is. I've always known."

"I always had a feeling you knew. Just like I had a feeling my mom knew, but now, I don't care."

"Bullshit, you do, and you need to know."

"Sylvia lives in Red Hook. I know. I asked the accountant about entries labeled 'support,' and he told me you had the bank cut checks out to her through one of our shells." Andrés chuckled. "You made fun of me for calling her my wife; meanwhile, you'd been paying her alimony and child support."

"I did that for a reason—"

"We held off from marrying because she didn't want her decision to say 'yes' to be influenced by how badly she needed health insurance. Once she got pregnant, we kept holding it off until Athena could be there with Andy and Daphne—all together, as our witnesses."

"Like I said, I had my reasons—"

"It doesn't matter anymore. I don't need to know why Sylvia left me or why she's hiding."

"But she's not! It's not Sylvia's fault; none of it is. It's Petra's. It's mine. Sylvia was in the hospital, just like you."

"She was?"

"After you left for Berlin, Sylvia lost it. She came this close to killing herself."

Andrés collapsed to the edge of the bed next to Elisa, stunned by the news.

She sat up and looked directly into his eyes. "If you had known everything that was going on, I know you would've been on the first plane back, and you would've lost your job, and that would've fucked Daphne up. My daughter comes first, and everything I've done since has been to keep you here with her, with us. I didn't want you running off.

"I don't know if you know this, but when the two of you lived in New Mexico and I knew you'd be at work, I would call Sylvia and ask about the plans the two of you had for the future. I needed to know, and I knew she would tell me because that bitch loves to talk about herself. That's when she would talk about the big plans she had with you—about moving to Taos for good, with Andy, with my daughter. It's like she forgot I was your ex-girlfriend and Daphne's mom. Then I began to realize that when she talked about taking my daughter away from me and living in this fantasy land you guys had dreamt up, she had gotten that idea from you, and I knew you must've been crazy to think I would agree and let Daphne go live far away from me unless you were getting ready to take me to court.

"A cross-state court battle? You had way more money than me and could afford lawyers. Who was I? I was a single mom from Bushwick with another daughter from another man, who's now dead. I'd be a single mom going up against a Wall Street tech bro and an Ivy League poet. I would be a stereotype going up against that.

"So yeah, that's why I did everything I did, including making Sylvia think I was into her, making Sylvia feel like she was so amazing that she could turn a straight woman into her plaything. Hello? Was there anything in that brain of hers that could make her see that while she was playing checkers, I was playing chess, gassing her up, feeding her ego—and yours—until I could make my big move? And that night, when I saw my opportunity to not be a victim and lose my daughter, I took it and called the cops. That's why I said what I said and kept saying everything I've ever said about you—to keep control of the situation, to be several moves ahead of you. No family court judge will ever side with a man with some questions about his background."

Andrés began looking around the room, as if wanting to run from the moment—from the truth that made him cover his face with his hands in shock.

Elisa leaned in closer, resting her body against his shoulder and pulling his hands away from his face so she could look directly into his eyes again.

"I'm sorry, but if you two were together, I would've lost that war, and you guys would be out in New Mexico right now, and Daphne would be a stranger to me, just like Andy is a stranger to Lydia. Those are my reasons. I don't know why Petra made you look like a drug addict."

He tried to pull away from her. "Stop—"

She threw her arms around him, holding him in place. "I don't know why she convinced Sylvia that you loved drugs more than you loved her. Petra made you look like the biggest loser to Sylvia."

"Stop—"

"It even got to me, what she was doing. I had to ask her, 'Why do you hate your son so much that you feel the need to tear him down like this, to Sylvia of all people?'"

"Stop, please," he said, pushing Elisa away and standing up.

"I'm not sorry for what I've done," Elisa said. "How could I be? My daughter is here. The moment I met Sylvia, I knew she'd try to take my place. I had to swallow the disgust I felt at going down on her just to make sure she didn't see me coming, and I'd do it all over again. We ended up giving Daphne as good a childhood as we could. With that said, nothing is stopping you from going to Sylvia's house now. None of this is her fault. Sylvia didn't leave you. I don't know what's going on up there, but it can't be good. You don't want her spending another moment in Petra's orbit. You can end it now."

After a long silence, during which Andrés stared blankly at Elisa, he snapped out of it and asked, "What if she doesn't want to see me?"

"You're stupid for thinking that—she raised your son by choice," Elisa replied.

"Fuck, I know."

"She did all the heavy lifting; she would want to see you."

"But I can't just come out of nowhere and surprise Sylvia with this. It'll destroy her."

"You're a smart guy. Put that big brain of yours to use."

"You're right. I'll figure it out, just as you need to figure out how to break the news to Daphne that you've been lying to her."

"I have?"

"Does she still think Sylvia and Athena weren't real?"

"Oh shit... I forgot about that."

"Yeah... You need to make things right. You need to tell her that they were real—"

"I know, I know—I'm going to fix that right now." Elisa called for Daphne to come.

She came from the downstairs family room, where she had been watching TV, and entered her mother's bedroom. "What's up?"

"Estefania, come and sit; we need to talk."

"Calling me by my full name? Am I in trouble?"

"Just some girl talk."

"Girl talk? Mom, you've been acting so weird ever since the operation."

"Be patient with Mom," Andrés said. "She's had a tumor, and it did a lot of weird things to her. Imagine having the worst headache of your life for twelve years."

"Great," Daphne said. "Exactly how long I've been alive."

"Go easy on her; your mother is exactly the way I met her, and that's why, despite everything, I love her."

"I love you too," Elisa said.

Andrés said goodnight and excused himself as Elisa began her girl talk with Daphne. He left the house to sit in his car in the driveway, trying to figure out what to do next with Sylvia. Just as he was thinking that maybe Elisa was right, that he was stupid, and Sylvia would want to see him, he felt his phone vibrate from a notification.

It was through the Facebook account Andrés had created recently, just in case he needed to carry out his threat with Myra. He opened the notification to see the subject line: Alene Rothbauer would like to be your friend.

Instead of the panic he had, over the years, expected to feel if he ever found himself in a moment like this—with Alene reaching out—he was curious. The notification opened a link back to Alene's profile. Based on her picture, it appeared time had made her into a proper woman. She looked nothing like the woman who came to the Love Parade to drop ecstasy and find an *exotic* man to fuck. Instead, she stood like a proud mother, behind twin boys in her profile picture. A portly man with a clueless smile proudly stood beside them. Aside from a more dignified style of dress, complemented by perfectly coiffed hair that projected a matronly and refined elegance, Alene looked the same. Slight wrinkles now framed her bright and tiny smile and eyes. Her red hair was longer.

Andrés looked through the photos in her profile. There were pictures of the twin boys at home or out and about in Berlin. Then there were also pictures of her with female friends on girls-only trips in exotic locales like Phuket, Thailand, and Hurghada, Egypt. Some showed Alene and her girlfriends drinking and laughing with the men they had met abroad. The last set of pictures Andrés examined were taken at home, showing her watching TV while her husband, appearing busy, was in the background. The caption of one photo read: "Lothar is doing what he does best: taking care of his family."

Just as he was about to delete the friend request, Andrés received a message from Alene. It read:

Surprise! I bet you never thought you'd hear from me again. It's coming up on eight years soon, and you came to mind the other day, so I looked you up (you gave me your business card that night, like you were some hotshot, remember), and holy shit, I found your profile. Anyway, speaking of hotshots, check out my pictures. Those two boys? Surprise! They're yours! Just kidding—or am I? OMG, that would be hilarious, though.

Lothar has been taking care of them all this time. They look like a pair of Afrikaner/Puerto Rican mixed-race beauties, lol. They have such exotic features. Andries and Liam could grow up to be models, but they're Lothar's; he's such a good boy.

Anyway, I'm still thinking of that shot you put in me, so yeah, friend me. You know you want to. Let's chat soon. xxx

Andrés deleted her message and blocked her profile before she got another chance to message him. He realized that blocking would solve nothing, and he panicked. Andrés didn't know what to make of the message, what it meant, or what it implied. All he knew was that the smell of plane fuel was now everywhere for him.

He took a deep breath and was about to pull out of his driveway when he received another notification of a new message. It was from someone named Skye de Vos, and her profile didn't have a picture. The message read:

This is Alene. I'm reaching out from a profile I keep hidden from family and friends. I didn't mean to freak you out—I know it's a surprise. I thought it would be fun to, you know, connect.

There's not a day that goes by where I don't think about the way I danced with you at the Love Parade. There's sex, but then there's a dance that—I don't know—I had never felt as connected to another man as that night when we danced under the laser lights. It's why I kept coming back to your room and knocking on the door. I wanted a chance to do things right. Not take it, but see if we could have a night where I could feel that boil I felt in our dance—even now.

Do you still remember our dance?

It was at that moment that Andrés understood the enormity of what Dr. Patton had tried to teach him so many years before. The psychiatrist had spotted behavior in Andrés that made him come off as a delusional stalker. It could be enough to scare off someone as important to him as Sylvia.

Alene was delusional to think she was anything to Andrés.

It didn't matter what Elisa had said. When it came to this, why trust her now? Despite the history and the permission Sylvia had given him long ago, death changes everything. Sylvia would always have to cross the boundary herself. Andrés couldn't risk coming off to Sylvia the way Alene was coming off to him.

"I have absolutely no desire to ever see you," Andrés said to himself about Alene. That's when the idea of what he needed to do started to come to him. He placed his car in park, jumped out, and began pacing back and forth in the driveway, trying to work out the idea some more.

In the chill of what felt like the longest winter that began in 1997—punctuated by the news Elisa shared with him and the messages from Alene—he reached deep down, squeezing just a bit more from within, and whispered to himself, "It is what it is."

All for his heartbroken twelve-year-old daughter, Daphne, who, in the distance, was yelling at Elisa in anger.

All for his estranged eighteen-year-old son, Andy.

All for his depressed twenty-one-year-old stepdaughter, Myra.

All for his dead daughter, Athena.

Up in the night, in a clearing of clouds, he saw the constellation Orion: the belt of stars, the otherness of life, of this world—beyond the mundane, and the Him, and the Her, and the Us.

Andrés remembered waking up in a military hospital in Landstuhl, Germany, broken, with a chaplain hovering over him. The chaplain said something had told him to stop by the room to minister to him, and there Andrés was, opening his eyes. The chaplain began to read him a passage from the *Book of Job* in the Old Testament:

"Can you bind the chains of the Pleiades? Can you loosen Orion's belt? Can you bring forth the constellations in their seasons or lead out the Bear with its cubs? Do you know the laws of the heavens? Can you set up God's dominion over the earth?"

Andrés remembered laughing at the chaplain, forcing him to leave the room. Job could do none of that. He just had to take it and deal with the hammer that had been dropped on him because God is an asshole, and the Universe is absurd, and for Andrés, they're one and the same. Yet, out of it all, Andrés could claim a small victory in being able to carve joy out of taking solace in his smallness when framed against a night sky so big.

It was still all so beautiful.

And if God says Andrés is nothing, then his problems are nothing as well.

And if God said to Job, "Don't worry, I got it," then don't worry, He's got it.

Since that moment with the chaplain, God had taken much more from Andrés, but he was now suddenly calm and happy. It made the burden of the rock he shouldered for his family a joy to carry across his back. When it became too great, he could always scream at the night sky until it was out of his system.

He smiled, whispering to himself, "It's going to be okay, I guess... Keep it moving."

There was more to life than this. Just because Andrés couldn't see it didn't mean it wasn't there.

Sylvia had been there all along, but he couldn't fully see her. Now that he could, and with something within him feeling as if it had come full circle, the flood of ideas on how to entice Sylvia to cross the boundary herself coalesced into one singular thought: Andrés had to develop a plan to draw her out through desire and make it her choice. It needed to feel like an invitation to a new dance while preparing her for what would be the biggest surprise of her life.

And that's when it came to Andrés—how to draw out the most passion, how to wake everything up inside Sylvia. He couldn't take a chance that time had killed the spark.

He reached into his coat pocket for his phone and called Andy. When Andy answered, Andrés began talking about Isabella. He made up a story, explaining that since his return to New York and Andy's refusal to see him, it had become easier for him to decide to fly Isabella out and find a symbolic spot to propose to her.

"You've got to be kidding," Andy said.

"No, I'm not. Isabella is willing to move to New York to be with me. She might be the One."

"But I thought you said Mom was the One."

"Which mom?" Andrés asked.

"Don't be stupid; you know which mom."

"Sylvia? She left me."

"You don't know the story," Andy said.

"It doesn't matter anymore. I'm picking Isabella up from the airport tomorrow, and on Sunday, I plan to take her out for an early dinner at this new lounge that just opened up—Sylvia knows the spot. It used to be the diner we would go to but closed down years ago. I figure it would be the best place to begin this new chapter of my life— at the spot where I began the last one with your *mom*. I think I'll be there around four—"

"But Dad, you can't do that to her."

"Why not? Both of your moms left me. I used to think I was a good man, but maybe I'd been deluding myself. Maybe the reality is that I'm a scumbag. It doesn't matter anymore. I'm old and tired, and Isabella is younger than me and hot. Lydia and Sylvia are old as fuck. I may even make Isabella the beneficiary of everything I have."

Andy hung up on his father.

Andrés looked at his phone and placed it back in his pocket. He looked back up at Orion in the night and laughed.

V

MEDUSA

And I'm a woman made of sorrow.

— EURIPIDES

❧ 40 ☙

THE ARENA

THE HAZE OF THE SUMMER AFTERNOON RAISED SYLVIA'S ALREADY high blood pressure to dangerous levels. Despite the dizziness from her pounding headache, she remained committed to her goal—to what she had come to the city for: taking pictures of the people around her, all gathered to stand up for those who didn't have a voice—who no longer had a voice.

Because they were dead.

Sylvia looked up at the space in the sky where the Twin Towers had once stood. She looked around at the people—members of the War Resisters League—who had gathered for the occasion of the Republican National Convention to say, "No more war!"

She looked back up at the haze and squinted at the blown-out sky, took a deep breath, and said, "It is what it is." Sylvia looked back down and kept taking pictures. She aimed her camera at the face of a police officer who was announcing that the crowd was engaged in an unauthorized protest and that everyone blocking the road would be arrested.

Sylvia shoved the camera closer to his face as he continued barking his commands. She then took pictures of the police steering the crowd onto a side street and pinning them against a set of iron gates outside St. Paul's Chapel.

"We're doing everything you ordered us to do!" she yelled.

The police arrested everyone around Sylvia, then came to her.

"Of course," she said, letting the camera Andrés had left behind when he abandoned her to dangle from the straps around her neck, freeing her hands for the officers who pulled her arms back. They placed zip ties around her wrists, led her into a transport van, and crammed her in with the others.

An officer sitting in the back corner said to Sylvia, "I recognize you. You were on TV."

"Would you like my autograph?"

He stood, came over, and hunched down so that he was face-to-face with her, grabbing Sylvia by her face as she sat, his thumbs on her cheeks. "You're not such a hotshot now, are you?"

Sylvia hocked phlegm in his eyes.

The officer punched Sylvia in the face.

In the blackout, Sylvia touched the darkness in the Underworld. She looked for Andrés, reaching out as if to grab him, but grabbed nothing instead. As she emerged from the Underworld of all her memories, she found herself on an oil-soaked floor in a small, fenced pen, coughing. Sylvia looked up at the signs warning of the hazardous chemicals that had been stored in the space. She pushed herself up to avoid being stepped on as the pen filled with everyone the police had rounded up.

Sylvia asked a woman standing next to her, as if she had been standing guard, "Where are we?"

"Hudson Pier Depot, I think," she replied. "I'm Angel... I was sitting next to you when he punched you. I tried getting his badge number, but you know how it goes—he had it covered."

Sylvia grabbed her jaw. "Of course."

"It looks like the NYPD set this up to be their own little Gitmo."

"That tracks."

Angel paused before saying, "I know who you are."

"So?"

"So? Don't be flexing in here. They'll make you disappear."

"You think I don't know that?" Sylvia said.

"All I'm saying is, keep your head down. While you were out for the count, they were talking about getting some more payback."

"If you know who I am, why are you talking to me like I don't know?"

"Bitch, do you wanna get clocked again? I'm trying to help."

"I'm sorry, I'm so sorry... Give me a moment." Sylvia shrank down to a crouch and then hunched her body over.

She cried and cried and cried.

As much as Sylvia believed in what she was doing, and as much as she believed in the cause, if she were honest with herself, this was all just to keep herself busy. It was to keep herself moving, because there were no doors in this room she had been in since her soulmate made a choice—how he was going to cope with the death of Athena.

Andrés wouldn't deal with it with her. He dealt with it by getting on a plane and abandoning her. He dealt with it through drugs because Petra told her Andrés loved the drugs more than he loved her.

Instead of being at home, out west—under the stars—Sylvia was there, trying to keep busy and stay off the drugs herself.

Sylvia screamed.

Angel knelt beside her and whispered, "Don't do that—not here."

"I said, 'Give me a moment.'"

"Don't you cry—"

"Back the fuck off!"

Angel became quiet.

Sylvia closed her eyes, took several deep breaths, and then swallowed. Calm returned to her face as she looked back up at Angel and said, "It's all good."

Angel stood and extended her hand, but Sylvia slapped it away and pushed herself off the floor.

Just as Sylvia was straightening herself, saying, "Game face on—it is what it is," Police officers barged into the small pen.

They were yelling with booming voices that they were transporting everyone to the Tombs for processing.

Angel became frantic, grabbing Sylvia's arms. "What does that mean?"

"This is good. The sooner this happens, the sooner we're out."

Angel became calm. After a pause, she asked, "Do you think, when we get there, you could represent me?"

"This is pretty much straightforward. Just keep your mouth shut and cooperate—"

"You mean like you in the van?"

Sylvia looked at her with dead eyes. "Do you want my help?"

"Yes—"

"Then shut the fuck up. There's no cooperation when someone violates you, ever!" Sylvia paused to calm herself. "With that said, don't give them a reason to keep you longer. That's it. And if there's anything more and I'm on the other side of this, I'll represent you."

SEPTEMBER 18, 2007

A police officer walked into the holding area and yelled, "You're free to go."

Sylvia looked up from the corner of the holding cell at the United States Capitol Police Station building and said, "I am?"

"You would've been out sooner, but you had to take a swing."

"I would've been out sooner, but you motherfuckers don't know how to keep your hands to yourselves."

"Do you wanna stay? No? Then shut the fuck up and go."

Sylvia got up, sauntered over to the open cell door, and followed the officer away from the holding area and out into the station's open room. Andy and Petra were waiting at a counter.

"You had to tell her?" Sylvia said, approaching Andy.

"Of course he's going to tell me," Petra replied. "He was scared."

Sylvia said to Andy, "I told you they were going to drop the charges —I was going to be on the first train home."

"Take this conversation outside," the desk sergeant said to them.

"Fuck you!" Sylvia replied.

Petra pulled her away from the counter, dragging her outside, and yelled, "What are you, stupid? They dropped everything!"

"Of course they did! No sane U.S. attorney would take a case like this before a judge who'd question why someone like me—who was only looking at unlawful entry—risked being charged with assault on a Capitol Police officer. They wouldn't dare attack my credibility. They know who I am. I'd represent myself, too!"

"You think too highly of yourself."

"Yes, I do—I've earned that right."

"You're playing a dangerous game."

"I don't care anymore."

"You should," Petra said. "You need to be there for Andy."

Sylvia waved her off. "He's fine. He drives himself to school, he takes care of himself, he has his own life. What do I have?"

"Your career? Your friends?"

"That's not a life. I don't have passion. I have nothing, and it means nothing without Andrés, and he's gone. He believed in me, and he's gone off, and he's not with me. So fuck it. This is part of my work—these protests. Everything counts, even my voice, even if it's small—everything counts."

"You're fooling yourself, thinking getting arrested counts. It doesn't." Petra wrapped an arm around Sylvia, trying to lead her away. "Come on, *Mamita,* let's go home."

Sylvia broke away. "I want to go home—I want to go to New Mexico and be with him."

Petra and Andy appeared surprised.

Sylvia snickered. "You thought just because I stopped asking, that was that? I hired a private investigator. My P.I. finally got a hit on something—on Elisa, where she works—and I went there last year. I followed her to that house, confronted her, and she told me Andrés had left them the week before. Just like that."

Sylvia turned to Andy. "Why didn't you tell me he had a big house? Like, what kind of drug addict has a house like that, lives in a neighborhood like that? I know Elisa doesn't make the kind of money needed to pay the taxes for that place. That's Wall Street money. It doesn't make sense. Nothing has ever made sense, and I don't like the feeling that you're fucking with my mind."

"That feeling is all in your head," Petra said.

"*Mama,* stop! I don't want to fight with you!"

"You're the one who needs to lower your voice. I'm standing here calm."

Sylvia grabbed Andy. "I know you still talk to Dad. I tried to respect your boundaries, but fuck that—where is he? Where does he live?"

"I don't know," Andy said.

"Yes, you do! I can feel it!"

"Alright! Dad is homeless—he's living out of his car."

Sylvia grabbed Andy. "Why did you keep this information from me?"

"Because we don't involve ourselves with addicts. Do you remember saying that to me?" Petra said.

"I remember," Sylvia said, dropping her hands to her sides. "But that was about Auntie Birdie, not Andrés. I know him. This is not like him. I can feel him."

Petra sighed. "I love my son, but the last time I saw him, he was not the same. You wouldn't recognize him."

"But that's my choice to make, not yours."

Petra looked at Sylvia dismissively. "You're acting like a child."

"And you're acting like you don't know what this feels like."

"I do; believe me, I do, but you need to move on."

"Are you for real? You're his mother. Why do you hate him so much?"

"I don't hate him," Petra said. "I hate what he's become. He's not the man you know."

"Again, that's for me to decide, and I've decided I'm going to go out there and find him." Sylvia grabbed Andy by the arm. "You better tell me where he's at. I know him—I know he'd pick a spot to keep too. I'm catching a flight out tonight."

"Mom, I don't know—"

"Then call him now!"

"No!"

"Call him! I need to talk to him!"

"No!"

Sylvia reached into Andy's pocket for his phone.

Petra placed her hand on Sylvia's shoulder.

Sylvia turned and pushed Petra away.

"Mom, stop! You're acting crazy!"

"It's okay, Andy," Petra said. "This is what crazy people do."

"Stop saying that! I'm not crazy!" Sylvia turned to Andy. "Please call him—tell him to meet me at the Bridge—he'll know what that means. Tell him I'll be there tomorrow. I'll be there in time for sunset. It'll be the golden hour."

"No, Mom, I don't want you getting sick again."

The mention of her hospitalization made Sylvia go silent.

Andy grabbed her hand. "Come home, please?"

She looked at Andy. "Tell him, that's all I'm asking."

"Okay, Mom, I will, but we have to go."

"And tell him that *1968* was just a poem I wrote for my dad, not for him. He can cry; it's okay for him to cry. I'm here to help him cope. He has to help me cope, you know?"

"I know, Mom."

Petra wrapped an arm around Sylvia and began leading her away again.

Sylvia abruptly stopped walking, swung herself in front of Petra, and looked at her with pleading eyes. "How would you feel if Andrés had never woken up after falling off the bed? Wouldn't you still be sad? Oh, wait—he's dead to you now, and I've never seen you happier. You don't have a soul."

"I do have a soul."

"I don't understand you."

"*Mija,* one day you will, I hope. Now, let's go home."

Sylvia allowed herself to be led away by Petra, with Andy following. Together, they walked several blocks to the public garage where Petra had parked her car, climbed in, and drove away, back to New York.

❦ 41 ❦

SHADOW DANCING

[1]

A hostess greeted Andrés and his date as they entered the lounge. The date asked if they could sit at a table next to a set of large windows with a view of the Williamsburg Bridge.

"Unfortunately," the hostess replied, "the manager likes to hold those in reserve for VIPs. Now, if you will, follow me."

"I don't understand," the date said, following the hostess to a table in the middle of the empty room. "No one is here, and I'm a VIP. I have, like, a lot of friends on Facebook. They care about what I do."

"That doesn't count," the hostess said.

"It should."

"Like I said, the manager holds those in reserve."

"But there's no one here, and I wanna sit there. If someone comes, we can get up. How hard is that? How hard is it for you to check with the manager? Can you do your job and check for me? Okay? Thanks. Bye."

The hostess dropped two menus on the table.

"What a bitch," his date said as the hostess walked away.

Andrés and his date sat.

She looked at Andrés and smiled. "You weren't supposed to see that side of me until our third date. I'm sorry—not sorry." She looked around the empty room. "I don't know why you wanted to meet this early. What kind of psycho are you?"

"I have plans tonight," Andrés said.

"Do you? How do you know you won't be with me?"

"Because I won't. Most women I meet for the first time double or triple book. I'm sure you have a date later on."

She laughed. "That's not true."

"See? You're guilty."

"Maybe."

"I know the game," Andrés said.

"Okay, you got me. But I always cancel my other dates if the vibe feels right. You're gonna have to show me if you're worth my doing that."

Andrés sat back. "Nope. Whenever I meet someone for the first time, I treat it like an interview—I don't go for more than half an hour. That's enough time to see if I like *your* vibe. Then we go our separate ways."

"Are you serious?"

"I am."

"So we're not having dinner?"

"Dinners are for girlfriends, and this is the only time I had available. I told you it would be a quick meetup, and you agreed."

"I know I did, but I thought you weren't serious."

"Take me at my word."

"Are you always this literal?"

"I am—"

"No wonder you're single."

"I may be single, but I'm never alone, and now you're here, so don't even play yourself."

The date gave him a knowing look and smiled. "I'm not playing with myself."

"I can play with you."

"Can you? You'd have to buy me dinner first."

"Let's see how everything goes. If we get along, then maybe by the third date, I'll pay for your dinner and a ride home. Maybe you're worth that."

"I'm paying for my meal? I didn't bring any money."

"This isn't a foodie call."

His date stood. "I'm done!"

The doors to the lounge swung open, and Sylvia entered.

She was wearing a purple headscarf wrapped around her head, with auburn curls peeking out at the sides of her gaunt face. Sylvia appeared surprised by the emptiness of the room and how exposed she was to it. She then smirked at Andrés as the hostess greeted her and automatically led her to a table by the large windows.

After taking off her long leather coat, Sylvia sat down and tried her best to focus on the menu, but she seemed flustered. Instead, she looked up at him from across the empty room. Her eyes, as bright and beautiful as the day he first met her, locked onto his.

She pushed back her headscarf to reveal—with the same breathless, vulnerable hesitancy she had shown years before, when she first revealed her body—the thick locks of hair cascading down to her shoulders.

Andrés's date placed her hand on him and sat down, her stare locked on a smirking Sylvia. "Why does that old lady get to sit by a window?"

Sylvia stood and sauntered over, placed both hands on their table, and leaned in close to her. "Would you like to repeat that to my face?"

"No—"

"Did he propose? Did you say 'yes'? Because if you did—and if he hasn't told you already—you need to know that this douche has three baby mamas, and he owes this baby mama eight years' worth of child support."

"Owe you? I didn't even know where you lived," Andrés said.

"Yeah, right," Sylvia said.

"Your *girlfriend* kept your address from me."

Sylvia laughed. "I wouldn't call her my 'girlfriend.'"

"Whatever, you got your money—Elisa made sure of it."

"I'm fucking with you—I got your money and more, but money is not love. You can't snuggle up to a bank account, and—you know what?—you knew where we lived. You took our son to an appointment." Sylvia shook her head in disbelief. "I never thought you'd end up like my father—a deadbeat dad. You abandoned us."

The date was taken aback. "You abandoned your son?"

"Fuck him," Andrés said with a smirk.

"That's an awful thing to say—I'd never let you near mine."

"Your profile said you didn't have any kids," Andrés said.

"Wait, did you just meet him?" Sylvia asked.

"Online... This is our third date," she replied, grabbing Andrés's hand.

"Third date?" Sylvia looked at Andrés. "And here I thought you were going to—"

"I was going to do what?" Andrés said.

Sylvia began to smile, as if realizing what Andrés was trying to accomplish. "I'm going to fuck you up; that's what I'm going to do."

Andrés shook away his date's hand to grab Sylvia's. "I needed something to get you back in the theater—back on a stage that only you and I can see. And it's *showtime*, this being our opening scene."

"Oh my God, I knew I recognized you," the date said excitedly. "I was trying to figure out from where. You're Sylvia—*Spacer Woman!*"

Sylvia looked back at the date, amused. "Yes, I am."

"I love you so much—wait a minute... You know him?"

Sylvia glared at the date. "What a stupid fucking question to ask. You see that we do. This deadbeat is my baby daddy. Back in the day, when I was a pimp, he was also my moneymaker—my bottom bitch."

Andrés laughed.

Sylvia glared at Andrés, not amused. "You like that throwback, huh? You get one, just one. I'm done with nostalgia. I'm dead serious about that."

"So wait," the date asked. "I thought all this time you didn't like men."

"What gave you that impression?"

"Your work."

"What I don't like is stupid people." Sylvia paused. "You know what? I don't like you. There... That I know. I don't like you."

"But why?"

"You said *Spacer Woman*... Did you read it?"

"Of course. So did a lot of my friends," the date said.

Sylvia pointed at Andrés. "That's Soldier Boy—he belongs to Emma."

The hostess came over to the table and said to the date, "After talking with the manager, she decided she can't accommodate your request to sit by a window. You're a nobody."

"You're more than welcome to join me at my table. I'm kind of a somebody." Sylvia pushed the date back down into her seat to keep her from standing up. "I was talking to him."

Sylvia looked at Andrés and held up her hand to his face, showing him the diamond ring on her finger. "Eight years. Eight motherfucking years, and I took it off only once, and that was when I got sent to the Tombs." Sylvia balled her hand into a fist. "I'm not fucking playing. I'm not waiting. You know what to do. Do it!"

Andrés stood.

"You're gonna leave me here like this?" the date asked.

Sylvia grabbed him by the hand. "Yes, he is." She led Andrés away to her table, and the two sat across from each other.

The date walked by, stopped, and stared for a long moment, then stomped out of the lounge, all while Sylvia mockingly laughed at her. Sylvia placed her headscarf back over her hair and shifted her focus back to Andrés.

"I knew you'd love that scene," Andrés said.

"Oh, did you? What makes you think you still know me like that?" Sylvia replied.

Andrés looked closely at Sylvia, noticing that she was not only still wearing the engagement ring he had given her the night after he watched her play with their kids in the park—like dust in the golden hour—but she also continued to wear the silver choker necklace with an infinity insignia, with a heart inscribed with "forever" hanging from one of its loops.

He understood he had her permission—barely. The covering of her hair with her headscarf, which confused Andrés as to why she would be wearing one to begin with, signaled that everything that had been given once before had to be earned again. Otherwise, not only would that ring come off her finger, but the collar would come off her neck as well.

After the long silence where they looked at each other, Andrés began their new dance by asking Sylvia, "What's my name, my government name?"

She smiled. "Andrés... What's mine?"

Andrés smiled as well. "Sylvia."

"That's right, but it seems like you forgot."

"I didn't forget."

She crossed her arms. "Whatever. What if I don't feel like dancing?"

"What's my name again?"

"Soldier Boy. What's mine?"

"Emma. Now that we're clear on that, let me be clear on this: we're not doing any of that Beautiful Ballet crap."

"We're not?"

"We're going to be doing the Tango: I lead, and you shut the fuck up and follow."

She smiled, amused. "Oh, it's like that?"

"Yeah, it's like that. While I was gone, have you tangoed with anyone else?"

Sylvia leaned forward, elbows on the table, a small black tattoo of a semicolon on the wrist of her left hand visible beneath the hem of her long-sleeved black top. "No, asshole—I was engaged. Did you? Did you Dance with anyone else? Yes, you did." She paused, anger flashing across her face. "You've hurt me, and I'm trying to keep from hurting you, but fuck your feelings! After you dropped Andy off at my house like you were leaving him at a bus stop, I tried finding new Dance partners. And you know what? Fuck this back and forth. I've waited eight years! I want answers!"

"I want answers too, but after we do our little dance, okay?"

Sylvia hesitated. "Okay."

"Are you sure?"

"Yes—get on with it."

Andrés leaned back in his seat, a wry smile on his face. "So, what brought you here? To this lounge, of all places. It's too much of a coincidence."

"It is, isn't it?"

"How do you know about this place?"

She sighed. "Back in the day, I was a dumb poet, involved with this pretentious guy who lived with his mom. After we broke up and then reunited, he moved in with me in an apartment not too far from here." Sylvia chuckled to herself. "Sometimes I think I was too good for him."

Andrés smiled. "You were."

"I'm glad you think so." Sylvia paused. "Because sometimes I also thought I would never be good enough. I used to bring him here all the time. He would be more interested in that view of the bridge than in this view of me... As you can see, I'm still pretty to look at."

"More than pretty. I can't take my eyes off you."

Sylvia smiled. "Thank you. Now, back to that douche... I think he took me for granted—focusing on that bridge instead of me."

"I can see that being a douche move."

Sylvia smirked. "Mm-hmm."

"Maybe when you used to bring him here and he would look at that bridge, he had visions of the future—that he would find himself standing on a bridge with his soulmate?"

Sylvia waved off the approaching waitress without breaking eye contact with Andrés. "I can see that. I know that—I think about the Bridge every fucking day. Like how, every Friday, after that douche would come home early from work, he'd drive me there just to watch the golden light spread across the snow-capped mountains and the gorge... Looking back, I can forgive that douche for being rude, looking more at that bridge instead of me. Those kinds of visions are hard to ignore. Trust me, I know—look!"

Sylvia pointed at the snow suddenly streaking beyond the large window outside at a hard angle, the streets rapidly turning solid white. "That came out of nowhere."

Andrés turned in his seat to look out the window. "That's gonna be a fun drive tonight."

"Tell me about it."

Andrés turned to focus back on Sylvia. "Since you're in the area and it looks like the roads are gonna be rough tonight, why don't you hit that douche up? See what he's up to?"

Sylvia turned her focus back to Andrés. "He doesn't live there anymore. Neither do I. Even though he told me not to, I gave up the apartment a month after I moved out west to be with him. It was a sign of my commitment to the relationship. We were going to be together forever. Where that douche goes, I go. Where I go, the douche goes. We both wanted to go to where we felt safe, in the silence, under the stars."

Sylvia sat back in her seat and wiped at her glistening eyes. "I don't know what happened to us. I don't think it's worth figuring out. Nostalgia isn't my thing anymore. I can't think of those mountains... I can't think about that home we talked about. And to be honest, I'd forgotten how much this kind of dancing hurts—going back into our past... I'm not that poet anymore. I haven't been for a long time. I have to be in the present. I have to make new memories because I can't tell you how much it hurts to have the old ones playing in my head on a loop."

"Then let's stop."

"No—don't give up so quick. I'm just saying, it's been years. I'd forgotten how to dance. The memories... It's hard making light of it, that's all."

"If it's any consolation, we're making new ones."

Sylvia smiled. "That's true."

"It's the first of many."

"I hope so."

"Are you willing to tango a little more?" Andrés asked.

"Just a little."

"So what brought you here?"

"I was in the area, and I always enjoyed the food here, so I said, 'Why not,' and there you were, with her."

"Did you know this place opened a month ago?"

"No," Sylvia said.

"So you must've come when it was a diner, expecting to see that."

Sylvia sighed. "Yeah."

Andrés smiled. "What did you think of her? My date."

Sylvia leaned forward from her seat. "You've got some nerve."

"This is the embrace in the Tango."

Sylvia laughed. "Okay, but don't forget, I can get you jealous too."

Andrés leaned forward from his seat. "Wake me up. Let's wake everything up."

"It's been awake. And if you weren't so fucked up, you'd know I've never gone back to sleep."

"Did you know I would be here? I mean, there are no coincidences."

"No, they are not."

"How did you know I'd be here?"

Sylvia rolled her eyes and smirked. "God, you're so fucking dumb."

"It's why you enjoyed being around me—you feel smarter."

"That's because I am—and we're done with this back and forth. What the fuck was New Mexico about? You found the willpower to push your way out there. For what? Is meth that much more important than me?"

"It's complicated."

"And the things I just found out from Andy about you."

"Like what?"

"You're going to make me say it?"

Andrés sat back in his seat. "Why not? I wanna get you more jealous."

"Fuck you—I knew something was up. Every time you called, I noticed he would disappear. He never did that with any of his other calls. I tried to get your number off his phone, but he'd guard it. I tried to port his number to my plan, but he refused. I stopped trying once he began talking about you late last year, telling me what you guys had talked about that day."

"Doesn't that tell you something? That I had a phone plan? Think."

"It never did make any sense: someone on drugs, homeless, living out of a car with a phone plan? What I want to know is, why did you move there and not come home to me? I've read about meth—is it that good over there that you'd rather live out of a car instead of with me? That's what Petra said—that you probably went out there because of the meth."

"Jesus Christ, my mother."

Sylvia slammed her hands on the table. "You left me!"

Andrés pushed the table at her. "I thought you left me!"

"Why would I leave you?"

"Because I got on the plane! Because when I was in Berlin, I called you! I sent you email after email! I left you voicemails telling you what was going on and that I was coming home in September, but I didn't hear from you."

"You're fucking with me!"

"No, I'm not," Andrés said.

"*Mama* had my phone—I was in the hospital! She was supposed to tell you!"

"I just found that out! You know who told me? Elisa. On Friday."

"Why would Petra do this?"

Andrés sat back in his seat. "Yeah, why? You never questioned anything she told you? If I were a drug addict, how could I afford to keep a phone plan with Andy? How could I send you all that money over the years? Yeah, it was Elisa sending it for me. I'll tell you later what was going on, but for now, you know she didn't have that kind of money—at least not back then. And what was sent to you—for you and Andy—equaled my disability from the DoD and VA. So how was I taking care of Daphne? Myra? I'm sure Andy told you about the house."

"Yes, *that* house—Andy never said anything, but I found out about it anyway."

"How?"

Sylvia sat back in her seat and smiled. "Emma's no snitch, but when you were in New Mexico, I drove down and saw it myself. That kind of money gets you a ranch in Taos."

"I know! Elisa bought it with *my* money, which she *controlled* through a guardianship."

"Petra placed one on me! But I needed mine because of school. She saved my ass on that."

"Mom helped Elisa place one on me. Elisa was the one who set up my retirement and disability from my job."

"Retirement? Disability? What the fuck? Why?"

Andrés paused. "I think everything I'm about to share with you will be one of the biggest surprises of your life."

Sylvia leaned forward in her seat. "Worse than Athena?"

"Nothing is as bad as Athena, but I think it comes close. I think it'll change everything forever."

Sylvia shot up from her seat and backed away from the table. She looked at the exit behind Andrés.

He said, "You think there's a door there, but there is no door. We have to face this. We'll always have to face moments like this. It's life."

"It's fucked up."

"I know, but I'm here. If you still want me, I'll always be here." Andrés stood and extended his hand.

Sylvia grabbed his hand, took a deep breath, and together they sat.

✣ 42 ✣

THE WATCHER

[2]

IN THE HEAVY SILENCE, ANDRÉS SAT ACROSS FROM HER WHILE THE waitress, whom Sylvia had waved off, stood a few feet away, watching.

"Who told you I was on drugs?" Andrés asked.

Sylvia replied, *"Mama."*

"Did she give you a reason?"

"Because of Athena."

"Any other reason?"

"What's the surprise?"

"Did she give you any other reason? I mean, what do you think happened after I got on the plane?"

Sylvia sat forward. "When I got out of the hospital, *Mama* said you had come back from Germany already hooked on drugs and saw that I wasn't home. You took your anger out on Elisa, in front of the girls."

"What the fuck?"

"It didn't make sense. I mean, the way I'm with you, and you've never hit me."

"You should've known," Andrés said.

"But I still wasn't right with myself, and I was so fucking sad that I stayed with *Mama* for a little while. She was handling everything for me. Everything. I wanted to stay in bed, but she'd yell at me to get up.

"*Mama* would say you were gone, and the man I used to know would want me to get out of bed and move on. 'Be strong,' she'd say. That I needed to focus on my writing and on finishing school. I knew she was right. You'd want that for me. I got out of bed.

"Months later, Petra said you were coming back... from where, she never said... and that you'd be staying at Elisa's, and that you were doing a little better, but you still had problems. *Mama* suggested I send Andy to Elisa so I could focus on finishing my work once and for all. I only agreed because I wanted you to get better, so I could see you sooner. I thought if you'd see Andy, he could remind you to fight for your life, you know, as you did once before, on that *day*."

Andrés placed his hands on his face.

"Antonio, Tony, Elisa..." Sylvia said, "they all told me it was for the best that I didn't see how bad things had gotten for you. But if that were true, why encourage me to send my son away to his dad but keep me away?"

"That should've been your sign," Andrés said.

"But I wasn't thinking straight. Everything I had was going to my writing and school. I was still taking stuff like buspirone, bupropion, and lithium. It was awful, so I didn't see the signs.

"When Petra brought Andy back, I gave up hope that you were going to get better, but I never gave up on you. I buried myself in work and the causes I believed in. I was waiting for you to get better. And I would not allow Andy to go back to you again unless they gave me Elisa's address.

"I am his mom, after all—Lydia signed over her rights. Now, not only does Andy have your last name, but he also has mine. I should have the addresses of everywhere he goes."

"You should," Andrés said.

"Thank you... I hired private investigators to find you. It felt like you were being kept away from me. I mean, no one would tell me where you had been before moving back with Elisa or where she lived. I went down to Bushwick and found she was gone, and Andy refused to tell me where she'd moved.

"He said he didn't want Grandma mad at him, but I never understood that. That shithead. Why would he be part of the problem? What's the fucking surprise? You always do this shit! Tell me!"

Andrés paused. "Did no one tell you what happened to me on 9/11?"

"No... Were you there?"

"South Tower—the 105th floor. I did as I had promised: I came back to New York as soon as possible. That was supposed to be my next job."

"Fuck!"

"It's the reality."

"I know. Fuck! You should've stayed in Berlin."

"No. I shouldn't have gotten on that plane. I shouldn't have left you behind. That's the real answer."

"You shouldn't have!"

"I know. I survived because I heard your voice saying, *'Get out! Let's go!'* I felt you pull me up after the second plane hit—"

"You felt my hand? I dreamt I did that! I saw you on the ground, and I told you, *'Give me your hand and don't worry...'*"

"'I'm with you. You're safe with me.'"

"I said that! I knew you were there! I knew it! *Mama* made me feel like I was fucking crazy—*una loca.* Every time she'd visit me at Bellevue, she'd tell me to shut up about my dreams, but it was the truth, and I always tell the truth. With God as my witness, I always tell the truth. I told her, and I told the doctors, that I'd have these dreams—watching you, waiting to be seen, then going down a stairwell. I felt you scared; you were so scared, and I'm screaming, *'Get out, let's go,'* and I watched you coming out by the Millennium Hotel, and then watched the dust swallowing you—swallowing everything.

"And the beeping—oh my God, the beeping—those poor firefighters. And I watched you get up and cross the Brooklyn Bridge, covered in dust. I watched you get to Elisa's apartment. I watched you watching cartoons with Daphne, and then she ran to you, crying because she thought you died."

"All of that happened," Andrés said.

"It did? Holy shit—we're connected—we're soulmates. The doctors told me that wasn't real, that my dreams meant nothing. That no such magic connected me to you like that. They said it was a coping mechanism because we'd lost Athena, and I was trying to escape reality. That I was losing my grip on it. But the dreams felt so real, and they were! I was there! I'm not crazy!"

"You were never crazy—it was all real."

"Then I would dream I was in Union Square, and I would see your picture posted on this long billboard. Your picture would be among these other pictures of everyone who didn't make it home." Sylvia became silent.

Andrés grabbed her hand. "Tell me, what's going through your mind?"

Sylvia looked past him at the window, the snow streaking harder with each passing second. "My doctor would say I was having those dreams because you didn't come to visit. Petra was the only one who came. She'd tell me we lost you to the streets, but that she was there. She'd never leave me behind like you did. You never made it home, just like everyone in my dreams, with their faces on a billboard, never made it home. The old Andrés was dead, like everyone else."

"I'm alive, and I'm here," Andrés said.

She looked at Andrés. "Why didn't you visit me?"

"I was in the hospital too."

"You were?"

"For a year. The world became too much."

"Petra didn't tell me. I didn't understand why you never came. You used to say you'd never leave me, but when it mattered most, you got on a plane and left. What was I supposed to think? It was only Petra there, and she's your mother—she's always taken care of me.

"She'd tell me to stop talking about the dreams. The more I talked, the longer they kept me, and the more time I missed from my work. So finally, I told them I stopped having dreams. I told them I didn't believe in soulmates, that there was no magic in the world. Eventually, they let me out, but I never stopped having those dreams—especially the one where I saw your face on a billboard. I had it yesterday. I'll never forget that feeling of being abandoned."

"I'm here, my love; I'm here."

"Petra told me it was all in my head, and she knew the truth? She made me feel like I was fucking crazy because of these dreams, and she knew the truth? She made me believe you loved drugs more than me, and she knew the truth?"

"I'm here, my love; I'm here."

"My love? My love?" Sylvia shook his hand away. "Shut the fuck up with that 'my love' crap! You don't love me! You were at my house and could've ended the bullshit that day."

Andrés sat back. "Let's go there—you knew I took Andy to an appointment once."

"There's a good reason I know."

"Whatever. Let's imagine I did end the bullshit that day. For what? For years, I thought about it. If I hadn't been so doped up on medication back then to realize it was your house—what would it have been like to come back into your life? You would've accused me of spending all that time apart eating cheese fries in the middle of the night.[1] Then you would've told me something didn't feel right, that you didn't feel the same. Then you would've kicked me out that night for falling asleep in the middle of sex, and that would've been the end of our eternal one-night stand.[2]"

Sylvia laughed. "Goddammit."

"Do you like that throwback? You get one, just one."

"Stop trying to make me laugh. I don't wanna laugh. I wanna be mad."

"Yeah, let's stay mad and cut the romantic crap, because I'm not laughing. This is you back in the day: 'Hey, Mr. Bullshit—I'm Sylvia, and I don't want to be in a codependent relationship with a fat fuck. I'll cut you out of my life.' Remember her?"

"I remember."

"For so many years, I thought about that. A small part of me kept saying that if there was a chance of coming back into your life, I needed to get my mind and body right. I think part of going to New Mexico was for that—a clean break from the past. Going into the

---

1. *Book Three: The Labyrinth*, "Chapter Nineteen: The Sunflowers."
2. *Book One: Orpheus*, "Chapter Six: The Purple Room."

desert to die without dying. And let's be real here: how do I know this whole bullshit scenario isn't one big motherfucking game you created to ease your way back into my life? You watched through your little *mama's boy* that I'd lost all my weight, built my body back up, was no longer on meds, and I was out there fucking."

"Jesus, you give me too much credit—I'm sad all the fucking time. I never got over Athena. Have you?"

"No," Andrés said.

"The woman who said she'd cut you out of her life said that before we entered The Labyrinth. After that, everything changed. Now I know what happened: you didn't leave me for drugs."

Andrés leaned forward. "You didn't leave me because I got on a plane. Are we still a family?"

"Yes, of course, you idiot." Sylvia reached out and grabbed his hand. "The one thing this has taught me is to never, ever let you go again. You're coming home."

"Before I do, we need to get answers," Andrés said.

"We need to see Petra."

"We're not going anywhere. It's snowing hard, and I don't want us on the road."

"But I need to face her."

"No, you don't; think game with Medusa."

"Medusa?"

Andrés squeezed Sylvia's hand. "Emma—focus."

"If I'm thinking like her, she'd probably have something planned for the moment we figured everything out. She'd expect me to come through those doors like—"

"Like Guns Blazing Constance[3]—and my mom would throw everything you'd trusted her to know right back at you. You'd freeze. Whenever she's losing an argument, I've seen Petra do that. It throws a person off, and she comes out on top."

"Fuck, I should've never told her everything."

"I told you, but you believed you were different. That's why I tried to get you to set boundaries with Mom. She's not like your grand-

____

3. *Book Two: Underworld,* "Chapter Ten: The Titans."

mother. Constance would never have worked to put your dad to sleep just to keep him home with you. And that's the reason for Elisa's part in all of this—she wanted to keep me asleep for Daphne. She also knew about our plans to maybe move out west and take Daphne with us."

"Oh, fuck," Sylvia said.

"We got too comfortable in our bubble, thinking everyone was down with our dreams and forgetting how it would affect them."

"Fuck it—what's done is done. We paid the price."

"We paid it, and now we're here. I'm over it."

"I wanna be over everything. The past dies tonight. Tomorrow, we're waking up new, but I'm still angry. What do we do about that? We can't go into a new day with that."

"Let's go grab a room and continue talking about it."

"Yeah—this poor waitress keeps looking at us. We're costing her money," Sylvia said.

"I know."

"The Rivington is up the street. Let's go."

The two stood, and Andrés helped Sylvia with her coat. They each left forty dollars[4] on the table and thanked the waitress for her patience.

"When I get old, I want to have a love like yours," the waitress said.

"No, you don't," Sylvia said. "Love like this hurts."

"This kind of love is too painful. Stick to square love... Vanilla love," Andrés said.

"No," the waitress said. "What good is life if it doesn't have passion? I want that—I want your passion."

Sylvia and Andrés walked out of the lounge and onto Delancey Street. In the heavy snowfall, they headed toward the hotel.

"I could never understand why Andy refused to tell me exactly where you were or where Elisa lived," Sylvia said, her shoulders hunched against the cold wind. "My P.I. finally tracked her to her job. I know now, but before that, we could never nail down an address—we

____

4. *Book One: Orpheus*, "Chapter Four: Eurydice."

just knew it was somewhere near Oceanside. So one night, I got Andy in the car, and we drove down. I drove through every street in the area. Boy, was I off."

"You did that?" Andrés said.

"Of course I did. I would look at Andy. If the house we were driving by was one he knew, I would wait for him to flinch. He'd tell me, 'No, Mom.' He was afraid of Grandma—afraid of what she'd do if she found out we were searching for you. But I would've protected him. I knew that no matter what, you would've protected him. Why was he so afraid? But something just hit me."

"What?"

"When Petra brought him back that day because she said you went crazy[5,] I remember him running over to me like he was still a little boy and hugging me tightly. I remember him asking, 'If my dad ever comes back, does that mean we're moving?' It didn't make sense why he'd ask, but I answered him with the truth. I said, 'Maybe. Dad and I always thought about moving to New Mexico.' He got so angry, saying, 'But I like it here. I don't want to move anymore.'"

"Fuck," Andrés said. "Let's tackle Medusa before we deal with him."

"I don't even wanna go there," Sylvia said. "To think Andy may have been working against us all along. I don't know. But tonight, we bury the past. We have to. It doesn't matter anymore if he worked against us."

"I just want to focus on the good stuff, like giving you props. Despite what he may have done, he's still a child, and you took care of him. You did an amazing job."

"You're damn right I did," Sylvia said. "I'd done such a great job that even Lydia gives me props. She'd tell me, 'I never wanted to be a mom. You're a natural.' And you were worried about having me in his life. You're the fuckup, not me. Now I'm worried about having you in his life—wait, I'm sorry. I take it back. I still see you through Medusa's eyes. I'm sorry."

"It is what it is."

---

5. *Book One: Orpheus,* "Chapter Three: A-Okay."

"I didn't mean it like that."

Andrés smiled. "Yes, you did. And it's okay."

"No, it's not. I'm still thinking what Petra said about you was the truth. I know what that is now."

Andrés huddled closer to her while walking in the snowfall.

"Speaking of truth," he said, "what's yours? I know nothing about your life."

"Nothing?"

"All I know is the hospital and just what you shared."

Sylvia stopped walking to look at him with disappointment. "Are you for real?"

"I've searched your name, but after 2003—"

"You mean to tell me that you had all that time to push your way out to New Mexico—meditate under the stars—be with other women —*Isabella*—but you had no time to search for my name on the internet? Instead of sending text messages to other women, which I know you've been doing, you couldn't take one fucking minute to search for me again? I got in a car and drove five hours, round trip, from our house upstate, with your son—who I adopted—to find you and bring you back from hell? Fuck you! I hate you!"

Sylvia rushed ahead.

Andrés followed her.

❦ 43 ❦
PRIVATE PYLE

[3]

Sylvia and Andrés entered the dark hotel room, a soft light emanating from a nightstand in the corner. Andrés took off his coat and everything else soaked by the snowstorm, while Sylvia looked around the room, inspecting the bedding and rug for stains. She went into the bathroom and then came back out.

He turned to Sylvia. "Aren't you going to take off your coat?"

"Don't worry about me," Sylvia said. "I've been fine all these years without you. You'd know that if you had searched for me."

He shrugged. "Suit yourself."

Sylvia gave Andrés a long look before removing everything that was wet, including her headscarf.

He went into the bathroom, came back with a towel, and handed it to her. "In case you need it. I don't want you to catch a cold—and also for the moment you feel safe enough around me."

"I already do."

"You took the headscarf off because it was wet, not because you felt comfortable enough to show me your hair again. I get it. When you take off that towel, I'll know it's because you want to."

Sylvia wrapped her damp hair in the towel, looked at him with soft eyes, and, with a slight smile, said, "Thank you."

"You're welcome." Andrés paused, looking at her with deep reverence and longing. "You're so beautiful. I love how much more beautiful you've become."

A glimmer of joy came to Sylvia's eyes. "Thank you. I still hate you, but you've always been handsome. You're a lot more solid now—I caught a glimpse of how fat you'd gotten."

Andrés laughed. "You did?"

"I have a security system at *our* house. If you'd searched my name, you would know why. Back then, when I got home from work, I would go through the day's video before moving on. When I got back from my business trip, I thought Antonio had taken Andy to the appointment, but I got excited when I saw it was you—fat and all—who'd taken him instead."

"Because of the meds, I had packed a solid hundred to my frame," Andrés said.

"I had packed a solid thirty onto mine. For someone as small as me, it might as well have been a hundred pounds. So it wouldn't have mattered if you were big. It was still you, just as I was still me. Besides, I would've made you lose it."

"Those years are all a blur. My psychiatrist maxed me out on everything. I wanted to stay awake, but he needed to keep me down. It was a time in my life when Elisa would hide the car keys because I had a habit of falling asleep while driving. When I started having these dreams—feeling you calling for me, feeling your suffering—my psychiatrist put me on lithium and warned me not to look for you. He reminded me at every session that there was a reason you disappeared from my life. It was obvious—you didn't want to be a part of it. You left me. Couples break up when they lose a child. You even said so."

Sylvia looked away. "I did say that."

"Yeah, you did... The psychiatrist helped me understand that, with all the signs that were there, searching for you would be like stalking. Every session, he warned me I couldn't turn into that kind of man. I couldn't do that to you."

She looked back at him. "How could you be a stalker? I had Andy!"

"I wasn't even clear about that!"

"How could you not be? You went to the house! He calls me 'Mom' and Lydia, 'Lydia.'"

"I was so far gone on Klonopin that I had even forgotten that—but what I'd never forgotten was how we've always thrived on permission. We've always thrived on understanding boundaries. We developed a Dance that depends on that—knowing when to lead and when to follow. Even in our absence, we were still dancing. So it didn't matter that, to you, from your end, I got hooked on drugs. To me, you had left. Your house was beyond the boundary, and you were safe behind it. Crossing the boundary and knocking on your door—would you see it as part of the Dance, or would you see it as the act of a stalker? A man you had left because Athena died, because I got on a plane instead of staying with you? Did you need to protect yourself from me because of that? Because I had already hurt you? From my end, that's how I began seeing things."

"Fuck!"

"I know."

Sylvia walked over to the bed and sat on its edge, appearing stunned.

Andrés sat next to her. "The psychiatrist helped me understand that if it *were* you in that house, I no longer had your permission. I had no right to show up and demand we pick up where we left off. When I called from Berlin, it appeared you had taken back all the power you had trusted me to have. You took it back the moment my calls started rolling into voicemail. You never called back. You never answered my emails."[1]

"But I didn't have access to my computer, my emails—my phone. I'd asked the nurses if they could give it to Petra. When I got out, Petra said the nurses had never given her my phone. But she told me not to worry—she'd taken care of everything else, including getting me a new one."

"I didn't know any of that. To me, silence became your new safe

---

1. *Book One: Orpheus*, "Chapter Two: Meet Her at the Love Parade."

word, and you were telling me, 'No.' You were so angry at me for what I couldn't do."

"We were both in shock!"

"But you were right to demand it." Andrés grabbed her hand. "You were feeling so alone."

"I should've been more patient with you. We deal with death in different ways, and that's how you dealt with Athena's—"

"Don't make any excuses for me. You hate me, remember? Your feelings are valid. I hate myself too—for what I couldn't do. And I couldn't cross that line and show up at your house with my issues, just because I felt like you were calling my name."

"But I was calling. We're believers, remember? And I don't give a fuck about boundaries. It's called devotion—that's the part of love that's not a game. There are no fucking rules to that shit. You just do it."

"That's easy for you to say. What looks like devotion from a woman looks like stalking from a man—that's the truth. So, I set up this elaborate Tango today to get you to cross the boundary for us, to see if you still feel desire for me. I didn't know if you still felt the same way, so fuck it—let's wake everything up."

Sylvia yanked the towel from her hair and tossed it to the floor. "Oh, I'm awake. Too awake. I've been stalking you since New Mexico. I tried reading your license plate from the video, but your car was too far, and zooming in made it fuzzy. If I had your address, I would've gone and pulled your ass out because you belong to me. Give me your fucking phone—now!"

Andrés reached into his pocket.

Sylvia snatched his phone away. "What's your passcode?"

"0626."

Sylvia paused for a moment before saying, "That's mine too." She opened a web browser on his phone and entered the search terms: Sylvia James and Private Pyle. The search results filled with video clips of her appearance on a news program from March 31, 2004. "If you had stalked me, you would have come across this badass right here. This is where I was that day you came to the house."

Andrés read the title: "Full, Uncensored Leaked Footage of Sylvia Owning News Bros, 2004."

"Shut up and watch what you missed out on."

She pressed play on his phone's screen.

A news segment began with a moderator sitting at a desk next to another man in a blue suit, with a large American flag waving on a large-screen video backdrop. Their body language suggested their professional relationship was more familiar than expected from a news organization. Seated alone at the far end of the desk, on the other side of the moderator, was Sylvia. She wore a black jacket and a white blouse, open wide enough to reveal a silver choker necklace with an infinity insignia. Her hair was combed back into a conservative bun.

The moderator began: "Joining us today is Sylvia—a spoken word poet and author of the novel *The Little Girl of the Valley.*" He gave her a quick glance and chuckled. "Are you trying to be like Prince or something?"

Sylvia continued to smile, not acknowledging the moderator, keeping her eyes locked on the camera.

"Also joining us is Colonel Jeff Willings of the United States Air Force. Colonel Willings served in the first Gulf War and in Afghanistan. He took part in the Battle of Tora Bora, where he was awarded a Bronze Star. The colonel is now retired and is an analyst with our network. Thank you for joining us."

The colonel and Sylvia both thanked the moderator.

"Sylvia," the moderator said, "your poetry has been published in anthologies and as stand-alone books. How are you able to go from writing about your *vagina* to writing about *war?*"

"Writing about my *vagina* is as serious to me as writing about *war,* but I'm going to entertain the false premise of your question."

"I'm honored."

"As you should be, because you can't be helped—I imagine it's the same way you're able to transition easily from playing beer pong to reading from a script. I'm still writing about my vagina. It's important to me, as much as war is, and I'm always willing to go to war to keep control over my body."

"And why is that? I mean, why is war important? When have you served?"

"When have you?"

"I come from a military family—my father served in Grenada."

"My aunt was an Army nurse in Vietnam. My father served with the 1st Cavalry in the Battle of Hué. For his troubles, he has a Distinguished Service Cross, and by the time he was done, he'd earned a few Purple Hearts—but that's beside the point. I know what war does to people... to families. Since you've made a deep dive into my work and read about my vagina, you must've read my poem *1968*."

The moderator said, "Never read it."

"Sure, you have. Over the years, I've received a lot of feedback about that poem, but I don't think the attention I've received is good. That's why I wanted to tell a story about what war does to the real victims—the families in the war zones. The people the United States claims to be 'liberating:' the Iraqi people."

"Here we go," the colonel said.

"Who speaks for them? Where's the justice? They're not just numbers. Each number is a human being."

The colonel interjected, "This is silly. This woman is nothing more than an instrument of Al Qaeda's efforts to spread propaganda under the guise of so-called literature. Everything in the book does nothing but promote the notion that our armed forces are the bad guys."

"That's how you've read it. Talk about projection."

"That's how the insurgency—and anyone else who supports them— will take it. By the way, we're coming off a bad month. We've lost a lot of American lives."

"For a woman who writes about her vagina, I didn't realize I had that much sway over the insurgency. I just wrote a story."

"Okay, we get it," the moderator said. "They're more than numbers. But why did you write the story?"

"I had planned to write this story long before the Iraq War. I grew up in Appalachia and was influenced by what I heard from the men and women in my community who had served in Vietnam and came back broken. I may not have served, but I can tell you, Colonel, that for the families of everyone who served there, they brought the war home to us. We suffered with them. But our suffering was nothing compared to the suffering of those who live in the countries we invade—the ones the United States supposedly liberates."

The colonel laughed. "You're repeating yourself."

"Excuse me, I'm speaking. While I wrote the book, I kept thinking about my father and the difficulty he had coming to terms with what his commanders ordered him to do—the suffering he caused. The American people need to brace themselves for a new generation of young men and women who will come home broken."

"This is silly. Vietnam? You wrote a book set during the first Gulf War about a fictional event that, given the time and setting, couldn't possibly have happened—north of the Euphrates River? Give me a break."

"Maybe it's not a fictional event. Maybe, if you care to file a request under the Freedom of Information Act and do some research, you'll find that I might know something you don't. Would that be possible?"

The colonel talked over Sylvia. "You know nothing. It's ridiculous to think that a story involving U.S. Special Forces, Iraq's Republican Guard, and a Bedouin family caught in the crossfire could be real. I'll tell you what's real—a drug addict from the East Village got hysterical and took out her daddy issues on our men in uniform."

"Excuse me, Colonel, what did you say?"

"This crap isn't worth a book. It's not even worth three minutes at an open mic in a cheap coffeehouse."

The moderator interrupted. "Let's circle back to the colonel's accusations. You wrote this book as a hit piece for Al Qaeda against our men in Iraq. After all, it was our bloodiest month yet. What do you have to say about that, Sylvia?"

"Excuse me? What's my name?"

The moderator looked at her, confused. "Sylvia? Is that not your name?"

"It's Dr. Sylvia Hadid James."

The colonel laughed. "Oh, you're one of them."

"I am—"

"What kind of doctor are you?" the moderator asked.

Dr. James smiled. "I have a Master of Philosophy and a Master of Arts in Political Science. I recently finished my law degree—something I started in the '80s when I was a stripper—and I was just admitted to the bar. So, yeah, I'm a lawyer. Oh, but you asked what I'm a doctor of —I have a Ph.D. in Political Science. By the way, all my degrees are from Columbia University. I'm like a Kennedy—an Ivy League junkie."

The panel ignored the cameraman when he said, "We're no longer on the air."

The moderator said, "We get it."

Dr. James continued, "No, you don't. My minor field is political economic theory, so I understand game and power. I enjoy the exchange. I see the exchange with your audience. Whatever the two of you say—even though it's a lie—you'll convince your viewers it's the truth. It's even within your power to convince them that women like me are part of the problem, that we're the reason we had our bloodiest month. If we didn't have crying mothers to contend with, we could throw our men and women further into the slaughter. Somehow, we're the enemy."

"See? Sylvia is emotional," the colonel said.

Dr. James replied, "There's power in titles. As such, you'll address me as 'Doctor,' just as I've addressed you as 'Private.'"

"I'm not a private."

The moderator interrupted. "You're not a real doctor—you're not curing anyone."

Dr. James gave the camera a wry smile. "This is not a real news network, and you're not a real newsman. You're a mouthpiece. But I'm here, and you're peddling outrage while selling my book at the same time. So, I'm *supposed* to say, 'Thank you.'"

"You haven't answered the question," the colonel said.

"I'm sorry—what was the question?"

"Did Al Qaeda pay you to write this book?"

"Pardon me, Pyle; I can't hear you."

The colonel said, loudly, "My name is not Pyle—"

"Again, Private Pyle, I'm sorry. I still can't hear you."

"I told you, I'm not a private—I'm a colonel!"

Dr. James laughed. "Geez, you don't need to get *hysterical*. It's okay —most officers never become generals."

The moderator tried to interrupt. "That's all the time we have."

Dr. James ignored him. "You're not a real colonel... Air Force? What a joke. That's not a real branch of the military. Even the Coast Guard makes fun of you guys. Tora Bora? You look too soft for anything else other than support. I'm sure you have some stolen valor going on. I'm going to ask Colonel Hackworth about you—confirm that Bronze Star is legit. Now that guy is the real deal—the U.S. Army. I bet he has sex with his boots on."

The colonel stood and took off his microphone.

As he walked away, she shouted, "Colonel Hackworth made Admiral Boorda see the dark! Six feet dark, if you know what I mean! Imagine what he'd do to you! You can't live a lie with honor! Would you like the same treatment, Colonel?"

The moderator asked the cameraman, "Did we cut too commercial?"

"Bro, a long time ago," he replied.

Sylvia shouted at the camera, "Boys are so easy to mess with. Guys, this is what you get! You brought me on, hoping to get a sound bite you could play on a loop. Here's one: the only way to answer bullshit questions is to give bullshit answers. The moment you give a serious answer, those bullshit questions somehow become legitimate, and I'm not here for that. I'm not the one. Am I right, ladies? In the control room back there? You know what I'm talking about. Some young guy is explaining your job to you—like you don't know. How many times have you given them a bullshit answer?"

Laughter could be heard in the background.

Sylvia said, "You guys are not using me for a sound bite. I'm using you to sell books. And if you've not cut me off by now, fair warning: I'm about to give your network its own Janet Jackson moment. I may be older than she is, but I'm holding up far better. I hope the FCC fines this network. This is for asking me bullshit questions."

There was more laughter on set as Sylvia stood and unbuttoned her blouse to reveal her breasts.

"You like that, huh? No bra! Parents Television Council, I have no agency! They made me do this! I'm emotional! Come for them, not me!" She laughed. "I'm just fucking around. Come for me. I know what I'm doing. Get mad. Buy my book. I need a new roof."

The segment ended.

The video clip ended.

❧ 44 ❧

THE DOMINATRIX

[4]

Andrés looked at Sylvia with immense pride. "You finished the Master Plan!"

She beamed. "Yup. It took me, what, twenty years? Several long leaves of absence?"

"I love how you handled the colonel. It's like, something in you snapped."

"Only you could see that! Everyone I know thinks that's normal, but they just don't know. They don't know what it took for me to speak and own it, to use my voice. You've been there, and, baby, I'm still on the dark side. I can't let up. Out there, I can never be soft. From the moment my research for the book caught the attention of the intel community, it has been non-stop bullshit. That's why I have a security system, and I've been on my own. That's my world. I handle men like that every day, but it's easy because they're so stupid and full of themselves."

"I'm so proud of you."

"You are? I was hoping you were out there, somewhere, seeing me do that."

Andrés paused. "When I told my psychiatrist I'd seen a quick flash of you on TV and had been having dreams—feeling as if you were calling for me—that's when he put me on lithium. He thought I was experiencing a break from reality."

"That had been the only time I was on TV for something like that; it was that night. Before heading to D.C., Petra wanted me to wear your grandmother's pearl necklace, but I was like, no, I'm not covering this up."

Sylvia touched her silver necklace.

"I told her, if he's watching, I want him to see me with it on. I almost didn't go—I had Andy's appointment scheduled months in advance, but Petra was like, I'll get his grandfather to take him."

Andrés sighed. "My mom..."

"I know she's no Constance, but she's the mom I never had. I know Nana did her best—and my dad would always say that Miss Alma battled the worst depression, and that it wouldn't be fair to her memory to hold it against her—but I can't help feeling what I feel. One of the few memories I have of Miss Alma is of her on a couch, ignoring me. Petra is the only one who looked after me, like a mom. I mean, a mom is supposed to teach her daughter how to take care of her hair, right?

"Do you know how many times girls bullied me in school because of my hair? Because Nana didn't know how to take care of my hair? She thought all hair was the same. Because of Nana, I was no homecoming queen, and I always felt ugly. I love Nana, but it was Petra who taught me how to take care of my hair, with that whole thing of wrapping it in a silk bonnet or using a satin pillowcase."

"I remember Mom getting on you if it looked like you went more than a day without taking care of your hair."

"'Stop being lazy,' she'd say. That we'd have to take care of our hair the same way we'd take care of our dignity. Our hair is everything. Nana never taught me that—and *definitely* not my real mom... Why would Petra do this shit? I don't understand..."

Sylvia paused, her eyes drifting past him.

Andrés grabbed her hand and asked, "Why were you in the hospital?"

Sylvia looked down. "When you got on the plane and left me behind, I was in pain. Yes, I was angry. I was in our new apartment, and I thought I would be okay until you came home, but I was not okay. I know you said the apartment was temporary until we found a better place, but I felt like I went backward. You were gone, she was gone, and that life out west felt like one beautiful dream.

"I couldn't sleep. Baby, I couldn't sleep, and I found myself wandering outside, like the way I used to walk the streets. I knew what I was looking for. I just wanted to sleep, and I knew I was gonna lose. I wasn't gonna let myself lose that battle. I am not a junkie! So I went back to the apartment, grabbed a knife from the kitchen, and walked over to the bathtub. I ran the water as hot as I could and got in. I kept looking at my stretch marks, and my breasts hurt so much—they were so swollen. I lost it. I was so tired. I just wanted you home, and I didn't wanna need you like I do.

"I hate this shit. I hate love like this. So I held the knife to my wrist. I was gonna do it. But I looked up at the ceiling and remembered looking up at the sky over the Bridge that night—and every night we would go there."

Sylvia looked up at the ceiling, her eyes glistening.

"Oh, the stars... The stars," she whispered. "The ceiling began to look like a vast cosmic ocean... Then I remembered my turtle—my beautiful turtle."

"Thank God for Kalpa," Andrés said.

"I dropped the knife and called 911. I voluntarily checked myself into the hospital. I didn't get out until I declared magic wasn't real, and the doctors felt they'd stabilized me enough that I was no longer a danger to myself. That was January 2002."

"Can I hug you? Is it okay?"

Sylvia looked back at him. "Please?"

Andrés wrapped Sylvia in his arms, her face buried against his chest.

Her voice muffled, she said, "I felt Daphne crying on your chest because she thought you had died. And you were dead to me—you were gone."

"That's all over, and you're alive, and you were right. You were always right… If you wanna talk more about your feelings, then please talk to me. I wanna listen, but I don't want this to be about me. Tonight, we're breaking the loops in our memories and starting new ones. We can end anything having to do with your dreams of 9/11. Can we?"

"Yes, please."

"Done… Tell me more about who you are now, Dr. James."

She pushed herself away from Andrés, looking at him with weepy eyes and her nose running. "I'm not a loser anymore."

"You never were."

"But you made me feel like one, and I promised myself that when I got the chance, I'd bring it up. My therapist helped me understand that when you made me feel like a loser in front of my friends, you did me wrong.[1] I know I asked you to roll with it and have fun, and if it were just us, it would've been funny. But those words, coming out of your mouth in front of Katherine and Jessica—who'd done nothing but bully me at that time in my life—made me feel so small… It felt too natural coming out the way it did, like you believed it.

"I've played that moment in my mind over and over, like a loop. It drove me to work harder, if only to shove my accomplishments in your face. But I don't know. I got here. How would I have gotten here without that?"

"You would've made it without me saying any of that."

"I don't know about that."

Andrés sighed. "I'm sorry."

"Is this a real apology? Or an 'I'm sorry you took the joke the wrong way'?"

"I'm sorry. I fucked up. You're right, and I'm wrong. Please forgive me. You're not a loser. You were never a loser, and I'm so lucky to have your attention, your love, your loyalty, and your devotion. There's no other explanation—you heard what you heard, and there's no excuse for what I said or how I said it. Your feelings are valid."

"Thank you."

"Do you wanna tell me more about how I've hurt you? Is there

---

1. *Book Three: The Labyrinth*, "Chapter Twenty-Four: Let Me Be Evil."

anything I need to know? Are there any other ways I've hurt you? Anything I've said or done? Because if so, please tell me so I can make amends."

"No. That's the one and only time you've hurt me."

"No, it's not," Andrés said. "I'm sorry for getting on the plane."

"I blame Antonio and Petra for that. I tried teaching Andy to be different. I've shut them down whenever they talk about Andy growing up to be a real man—a good provider—like they're both the same thing. Fuck that."

"Thank you!"

"Do I need to make any amends?" Sylvia asked.

"Stop. This moment isn't about me. You have nothing to make amends for. Tell me more about your life—do you have a boyfriend? A girlfriend?"

Sylvia was silent.

"If it's none of my business, that's one thing. I respect your boundaries. But you've seen me on a date, and you keep bringing up New Mexico."

"It's not a boundary thing—I feel weird telling you about my love life."

"Tonight, we're waking everything up. I want to get jealous. I want to get angry and jealous and never let you go again so easily. I want to be the kind of man who won't find it so easy to get on a plane and leave his fiancée behind, thousands of miles away, taking for granted that she won't fuck around."

"Yes, let's put that fear in you, asshole. I like that! Don't take me for granted. Let's add that step to the Dance."

"Agreed—yes."

"I moved on only because I found out about New Mexico. I can't believe you. I still have this ring on my finger. Never mind, because none of this is your fault. You thought I left you; you were respecting my boundaries; my absence and silence were my safe words to stop. And you're so fucking stupid. Okay, let's do this—I had a girlfriend, and we didn't last long. She'd say I was cold. I had to break up with her because she was the sweetest, kindest woman I had ever met, and she didn't deserve to be treated that way, like whatever she was feeling didn't register.

"I tried having a boyfriend. He'd get mad that I was raising Andy for someone he'd say was a bum. He didn't like Petra and Antonio being an active part of my life. I'd tell him to read the room, to look at my son, at everything in my house and office, and see there were no signs of his importance. But there were signs of the importance of the father of my son... and my late daughter. He'd say the only sign he could see was your weakness in becoming a drug addict. The idiot forgot he said that to a woman who counts every day of sobriety.

"Before there was a Dr. James, there was a Spacer Woman. He'd go on about how much better he was than you because he had these degrees. I'd say, 'Don't kid yourself—you're just a time filler for my man in the arena. I'm still with him, but he's sick.' This idiot asked if my fiancé would care if I was having sex with him."

Andrés laughed. "What a chump."

"I know, right? Oh God, I took pleasure in beating the shit out of Time Filler—he was a big pussy. It was a mistake to date a colleague. I dated him out of boredom. He resigned and left after I made him say your name while pegging him. I only did that after that piece of shit made an issue out of what I had written in one of my books. I should've known better. Something was off about him—guys who put themselves out there as the biggest feminists are the worst misogynists. His bullshit comments about the book caused so much drama at work, and I was like, I am who I am, and I stopped saying sorry years ago. I showed him that this doctor was a dominatrix. While those fuckers talked theory, I put what I had learned into practice. I'm the woman in the arena, walking the walk, talking the talk, and fighting the fight. I've lived life, not theory.

"After pegging him, he couldn't face me anymore. But I had to resign soon after he left because of the shit he stirred up in the aftermath. It was bad—so, so bad—that I was at a social event in the city not too long ago, engaged in *boring* small talk, when I was approached by this much older man. He touched my arm in a way that sent shivers up my spine, then, in front of others, said, 'I can never forget the hair

—your hair.' Then, he reached into his pocket and tried handing me a hundred-dollar bill, saying, 'For old times' sake, how about a dance?'"

Sylvia paused. "I kept my cool. This was someone who I must've, at some point, given a lap dance, but I wasn't having it. So, rather than respond, I walked away. And it was then that I decided to start wearing a hijab."

"I understand now."

"My other memory of Miss Alma was of her wearing one once. To me, it just made everything about her face so much more beautiful. So, no, I didn't convert to Islam, but after the life I've lived, I enjoy the idea that this is the final step I needed to take to reclaim everything that had been robbed from me, so that it would only be you—and our son—who truly sees me. The real me.

"But even now, as I'm trying to play it off like that experience somehow became something positive, it still hurts. It hurts so much, so I'm done. I am so done... dealing with people... Nothing is the same. I hate feelings, and I fucking hate people, and I've tried to move on—I really did try—but I only want you. So, I buried myself in work. I've lived my days out like a monk while trying to figure out a way to crack Andy's phone. I told him to tell you to meet me at the Bridge, giving him a specific time and date."

"He never told me anything."

"I realize that now. I showed up, and you weren't there. I wanted to fling myself off the fucking bridge."

Andrés grabbed Sylvia and hugged her.

"I went out and bought one of those new phones," she said, her face buried in his chest. "I told him that if he wanted it, he'd have to come over to my plan. Andy said, 'No, thanks.' The little fucker didn't even want an upgrade—he wanted to keep his *potato*. All I needed was your number."

"Elisa had set up an anonymous shell corporation for the family, which she had managed alone. Everything of mine was under it."

Sylvia looked at Andrés. "That's fucking evil because I searched for you. I looked for you. I swear, I mean, I even asked Tony, and the fucking pussy was like, 'I need to speak to *Ma*.' Didn't you ever look at your phone bill? The calls Andy would make? My number would've been there."

"Elisa managed all the bills, and I didn't have access to my accounts. Then my doctor made me promise—"

"If you'd done one more search on the internet, you would've seen where I'd been all along. I don't give a fuck what your shrink said. To love like this, you should've known better."

"To me, you'd left, and that silence was the same as you saying, 'Constance.' If we were to have a future, I had to keep the boundary. Even in our absence, I had to respect you. How could you ever trust me again if I didn't respect your word?"

Sylvia screamed.

Andrés brought her close.

She buried her face in his chest, screaming until her voice gave out, leaving her breathless.

"Do you still trust me?" he asked.

"With my life... With my soul."

"It had to be this way; we have to move on."

"We have to... Nothing else matters. I can't let this eat me inside out. I'm gonna close the loop, or it'll just play over and over."

"No need to go back to it—tell me about your work."

Sylvia took a deep breath and came out of Andrés's embrace. She wiped the edges of her eyes and smiled. "You've seen the house. My first book got me—well, it got me a mortgage."

"It's a beautiful home."

"Thank you. I can't wait to show you the inside. For my second book, I tried to make it funny but ended up kind of serious. It's about a stripper who's always broke and always gets into some bullshit. The total opposite of my first book."

"Did you include *Raylon?*"[2]

"Yes!"

"I love that story."

"It's that story and more. I called the book *Spacer Woman*. It's what your date called out when she recognized me. It's what Time Filler

____

2. Raylon is a chapter in the novel *Spacer Woman*.

tried to get me to feel shame over. But you loved those stories, and you met me during that time in my life, and you wanted to love me."

"I can't wait to read it."

"You'll be surprised at how brave I am with what I shared."

"No, I won't—I already know how brave you are."

Sylvia smiled. "Thank you... You know, I wrote about how we met."

"Did you?"

"Yes," she said.

"God, you were so damn hot. I love bad girls."

"I love guys who look like they 'eat dirt.' I still can't get over that was you—and it's gonna be twenty-three years. *Spacer Woman* opened my audience beyond the more political one I gained from the first book. The voice in *Spacer Woman* is me from The Loft, and because of that, my publisher took work that had been out of print and republished it. I'm being asked to perform again, but I turn down most offers because I'm not that person anymore. Now, I'm an associate professor of political science at Vassar College."

"Holy shit!"

"Yeah, and don't forget, a novelist. I have an idea for a third book, but I don't know how to approach it yet. That one will be the one that tears me apart, but I need to write it—and I will when the time is right. See? I made it. Not bad for a *loser*."

"I knew you would."

"I can't say this enough—my biggest accomplishment is staying sober for 6,555 days now. Each day is a struggle, and I almost lost it, but I wasn't going out like that—not because of you or Athena. I can't fail myself. I'm strong enough to know when I need help. Thank God I can see beyond myself. I'm glad I checked myself into a hospital."

"I'm glad that you did," Andrés said.

"I told you we would figure it out. Well, I figured it out—I used that time in the hospital to come up with a new plan for us, but you know what happened with the rest."

Andrés reached out and pulled Sylvia close, wrapping his arms around her. "It doesn't matter anymore. We're here in this room. This moment is what counts."

Sylvia took a deep breath and exhaled. "I miss this feeling."

"Me too."

"Can I ask you something?"

"Anything."

"How did you *handle* Caleb? Can you tell me? Because I thought about him that night, and man, if I'd known where he was, I would've called him instead of help. You let me believe one thing... you've always implied one thing, but I was never sure. You've let me think there was a possibility he was still out there—that you scared him enough to disappear."

Andrés paused, silent for a long moment.

"Tell me, please," Sylvia said.

"I wasn't gonna let him hold your sobriety hostage, back then or ever. He fucked himself the night he slipped that little packet into that takeout and began stalking you—we've talked about this."

"But I need to know everything."

"If you need to know everything, we need to be married. You, of all people, should know there's no statute of limitations for how I *handled* him. I can't let you get in trouble with that information. You'll need spousal immunity."

Sylvia squeezed Andrés harder. "This is why I could never work with anyone else. You—the moment I saw you, I knew you were my one. I knew I loved you. I'm talking 1986."

"Damn, you wanted to lock down that dick? You didn't even try it."

"Shut up! Did you know?"

"I knew I wanted to see your pussy, and I'm talking 1986."

Sylvia laughed and pushed Andrés away. "You asshole."

"I bet it was hairy back then too."

"Fro for life—but I'm serious—when did you know?"

"After I got mine, then I knew—"

"Stop joking—"

"I knew the moment I saw you dancing on the pedestal and we locked eyes—I wouldn't throw my body on top of just anybody with bullets flying like that. It was instinctive how I wanted to protect you, like you were mine."[3]

---

3. *Book Two: Underworld*, "Chapter Fifteen: Emma."

"I knew it. I fucking knew it. I cried that night because you opened your mouth, and out came these words that only a stupid teenager would say. And I was like, 'Fuck, he's not ready, and I'm still out here on the streets.'"

"We weren't ready for each other yet," he said.

"You're right, but I'm ready now, and I still wanna know the whole truth about Caleb. So, we get through this night, and we get a civil ceremony done—once and for all."

"As soon as possible."

Sylvia and Andrés kissed.

"Alright, time to do battle with Medusa," Andrés said.

Sylvia pulled out her phone and began dialing. "She played this game with us? Then let's play."

❧ 45 ☙

THE BROKEN CUPS

[5]

Sylvia dialed, placed the phone on speaker, and looked at Andrés, who was biting his nails while waiting for his mother to answer.

"*¿Dime?*" Petra said.

"Guess where I'm at," Sylvia said.

"Home, where you should be if you're out. It's going to snow, and the roads are going to be bad."

"It's already bad... I'm in the city."

"What are you doing there?"

"I'm on a date, and I'm calling to let you know, just in case something happens—you'll know I was with someone."

"But you work tomorrow."

"I should be home tonight, but if not, I'll call in."

"That's not responsible of you."

"What do I care? Nothing matters anymore. I lost him—I lost him."

"Lost who?" Petra asked.

"You know who. Don't play dumb. I lost *mi hombre.*"

"I hate when you talk Spanish. Are you drunk?"

"Yeah, fuck it. What does it matter? Andrés is dead! *Mama,* he's dead!"

"Wait a minute! Who told you that?"

"I have a news alert set for his name, and I got an email. Let me read it to you." Sylvia paused, closed her eyes, took a deep breath, and said, "From Taos News—headline: 'Body of New York Man Recovered from Below Rio Grande Gorge Bridge.'"

"Okay, and?"

Sylvia exhaled and opened her eyes. "Taos County Sheriff's deputies recovered the body of a New York man from below the Rio Grande Gorge Bridge on Friday, February 27, Sheriff Jeffrey Hidalgo has confirmed. Hidalgo identified the man on Saturday, February 28, as thirty-nine-year-old Andrés de León of Hewlett Harbor, New York. The man left a suicide note before apparently jumping to his death just before midnight Friday evening, February 27, making him the second person to commit suicide at the 600-foot-high steel arch bridge in 2009."

"Stop! That can't be him!"

"It's him! We used to go to that bridge all the time."

"I don't believe you. Why are you not crying?"

"Because I'm drunk and high, and this broke me. I'm tired of crying. I didn't care if he was a junkie. What was Andrés supposed to do? We'd lost Athena, and he'd seen things and done things that no one could sleep through unless they were on drugs. I was the only one who could help him sleep—I was his nightlight, and he was mine. He was mine to take care of, and that's what love is, is it not? What is love if it's not that? Andrés was my soulmate, so I'm gonna join him."

"Join him? What about Andy?"

"You're thinking about him now? He's gonna be nineteen—he can take care of himself, I guess. I'm done raising him, and thanks to you, Andy already lost his dad. Fatherhood was everything to Andrés. He did some unspeakable things just so he could be a part of Andy's life, and you took it away from him—you threw Andrés away like he was garbage. Disposable. Think about that." Sylvia hung up on Petra.

Andrés looked at her for a long moment. "You were really crying as if that had happened."

"Because it did. They'd already made you dead to me."

"Thank you... thank you, thank you for being my witness."

She composed herself, flashing a smile. "It's what I do."

"Why does it scare me that you had those suicide details at the ready?"

"It was just there. I don't know." Sylvia laughed. "I'm a gifted writer, that's why, and not a *loser*, you asshole."

"You're not gonna shut up about that, are you?"

"Make me."

Sylvia's phone rang. It was Petra.

She looked at Andrés. "Let her stew. Wanna see my pussy?"

"Now?"

"Let's make this twisted—answer and put it on speaker, and don't say a word. I'm so done with the square shit, and it's been a long time."

"Too long," Andrés said.

"I'm just relieved that I was right—I was right all along. I'm not crazy."

Andrés answered the call and placed it on speaker.

The two began to moan.

Petra hung up.

———

Darkness covered the lovers in bed until a bright light pulsed from Andrés's phone, showing an incoming call from Elisa.

Sylvia smiled, grabbed the phone, and answered on speaker. "What's up, bitch?"

Elisa's laughter came through from the other end of the line. "Please tell me this was your idea."

"Of course. Imagine if I had a tumor? I would've come up with more evil shit."

"So, you know?"

"Of course I know. Andy ratted you out—sounds like bullshit."

Elisa laughed. "Well, it's not."

"So, were you like Dr. Jekyll and Mrs. Hyde?"

"Kind of? It made me do crazy things, but it was still me. I'm not going to blame a tumor for the fucked-up things I've done—for everything I've done for Petra. I'm sorry."

"Stop!" Sylvia said. "I know. Tonight, we're burying the past."

There was a pause as Sylvia and Andrés looked at their reflection on the black mirror of their phone, waiting for Elisa to respond.

"If we're burying the past," Elisa said, "you wanna know something messed up? This whole time, I'd been waiting for Andrés to say, 'Constance.'"

"For real? You're not joking?" Sylvia said.

"I'm not."

"I wish that tumor had been cancer," Andrés said.

"Don't be mad," Elisa said. "I was on top of the two of you, and it felt good. But we're burying the past, right? If he would've said it, I would've taken my foot off his neck. I would've taken it off both of your necks. For years, I was the Domme. You two were my Subs."

"That's not how any of this works. That's so fucked up!"

"Yeah, I know. It sounds horrible now that I think about it, but you were going to pull that bullshit move out west and take Daphne away."

"A frontal lobe thing? I get it," Sylvia said, standing up from the bed. "Now all I'm saying is don't get hooked on painkillers, or else I'm coming for Daphne and completing the set 'cause I've already got Andy. So you better stay motivated to get better, 'cause I'm waiting for that moment when you get hooked on drugs to put *my* foot on your neck."

A bright light pulsed from Sylvia's phone, showing an incoming call from Petra.

"I gotta go. Medusa's on line two." Sylvia looked at Andrés. "Please answer it. I can't..."

Andrés grabbed her phone from next to him and answered on speaker. "You're playing a dangerous game, *mother*."

Petra gasped, "Andrés?"

"That feeling," he said, standing up from the bed, "that uncertain feeling you had where you knew something was off—you had it, what, for an hour? Yes? That's what Sylvia's been feeling for years, and you told her she was crazy?"

"It is you! Thank God you're alive!"

"I've been alive all this time, and you treated me as if I were dead!"

"I have my reasons."

"I don't care!" Sylvia yelled.

"Wait, why are you together? How did you get together?" Petra asked.

"Because we are written in the stars," Andrés replied.

"I am his fate," Sylvia said.

There was silence as Sylvia and Andrés stared at their reflection again while waiting for Petra to respond.

"Are you there?" Andrés asked.

"I'm here," Petra said. "I knew this day was coming... I've prepared a story for this moment... It's about a broken warrior and a poet who was his fate."

Sylvia interrupted her. "Now's not the time for stories."

"If you two can keep your mouths shut for a moment and let me tell you their story, when I'm done, you two will understand... The Poet loved Anne Sexton and Pablo Neruda. She couldn't get enough of Anaïs Nin.

"One day, the Poet met the Broken Warrior at a gallery reading. He was twenty-three, powerful, and fearless—a Marine who had already served in Vietnam at Huế in 1968. The Broken Warrior listened to her and told her the poems she had read were beautiful. He saw her soul, and she saw his, and they fell in love.

"They had a baby boy, and she thought they would be happy forever, but the nightmares of Huế became too much for the Broken Warrior. Poetry wasn't the cure she had hoped it would be. It was no match for the darkness. His darkness—his anger—made her feel as if she were going to drown.

"All the Poet wanted to do was love the Broken Warrior, but she had to escape for her own good because she had a higher purpose— their son. Her higher purpose left no time or energy to fix the Broken Warrior. The Poet was not an empty cup into which he could pour all his trauma. It would have gotten in the way of the Poet being a mother. Andrés, that man is your father. There is so much of him in you, and all your life, I worked hard to bury that. It's in your nature to be like him."

"This is fucked up. This is so fucked up. Mom, I'm not him."

"Then why did Elisa have to call the cops on you after 9/11?"

"To build dirt on me—nothing else—so that if I ever took her to family court, I would have that against me. She was afraid I was gonna take Daphne away."

"Are you sure you didn't hit her? Because that's what she told me."

"Mama," Sylvia said, "I used to hit Andrés—throw punches at him—and he's never hit me back. Elisa was lying. She will tell you that now."

"I know what I know... Andrés is like his father: angry."

"That guy is not my father."

"Antonio may be your dad, but the Broken Warrior is in your flesh and blood."

Andrés paused before turning to Sylvia to ask, "Can I dance with Petra for a little bit? Before I smack down her bullshit? I promise I'm going somewhere with this."

"Make it quick," Sylvia said. "I don't want to dance anymore. Not with her."

Andrés focused on the phone as if he could see Petra through his own reflection on the black screen. "Mom, did you ever experience postpartum depression?"

"No," Petra replied.

Sylvia snickered. "Lucky you."

"Sylvia has, and I'm the asshole that left her behind to deal with it alone. Did you ever lose a baby?"

"You almost died."

"I'm here, so you have no clue. I left Sylvia behind to deal with the death of Athena alone." He turned to Sylvia. "Be honest... Are you still angry with me?"

"Yes."

"Why?"

"You know why. Don't bring me into this; this is your dance. I can't dance anymore."

Andrés returned his focus to the black screen. "Boys. Don't. Cry.

Remember that, Mom? Boys don't cry? Remember beating me up that night because I couldn't stop crying? Because I was terrified of nightmares? I was afraid of the dark?"

Petra was silent.

"You beat me with my fucking storybook! You yelled at me! Dad made me wear your panties! I was seven! 'Don't become Estefania!' That's what you yelled at me. Remember? You even called me by her dead name, you fucking asshole. I'm the asshole who watched Sylvia cry. I watched her beg me to cry—she was banging on my chest, begging me, screaming at me—because she felt so fucking alone. Like an asshole, I watched and held it in because the only voice I heard in my head was yours, saying, 'Crying is for faggots. Real men don't cry.' Fuck you, Petra. If I'm getting my anger from anyone, it's from you.

"And when I was in Berlin and Sylvia didn't call back, I thought she'd left me—I called her every night. I sent emails. I left voicemails that I'm sure you had erased. You erased everything! So yes, I'm angry! I was not a man! I failed at being a man when it mattered the most— being there for her! What man leaves his family behind? Me!"

Sylvia hunched closer to Andrés and yelled at the black screen, "I told you to tell him where I was, and you said you did!" She looked back at Andrés. "When they came to take me home from the hospital, I asked about you, and it was as if they didn't hear me. Like I wasn't there."

Petra was silent.

"Are you still there?" Sylvia asked.

"I'm still here."

"Did you hear any of that?"

"The call is clear. Go on with your tantrum. Get it out of your system."

Andrés shook his head. "You do this shit all the time."

"All the time," Sylvia said. "The silent treatment."

"I don't owe the two of you my attention," Petra said.

Andrés said to the black screen, "Fine, whatever. If you would've told me, I would've known she was safe. I wouldn't have freaked out, you know? You had information for me, Mom! I had called and asked about her. You made her think I loved drugs more than I loved her.

And by the time I wound up at her house, my thinking had already gone to mush, and I'd forgotten that I had every right to walk into her house and say I came back for her! Instead, my psychiatrist convinced me that Sylvia would've seen me as nothing more than a stalker!"

Petra laughed. "You see? What did I tell you? Anger."

"If anger is an issue for you, then why did you continue seeing this man?" Andrés asked.

"What are you talking about?"

"I know about Playtime. I know absolutely everything. You don't think I'd notice things, like how Dad would drop all of us off at Grandpa's on the weekends so you could be with *Tití* Estefania and *Tío* Victor while he worked double shifts? Then you'd disappear and leave me with Tony and *Tití*."

Sylvia laughed.

"Grandpa would point you out to me: 'Pay attention to what people do, not what they say...' You can say what you want, *Mother,* but do you think I didn't notice how the same guy would start appearing at family parties? And how he'd kind of look like me? Hanging out with you?"

Petra interrupted, "Wait a minute."

"He was at Grandpa's funeral. *Tití* Estefania—God, I miss her—she came right out and said it: 'That man right there, the cure and the cause for your mom. Too bad passion don't put food on the table or pay the rent, 'cause if it did, your father would be rich.' So this anger excuse is bullshit. You kept seeing my father for years."

"Please say nothing to your dad," Petra said.

"You have some fucking nerve lecturing me about what Andrés had with Elisa and me," Sylvia said. "At least we were all open about it—no one was sneaking around."

"My father died lonely because of his choices," Petra said.

"Grandpa chose to be alone!"

Sylvia cut in, "Andrés! We're not talking about the Old Man... Petra, enough with the deflecting. If you don't tell me right now why you did this to me, I'm going to call Antonio."

"Fine, I'm going to tell you, but I'm warning you—and when I say 'you,' I mean Andrés—don't interrupt me, because this isn't about you. I'm talking to Sylvia."

"Okay, Mom," Andrés said.

"Sylvia, if I had told you what happened to Andrés, you would've gone right back into the hospital. Surprises, right? If we had told Andrés what happened to you, he would've gone straight to you, and you would've become more anxious. Your focus would've shifted to him and not stayed on the person who was more important—you."

"But *Mama,*" Sylvia said, "I had a plan, and it was important to me."

"Yes, that plan. I remember that plan. I decided you couldn't start a new plan for your own good until you finished that Master Plan. You couldn't spend any more money on IVF. You couldn't take any more leaves of absence. You needed to make progress, or they would've dismissed you from the program for good.

"When I went to your apartment to clean it out, I read through your papers... Columbia had given you so much leeway when they allowed you back into the program, and you were this close to taking more than what they'd already given you. You had pushed their generosity enough—so it was your new plan or your father's Master Plan."

"Okay, but you didn't need to do that to Andrés. Don't you love your son?"

Petra didn't answer.

"Hello, can you hear me?" Sylvia asked.

"Now I can—what did you say?"

Sylvia became frustrated. "I said, 'You didn't need to do that to Andrés. Don't you love your son?'"

"*Mija,* I love him with everything in me, but it's different with sons than it is with daughters—and you've become my daughter too. Andrés has already gone as far as he could in life, but you have not. Am I still on speaker?"

"Yes, *Mama.*"

"Andrés?"

"Yes, Mom."

"Now, I'm talking to you. You brought Sylvia into the family. Did you not ask me a long time ago to look after her?"

"I did."

"When you worked overtime, what did I do?"

"You helped her with Andy while she would be studying."

"And when you started traveling, what did I do?"

Sylvia said to Petra, "Spend a lot of time with me."

"*Andrés,* I did as you asked; Sylvia is family. But the two of you became sick, and what was I to do? I love you, but I also love her. I didn't want you to be the reason she didn't make it—for what happened to you to be the reason for her failure. No! She had these goals before she met you.

"And I read *1968*—it was her father's last wish... I couldn't do that to her father or to her grandmother, who gave her everything a mother could give. That would be a tragedy not only for Sylvia but for that poor lady who, from what I've been told, sacrificed her life for Sylvia. *Mijo,* you know I'm right."

"You have a messed-up way of showing love," Sylvia said.

"Listen," Petra said. "Andrés is a good boy—and if he loves you, he knows I speak the truth. If he knows how important making something of yourself was to you, especially after what you told me happened to you and what you had to give up, he knows I speak the truth. He's not selfish."

"I'm not selfish, but this is fucked up," Andrés said. "If you truly knew Sylvia, you'd know just how much you lost her love."

"*Mama,*" Sylvia said, "you took away my power. You needed to trust me to make the right choices. I'm an adult, and that was not your choice to make—it was mine. Andrés and I were great at setting boundaries and talking things through. I think it was one of the best things about us."

Petra interrupted, "I see a lot of Estefania in you."

"Stop with that!" Andrés yelled. "You don't get to use her in this argument—especially after all the horrible things you said about her when you beat me up that night."

"I get to say and do what I want," Petra said, "especially since it was Victor and I who protected Estefania all her life. I see her in Sylvia—in the way she talked about the choices she made after Constance died, how she regretted them."

"I never said that," Sylvia said. "I would do things differently, but there's no regret. You're the one with regret. Anaïs Nin? Yeah, I lived the life you wanted. Let's face it."

"I'm going to ignore that because, obviously, the moment has become too much and has made you angry and emotional," said Petra.

Sylvia laughed and said under her breath, "If you were someone else..."

"Like I said, Estefania made a lot of bad choices. We didn't have our mother to guide us, and it killed my sister. Sylvia, you wanted me in your life like that? This was the deal. What would your mother and father have wanted? Your grandmother? In your head, can you hear her?"

Sylvia closed her eyes and nodded. "I can hear her."

"What is she saying?"

"She's saying you're right and that I'm hard-headed, as always. She's saying my dad had a master plan, and he gave up a lot to make sure he funded it."

"That's right! And you made it! Can't you see? If Andrés had been around, he would've distracted you! I mean, God did not place you in this world for anyone other than yourself. You do not exist for Andrés, just like he does not exist for you. Andrés made his choice, walked through that door, and got on the plane. He went through what he went through, but his suffering is his—just like you had already gone through yours way before he came into your life.

"No boundaries the two of you could have set could've protected you from seeing Andrés in the pain he was in when you had just come out of the hospital, after you wanted to kill yourself. Sylvia, *Mija*, you're not a cup Andrés pours his life into. You're not an empty cup; you are not an empty cup! You are you! Your cup was already filled—with you!"

"But this is my relationship, and I'm forty-six years old. These are my choices with him. It would've been my choice to take care of him if he were broken. Do you know how many years he's put into me because I've been broken? That's love.

"Andrés had been the one to tell me, my cup is my cup, and his cup is his cup. That's love. He's the one who reminded me I needed to do whatever I needed to do so that I wouldn't find myself on stage again, crying, like I'd done once before—to be on top of my shit. That's love.

"We used to fight because we weren't spending enough time with each other and needed more, but we would always work it out. Andrés would tell me everything I was doing—I was doing it for that girl on the stage. Do it for her. Go all the way. He said we would carve out our time together however we could, like Greece, like New Mexico. It made us hungry for each other, and it always brought us closer. And then we would fuck. Oh my God, we would fuck. The passion brought us closer. That's real love."

Petra laughed. "So many young people think passion is like love. No. Passion is overrated. This is real love—the letting go because you know real love will come back." She chuckled. "Yours is written in the stars..."

"Fuck you, Petra," Andrés said. "You're not gonna wrap this all up with some feel-good magic bullshit. I got on the plane because you and Pop programmed me to be a mindless-fucking provider. I should've followed my heart, stayed with her, and lost my job. No! I didn't make a choice to let go."

"Neither did I," Sylvia said.

"No one did any letting go."

"And I had a plan, and I still want that plan, but it's too late! There's no happy ending here."

"And don't forget," Andrés said, "we know your secret. You say one thing, but for years, you had your side dick. You needed passion."

"Petra, repeat after us," Sylvia said. "Passion is not overrated."

"Passion is love," Andrés said.

"Passion is every-fucking-thing. And you're in your comfortable home, judging us? You got to live a bit of that dangerous life with Andrés's father, with your Playtime, while Antonio, who made the choice to be his dad, worked long hours for that comfortable home you'd always wanted."

"Petra," Andrés said, "you're right... I am angry. I'm angry at God that our daughter died and that He's hurt Sylvia, who has known nothing but pain for most of her life. I'm angry at you—and I will be for the rest of my life—for hurting her. Mom, you don't understand.

What you did to her makes you no better than the monsters in Austin —the ones who took away her childhood."[1]

Sylvia grabbed Andrés, nearly knocking the phone out of his hand as she hugged him hard. "Thank you, thank you, thank you for sticking up for me! For being my witness."

After the hug, Andrés stepped back. He took a deep breath and swallowed the pain of what he was about to say: "Goodbye, Mom."

Sylvia took the phone from him and said, "Thank you, Petra, for everything, but you should've trusted me to make my own choices. I would've done the right thing for what I wanted—not what Constance or Wendell wanted when I was a kid. I love you, Petra, but when you made me question my own reality—when you hurt him—when you threw him away—you killed me. *Mama...* goodbye."

Sylvia ended the call.

---

1. *Book Two: Underworld,* "Chapter Ten: The Titans."

❧ 46 ❧

THE SAD TURTLES

[6]

SYLVIA AND ANDRÉS TURNED OFF THEIR PHONES AND TOSSED THEM onto the bed. She walked to the window, and Andrés followed. Snow blanketed the night in white. Random people wandered the empty street below. There was no traffic.

"Why do I feel like she was trying to get me to say, 'Thank you?'" Sylvia sighed. "I don't know how I feel about her anymore. She's done so much good, but I had a plan for us. I mean, I figured it out."

"What was the plan?" Andrés asked.

She shifted her focus from the window to look directly into his eyes. "To try again. We needed to try again, right? Try for another baby. But it's too late. It's too late now."

Sylvia turned back to the window, staring blankly at the white night as if lost in thought. "I haven't been back here since that night... I need to take back that night—I need to take back this space. Let's take a walk."

"But you'll catch a cold," Andrés said.

Sylvia looked back at him and smiled. "We only live once. Besides, it'll be like old times when we used to play in the snow. We can take back that memory too. We can place it here." She clutched her chest, as if grabbing her heart. "That's good nostalgia."

Sylvia and Andrés dressed in damp socks and shoes, pulled on their wet coats, left the hotel room, and stepped outside.

They ran up snow-covered streets, Sylvia laughing out loud as Andrés chased her. They stopped running and wandered along the avenues of the Lower East Side until they found themselves in front of what used to be Robots.

It was gone.

A hookah shop and an ATM had replaced the old storefront entrance.

Andrés patted Sylvia on her behind and said, "Tag, you're it."

Sylvia chased Andrés through the snow, running up the streets. A scattering of cars struggled to make their way along the avenue. She caught up to him in front of what was once The Loft.

It was gone.

A chain coffee shop had taken its place.

Sylvia began choking up with sadness.

Andrés grabbed her hand and led her away.

Together, they walked through the blinding snow. Sylvia coughed, and Andrés pulled her closer, huddling against her for warmth.

In the distance, the chains on the tires of city sanitation trucks rumbled as they plowed the snow off the streets.

An iron gate lining the outskirts of Tompkins Square Park came into view. Sylvia led Andrés around it and onto Avenue A. They continued until they were back in front of their old apartment building.

They sat on the snow-covered staircase. Across the street, the playground where Andy and Daphne used to play stood empty.

Sylvia and Andrés looked up at the window of what was once their home.

"I told you what my plan was. What was yours? You came back in September." Sylvia looked back down at Andrés. "What was next?"

Andrés looked at her. "Do you want to do this?"

"Yes, I need to know what could've been."

Andrés sighed. "We would've tried again. If I had landed that gig, we would've moved into a new apartment. I would've picked up more experience and found a better job that didn't leave me at Paul's mercy. I'd be home with you and our kids."

"You're talking as if it didn't happen. We know there's no happy ending here. Had I known the truth, what was your plan? What was next?"

Andrés paused. "We would've reunited and reconciled. I would've told you I wanted to try again too. You would've had our baby. I would've worked out a shared custody agreement with Elisa—on paper. She would've gotten her happy ending. We would've gone back to being civil with each other, with clear boundaries. We would've bought a house where Andy and Daphne would've lived with us. I would've been a stay-at-home dad to our baby and raised our child while you, Dr. Sylvia Hadid James, became who you were born to be because you would've succeeded. I would've made sure of it.

"We would've had a special room. We would've faced our challenges, had our fights, and grown closer. I would've never melted down and sunk into the depression and despair that I did, thinking you were out there calling my name and the only place I could get to you was in my dreams. I would've been awake, active, and fit. I would've been by your side every step of the way, supporting your choices, protecting you every moment because I would've never allowed anything to bring you pain. Just joy. I think that's the life we would've had."

"I think you're right," Sylvia said. "Do you know what I also think? I think you should've just kept your fucking mouth shut that night in Chicago and not played Captain Save-A-Ho. If you had, I would've had you. I would've had all of us together.

"Paul wouldn't have exiled you to New Mexico. He would've never sent you to Berlin because he thought it was funny to keep you away from your family after Athena died. Maybe we'd have her.

"You know, sometimes I wonder if the stress of flying cross-country to join you did something to Athena. Maybe this is your fault. This is your fucking fault, and it's not all on me. If I hadn't gotten on a plane and followed you across the country—and lived at such a high altitude —maybe Athena would still be alive?

"I don't know. I'm trying to make sense of it. Athena felt fine. I did everything right. I never missed an appointment. I ate right. I exercised. The only thing about me was my past and drugs. So it's got to be my fault, right?"

"No, it's not," Andrés said. "Maybe it's mine. I was exposed to depleted uranium. You know what that does."

"I do."

"All that radiation, all that smoke, and other shit my body absorbed. We made our baby. If you're thinking this way, throw the blame on me."

"But this is my fault. I should've listened to common sense and never given up the apartment. I should've stayed in New York, but I was so driven to follow you that I left Andy and Daphne behind. What kind of mother am I?"

"You're the best—"

"Stop! I don't need you bullshitting me! I left them behind! Maybe God saw something in me that could've left Athena behind just as easily—that I took Her gift for granted, that I considered you more than my own children! You were a big boy who could've done without me out there. I'm a big girl. I've had to learn how to sleep without a nightlight. This is our fault."

Andrés paused, looking at the ground. "Maybe."

"Maybe?"

Andrés looked back up at her. "Sometimes, people die because they die. We don't know. We can't know. Look at us. We'll never know."

Sylvia looked up at the night sky. It was white. The snow was falling hard. "It's God's fault... Orion..."

Andrés sighed. "Orion..."

Sylvia looked back at Andrés. "I would give up everything I've earned for a chance at that life—the one that could've been before you opened your fucking mouth and checked Paul. But I can't be mad at you for that. It's my fault too. You know me, and you love everything about me."

"I love everything. I couldn't let that go."

"I know. And I'm glad you couldn't—that you're the kind of man who couldn't let that go. I mean, I needed someone like you at that time in my life. It would've made the difference. I would've completed the Master Plan a lot sooner. I hope what you did made a difference for Estrella."

"I hope so too, but... you know the truth."

"I know... and it's why I'm still mad because it probably didn't make a difference for her. She is not me, which is why you should've kept your mouth shut. From now on, keep your mouth shut and only think of us. Understand? You're done saving people—I'm the last one. I'm the only one. You got that, Soldier Boy? You understand? I'm the only one."

"Always will be," Andrés said.

"I think I'm done being angry. Any last words? For Athena? I've done my crying."

Andrés was silent.

Sylvia wrapped her arms around him and whispered, "I'm sorry for attacking you on stage that night with my poem.[1] I think that's why you closed up, and it's my fault."

Andrés was silent for a long moment.

"It's okay. You're safe with me. I promise."

"I can't believe Athena went just like that. I held her, and she was moving, and she opened her eyes and looked into mine, then closed her eyes and was gone."

"She looked at you? She got to see you?"

"It's all I remember of her. Her eyes..."

Sylvia broke down and cried.

"She would've been eight," Andrés said.

"Can you imagine?"

"I can..."

Sylvia paused. "I like to think she's out there—that Athena was an old soul reborn, and her being here, even for a second, was a rare miracle. Like the Buddha's blind turtle."

Andrés broke down and cried. "The turtle."

"Kalpa... Oh, my beautiful little Kalpa... She was my reminder that my being here, alive, was a great miracle too. Like Andy and Daphne,

---

1. *Book Three: The Labyrinth*, "Chapter Twenty-Five: The Minotaurs."

like Myra—Athena is a miracle. Since she died, I don't want to be here anymore. I'm tired."

"Me too... but I have to be here, and if I have to be here, you have to be here with me. So, feel my back."

Sylvia hugged Andrés, running her hands up and down his back.

Andrés whispered, "Doesn't it feel hard, like a turtle shell?"

Sylvia laughed. "Yes, you idiot."

"Your being here is precious to me. You're my rare miracle."

Sylvia whispered, "You're mine too."

"We have to move on. It's why I didn't go after Paul; he has daughters. I can't hurt them like he'd hurt ours. I have to be the one to end the cycle. No more violence. No more pain—I can't lose my soul anymore."

"No more. We have to end this loop. Oh God—Athena, old soul, we have to go."

"We have to go. Until we meet again."

"Until we meet again, my love," Sylvia said.

Together, they got up and made the long walk back to their hotel, crying every step of the way. Once in their room, they stopped crying, undressed out of their wet clothes, and climbed into bed together.

Andrés played with her hair and smiled down at her. "Goodnight, Sylvia."

Sylvia looked up at him and smiled. "Goodnight, Andrés."

It was the end of the longest night of their lives. For the first time since June 25, 2001, Sylvia and Andrés had an uninterrupted night of sleep with no bad dreams.

❧ 47 ❧

ELYSIUM

MARCH 6, 2009

When Sylvia and Andrés woke up Monday morning, they decided to focus on obtaining the marriage license as soon as possible, and that she was going to take personal time off from work to help him settle in.

"This is a major life event, and it's time for me to have a life. I'll call later today, talk to my assistants, and make all the arrangements," Sylvia said.

By late afternoon, they decided the roads appeared safe enough to drive and checked out of the hotel. They drove their cars out of the nearby garages, with Andrés following Sylvia up the long, slippery roads until it was night. He pulled into the driveway behind her car.

When they got out, Andrés reminded Sylvia of what they had discussed.

"We're going to act like Andy didn't work to keep us apart."

"It's behind us," she said. "The loop is closed."

Sylvia led Andrés from the driveway to the door of their home. Inside the family room, she pointed at the three large, framed pictures hanging on the wall.

"Look," she said.

The first picture, taken during Sylvia's first visit to New York, showed Wendell—his face haggard and gaunt—hugging his smiling daughter in a yellow sundress, with the bronze statue of Atlas at Rockefeller Center looming above and behind them.

The second picture, taken during Sylvia's last visit to Virginia, showed a looming Constance hugging her smiling granddaughter from behind. Constance was wearing a gold head wrap; her lipstick was a bold red, her eyes bright. With her chin held high, as if staring at death, her expression seemed to say, "You're not taking me without a fight."

The third picture, taken during Sylvia's maternity photoshoot at the crest of the Sandia Mountains in Albuquerque, showed Andrés— his face bright—hugging his smiling fiancée from behind. The light of the setting sun loomed behind them, making their bodies glow with a golden aura. Sylvia was wearing a golden maternity sundress with a crown of sunflowers heaped upon her curly auburn hair; her lipstick was a bold red, her eyes bright. With her head tilted to the side, signaling her comfort and joy, her expression seemed to say, "I'm on top of the world."

"These were the first things I put up when I bought the house with the money I earned writing *your* story. I told you I was going to get me some payback," Sylvia said.

They both laughed, and that's when Andy came downstairs. He looked uneasy seeing his father for the first time since the doctor's appointment in 2004.

"Damn, you look different," Andy said.

"Is that all you've got to say?"

"You're not fat."

"Come here," Andrés said, reaching out to pull his son into a long hug. "I've missed you."

"I've missed you too."

"You did a great job taking care of Mom. I'm proud of you."

"You are? You're not mad at me?"

"For what?" Andrés asked.

"I don't know."

Andrés released his son. "Don't worry about it. Everything is good."

Sylvia placed her hand on Andy's shoulder. "Dad is here to stay."

"Does that mean Daphne is moving here too?" Andy asked.

"No—her life is on Long Island," Andrés replied.

"Thank God. I was worried about that."

"Wait—you were worried?" Sylvia said, surprised. "What if I want to move her here? You don't have a problem with that, do you?"

Andy said nothing.

Sylvia's face turned red. "When you live on your own, you get to decide who lives in your space. This space belongs to me, and it has always belonged to Dad. Look who is on that wall—the Titans. As much as I love you, you are not on that wall." Sylvia laughed to herself. "This was never about taking care of me."

"Mom, wait—"

"No. I don't want to talk to you anymore. This conversation is over. You need to leave this space right now."

"But Mom."

"What did I teach you about no? When someone says it, they mean it. Now go."

"Yes, Mom."

Andy went back upstairs. All that could be heard was the door to his room slamming shut.

That was the welcome Andrés received upon his return to the small house in Red Hook. By crossing the boundary, it truly became his home.

Sylvia and Andrés spent the week personalizing the spaces they would share. Sylvia had two small rooms she kept empty. One was a white room with a golden urn containing Athena's ashes on a pedestal. The original purpose of the room had been for a new baby, but it was too late. That empty room was now held in reserve, should Daphne ever need it.

They began converting the other empty room into their personal playroom, a room that would be kept hidden under lock and key from everyone living or visiting the home. Sylvia and Andrés had decided that what they did together as a square couple in the bedroom needed to be separate from what they did together in their dynamic. Sylvia and Andrés remembered how, when they lived in the city, Andy and Daphne would climb into bed with them to watch TV. Knowing what went on there when they were alone made them cringe as parents. Going into another space would help them forget they were older—and still parents. Their bedroom might not only see future late-night check-ins from their now-grown children but perhaps grandchildren as well.

As Sylvia said while they were painting their playroom red, "We needed to do this—compartmentalize our kinks into a space devoted to it. I don't want our grandchildren to know this about us."

On Thursday, Sylvia and Andrés drove to the south shore of Long Island, where Andrés unlocked the doors to his other home.

When Sylvia saw Elisa in bed, groggy and out of it, she said, "Oh, hell no," and rushed to her side.

Andrés followed, asking, "Where's Myra?"

"She has her own life," Elisa replied.

"What about you? What about your life? What are you doing to take care of it?" Sylvia asked.

"I have my pills—wait, why are you here?"

Sylvia's expression shifted from concern to annoyance. "I came to see Daphne, but I wasn't expecting to see you like this. I meant what I said. It's up to you—stay motivated, or I'm taking her. You laugh and think I'm joking, but I'm not. Whatever you need to do to make sure I don't follow through, do it. Because you look like shit, and this is the last time Andrés comes here and we do this."

Andrés and Sylvia pulled Elisa out of bed. They gave her a bath and cleaned her up. Once they were done helping Elisa get dressed, they all sat together in the family room, waiting for Daphne to get home from school. When she arrived, Daphne looked surprised to see her dad—not haggard, but well-dressed and clean-shaven—sitting between her mother and the woman she had called, when she was younger, the "beautiful lady who had her little sister in her belly."

"Hi, Dad—hello, Andy's mom," she said.

Sylvia and Andrés exchanged confused looks.

Daphne laughed. "You assholes didn't think my brother would talk to me? That he wouldn't tell me everything? We've been texting each other almost every day—I'm not stupid. I kept my mouth shut—I don't want to move to New Mexico! I don't want to move upstate! I like it here with my mom. My mom is better than you!"

Sylvia glanced at Elisa.

"The girl talk was not long—she wanted to keep her dad here too. We all wanted the same thing: for him not to pull a 'Wendell' and bounce on us, but I messed that up too," Elisa said.

"I don't know why I told you anything about my father—my family."

Elisa laughed. "Because you love to hear yourself talk."

Sylvia sighed and turned to Daphne. "Since you know everything, then you know?"

"Yeah, Andy told me. Get married. I don't care what you assholes do... Mom, can I go to my room? I have a lot of homework to do."

"Go on ahead."

"Thanks... Bye, Dad—goodbye, Andy's mom." Daphne walked away, heading upstairs.

"What a cunt," Sylvia said.

"She called us assholes," Andrés said.

Sylvia pointed at Elisa. "Daphne lumped you in with us."

"I guess she did. I don't blame her. This is my fault—she used to talk about you a lot, about how you had her little sister in your belly. She'd say, 'Where did she go?' I spent years telling her you didn't exist. Our girl talk was her yelling at me for making her question her reality." Elisa put her hands on her face. "Fuck my psycho phase. She knew I'd been lying. She'd been going through my stuff for whatever reason and found that picture I had of you holding her in the park. You'd become extra real to her since then."

"That's karma for you," Sylvia said.

Daphne came back downstairs. "I didn't go to my room."

"I knew you wouldn't. Come sit over here with the rest of the adults," Sylvia said.

Daphne did as she was asked, taking a seat on one side of Sylvia while Andrés sat on the other. She glanced awkwardly at Sylvia, who smiled down at her.

"I'm sorry for calling you a cunt," Sylvia said.

Daphne sighed. "It's okay. You're kind of a cunt too."

Sylvia grabbed Andrés's hand to signal him not to react, then said, "I can be, and that's okay. I enjoy making men call me that. It means I made them mad, and they can't do anything about it. I'm in their head."

"I like that."

"Good. Now tell us what you know."

"Andy didn't want me to be surprised by what you assholes were doing. I think I was eight when he started telling me everything, but he made me promise not to say anything because if I did, Dad would move me upstate, or he would've moved us all to New Mexico. Is that true?"

Sylvia paused, the weight of her dreams' consequences finally hitting her. "It would've been selfish for us to do that. You would've stayed with Mom because she is great, and Dad and I wouldn't have moved out west."

"That's a relief. It's a big surprise to see my dad with another woman. Then that woman takes him far away from me and—"

"Leave you behind?" Sylvia asked.

"Yeah."

"I would've never done that to you." Sylvia looked at Elisa. "I'm sorry. I'm sorry for everything."

"I'm sorry for everything too," Elisa replied.

Sylvia turned to Daphne. "Did Andy tell you everything, everything?"

Daphne looked down. "Yeah."

"Do you have questions?"

Daphne looked up at Sylvia. "It's just weird how my mom and dad lived with each other but weren't together. You and my dad didn't live with each other but *are* together. You're my brother's mom, but you're not his mom, 'mom.' What does this make me?"

Sylvia said, "You're my kid too, like you're your mom's daughter. Life is weird, and love is big and fucked up, but it's also so beautiful, and we're here. And I asked your dad to bring me down because I had made a promise to you. But now... I'm checking on your mom because

I think she's going through something I went through, and that's what you do when you share experiences. And, like I said when I last held you, 'until we meet again,' I came back. Here I am. Like I promised. I came back, and I wanted to show you the respect you deserve as the number one woman in Dad's life. I wanted to make sure it was okay with you. I'm asking you in front of your mom. Is it okay if Dad and I get married?"

"Do you need me to say yes?"

"I think so. If you don't like me now, we can work on becoming friends. I could never replace your mom, but do you remember? In the playground, and I would say, 'Touch my belly?'"

"I remember."

"Do you remember Mom bringing you in a stroller to us, and you would stay, and we would all watch TV in bed—Dad would be home?"

"I remember."

"That's me! I'm home to you, too. And Mom was a big part of that —we helped her, and she helped us. We were all family once. We can be again. Do you give your blessing?"

"Yes."

"Can I give you a hug?" Sylvia asked.

"Of course, you cunt."

Sylvia laughed and gave Daphne a big hug.

"I'm so glad you're real—that I didn't imagine you."

"Me too." Sylvia turned to Elisa. "Is it okay if we bring her back with us tonight? We're having our ceremony at the town court in the morning, and we always imagined the kids would be our witnesses."

"You can keep her if you want, but have her back by Sunday night."

"Daphne, is that okay with you? Will you be our witness?"

"Yes."

When Daphne arrived at Sylvia and Andrés's home upstate, she was happy to see her brother for the first time since 2003. She appeared taken aback by just how much of a life her father had that she hadn't known about. Looking at the maternity portrait on the wall, Daphne said, "It looks like you were living in a dream. Where was I? Did you think of me when this picture was being taken?"

"Don't worry, they weren't thinking of me either. You're not the only one. They left me behind with Lydia. It was all about her—it was always about Athena," Andy said.

Sylvia and Andrés walked away as the two continued to talk. For Andy and Daphne, Athena was an abstract thought—alive only in concept. They never got to hold her the way Sylvia and Andrés had before giving Athena back to the hospital staff. Andy had only ever known Athena as ashes in a small golden urn in the White Room. The loop was now closed—no more crying.

On Friday morning, Sylvia and Andrés were at the town court, with Daphne and Andy standing at their sides as witnesses to the exchanging of vows. After the ceremony, they all returned home. Once alone, Sylvia led Andrés into their playroom. Before closing the door and reconfirming the boundaries of their play, Sylvia said, "Now's the time. Tell me what happened to Caleb. I have spousal immunity."

Andrés shared everything that had happened the day he *handled* Caleb. That day, Andrés had told Sylvia he needed to go back to the VA hospital. The red bumps that had been sporadically appearing on his face had opened into lesions. Instead of going with him as she had wanted, he encouraged Sylvia to take that time to visit friends. Andrés spent the afternoon out of sight, tracking Caleb from a distance. By then, Caleb had become unrecognizable; his obsession with stalking Sylvia—the apparent singular focus driving him to hover just outside her awareness—had led him to abandon himself entirely, transforming him into someone who looked like one of the homeless loitering in the park.

From a distance, Andrés followed Caleb as he tracked Sylvia through the Lower East Side. Sylvia, doing as Andrés had suggested, was visiting Reginald, who was privately battling HIV. When Sylvia entered Reginald's apartment building, Caleb went into a nearby discount store and came out with a ski mask and rope in an almost-clear plastic bag. Andrés didn't need to guess Caleb's intent. He went on to tell Sylvia how he sprang into action.

Sylvia smiled, taking pleasure in hearing the gory details—especially how Andrés had called his long-estranged cousin, his uncle Victor's son, who, like their grandfather, remained connected to the criminal underworld, to help dispose of the body. It was the same way their grandfather had called up his connections to dispose of Carmen, the cousin's mother.

It wasn't until the day before Andrés had gone to Caffè Reggio with Sylvia that he received confirmation from his cousin: no trace of Caleb remained.

The family that had taken Sylvia in as one of their own had made Caleb disappear.

"I know you must think I'm twisted," Sylvia said, "but you already know Caleb was my dealer. What you didn't know was that he had stopped taking my money. He wanted sex instead. He'd say, 'Why the fuck not? This way, we'd cut out the middleman. You give me all your money anyway. It's not like you give a shit, right?' I did give a shit, but —in my not-so-sane way of thinking—I told myself it didn't matter. I'd give him what he wanted, but first, I needed to get my fix.

"He must've laced the heroin with something. I swear it was fentanyl. I never injected; I always snorted. And the moment I did, I knew it was different. It was going to kill me. In fact, I know it killed me. But somehow, I came back. I woke up on the floor in my poop and with a gash on my forehead. I got checked out at the hospital, and apparently, shitting on myself is what saved me from Caleb." Sylvia paused. "I couldn't tell you that when we first met—not the whole story. I'm sorry."

Andrés grabbed and hugged her. "You could've told me everything, and it wouldn't have made a difference to me. I think I would've gotten rid of Caleb sooner."

Sylvia pushed Andrés away to look at him. "I was keeping him close, letting him linger—planning a solution myself to *handle* him— but then you happened. You came into my life." Sylvia laughed. "God answers prayers."

Andrés laughed along with her before locking the door to their new playroom.

Friday night came, and Sylvia and Andrés left Andy and Daphne at home to eat takeout and play video games. The newlyweds were heading out for a brief honeymoon in the city.

For two hours, Sylvia drove until she pulled up in front of a boutique hotel in Manhattan's Meatpacking District, rising high above an old warehouse along 10th Avenue.

With a mischievous smile, Sylvia asked, "Does this place look familiar to you? Imagine a row of taxis dropping people off, the door queen rejecting them before they even got close to her."

"No, you've got to be kidding me," Andrés said, laughing.

"Yup. We have made our return. But instead of going down into The Labyrinth, this time we're going up."

Valets rushed over to help Sylvia and Andrés out of their car, parking it for them as they entered the hotel. They stepped into an elevator and rode it to the penthouse floor, which had been converted into a nightclub called Elysium. The elevator doors slid open, and they walked onto the dance floor. Red laser lights shot from the corners, reflecting off a giant strobe mirror ball hanging from the ceiling. Soulful grooves blared through the sound system, with everyone swaying about the space of the dance floor, their faces illuminated by the glow of their phones.

"It's not the same, but it'll do," Sylvia said. "At least we're still surrounded by junkies chasing dragons. That'll never change. Let me put that up as a status. Not."

Andrés laughed, and the two closed their eyes and danced. They smiled as they lost themselves in the groove for what seemed like a moment but turned out to be hours—until Sylvia's cough broke the magic spell of the dance.

Andrés opened his eyes.

In her hand was mucus, speckled with blood.

Sylvia gave Andrés a long, worried look.

Rather than let her mind spiral over what that meant, Andrés pulled her close, bringing her back into the moment of joy.

"Hey," she said, laughing in his arms.

"Hey, what?" he replied.

She relaxed her body and smiled. "I don't know you like that, to be pulling me."

"What the fuck are you talking about? You had me checking you for hemorrhoids our first night together."

Sylvia laughed. "What the hell was wrong with me back then? Oh right, I was trying to fuck with you."

"You had issues."

"No... I was testing you... I was always testing, and nothing phased you. Holy shit, and it felt like I'd never see you again, but I have a secret..."

Sylvia paused, her eyes signaling the moment for a great revelation.

"I knew I'd see you again, like this, healthy," she said. "It was not a matter of 'if,' but 'when.' I can't explain it, but I knew this moment would come. The hardest part was living through 2,785 days of pain just to get here, to our Sixth Memory Loop. I counted each stage of our lives together, starting that night when you met Spacer Woman. We've lived through five memory loops. The last one started when you got on the plane. And throughout that time we were apart, I played the memories we'd created together over and over in my head—on a loop. It was my personal TV station. I had nothing else. It was so painful."

"It was so painful—I gave up," Andrés said.

"But I didn't. You don't see the world as I do. I'm a watcher. I'm always looking for signs, and all the signs were there, saying not to give up on love. Not to give up on the vision I had, where I'd seen us, here, on the other side of night. Here, like this, with you dressed and healthy, and me happy. I used to think it was déjà vu. I can't explain it; I have to show you."

Sylvia led Andrés off the dance floor, through the open-air patio entrance, and out to the railing. The night sky over lower Manhattan stretched endlessly, the stars shining brighter than the city lights.

"What do you see?" Sylvia asked.

Andrés paused. "A hole in the skyline."

She smiled. "I see us as we were that morning."

"I've played that day—that weekend—over and over in my head."

"Like a loop?"

Andrés chuckled. "Yes, like a loop."

Sylvia turned away from Andrés, staring wistfully at the hole in the skyline.

"What I see now is me, as I was—a scared young woman, looking up from the observation deck of the South Tower, saying a silent prayer to the tenement sky, wondering if she should make the leap and accept that feeling that was developing between her and the young man she had taken home the night before—of unconditional love, unconditional acceptance. I can see her now—this is not déjà vu. That day you brought me up there, God had shown me our future, and I had to trust... I had to hold on."

Sylvia stepped away from Andrés, looking up at the vast night, her gaze fixed as if mesmerized by a spirit in the sky. Tears streamed down her face, and her voice trembled with joy.

"God... that morning, I made a wish. I said a prayer. And You gave me all the signs I would need on my journey to now. Even signs I was not expecting... that I did not want to see. I did not want to experience, but I held on. God, I held on, and I was angry at You for so long —but not anymore.

"I now understand Your plan for me: pain is a gift, too.

"God, I would not know this joy if You had not shown me those dark nights. Now, because of what You put me through, I know real love. I know I'm unbreakable. I will never be scared again, ever in my life. Thank You, God, for granting me my wish. You have answered my prayers."

The wind howled, as if the Divine were responding. The stars shone even brighter.

Sylvia looked back down at where the towers once stood. Suddenly, she jumped for joy, spotting something in the beyond, and began waving furiously as if trying to get its attention.[1]

She yelled into the distance, as though yelling across time and space, "Emma! Don't be scared! It'll be okay! Go for it!

"There's magic in the world!

"Just believe, Emma!

"Believe!"

---

1. *Book One: Orpheus*, "Chapter Eight: Tenement Sky."

THE FURIES

Stop the murder and the suicide!
All's well!
I am the Guard

— JACK KEROUAC

48

NEMESIS

In Our beginning is Our end.

And in that space before Our coming through that cosmic yoke—where We would ultimately enter the Master Loop that Sylvia Hadid James and Andrés de León would become bound to, Their Eternal Return to become Us, again and again—We watch.

We are bound in Our duties bestowed, upon Us by the Highest Light of the Universe, to observe—at key times dictated by prayers—quantum particles, so that in Our observing, We force them to take a definitive state instead of existing in multiple possibilities at once.

The God of Abraham is the God of the Quantum Realm, and if We are not watching for God, there is no such thing as divine justice. The Furies must always be on guard, always watching. And We, in that capacity, watch specifically Their Eternal Return—looping through the memories of Sylvia, when she was in her catatonic state while hospitalized, seeing what has passed and what will be—so that even through her point of view, that specific, definite state of the quantum particles needed to get Andrés to that spot in the desert—where the land is flat and the desert landscape glows gold—will come to pass because it must.

And in her catatonic state, Sylvia watched, sorting those states in

Memory Loops—the first of which began on May 17, 1986, when Andrés threw his body on hers as bullets whizzed past them in the dark.

The Second Memory Loop began when Andrés met Sylvia again at The Loft on September 11, 1992.

The Third Memory Loop began on March 6, 1993—the day after Sylvia and Andrés broke up—so that she could discover firsthand that fame was not what she thought it would be. She was meant to do more with her life than become just another self-absorbed spoken-word poet.

And that moment came on April 12, 1997, when she ran into the coffee shop after being assaulted to find Andrés there, set to read a poem. Because of Our watching, We brought into existence that specific state—a moment that lovers and believers in magic would call serendipity—what We know as the Fourth Memory Loop.

And that family life they had built in that Loop came to an end when Andrés got on the plane to leave her behind on July 15, 2001—the beginning of the Fifth Memory Loop.

It is in that Loop Sylvia hospitalized herself because of what Andrés had done, leading to their great separation that ended on March 1, 2009, when they were reunited—kicking off the start of the Sixth Memory Loop.

Three years, two months, and sixteen days into that Loop, Sylvia and Andrés were at home when an early morning phone call woke them. She answered. The call came from an unknown profile through one of his social media apps. A video window opened, and on the other end was Alene. She was thin and pale, her red hair styled in a pixie cut. Alene's startled expression made it clear she hadn't expected anyone but Andrés to answer.

"Who are you?" she asked.

"You know who I am," Sylvia replied.

Alene smiled. "Ah, yes—*the girlfriend.*"

"No, *the wife.*"

"Wife?"

"He should've told you we were engaged, but he didn't know what was going on with us—and calling me his girlfriend was his way of coping."[1]

"By dancing with me?"

Sylvia gave an evil laugh. "I'm so glad I did what I did. You couldn't leave him alone; you had to keep stalking him."

"Wait a minute? I know who you are! You're on TV!"

"Bye."

"Wait," Alene said. "Don't hang up. I'm sorry; I know I fucked up. My husband just left me."

"So? Who gives a fuck?"

Alene appeared to force herself to cry. "I know I deserve it, but my boys don't deserve to pay for my mistakes."

"Fuck you, that's the consequence."

"I know, but my boys are asking questions, like, 'Why don't we look like *Papa?*' Please don't punish my boys for what I've done. They're innocent. I'm going to tell them the truth. I just wanted to tell Andrés not to be surprised if my boys come looking for him when they're older. We all want to know where we came from, but make no mistake —they already have a *papa.*"

In the background, Andrés woke up.

"I know about the boys," Sylvia said, motioning for Andrés to remain out of view of the video call. "He tells me everything, and I don't believe you. You still want a chance and not to *take* it from him like you had done, but every time you track him down, you take something more. So, I have one question, and I hate that you're making me go there, but did you fuck anyone else at the Love Parade?"

Alene looked away.

"I'm going to presume that's a yes. Because I don't want *my* Andrés to feel any more pain from that day, I need you to say right now that, without a DNA test, those boys are not his. Say it! Because if you don't, I'll get those same lawyers who fucked up your marriage to bring about more pain. If you recognize me and have seen me on TV, then you know how far my reach goes. I have an apolitical client list that spans the United States and Europe, and they love that I've put my

---

1. *Book One: Orpheus*, "Chapter Two: Meet Her at the Love Parade."

specialty to good use for them—I make monsters eat bullets. I make monsters *end* themselves. And you're a monster to Andrés, and you're a monster to me, and I will fucking bankrupt you and make you end yourself if you don't say it—"

"Okay, Andrés is not the father!"

"Say it one more time."

"Andrés is not the father of my twins!"

"That's my good girl."

Sylvia ended the call and dropped the phone on the bed. She looked at Andrés.

"I knew she was going to call."

"What did you do?" he asked.

"I'm not saying—you handled Caleb your way, I'm handling Alene mine. By the time I'm done with her, she'll feel like I've chopped her up into pieces and scattered her body all over Berlin." Sylvia laughed. "I guess I learned that specialty from you."

Andrés smiled. "I knew your aura was starting to seem off."

"What did I tell you a long time ago? I can be evil. Alene's gonna find out the hard way. There's more to come."

"Well... I can't go back to sleep."

"Might as well start the day," Sylvia said. "This semester's been one long shitshow, and today's gonna be awful, but thank God it's ending."

"I'll start breakfast. Boiled or scrambled?"

"Today, I want my eggs scrambled... Can you make me some toast?"

"Sure thing, my love."

"And remember: routine, routine, routine. We can't get lost in our feelings."

"I know, I'm trying not to."

"The only time we need to worry about Andy is if a chaplain comes looking for us, okay? Otherwise, he's fine."

"Okay. Routine."

Sylvia paused.

"What's the matter?" Andrés asked.

"I can't help but put myself in Constance's frame of mind... This is what she *was* feeling in 1968." Sylvia grabbed a notepad from her nightstand and began writing.

Andrés got up from bed and went into the bathroom. He came back with a spirometer.

"Did you get it?" he asked.

"I did."

"Good—you know the drill. Blow."

"Do you want me to give you a blow job?"

Andrés laughed. "Emma, focus."

"Alright."

She grabbed the end piece, inserted it into her mouth, and blew as hard as she could.

"That's my good girl. Amazing, as always," he said.

"I feel like passing out, as always."

"The numbers are solid."

Andrés placed the spirometer on her nightstand and extended his hands so she could grab them and pull herself off the bed to stand.

"Take your time; I'll meet you downstairs," he said.

"No, stay, please." Sylvia trudged into the bathroom.

Andrés followed and helped lower her onto the toilet.

"My joints feel all achy. I don't want to get stuck here," she said.

"I've fallen asleep on the toilet."

Sylvia smiled. "It sounds like I skipped the best parts of being with you. I wish I could've been there."

"Emma, the loops are closed."

"Yeah, yeah, I'm just saying."

Sylvia finished her business, and Andrés helped clean her up, then grabbed her from underneath her arms and helped her stand.

"You good?" Andrés asked.

"I think so. I think I'm going back to bed. You can start your morning if you want," Sylvia said.

"I'm coming back to bed with you."

"Then don't worry about breakfast."

Sylvia and Andrés washed up, then Andrés followed Sylvia out of the bathroom and helped her to bed. He climbed in and wrapped the comforter around their bodies. She backed up against him so that her cold feet could rest on his.

"I've got something to tell you," Sylvia said. "The department chair asked if I'd considered going on disability—like taking a long-term leave of absence. Use that time to see if I can get better."

"Have you considered it?"

"I have."

"And?"

"I've worked hard to get here, but..."

"But, what?"

"I don't want it anymore. It's not what I thought it would be."

"What do you want?" Andrés asked.

"I want to write. I don't want to feel tired all the time." She turned in bed to look at him. "What do you think?"

"Are you a writer or a professor?"

Sylvia rolled onto her back and stared at the ceiling for a long while.

"I'm a writer," she said.

"Then take the leave of absence. You can go back to your job when you feel better."

Sylvia paused. "I'm going to shut down my consulting work too. Would that be okay?"

"You don't need my permission. It's your business; those are your clients. You can always start over when you want. The clinic will run fine on its own—I'll see to that. Don't worry."

"Okay, that's what I'm going to do. I can use the time to write my book. I'm going to need that time."

"There you go," Andrés said.

"The leave and disability would be a lot like yours. I'd keep my position and office. I'd still have my privileges, whatever the hell that means. The thing is, will you be okay if I'm not working?"

Andrés chuckled. "Do you forget who you're talking to?"

"No, I mean, will you get tired of having me around you all the time?"

"Stop, stop; we went through so much to have this. No! I will never get tired—this is the dream. If I could spend every second of the rest of my life with you, that's what I would do. I want eternity with you."

"Are you sure?" Sylvia asked.

"You're all I've ever wanted. For years, I'd dream of coming home to you, but you wouldn't be there. It was the worst feeling—especially after it felt like something had taken you away from me. I'd be in a car along a desert road at night, looking because I had to find you, and I'd hear you calling, so I'd keep searching in the only place I was allowed… in my dreams. I needed you back, and here we are—at the end of that road. We're home. Every day with you is a relief and a dream come true."

"You make me so happy," she said.

"You make me so happy too. I can't live without you. I don't want to."

"Me neither."

"So, it's okay. Don't worry. We're in paradise."

Sylvia smiled. "Okay… I feel much better about it now. I know what I need to do. Let's squeeze in some more sleep and then start our routine. We can't get into our feelings about Andy. He made his choice. I don't like it, but it's his."

"Every young man needs to feel like they've gone through a rite of passage."

"Yeah, I know," Sylvia said. "Men are stupid."

"Men are hardwired for it… I don't like what he chose, but it is what it is. You sleep in. I'll wake up in an hour and take Daphne to school, then I'll call in for you. You can relax now. Get your sleep."

49

HOMECOMING QUEEN

IN THE SIXTH MEMORY LOOP, SYLVIA USED THE NOTE SHE HAD FIRST jotted down after that early morning call with Alene as the starting point for her new book. On days when reopening the memory loops of her childhood felt like too much, and when Sylvia physically felt up to the adventure, Andrés would drive her out into the Catskill Mountains. Together, they would hike until sunset. Then, they would find a flat rock to rest on and look at the stars while holding hands in silence.

Sometimes, Sylvia would talk about her mother. She remembered wanting a hug—just one hug. "I got that flashback today, and it was my dad who scratched that itch. I would've called him Mom if I knew I could. My dad would've been cool with it."

On those nights of silence under the stars, Sylvia and Andrés had no worries about Daphne. Their daughter had grown to be independent and resourceful, always finding her way home. Daphne was a self-starter, like Elisa.

In the Sixth Memory Loop, Sylvia finished writing the book, and it destroyed her. To help her recover, Andrés took her to Ibiza for the summer before Daphne started her senior year of high school.

While there, Sylvia and Andrés would watch the sun reflecting on the waters of the beaches at Cala Benirrás as it set late on summer nights. In the silence, they relaxed while a scattering of stars twinkled, and together, they breathed under a sky at twilight.

Sylvia said she wanted to dance while in Ibiza, but when the time came to leave the beach at night, she wanted to stay, sleep, and wake up to watch the stars fade out above them and watch the sunrise. To have the moment to breathe the way she could with Andrés, while watching the sky at twilight, was her new way of feeling alive.

Sylvia and Andrés were both in massive physical pain, though she didn't know he was. All they wanted to do was not move, but just hold to each other and not move, and just enjoy the sounds of the ocean, and the feel of the sun, and the feel of the wind, and the feel of being alive together, and feeling her breathing, and seeing his chest rise and fall, and feeling their feet and legs tangled together in the sand.

Yes.

They did this under the sun and stars until they made their return to New York.

In the Sixth Memory Loop, Sylvia and Andrés lived a quiet life of joy, even when she persuaded him to see a doctor. After a battery of tests, including MRIs, CT scans, and a bone marrow biopsy, they diagnosed Andrés with advanced-stage multiple myeloma. Sylvia asked how that could be possible. The doctor said it could be because of his deployment… it could be 9/11. An increasing number of survivors were continuing to die from the terror attack.

"How much time do I have left?" Andrés asked.

"Maybe three years. Maybe," the doctor replied.

When they left the doctor's office, Sylvia was quiet.

"Are you okay?" Andrés asked.

"I have to be honest—the way I've been feeling the last few years? It's hard to say," she replied.

"It's okay. Say whatever you feel. Everything's good. Gratitude, my life—I'm just so happy."

"It's gonna be a race to the cliff's edge. You and me."

"You and me."

Sylvia began to cry. "I wish we had more time."

Andrés cried with her. "Me too."

"We can't run away from this, can we?"

"No."

Sylvia choked back her tears. "Please... let's not say anything to the kids... If I'm the first to go, you already know my wishes—"

"No wake, no funeral—"

"No networking over my dead body—but I've got one more. Take me and Athena back to the Bridge. You'll know what to do from there."

"I know."

"If you're the first to go? What's your final wish?"

Andrés choked back his tears. "Emma... let me show you that I'll always trust your word. If I go first, it'll be our final trust exercise. I'm leaving it to you to decide, as long as it shows just how much I loved you—more than I loved my own life."

"I love you more than my own life—yes—I know what to do."

Sylvia and Andrés collapsed into each other's arms in grief, crying as people walked around them to enter and exit the doctor's office. They cried until his phone began to vibrate in his back pocket. Andrés choked back his tears to answer.

It was Daphne. She called to ask what was for dinner. She would be home soon and was bringing friends over. Sylvia and Andrés regained their composure and told Daphne they weren't cooking, but they were bringing pizza over for her and her friends, which made her happy.

In the Sixth Memory Loop, Daphne excelled in high school, and several top-tier colleges accepted her. Sylvia and Andrés sat down with Daphne to go over her options, and after much discussion, Daphne decided that the University of Virginia was the one she wanted to visit. She needed to see if she could spend the next four years of her life living in Charlottesville.

"My dad graduated from there," Sylvia said with a bright smile.

"Oh my God, woman. I know. You've said it, like, a thousand times. I get it," Daphne said.

"That was my way of trying to get you to choose UVA instead of MIT, without actually telling you, and it worked."

It was the blue hour of Friday morning when Daphne, Sylvia, and Andrés got in the car and began the drive to Charlottesville. Once in Virginia, they took the scenic route. With eyes bright and wide, Sylvia's face pressed against the window as they rode through the Shenandoah Valley.

"While we're in the area, I'm taking you home. We can see her together. Would you like that?" Andrés asked.

Sylvia looked at Andrés and nodded.

"That's not an answer."

"Yes, I'd like that."

When they arrived in Charlottesville, they checked into a hotel, then went for an early dinner before walking to the campus. Sylvia and Andrés hung back and watched Daphne get a feel for the area on her own until she came back to them and said she was tired. They then went back to their hotel room, where they ended the day by relaxing and watching TV.

The next day, they returned to the campus for Daphne's tour for accepted students. The organizers paired her with a student guide—a junior majoring in aerospace engineering, the same major Daphne hoped to pursue.

With Daphne gone, Sylvia took the opportunity she had alone with Andrés to tour buildings and locations her parents would have visited as engineering students. Alma had come from Syria to study at the University of Virginia, meeting and falling in love with Wendell instead.

Hours later, Daphne returned, and they all got back in the car and drove away. During the golden hour, they arrived at Sylvia's family plot near Big Stone Gap and parked in a dirt lot.

They all got out of the car.

Daphne looked around. "Is this where you grew up?"

"Not too far from here," Sylvia said. "If we'd kept driving, we would've passed the dirt road leading to a small shack, way in the back. I doubt it's still there."

Sylvia looked around as if trying to regain a sense of the place.

"I know where they're at now," Sylvia said, walking in the direction of the graves.

Andrés and Daphne followed her until she stopped to kneel at the side of her mother's grave, looking at it for a long moment before shaking her head and looking over at Constance's grave, buried alongside.

Daphne ran back to the car and returned with paper towels and a bottle of water. She helped Sylvia clear the stone markers as Andrés began looking for large rocks.

Sylvia said to Daphne, "I could never bring myself to come back... Coming back would've meant coming here and seeing her gone... Auntie Birdie would always leave me a bus ticket every Thanksgiving—every Christmas—but I'd always find one thing or another to distract me from the reality that she was gone. Nana went out in the most painful way."

"That picture—was that her last picture? The one in our living room?" Daphne asked.

"Yup. She threw up after taking that picture, and I had to take her back to bed. I undressed her, and cleaned her, and kept the head wrap on. I had to come back to New York for my graduation ceremony. She died after I left."

Daphne hugged Sylvia. "I'm sorry."

"It's okay. That's life... I think the one thing I'd do differently is that I would've come and visited her instead of waiting this long. I think avoiding this visit—I don't know—avoiding it made finding other stuff to distract me easier? You know? I got lost in the night."

"I know, *Mama,* I've read your book."

Sylvia pushed Daphne away to grab her by the shoulders and said, "Okay, then, if we're being real, listen—promise me, please promise me, you'll face your emotions. You'll face your feelings. You'll make peace with it; otherwise, it'll twist inside you, you know?"

Daphne looked at Sylvia with alarm and confusion. "I don't understand."

"Just remember what I'm saying, and you'll understand when the moment demands that you do, okay?"

"Okay?"

Andrés came over. He asked Daphne if she could find two large rocks. He said he would explain when she came back with them, but that it was necessary. Daphne left her parents alone.

Andrés knelt alongside Sylvia and looked longingly at Constance's grave with her.

"We can think of all the things that could've been, what you could've done differently, but what good does that do you? Want my opinion?" he asked.

"Of course, as always," Sylvia said.

"In looking back, I think you're undermining the woman you were in 1984—the one who knew herself, who knew better. You're looking back as a fifty-one-year-old, and it's not fair to that kid who didn't want to get on the bus and come here to see her nana like this."

Sylvia kept her focus on Constance's grave, staring intently as though she were still that young woman, terrified of the world—of death.

"I was doing everything I could to keep myself from thinking about the last time I saw Nana," she said. "To keep myself from coming here —to see her dead and buried and her seeing me, and what I'd become. A loser, like my father... I know she didn't mean what she said on my sixteenth birthday, but damn if it didn't stay with me. There's no acting in front of Nana. I couldn't come back here, not until today, not without you...

"I can see why Petra did what she did. But if I'm being honest, I think all I needed to come back here was you. When we first met, I had already graduated from college. For Christ's sake, I'd been in law school. Now I can see I wasn't a loser when you met me. I don't need a Ph.D. for what I'm doing—I don't even use my law degree."

"Yes, you do—stop putting yourself down," Andrés said.

"I mean, it's all for ego. To tell myself I'm not a loser—to stand here without fear of what she'd think of me—to say, 'Yeah, Nana, I'm a doctor. I'm a lawyer.' Like, big deal."

"Stop downplaying everything—it is a big deal. This is bigger than you! This is bigger than us! That clinic has helped so many people! You've saved so many lives! You've done so much good with what you've earned."

"But that stupid Master Plan cost me thousands of days I could've had with you! More family time! More trips together! Hell, I was ready to live with you in one of those Earthships outside of Taos—just stars and silence."

"Stop, stop—close the loop! We can't think like this!"

"Yes, we can! I can't get back those days, and we're dying!"

"You want to think like this?" Andrés asked, choking back his tears as Sylvia began to cry.

From a distance, Daphne asked, "What's wrong?"

Sylvia took a deep breath, swallowed, and forced a smile onto her face.

"Just give us some space, dear—we're fine," Sylvia replied.

"Okay," Daphne said, then continued searching for the two largest rocks she could carry.

Sylvia whispered to him, "Why can't I think like this?"

"If we had gone through our new plan and tried again, and we had our baby, how old would she be now?"

Sylvia paused. "Best case—without IVF—conceived 2002. Born 2003."

"What year is it?"

"2014."

"How much time do you think we have left?"

Sylvia shifted her focus from Andrés to Constance's marker.

"We'd be leaving her behind," she said, beginning to cry. "Now I know why Athena died... We'd be leaving her behind too, and she'd be too young to survive on her own."

"It's the only thing that makes sense."

"It's not the *only* thing."

Andrés sighed. "I know... Karma..." He stood and looked at Sylvia. "But we need to keep that loop closed and drop it. We're not here to mourn Athena but to show Constance that the sole purpose of her life has become who she dreamed she would become. And after all these years, you're here, finally, to show her—because everything that happened was meant to happen—and my asshole mother made sure you honored Nana's dream. So enough—no more tears. Emma, stand up."

Sylvia stood.

"Look at Constance and say it with me—'I did it, Nana.'"

"I did it, Nana."

"Say it again—"

"I did it, Nana. I did it—I finished! I was scared, Nana, but"—Sylvia started laughing—"I found another asshole like you who pushed me and didn't give a shit if I hated her, to make me see I had to put me first."

"Good girl—I'm so proud of you."

Sylvia turned to face Andrés. "But you're not mad? I mean, we have a good life. We're happy; you're happy? Right?"

"Emma, being away from you for all those years has taught me never to take you for granted ever again. Do you know what I thought about a lot? Remember that morning? I was studying for a test. *Oedipus Rex*, I think."

"Yes! Our Second Memory Loop."

"God, I hate that guy sitting at the table. You made me breakfast, and I was so focused on the test that I forgot to say thank you. That's my regret—that I didn't say 'thank you.' You know, when we were apart, how many times I replayed that moment in my mind?"

"That memory loop?" Sylvia asked.

Andrés laughed. "Yes—that memory loop. What I would've given to be back in our kitchen, to have looked up for that one second and said, 'Thank you.' Thank you for doing something that was so out of your character back then, but you did it anyway because you saw something in me that made you want to do it.

"You know how many times I racked my brains trying to figure out if that house was your house? If I had your permission to cross the boundary? I wanted to show up at your doorstep so bad, just so the first words I could say to you were, 'Thank you.'

"Now, every second of my life, I want to be with you. Being apart all those years taught me never to take you for granted again. It left me with regret. I regret every second I didn't show you gratitude, just as much as I regret all those days we were apart—but it had to happen."

Sylvia paused to look longingly again at Constance's grave.

"Nana was worried about leaving me behind. She said it once—on my last visit—and I knew she didn't mean to say it out loud, 'cause she didn't want to scare me. There was so much pressure from her to do my best. I felt it even after she died—I'm standing here now, and I can feel her relief."

"Do you feel relief?" Andrés asked.

Sylvia took a deep breath and exhaled. "I do."

"Nothing worth a damn comes easy in life," Andrés said.

"We learned that the hard way."

"Knowing is everything."

"I know..." Sylvia paused. "Damn, I wish I'd brought flowers. But you know, if rocks are good enough for my dad, they're good enough for Constance. For my mom? For the water she helped put in my lungs, and all the issues I've had because of it—she gets nothing but a marker cleaning."

"Emma, be nice. Don't you think your mom may have suffered from postpartum depression, like you?"

"I didn't think of it that way."

"Why would your dad say Miss Alma battled the worst depression? That it wouldn't be fair to her memory to hold it against her, especially given what you'd said was the fucked-up spot your Syrian grandparents had placed her in? Would it have been fair to judge you the day you checked into the hospital?"

"No," Sylvia said.

"Why did your father continue to love the memory of her? Why would Constance have her body moved from Texas and have her buried here, with the only family that made her feel like she belonged? Because your *yamma* was a good woman who wasn't as lucky—who couldn't see beyond herself enough to know she needed help. You called for an ambulance; your mother didn't. My love, your mother paid the price for bringing you into the world. Forgive her—Miss Alma is the yoke."

"You're right. You're right... I want to leave a rock for *Yamma*."

"I'm so proud of you. Would you like to leave rocks for your dad? We can visit him on the way home."

"No, I don't want to go to Arlington. I'm having dreams again, and if I speak on them, they'll come true."

"Speak, it's okay."

Sylvia paused. "I see your name on a tombstone, but your coffin is empty."

Before Andrés could respond, Daphne returned. "Okay, I'm tired of holding these large rocks, and I don't care if you dorks are crying."

Sylvia wiped the corners of her eyes and smiled. "Changing the subject. The reason we want rocks instead of flowers is because flowers die, but rocks endure. I want the signs of our visit to last as long as possible. Maybe even after Dad and I are gone."

"Don't joke like that," Daphne said.

"We may joke," Andrés said, "but it's the truth. Everything that grows old dies—but that's good. That's what makes everything beautiful. Because it ends. And I know I'm beautiful."

"Stop, Dad, you're not. Sylvia is beautiful."

"I'm fucking gorgeous."

Sylvia took the rocks and placed one at the base of Constance's grave and the other at the head of Alma's grave.

"Would you like to drive around the area some more?" Andrés asked.

"What for? I did all my growing up in New York, not here. There was nothing left once Nana was gone, and I'm still mad at Birdie. She'll never grow... she'll never change. Let's get out of here and go home."

On the drive back to New York, Daphne sat in the front passenger seat. She asked Sylvia, who was focused on the dark road ahead, "What's the deal with you and turtles? Like, why are you obsessed with them?"

"I'm not obsessed," Sylvia replied.

"Come on, you've got a charm on your wrist that's a turtle. You and Dad have a picture of, like, a ninja space turtle in your bedroom, which is, like, weird."

"That's her fetish," Andrés said.

"Dad, that's super gross."

"Okay, well," Sylvia said, "it's a serious subject, but I think it's important for you to know. Is it okay if we talk about something serious?"

"It's okay."

"Might be a little upsetting, so that's your warning. Is it okay if I go ahead?"

"Yes, woman, tell the story."

"Okay, believe it or not, I was a lot like you. My dad died when I was a senior in high school, and when I started my freshman year of college, I was suicidal—not because I wanted to die. I'm scared to die; even now, I'm scared to die."

Sylvia took a deep breath, swallowed, and held her composure.

"I wanted to die because I was tired of being in pain, always sad and depressed. It scared me because it was becoming too much. I had one friend. He was sad and lonely too—it was his first time away from home, and he'd been living in a way that wasn't true to himself. He had to pretend for his religious parents, and if they'd known the real him, they would've told him he was going to hell."

"That's awful," Daphne said.

"Dad knows my friend."

"Reginald Horne, a.k.a. Reginald Superstar," Andrés said.

Sylvia smiled. "He was something—he's the one who got me into spoken word poetry. I miss him. He was my first real friend. You'll make a lot of them in college. Anyway, he caught me crying one afternoon, and he sat next to me, and we started talking about life. Reggie loved Jack Kerouac, and he began reciting a poem to me from memory called *The Sad Turtle*. It was a beautiful poem based on Buddhist scripture, and I'm the type who has to read the source myself."

"Me too!" Daphne said, excited.

"As you should. I found the actual sutra where the Buddha talked about how rare a chance it is to be reborn as a human. It is rarer than a blind turtle coming to the surface of an ocean once every hundred years, luckily finding its head has gone through a single hole in a wooden yoke that just so happens to be there, at that spot. Baby, what are the chances of that? I bet you could do the math on that."

"I know I can," Daphne said.

"I'd like to see you do it for me, but when we get home—not now. I want you to think about what I'm gonna tell you. I went back to Reggie with the scripture passage, and he told me all life is a miracle— and that my being alive is a miracle too. If that's true, then it means

I'm special. It means I'm meant to be here. I remember Reggie telling me that even though we'd just met, that miracle was precious to him because life itself is that rare. It's rarer than a blind turtle, innumerable *kalpas* old, finding that yoke and going through it to be born. So please —don't give up. Don't hurt myself. Reggie became the brother I never had, and he messed with me like I was his sister—sometimes, a little too much."

"We should bring him some rocks," Andrés said.

"Before we *retire,* Reggie deserves that. Because of him, I started keeping a pet turtle in my dorm. Sometimes I'd take Kalpa with me. She reminded me that no matter how awful I felt, I was lucky to be alive. I'm the one who made it through that hole in the yoke, at that moment, in that spot. My life's a gift. And in return, I need to show gratitude for it by maintaining good karma—by trying to do good in the world."

"I get it now," Daphne said. "And you with the protesting and stuff?"

"I was just trying to do what I thought was right."

Daphne paused. "I've always wondered—people who get arrested at protests, does it stay on your record?"

"Most times, no. But you still see the inside of a cell, and I've seen the inside of a lot of them. Did it make a difference? I don't know... Your brother did a tour in Afghanistan. He doesn't want to talk about it. What good did I do? My kid still ended up going off to war. I wonder if he's gonna need a turtle for himself."

"At least you tried. Dad's done nothing. While you were protesting, he was eating cheese fries and playing video games."

Sylvia pulled the car off the road and onto the shoulder, tires skidding as they stopped.

"Is everything okay?" Daphne asked.

Sylvia's face was filled with anger. "Do you even know your father?"

"I do... I think."

"Then tell me something about him that doesn't involve being your dad."

"He's with you? He was with Mom?"

"It's okay; it doesn't matter," Andrés said.

Sylvia looked at Andrés in the backseat. "Yes, it does—it matters." She turned to Daphne. "Estefania, if something happens to you while you're working, and you end up in a wheelchair because of it, would it be fair for anyone to expect you to get up and run?"

"No."

"What if you went blind? Would it be fair for anyone to be mad at you because you can't tell them if it's night or day, if the moon is in the sky or not?"

"No."

"Your father is disabled exactly like that, but with his brain—do you know the army awarded—"

"Stop. I'd rather she not know," Andrés said.

"Awarded what?" Daphne asked.

"I've never talked about it. Elisa barely knows."

"Are you serious?" Sylvia said.

"You only know because I used to talk in my sleep. By the time I met Elisa, I'd stopped... You were my leap of faith. You cured me. Besides, I saw what knowing stuff like that did to you. I learned from your experience. Andy doesn't know."

"Shit, I made him read my first book."

"What about your first book?" Daphne asked.

Sylvia pointed at her. "You're lucky you had your dad around. I didn't have that."

"Let Daphne think what she wants," Andrés said. "In a few years, it'll be like when you got Wendell's letter. You thought one thing but found out another."

"And I felt like an asshole." Sylvia laughed. "That's twisted. I like that."

Daphne looked confused. "What are you guys talking about?"

"I can't do that to her—having her find out after we've gone off and retired," Sylvia said.

"Let me be evil," Andrés said.

Sylvia laughed. "No! Not like that." She turned to look at Daphne. "Estefania, there's a black box in our closet that has all of Dad's stuff. You'll find more than the old pictures he's taken of you and me—stuff he earned. When you're ready to feel like an asshole, go open that black box. You have our permission. You'll see: if your dad hadn't earned what's in that box, Andy would've lived with Lydia and turned out differently. I'd still have an evil man in my life, would've lost my sobriety, and wouldn't have the life I have now. And most of all, you wouldn't be here... Dad is the yoke."

Sylvia drove off the shoulder of the road and continued the drive back to New York while Daphne kept asking, over and over, "What's in the box?"

In the Sixth Memory Loop, Daphne graduated from high school and lived with Elisa for the summer. It would be Elisa who would drive Daphne to Charlottesville and send her off to college.

Before moving away, Sylvia kissed Daphne goodbye and said, "Remember everything I've told you. Be good to Mom."

"Why are you like this? I'm coming home for Thanksgiving. It's not that long."

"Of course—I'm just saying, 'until we meet again.' I love you. I love you so much."

In the little house in Red Hook, it was now just Sylvia and Andrés, their memories, and everything they had worked hard to attain. After traversing the long, dark road that opened into a bright light of joy— like the sun on their faces—their journey together was coming to an end.

It was a Friday night, like every Friday night since they got married —Sylvia and Andrés drove into the city and began the evening in the Bowery. They enjoyed an early dinner in the lounge, where the Sixth and Final Memory Loop began. The lounge had frequently changed names over the years, which was fine for the two—for Sylvia and Andrés, it would always be the Diner. They sat together on the same side of the table, looking out the large window at the Williamsburg Bridge until the night prompted them to move along.

In keeping with the tradition of closing the loops, Sylvia and Andrés got back in the car. Instead of spending the rest of the evening in the Lower East Side, as they used to when they were younger, he drove over the bridge into Brooklyn. After navigating the back streets, Andrés parked the car.

The two went to a movie house in Williamsburg. There, just as they had when they were young lovers, Sylvia curled up against Andrés, and they watched the movie in comfortable calm.

After the movie, Sylvia wanted to spend the rest of their Friday night watching the city lights. After parking their car along the waterfront, Sylvia and Andrés entered Transmitter Park in Greenpoint. They walked down the long metal pier to the end, where she found a bench and asked that they sit.

In the silence, they enjoyed the skyline at night.

In the silence, they watched small boats sail up and down the East River.

Andrés grabbed her hand.

Sylvia squeezed his hand tightly in return.

She rested her head on his shoulder.

Not a word was said the entire time. It was a calm the two knew as home.

Then, just like that, Sylvia coughed.

Then, just like that, she clutched her chest.

Andrés placed Sylvia on the floor on her back.

She coughed and coughed. Her face turned red and blue. Her eyes closed.

Andrés pressed his palms against her chest.

He pressed furiously several times.

Sylvia's eyes opened, and she coughed and grunted. "No. Stop."

Andrés looked at her.

She tried to smile. "It's okay—I'm not. Scared."

Andrés placed his hand underneath her head. He took a deep breath and smiled.

"No fear, my shooting star... My beautiful sunflower... I love you," he said.

She looked into his eyes and smiled.

"I love you too. No fear—I see Us," she said, her eyes blinking once, then shutting forever.

The Sixth Memory Loop lasted five years, five months, and twenty-one days.

It was also the end of the Master Loop that began on May 17, 1986, when Sylvia witnessed a man who exhibited no signs of jealousy or anger. A man who had a woman taken away from him and acted as if it took nothing away from his manhood. A man she felt was the pull of her other half—someone she could trust to explore with her, someone who would not hurt her.

Andrés confirmed it for Sylvia when he threw his body on hers as bullets whizzed past them in the dark.[1]

The Master Loop ended as Sylvia crossed the boundary between the Land of the Alive and the Land of the Not-Alive.

God removed her blinders and restored Sylvia's sight.

Sylvia could see, at long last, the past, present, and future all at once. She would be whole once Andrés crossed the boundary himself to join *Her* in becoming who We are now, tasked by Our Maker to bear witness for every survivor who has ever been violated...

Who has suffered...

Who has had to hide—

Who has ever been doubted and questioned and put to shame and blamed when they were blameless—

We see you.

We believe you.

We are here to be Our Maker's Fury.

You are never alone.

Because...

We are the Watchers. We see all. We are the Beloved, now watching from outside of time.

Here, We wait for the day when he is led to a spot where the land is flat and the desert landscape glows gold.

That will be the day when the sky is at twilight.

His eyes will burn from staring at the sun setting on the horizon.

He will smile.

It will be December 21, 2014, Our wedding day.

Until then...

Andrés, Our Master Loop lasted twenty-eight years, three months, and five days. No fear—listen to that voice in you. It's me. I must steer you to that spot.

---

1. *Book Two: Underworld*, "Chapter Fifteen: Emma."

*To have our eternity and our peace, God must answer prayers. You must submit
to judgment.*

50

OEDIPUS

F RIDAY NIGHT WAS A BLUR; A NDRÉS REMEMBERED NOTHING AFTER the goodbye.

He woke up Saturday afternoon in a room at his parents' home, with a bottle of Klonopin that appeared to have been filled that morning on the nightstand and several messages from Daphne and Andy. Elisa had left Andrés a lengthy voice message in which she was crying and expressing regret for everything.

Elisa ended the message by saying, "I'll take care of Daphne and Andy; don't worry. Take your breath. Collect your thoughts. We're family, and I'm here."

Tony and his ex-wife, Jeanie, came over, sat at his bedside, and watched Andrés cry himself to sleep.

When Andrés would wake up, he would take a pill, furthering his relapse. Then he would see countless messages from Sylvia's friends and colleagues admonishing him for not having betrayed his wife's privacy. They all said the same thing:

"We didn't know she was sick—why didn't she share that with us? Why didn't you post about it on social media? We thought she had taken the leave to write the book."

After the *Spacer Woman* debacle, Sylvia would say her life was like her body. She wanted to maintain tight control over whom she would share it with and on what terms—even her hair, which she had kept covered in a headscarf for all except her family until the day she died. Andrés continued the tradition Sylvia had established for herself a long time ago: to never present justification to those who were not deserving of it. He let the messages go unanswered for now.

By late Sunday night, Andrés couldn't remember if he ate or drank anything. If he showered or talked to Andy. The number of completed calls listed in his call logs told Andrés he had spoken to his son.

Andrés received a text message from Daphne with a link to *The New York Times*. It opened to Sylvia's obituary:

Sylvia, Artist and Activist Who Walked the Walk, Dies at 51

Dr. Sylvia Hadid James, a poet, novelist, and activist, died on Friday in Brooklyn. She was 51. The cause was a heart attack following a long battle with sarcoidosis.

Dr. James was a longtime resident of Manhattan's Lower East Side before the neighborhood's gentrification. Her poetry, often humorous and self-deprecating, was written with unflinching candor about her body—years before *The Vagina Monologues* brought such themes into mainstream discourse.

"If men can talk unapologetically about their conquests and body parts, why can't I do the same without shame?" she told *The New Yorker* in 1992.

Born on Oct. 21, 1962, in Charlottesville, Va., Sylvia Hadid James moved to New York to attend Columbia University, later dropping out of law school in the mid-1980s. She discovered her voice while in a drug rehabilitation facility and soon after began her career as a poet. In her later years, she earned a doctorate in political science and a law degree from Columbia.

Her poem *1968* marked a shift in subject matter, signaling the direction her work would take as a novelist.

Her debut novel, *The Little Girl of the Valley*, explored the hardships of a Bedouin family during the Persian Gulf War. Their struggle ended abruptly when Iraq's Republican Guard and American-led coalition forces placed them in their crossfire. The novel gained notoriety for its harrowing final section, narrated by a child whose life is extinguished in a brutal, senseless manner. Dr. James's account made no distinction in culpability for what amounted to war crimes.

Released in March 2004, *The Little Girl of the Valley* coincided with the expansion of an insurgency in Iraq. When questioned on a news program about the timing of the book's publication and her loyalties, Dr. James's nonchalant response—amplified by a video leaked by the network's executive producer—brought her infamy.

She went on to write two more novels.

Spacer Woman drew from her brief time as a stripper while working her way through law school. The book caused controversy among her colleagues at a think tank, forcing them to confront the reality that she had, unapologetically, been a sex worker. Before resigning, she addressed them in an open letter:

"Back then, who was I to say no if men wanted to give me money? I was on my own and needed to eat. You, who judge, have never had to walk the walk because your family didn't leave you behind. I've walked the walk. I didn't have a family anymore, and I had classes to attend, rent to pay, and food didn't come out of nowhere—I had to be my own savior."

In 2010, Dr. James founded Estefania's Refuge, a clinic offering legal and social services to individuals at risk of exploitation. Through the clinic, she led a team of pro bono lawyers assisting survivors of sexual assault, trafficking, and domestic abuse, often filing civil suits on their behalf when the criminal justice system failed them.

Her final novel, *Atlas*, followed a matriarch struggling to keep her family together in Appalachia during the Vietnam War. The matriarch came to the horrifying realization that families like hers were regarded by society as only suitable for working in mines and serving in wars. They had been made to feel disposable by a government that had forgotten, "There are real people who live in those mountains."

Dr. Sylvia Hadid James is survived by her husband, Andrés de León; her son, Andrés James; and her stepdaughter, Estefania de León.

He called Daphne.

She answered. "Dad... I want to come home—I need to come home."

"My love."

"Yes, Dad?"

"Think... Can you hear Sylvia? Right now?"

Daphne paused. "Yes, Dad."

"Ask her if you should leave school and come home. Can you hear her response?"

She cried. "I can hear her. She's telling me to stay. She's telling me she loves me." Daphne ended the call.

On Monday, Andrés was out of the fog and lucid, remembering Sylvia's wishes: no wake, no funeral, no services. He messaged every one of Sylvia's friends and colleagues who made her death about them. The message was simple: fuck off. "Where were you when that guy tried to destroy her for what she wrote in her novel? Again, fuck off."

Andrés called his son, and when he picked up, Andy was not well. "My command won't let me take leave."

"Then I'm coming to you," Andrés said.

"No, Dad—what for?"

"To be there for you."

"Don't come. We're getting ready to *go* any day now, if you know what I mean. There's a chance I won't even be here."

"I have to head out by Fort Hood anyway."

"For what?"

"To fulfill one of Mom's last wishes."

"You guys knew she was dying?"

"We had an idea it was coming."

"Why didn't you tell me?"

"What's done is done—"

Andy cut him off. "That's easy for you to say. I was the one around her the most. You? You left her—not once, but twice. Your sorry ass got depressed after what's-her-name died, and you turned into the biggest pussy."

"Let it out," Andrés said.

"It's coming out. I was the one who took care of her, and she took care of me. You didn't do shit for us."

"Is that what you think?"

"It's what I know. The only reason you got to come back into Mom's life was 'cause she'd been hiding a bottle in the house. I found it, and it hadn't been opened. Then, when you started talking that *shit* about proposing, I knew I had no choice but to bring you back before it was too late."

"You don't know what I had to do to protect her sobriety, you little fuck!"

"You didn't think to tell me Mom was dying? I was the most important man in her life. It was a fucking mistake bringing you back—I didn't have to compete for attention with Daphne. I should've trusted Mom not to open that bottle."

"Shut up and listen, 'cause I'm gonna be real here. After what you just said, I don't give a fuck about your feelings anymore. You're on your own. All I care about is coming through for Mom's last wishes. Mom knew she was dying and didn't wanna tell you because she also knew you'd act the way you're acting now, and it would become about you instead of how it was scaring her. She didn't wanna worry about how you'd react, like a little bitch. You'd already showed her you were one, with that bitch move of yours—keeping us apart for all those years. You could've ended it when I came to the house."

"I could've."

"I'm gonna do this to you so you'll learn that choices have consequences. What do you think would've happened if I had come home that day? You think she would've taken to protesting?"

"Yup."

"No, she wouldn't have—Mom told me she was just trying to keep busy. She was coping with what you and your grandmother let her believe was the truth. You want the truth? The chemicals the police exposed her to when they locked her up at the pier that day triggered her sarcoidosis.[1] She already had a genetic predisposition, and it got worse because she'd drowned as a little girl. You really think she'd still be alive if I'd been home with her in August 2004? Think about that, asshole."

----

1. *Book Five: Medusa,* "Chapter Forty: The Arena."

"There's no way to know that."

"It's what the doctors told us. You made a mistake. Own it."

Andy was silent on the call.

"No sooner had I come back into her life, I helped her focus—and she did way more than just put herself in danger. She created that clinic. She's helped women like my aunt, who the system threw into a men's jail when she got arrested for credit card fraud. Fuck—she made sure she was there to fight for women like my aunt!

"She also helped this woman I met in Berlin, who told me she'd been abandoned by the father of their daughter—some army sergeant based in Landstuhl. Once I told your mother about Ina, she jumped into action, tracked the guy down, and made sure he paid what he owed to the mother and their kid.

"I don't know how she did it—I only knew her as Estrella—but Mom found her on social media. Her real name was Margarita. She was a dancer Mom convinced to take the company—and the partner I used to work for—to court."

"Why?" Andy asked.

Andrés sighed. "I don't want to say. But I'll tell you this—if you hang out with men who treat women like shit, and you don't call them out, and you just keep hanging out with them, then you're shit too. I did something about it. I stopped my boss from... and that's why we ended up in New Mexico.

"He wanted to hurt me because he knew Mom was pregnant. That's why we left you behind with Lydia—I couldn't leave your mom alone while she was carrying Athena. And Lydia, for whatever reason she had at the time, wasn't comfortable with me taking you across state lines.

"Mom went after all of them—and she won. Estrella got a massive payout. And because of that, she was able to rebuild her life instead of letting it end at the hands of the garbage human being I used to work for."

"Dad—"

"Mom got justice for Estrella—my ex-boss ate a bullet 'cause he got caught and lost everything."

"Dad—"

"Mom became the motherfucking Fury! That was her destiny! She was working with people in power to help change shit that actually mattered. People's lives. People like Lydia—I literally had to rescue her from her father's house because that man abused the fuck out of her for years—"

"Dad—"

"She tried going to the cops, but they didn't believe her—or your aunt Becky, who ended up killing herself. That's how I met Lydia—at her little sister's funeral. And once Becky was gone, he turned it all on Lydia. She tried reporting him again, and again, the cops didn't believe her. That's why we got married so young. She was ready to end it too. I had to pull her out of hell!

"It was your mom who showed Lydia that everything that happened to her since she was thirteen wasn't her fault. And *your* Lydia —your birth mom—is finally at peace. Lydia's the yoke for you.

"So don't talk to me like protesting was the best use of your mom's time, her education, her passions. Because I'd come back into her life, she accomplished so much more than just putting herself out there, getting locked up, and having jail guards take a quick feel of her body, you fucking asshole! That happened to her!

"You don't even know your mom! She had it worse than Lydia, worse than Becky, worse than Estrella, worse than Ina, worse than Estefania."

Andrés took a deep breath and swallowed. He took another deep breath and swallowed again.

"This is my fault—I fucked up with you," Andrés said. "I fucked up with everyone. I should've been more open about my feelings. I should've talked more about what I've lived through... Did you ever read any of your mother's work?"

"I don't like poetry. Mom made me read her first book. She quizzed me on it."

"Why would she quiz you?"

"Mom loved talking about her writing. I thought she was just crazy excited about it."

"You know that's me in the book, right?"

"It is?"

"I got into a fucked-up situation and had to fight my way out. A lot of people died who shouldn't have—just so I could make it back here to be your dad. And you get to call me a big pussy."

"Dad—"

"Did you know Elisa made sure Sylvia got my financial support?"

"I didn't know."

"Did you know I was in the South Tower on 9/11?"

"No."

"Petra was supposed to tell you."

"I'm sorry—I thought you were in bed because you were weak and couldn't get over Athena."

"Would you say something like that to your mom?"

Andy was silent.

"Of course not. But you can say it to me because who cares? I'm just *Dad;* my feelings don't count. I'm just weak. You know what? I've never talked about this, but I'm going there now—I got a Silver Star and a Purple Heart for what I did that day your mom had written about in her book. You think the Army just hands those out?"

"No."

"Am I still a big pussy?"

"No."

"Mom and I both felt something was off—like you were keeping us apart—but we let it go. What mattered was that we were all back together. But you're in a world of men now, and I want you to remember this—'cause that bullshit you put me and my wife through? It'll get called out, just like my uncle Victor got called out.

"He's an extreme case, but he still acted sneaky as fuck. From what your Grandpa Antonio told me, after my grandfather died and I joined the army, Victor snuck around and slept with a married woman. Her husband found out, shot my uncle several times, killed his wife, then turned the gun on himself.

"You fucked me over. You kept me away from my wife, you little rat bastard. I've got nothing left in me to worry about your future if you try to pull some sneaky, underhanded shit like this again. Life won't be as forgiving to you next time, and I'll be long gone. Taking years away like that from a man will get you shot, do you hear me? If I were still the man Mom met when I was sixteen—"

Andy started crying on the call.

"Stop—if you wanna cry, cry later."

"Do you want to shoot me?"

"Shut up and listen. Your mom is the only one who matters right now, so let me get through one of her last wishes. It's what I wanted to tell you face-to-face. I'm putting aside what I'm feeling toward you right now to say it. Are you ready?"

"Yes, Dad."

"Whatever you read in that book—I did it to make sure I stayed alive for you. I want you to see me as a man who made a mistake. A man who went against his conscience. I should've died instead. Your mom always thought Athena's death had something to do with our karma. And after you joined the Army, we started worrying about yours—if you were in danger of getting caught in our cycle of pain... or if you were starting a new one. So this is important. Are you listening?"

"Yes, Dad."

"If you have standing orders to do something that doesn't feel right —if it goes against your conscience—say no. Use your voice. Even if it means a court-martial, even if it means jail, say no. You chose to join the Army. That's the consequence."

"I don't understand."

"Yes, you do. You know exactly what I'm talking about. Out there, life is cheap, and they tell you, 'It's us or them.' Your mom and I didn't want this for you. We have a college fund set up, but we believed in the power of choice—and joining the Army was yours. Fine. But it's our last wish that you break the cycle. It's what I should've done. I should've said, 'No.' It's what Wendell should've done, but he didn't. One of your mom's memories of her father was him crying over the senseless killings he took part in, begging Constance to tell him God would forgive him."

"I didn't know," Andy said.

"Of course not. What man's gonna tell his family he did those things? Only a psychopath would talk about that. It's the only time I lied to Mom—when my memory started coming back. She had a feeling I wasn't being honest when I'd say I still didn't remember, but she never pushed. She'd just smile, 'cause she saw the bigger picture. I didn't want to talk about it. She played along until I was ready to make the choice and share. I miss her so much..."

"I miss her too."

"Andy, for a long time, I denied the existence of God—because if all that shit was real, I'm fucked. But your mom convinced me it's real—to open my heart, to love something deeper. That I had a soul—and it belonged to her. Andy, I'm a believer because of her. I believe in God because there's magic in the world. And if we're believers, then I know I've got to pay for my sins. But that's okay. That's the consequence of my choices. I got to be your dad. I helped your mom with her plan. I can't wait to die. I want to go home."

"But I don't want you to die."

Andrés stared at his reflection on the black screen of his phone, realizing he was talking to his son—who, despite being an adult, was still a scared child who had just lost his mother. He was not his adversary, as he had first come off as on the call. In that moment, he wished Andy was not set to deploy immediately so that he could drive out to Fort Hood, give him one last hug, and tell him face-to-face everything he needed to hear.

"My son," Andrés said, "karma is real. Break the cycle. That's what your mom and I want for you. Don't be like me, please. Don't be like her father. Be decent. Don't hurt people. Don't be part of the pain in the world."

"I'm sorry, Dad—please don't hurt yourself. Mom can wait."

"That's what she wanted me to tell you. And what I want for you is this—don't be like me. Be like her. Please tell me I'm not too late. Please tell me you haven't killed anyone."

"No, I swear. I haven't. I swear to God."

Andrés sighed with relief. "Thank God. Please don't cross that line. Don't cross that line and lose your soul. Please be like her. Life is precious. Your life is precious. It's so precious to me. I don't want you to lose your soul."

"I promise. I won't lose it."

"And get the fuck out of the Army as soon as you can. Take that money we've banked for you and go to college. Be like her! That's the Master Plan I've got for you and your sisters—to be like Sylvia, not me.

"I think of all my problems, and they all go back to that day I stood on a spot north of the Euphrates River. I've gotta find a way to make it right with God, because, as I've learned, God answers prayers. A lot of times, the prayers God answers aren't ours. Somewhere out there, there's a family that prayed to God for justice, and God's gonna make sure they get it.

"And when He does, I need to make sure you and your sisters don't pay the price for what I've done—for what the men before me did. Like Wendell. Like my biological father... Your mom tried to do a lot of good in the world. She worked hard to *try* to put our karma in the black. I've got to figure out how to pay off whatever balance is left, if any..."

"Dad, why do I feel like you're going to kill yourself?"

Andrés sighed. "I got caught up in the moment. I wish I had those years back. That was our only regret—we lost so much time we could have spent as one big, blended family."

"I'm sorry. I'm sorry I did that to you."

"I love you—it's done. Don't be like that again. Don't get involved in people's relationships. I won't be here to protect you. I wanted to scare you, that's all."

"You did."

"When you get between a man and his wife, you can ruin their lives."

"Did I ruin your lives?"

Andrés sighed. "No. In our case, it had to be this way. Mom was destined for more, and she needed that time to get there. It was God's plan... Orion."

"Orion?"

"When are you getting out?" Andrés asked.

"I have one more year left. When I get back from this deployment, I'm coming out."

"Good."

"Dad, I hate to do this, but I have to go."

"We've talked long enough. Let your command know what's going on, and if things become too much, go to a doctor—talk to someone."

"I will."

"Stay safe, and don't be a fucking hero. Glory is bullshit—there are dead people at the other end of that crap."

"You sound like Mom."

"Where do you think she got it from? Now go."

"I love you, Dad."

"I love you too, son."

51

THE SIREN

ANDRÉS WAITED UNTIL EARLY TUESDAY MORNING FOR PETRA AND Antonio to return home with Sylvia's ashes in a gold urn. Petra, who had been mute and like stone the entire time, approached Andrés, handed him the large cylinder, and kissed her son on the forehead.

"I'm sorry," she said.

Andrés said nothing as he left their home. He couldn't remember if he was the one who had driven back that night from Brooklyn or if it was his dad, but his car was in the driveway. Andrés got behind the wheel. All he could think about were Sylvia's wishes, especially her last one.

Andrés made a quick stop at his home to pick up the small gold urn containing Athena's ashes, which had been on the mantel in their bedroom. He also grabbed the other items he needed to fulfill Sylvia's last wishes and set himself back on the road.

It was almost 9 p.m. when Andrés arrived in Charlottesville. He called Daphne.

"Surprise, I'm here," he said.

"Why?" Daphne asked.

"I promised *Mama* I'd do something for her, and I was driving through. I wanted to see you—even if it's just for a late dinner."

"Thank you, Dad!"

"I'll come get you. Where do you want to meet?"

Minutes later, Andrés drove by the statue of Thomas Jefferson outside the rotunda. Daphne rushed over to the car, climbed in, and he drove off.

Over dinner, Andrés tried to engage Daphne in conversation, but it was difficult. She was quiet.

"Talk to me," he said.

"What's there to say? I knew something was up the moment I saw you two crying when we visited her grandma." Daphne took a deep breath and swallowed hard.

"Don't do that, my love."

"Do what?" she asked.

"Swallow your feelings."

"I don't want to cry here—especially not now." She paused. "Dad, can I ask you something?"

"Anything."

"You look sick. Are you okay?"

"I'm sick, but I'm telling you the truth—I'm okay right now. I'm with you. How could I not be okay?"

Daphne said, "I'm not okay. I've had dreams... I can't talk about them." She took another deep breath and swallowed hard.

Andrés grabbed her hands.

"Dad, can I ask you something else?"

"Of course."

"Are you dying?"

Andrés smiled. "I am, and so are you. We're all dying, right?"

"You're an asshole—you know what I meant."

Andrés tapped Daphne on the nose. "Boop."

Daphne laughed. "What the fuck?"

"I'm fine. But I want to go over the logistics of your fund and everything else you need to know, just in case something happens."

"See, it's that shit... What's gonna happen?"

"I'm getting older, and nothing is guaranteed. Look at what just happened. I want you better prepared than *Mama* and I were for life's surprises, because the truth is, life is the surprise. So let's do some emergency planning in case shit happens. That's all. God owes us nothing. Every moment we're alive is a gift. You're lucky to be here; I'm lucky you're here."

Andrés reached into his pocket and pulled out a silver wristlet with a turtle charm, handing it to her.

Daphne's sad expression was replaced with joy. "I love this charm."

"*Mama* knew that. She'd want you to have it—to remember to honor life, especially your own, and never give up on yourself. It's why she wore it all the time. We want you to wear it all the time now. You being here is a miracle—that means everything to me, Mom, and *Mama*. Don't you ever forget it. Mom risked her life to make sure you were born into the world. I know Mom told you the story. So if life gets tough, think of the Sad Turtle and don't give up."

"I won't." Daphne placed the charm on her left wrist. "I love you, Dad."

"I love you too. Now, are you hungry? Let's eat."

Daphne and Andrés enjoyed a long dinner together. Then he gave her a ride back to her dorm.

Daphne reluctantly got out of his car. "Text me later, please?"

Andrés nodded before driving away from the Charlottesville area.

Andrés stopped at Sylvia's family plot near Big Stone Gap. There, he scattered a portion of Sylvia's ashes across Constance's grave. For Andrés, it was only fair that, for all the work the Matriarch had put into Sylvia, Constance should be rewarded by resting with a part of her granddaughter for eternity. For everything his wife had told him about her childhood, the Matriarch had moved heaven and earth to make her the person she turned out to be.

He also spread a small portion across Alma's grave.

Based on what Constance had learned from the suicide note and subsequent investigation, then told Sylvia before she moved away to college, and what Sylvia later shared with Andrés when they began dating, Alma, overwhelmed by the sadness of being left behind by Wendell—who, prior to 1968, had volunteered to go to Vietnam—had taken her own life. She had still been battling postpartum depression, amplified by being disowned by her Syrian parents, who viewed marrying outside her race as *haram*. Alma, in her loneliness, made one

last call to her parents. They told her the only way to make things right
with them was to kill Sylvia, whom they referred to as *muwallad*.[1]

At first, Alma tried to drown Sylvia while giving her a bath, but that
maternal instinct most women have must have kicked in. Instead of
doing what she felt compelled to do to deal with the soul-crushing
loneliness and depression, she killed herself instead. She had the fore-
sight to keep the water running in the bathtub, knowing someone
would eventually break into the apartment she shared with Wendell
near Fort Hood and, in trying to investigate the cause of water
damage, would ultimately find Sylvia.

Andrés knelt to touch Alma's marker and, after a long silence, pros-
trated himself before her grave, kissing Sylvia's ashes upon the marker
before standing back up and looking at the night sky. It was so clear
and starry blue. As clear as that night on the Bridge so many years ago.
He looked around and saw all the last names on the grave markers and
tombstones around him—Osborn and Lawson, her ancestors. Andrés
understood that he had returned a part of Sylvia to the source.

"Emma, you always had a family."

We, the Watchers, see it all loop back around:

His Orpheus to my Eurydice—

AUGUST 27, 2014

He was in the dark woods near Big Stone Gap, standing in front of the
Matriarch's grave, surrounded by tombstones. How he arrived at the
grave was as unreal as the vast night sky, but not as unreal as the sky in
New Mexico. There, in the pockets of darkness, in dazzling clusters
scattered across the night, the stars shine brighter. God comes through
in the shine.

There was no shine in Virginia. No shooting stars.

A long time ago, Emma, his shooting star, had said:

*"There was something so beautiful about his devotion to Eurydice. It would
get to me that a man could love a woman so much that he'd try to bring her back*

---

1. *Muwallad*—in this context, a pejorative Arabic term for a mixed-race child, especially
one born to an Arab mother and a non-Arab father; it implies social or cultural impurity.

to life.... When I was a little girl, I wanted a love like that to be real. I prayed for love like that—a love that was so powerful, so strong, that it would drive my soulmate to go to the End of the World, into the Underworld, to come back for me, even if I were a lost cause. That's real love."

His undying love was real.

His undying devotion compelled him to walk away from the Matriarch's grave, get into his car parked nearby, sit in the driver's seat, and begin the journey toward the End of the World.

On that long drive, the heap of broken images flowed through a thought process hampered by the years he had spent on benzodiazepines and neuroleptics, compounded by the relapse after Sylvia's death. His mind bounced back and forth through every era and year of his life, caught in endless memory loops, until he finally arrived at:

The End of the World.

AUGUST 30, 2014

The road ahead twists around mountains and hills and descends.

The sky becomes clear.

It is just after midnight.

A crack on the surface of the plateau opens up in the distance, as if a dark entrance into the Underworld. It stands out darker against a night shining brightly with stars.

Andrés pulls off to the side of the road and parks. He jumps out of the car.

The deep, dark crack extends far into the horizon.

He falls to his knees.

Andrés grips dirt, gravel, and dust, unable to breathe.

He places his hands on his face, takes a deep breath, swallows dust, and coughs.

Andrés pushes himself up. He gets back in the car and drives off, entering Taos. The streets are empty. He follows signs for the Rio Grande Gorge Bridge, driving along the state road straight into the dark.

He crosses the Bridge, parks in the lot, and gets out of the car. He pulls out his phone—several messages from Daphne, all begging for him to respond.

There is no longer any cell reception.

Andrés walks onto the empty bridge.

He looks long over the rail and into the darkness below.

The stars above shine.

Andrés smiles.

He takes a deep breath. "Feelings no longer matter. It'll be over soon."

He walks back to the car and grabs the large bag he had used to stow the two urns. He carries it over his shoulder and walks back to his spot. Her last wish was to be brought back to the Bridge.

Here is Andrés, Sylvia's other half, pulling out the small golden urn containing Athena's remains.

He opens the lid and pours Athena into the darkness below. Andrés throws the small golden urn into the void.

Andrés pulls out the golden urn containing Sylvia's remains.

"Under a tenement sky."

He opens the lid and pours her into the darkness below. Andrés throws the golden urn into the void.

"As you had wished."

The calls begin again, as they have throughout the entire drive along the desert road of night:

"But I was calling. We're believers, remember? And I don't give a fuck about boundaries. It's called devotion—that's the part of love that's not a game. There are no fucking rules to that shit. You just do it."

"I'll never doubt you; I'll never leave you alone ever again. This is not a delusion—you jumped first. You lead, I follow—"

The bridge swings back and forth. A gust of wind pushes him on all sides. His heart races as it would when one is at the edge of a great height and feels the urge to jump, just to jump.

He climbs onto the railing.

"No fear—it's just a feeling."

The gates to the Underworld open below.

The darkness calls.

Andrés thinks he sees Sylvia waiting to wrap her arms around him. A supernatural entity—a siren—that looks like her.

Andrés blinks.

A buzzing in his pocket breaks the siren's magic spell—a buzzing from his phone—receiving a text message in an area with no reception.

It keeps buzzing and buzzing.

Andrés climbs down from the railing to read the message:

> ESTEFANIA
>
> Dad, I know you're sad, but please. I know what you're going to do. I feel it, and Andy has felt it too. He called me from Germany. I heard Sylvia's voice in my head telling me you have to stop your father, that she'd seen the same thing the first night you brought her there, wherever that is. I didn't want to say that because it seemed too weird, but damn— don't do this to her too! She didn't give up, so neither should you.

Andrés slumps to the ground, places his hands on his face, takes a deep breath, and cries.

We, the Watchers, say to Andrés: This is not your door. That is not your exit—not now. That is not *me* staring back at you, trying to lure you into the void—it never was. You can't run from this moment. Your door will open soon, and when it does, you will see the golden light and *me* on the other side, but not tonight. Be patient. If *I* was brave enough to stay to the painful end, so will you. Even if it means grabbing *my* camera and doing what you always wanted to do—be a voice through your pictures.

It'll be a way of bringing everything into the black. That's how you will get to that spot.

I need you to get to that spot.

Get to that spot, and you'll be fine.

He whimpers, "No, I won't."

It's okay, Andrés. Trust *me*.

Andrés stops crying and begins to laugh. He laughs and laughs and laughs.

"I hear you. It's you! Just like before—when we were apart! We're not crazy! Okay. I trust you. Yes. I'll grab *my* camera, and I'll trust what you're saying, and follow your lead to whatever spot."

Andrés sends Daphne a message:

DAD

I'm on my way to New York. No worries.

Daphne messages back:

Thank God, you asshole. You scared me! Text me when you get home. I love you.

I love you too. I'm sorry for the fade-out.

Andrés returns to his car and begins his long drive back to New York.

❧ 52 ❧

WEDDING DAY

IT WILL TAKE ANDRÉS THREE DAYS TO RETURN. WHEN HE WALKS through the doors of his home, he will begin the work of carefully wrapping up all of Sylvia's private papers and moving them into storage. He will keep every personal item signifying proof of their life in place. The house will be locked away, and a key will be given to Petra.

On that visit with his mother, Andrés will say, "She may have forgiven you, and I said nothing about it, but I was still angry. I let her think I forgave you."

Petra will say, "You're still angry about that?"

"About that? Like what you did to me was not a big deal? No, not anymore. I'm dying. I can't let that be the last thing I feel for you. Because of Sylvia, I choose love; I'm doing it for her. So, here's a key to the house for Andy. I'll be giving one to Elisa for Daphne."

"Where are you going?"

"I'm going to take my camera and keep busy until I'm no more." Andrés will turn to Antonio and say, "Thank you for choosing to be my dad. I love you with everything in me."

Antonio will laugh and say, "You're fine. Stop overreacting."

Andrés will pat Antonio on the back and say, "Never change, *mi viejito*. I love you."

Petra will walk with Andrés outside.

Andrés will ask, "Whatever happened to my father? Did he ever want to see me just to see me, without wanting to see you? Did he ever ask for me just to ask for me?"

Petra will say nothing.

"I'd like to see him."

"Your father is dead," she will say.

Andrés will shake his head and say, "Bye, Petra."

Andrés will visit Elisa for the final time and see Elisa thriving. She will have recovered from her surgery and from her addiction to pain medication. He will see Elisa in mourning over Sylvia's death, and they will sit together and cry.

Elisa will say, "She had warned me. She saw through my bullshit. I don't know where I'd be if she didn't come here every week and kick my ass to stop with the pills. To do it for me and no one else."

He will then share everything set to occur with him, and they will cry together some more.

Because of Elisa's past addiction to pain medication and Andrés's subsequent seizure of control over all their assets for their financial protection, Andrés will leave new instructions with Elisa on what to do for Daphne to make sure their daughter understands she will never need to worry about how she will pay for food, rent, and other bills while in college. The Athena Fund will provide everything for her.

Andrés will say, "Sylvia doesn't want Daphne to experience the nightmare she had to live through just to survive while going to school."

He will share with Elisa where every important document can be found in the small house in Red Hook. Andrés will say, "Andy and Daphne are co-executors of her literary estate. Everything of ours belongs to both Andy and Daphne. Everything that was personally mine belongs to you, Myra, and Daphne. I still have all of you as beneficiaries of the life insurance policy you had set up so many years ago. Our lawyer has our will. When the time comes, she'll contact you."

Elisa will say he doesn't have to go. That he could rest there until the end. "I love you," she will say.

He will say, "I love you too. That's why I want you to be happy. You've had enough of my bullshit. Thank you for taking a chance on me. Thank you for carrying our world for so many years. I can't imagine how heavy that must've been for you. Live your life—until we meet again."

Andrés will leave, and by night, he will be at the airport, with his phone off and looking out of the terminal windows at the faint glow of lights from the Manhattan skyline to the west. He will understand that he will never again find joy. Every morning, Andrés will wake up, feel weaker and weaker, and realize it is a matter of time. But as long as he is alive, he will put his time left to good use. He will be a freelance photojournalist and see if his pictures can be the voice.

OCTOBER 2014

Andrés will wander to Berlin, where he will search the internet for Alene's address and find her home in Dahlem. He will travel there, appear at her doorstep, and knock. A young teenage boy will open the door, followed by his twin brother. The two boys will look like Andrés at the age he was when he watched *The Day After* and first became aware he lived in a universe that didn't care about his existence. The young boys will still live in the relative bliss of childhood, which will make Andrés smile when he sees them.

Alene will appear at the door, smile, and mouth the words "thank you" before hauling the two boys away, as Lothar will suddenly appear, surprising Andrés. Lothar will grab Andrés by the shoulder and drag him out until they are far enough from the door.

Lothar will grab Andrés by his short hair, swing him down onto the pavement, and punch his face over and over. He will stand over him and yell, "How dare you come to my home? First, you force yourself on her, and now this? Have you no decency?"

Andrés will say, "Whatever helps you live. You know your wife best. As God and His Watchers are my witnesses, Alene raped me at the Love Parade."

Lothar will appear taken aback and will step away as Andrés pushes himself off the pavement. Andrés will look over at the windows to see Alene standing behind their two boys, and there will be no denying it —he was the yoke for them. The boys will all be watching the commotion outside. Andrés will wave at them, happy that the man raising them looks strong in their eyes and that they will continue to feel safe in his care.

Alene will return his wave.

Andrés will see her mouthing the words, "I got you. You're dead."

Andrés will be confused but will still walk away, feeling as if he has satisfied whatever curiosity might arise in the future for the two boys. He will wander toward Großer Tiergarten and over to the Brandenburg Gate. He will keep wandering until he finds himself inside the lounge where he sat with Alene years ago.

A middle-aged Arab man will approach Andrés and ask if he's a photographer. Andrés will appear confused by the question. The Arab will mention the bag Andrés has at his side, saying it's one many photojournalists use. "I'm a photojournalist too."

Andrés will feel unsure about the man and say, "I enjoy taking pictures, that's all."

"Are you sure? The bag has the Leica Red Dot. That's the mark of a photojournalist, a combat photographer." The Arab man will sit next to Andrés, introduce himself, and show credentials proving his association with a major German news outlet. "We're always in need of eyes on the ground, especially in Syria. The world needs to see what's going on. If you'd like to add eyes to the ground, I can make the arrangements."

Andrés will say, "No thanks."

"Are you sure?"

Andrés will feel nervous, stand up, and say, "If you'll excuse me, I've got to go."

The Arab man will say, "Are you sure you don't want to stay? I can get us a beer—perhaps whiskey? We can talk more about the opportunity of taking pictures for the Syrian people."

Andrés will laugh and say, "No."

"I understand. I've got to go as well; I'll follow you out."

Andrés will stop and say, "Back the fuck up."

The Arab man will place his hand on Andrés's shoulder and begin leading him out of the lounge. He will say, "What's the matter, my friend? We're just talking. You need to relax."

Andrés will be set to yell for help but will stop when he feels a gun pressed against his torso. The Arab man will whisper, "We have a friend in common—Alene. I was with her at the Love Parade before you, if you know what I mean. Take it easy, my friend—she said we would more than likely find you here, like a pathetic fool, thinking back about that night. Alene asked me to tell you that her reach is also long—longer than your wife's. It's a shame your wife was the one who made the threat and carried it out—a bigger shame she's not alive to suffer the consequences. But you are. Yes, we heard about her passing. It's good she died—presenting herself as Arab and profiting off the misery of our people. My friend, her fate will soon be yours—this is your door."

Andrés will be too weak to break away or fight. All he will do is submit to the kidnapper's force as he is steered out of the lounge and away from the entrance. The kidnapper will push Andrés into the backseat of a car sitting idle. They will pistol-whip Andrés and tape his mouth shut.

In the moment that they will place a hood over Andrés, submerging him in darkness, he will be six again, feeling the blows from the book that had rained down on his small body—guided by Petra's hand—for crying.

As much as he will want to cry from fear or yell with rage, he will hear only Petra's voice telling him not to cry like a faggot. If he could not shed tears for the love of his life, when it mattered to her the most, he will certainly not shed them for those who will be his executioners. So he will keep holding on to what was first taught to him by Petra and will not give in to the darkness and cry.

He will not give them the satisfaction when facing what he knows will be his death. Andrés will remain brave and resolute in the face of it, because he will know what comes—and what will come is the answer to the question he has asked himself since that moment he stood at a spot along the Euphrates River in the valley: *If there is a God, then why am I alive?* And he will understand this is why—because this needs to happen the way it needs to happen. With the violence he knows awaits—the only way of bringing everything into the black.

The kidnappers will pistol-whip him one last time, and Andrés will submit to the long, dark deep of sleep. Each time Andrés wakes, he will find himself still gagged, still hooded.

Again and again, Andrés will feel the pistol-whipping. Again and again, he will submit to the long, dark deep of sleep.

Andrés will emerge from the Underworld to find himself no longer gagged or blinded by the hood. His hands will be free, and he will look around and see the room he is in. It will be dark, except for the soft light coming from the corners. The kidnappers will have dressed Andrés in an orange jumpsuit.

Every day, Andrés will be beaten.

NOVEMBER 2014

Every day, he will be blindfolded and tortured.

Every day, Andrés will scream.

Every day, Andrés will question the choices he had made that landed him there—the choice to join the Army so that he could rescue Lydia.

If he had not made that choice, along with the many others that led to meeting Sylvia, Elisa, and Alene, he would not be hearing his captors say, every day, "We should put him down, like a dog," only to hear the response, "He'll die like everyone else, for the entire world to see."

DECEMBER 21, 2014

The doors will then open, and a man will come in. The same man who has come to him every day while Andrés is in captivity. Instead of torturing him, the man will ask if he is ready to admit guilt.

Andrés will play dumb and say, "Guilt? For what?"

The man will say, "Don't act stupid. We know everything about you: Sergeant Andrés de León, SFODA, Iraq, 1991. You know what you did. Today is the day. *Allāhu 'akbar;* you will meet your maker and feel His justice. You will meet His fury."

The man will leave the room.

Any minute, they will come. All Andrés will think about is his execution appearing on social media. His death will become a source of information and entertainment consumed through the internet, much like Andrés had consumed Death by Water through the poem *The Waste Land.* He had never given serious thought to Phlebas as anything more than a character in a story. Andrés will become a character in a video, judged by the number of likes and dislikes—the entertainment quality of his death—then be forgotten. The sum total of his life culminating in a news snippet that will be scrolled past within five seconds of appearing in a social media feed.

To then be disposed of and forgotten by all except his children—much like the way war victims had been disposed of and forgotten by invading armies, but not by the families they left behind.

And not forgotten by Andrés.

Andrés volunteered to be an instrument of death for an army. It will be a just end for Andrés—but not in the eyes of his children.

Andrés will decide, no matter what, to keep his face relaxed, his eyes wide, and wear a stone smile to show he was a rock until the end. And rocks don't die; rocks endure.

Just as his love for his children will endure.

Like the Sandia Mountains facing the sun setting to the west, all Andrés will want is for his children to see that his stone face will be cast in beautiful golden-hour light. He will want everyone to see he will be happy, for this will be Our wedding day with Eternity.

He will be joined again to Us, his love.

Yes!

This will be Our real wedding day!

Yes!

The doors will open in Our sky at twilight, and Andrés's eyes—swollen shut from the countless beatings—will open just enough to burn while struggling to stare at the sun.

He will offer no resistance as his captors lead him out toward a spot where the land will be flat, and the desert landscape glows gold.

His captors will position him in place, and before him will be a little boy holding a phone up and recording.

We will be there as pronouncements are made, declaring Andrés an enemy to the Arab world.

Andrés will see Us at this moment.

He will see Us, and he will smile from understanding and knowing this is justice.

And he will smile because he will know he will be coming home.

He will understand, for everything to be made right, he will need to make the admission.

Andrés will yell, "I'm guilty!"

He will hear Us declare, as We will be compelled to do so when the Highest Light of the Universe passes a judgment:

You,
Sergeant Andrés de León,
Son of Antonio and Petra Vargas;
Common-law husband to Elisa Refaeli;
Ex-husband to Lydia Torres;
Dad to Myra Refaeli, Specialist Andrés James, Estefania de León, and
Athena de León;
And most of all, beloved husband to Dr. Sylvia de León—
You've escaped death as a child.
You've escaped death as a soldier.
You've escaped death countless times as a man.
Your time under the sun and stars will be over, just as Orion will rise.
The Highest Light of the Universe will not be denied Justice.
The Earth is a witness to your transgressions.
A father in Iraq was demanding Justice for his little girl, too.
This will be your door.
This will be that father's Justice.
Our Creator has heard his prayers too, as He had heard Ours and had
given Us this wedding gift.
This will be the price.
For me to be the Fury for our Lord and lead you to this spot. And I had already
accepted on our behalf, when I died, that I will make it right. I will cleanse your

soul of your evil, regardless of your good intents. I will make sure the bad karma, the pain, and the trauma are not passed on to our children—that they can be free to make their own future, free of our mistakes and the mistakes of our fathers. For you will be dying for them, too.

Are you ready to die?

Andrés will have heard Us and will smile. He will yell, with ecstatic joy, "I'm ready! Yes! I'm so happy to have made the choices I made. I would do it again and again if it means becoming one with You!"

As THE BLADE HACKS AT THE SIDE OF ANDRÉS'S NECK, HE WILL SMILE at how the dust in the golden hour of the last rays of sunshine over the desert landscape dances all around him, like stars. As the blade hacks deeper into his neck, he will be back in the moments when Andy, Daphne, and Athena were born out of a gush of fat and bloody afterbirth foaming around them, as if each came into the world like Aphrodite upon a clamshell.

Andrés will be back in the moment when he first met Myra at seven years old and how she took to him, hugging his legs and saying, "Good to meet you, mister."

Andrés will remember the home booming with the sounds of all his children playing and fighting and running around and laughing, and he will realize that was the best time of his life—to have been blessed to have been a father to them all. And he will be grateful to have been awake and lucid for some of their moments.

He will remember seeing Lydia as he was setting himself to leave her behind in a hospital room after giving birth to Andy—the long goodbye he had given her and their little boy, and not wanting to let him go, and not wanting to let her go, and the fear that was on her face in being left behind, alone, with a newborn she didn't know how she could take care of by herself while Andrés was being deployed. And he will remember Lydia crying out, "Don't go, please, don't leave me. I can't be alone," as Andrés walked out on the mother of his son, cementing the trauma she had been working hard to overcome—

trauma inflicted by a father who had become her monster, whom Andrés had rescued her from, like Perseus did with Andromeda.

He will remember the bright golden mornings with Elisa, with Daphne sleeping between the two when she was first born, and the golden light dazzling brightly from the windows, with Elisa always smiling at the gift that is their daughter.

He will remember the bright golden mornings with Sylvia, with Daphne sleeping between the two when she was a toddler, and how she would wake up to climb on Sylvia's chest and hug her.

He will remember the moment when, after nurses disconnected all the tubes and sensors from her inflamed body, he climbed into bed to cradle Sylvia from behind while Athena was brought back into the room so their baby could rest—dead—on her chest as she cried.

He will remember Sylvia's eyes streaking across the dark like shooting stars when they first danced under the disco ball at Robots— just as her eyes flashed while they lay with each other on a beach at Cala Benirrás, watching the stars fade out above them before sunrise.

Andrés will smile, for he will be at the precipice at the end of his existence.

Andrés will be joined with his one, just as He will be bound to the Body of We:

Just like the way you joined me after our leap off the cliff, at the bottom of our dive, in the clear blue water, with bubbles of light swirling around us, where we rose to the top together, to breathe. And before you, my soulmate, my one, embrace the annihilation of your sense of self into me, to become whole again, you will understand when I had said before I died, "no fear," that I will be here, in the beyond, waiting to be joined to you, to become Us

—The Watchers—

Andrés will remember the moment he had come home from the hospital after the war and was resting in bed, and Petra coming into the room and reading to him to help the medication along in dulling his pain. And he will remember how Petra had grabbed hold of Andy from his crib and, coming to Andrés's bedside, read his favorite bedtime stories from memory—of Mother Earth and Father Sky, and

Eurydice and Orpheus, and of undying love that finds each other in the dark.

And in the last golden rays of life coming through the window of his consciousness and perception, Andrés will remember his mother, whispering, "*Mijo,* it's okay. Everything will be alright. Trust me. I'm here. I *will* always protect you."

The blade will have finished its hack, and just before Andrés's head falls to the Earth, he will be aware of the golden rays of light cutting to black, and whatever in him that could be construed as spirit will give, as its last whisper:

Shantih shantih shantih

We will be finally one!
Yes!

ABOUT THE AUTHOR

Viktor E. Marés is a novelist, poet, and essayist known for his raw, existential explorations of masculinity, fate, and the unseen forces that shape human lives. His works include the novels *Spacer Woman, FWB,* and *The Desert Road of Night,* as well as the poetry collection *Eulogy for an Old Lover and Other Poems.*

His writing cuts into the brutal, unvarnished truths of life, often weaving themes of faith, mortality, power, and longing into a stark, unrelenting narrative style.

Marés brings an unsparing intensity to his work, rejecting contemporary literary trends in favor of storytelling that cuts to the bone. His essays challenge modern ideological narratives, favoring a direct, unflinching look at the realities of men's lives.

When he isn't writing, he's photographing the night skies of the

American Southwest—chasing the same vast silence that lingers in his work. You can find his work at vemares.co, on Substack at vemares.substack.com, and on Patreon at patreon.com/vemares.